ᴍᴀ

Amanda Quick, the bestselling author of *'Til Death Do Us Part*, transports readers to 1930s California, where glamour and seduction spawn a multitude of sins . . .

At the exclusive Burning Cove Hotel on the coast of California, rookie reporter Irene Glasson finds herself staring down at a beautiful actress at the bottom of a pool . . .

The dead woman had something Irene wanted: a red-hot secret about an up-and-coming leading man—a scoop that may have gotten her killed. As Irene searches for the truth about the drowning, she's drawn to a master of deception. Once a world-famous magician whose career was mysteriously cut short, Oliver Ward is now the owner of the Burning Cove Hotel. He can't let scandal threaten his livelihood, even if it means trusting Irene, a woman who seems to have appeared in Los Angeles out of nowhere four months ago.

With Oliver's help, Irene soon learns that the glamorous paradise of Burning Cove hides dark and dangerous secrets. And that the past—always just out of sight—could drag them both under . . .

"The action-packed plot is kick-started at page one . . . Quick has a great time with the 1930s Hollywood-glamour atmosphere." —*The Seattle Times*

"There are fierce forces at play in every page of *The Girl Who Knew Too Much*." —*Redbook*

"The love story and the mystery are beautifully intertwined here." —*The Washington Post*

"All of the key ingredients—wit-infused writing, sharply etched characters, and plenty of simmering sexual chemistry—that readers have come to expect from Quick snap into perfect alignment in this stellar novel." —*Booklist* (starred review)

Titles by Jayne Ann Krentz writing as Amanda Quick

THE GIRL WHO KNEW TOO MUCH

'TIL DEATH DO US PART

GARDEN OF LIES

OTHERWISE ENGAGED

THE MYSTERY WOMAN

CRYSTAL GARDENS

QUICKSILVER

BURNING LAMP

THE PERFECT POISON

THE THIRD CIRCLE

THE RIVER KNOWS

SECOND SIGHT

LIE BY MOONLIGHT

THE PAID COMPANION

WAIT UNTIL MIDNIGHT

LATE FOR THE WEDDING

DON'T LOOK BACK

SLIGHTLY SHADY

WICKED WIDOW

I THEE WED

WITH THIS RING

AFFAIR

MISCHIEF

MYSTIQUE

MISTRESS

DECEPTION

DESIRE

DANGEROUS

RECKLESS

RAVISHED

RENDEZVOUS

SCANDAL

SURRENDER

SEDUCTION

Titles by Jayne Ann Krentz

PROMISE NOT TO TELL

WHEN ALL THE GIRLS HAVE GONE

SECRET SISTERS

TRUST NO ONE

RIVER ROAD

DREAM EYES

COPPER BEACH

IN TOO DEEP

FIRED UP

RUNNING HOT

SIZZLE AND BURN

WHITE LIES

ALL NIGHT LONG

FALLING AWAKE

TRUTH OR DARE

LIGHT IN SHADOW

SUMMER IN ECLIPSE BAY

TOGETHER IN ECLIPSE BAY

SMOKE IN MIRRORS

LOST & FOUND

DAWN IN ECLIPSE BAY

SOFT FOCUS

ECLIPSE BAY

EYE OF THE BEHOLDER

FLASH

SHARP EDGES

DEEP WATERS

ABSOLUTELY, POSITIVELY

TRUST ME

GRAND PASSION

HIDDEN TALENTS

WILDEST HEARTS

FAMILY MAN

PERFECT PARTNERS

SWEET FORTUNE

SILVER LININGS

THE GOLDEN CHANCE

THE GIRL
WHO KNEW
TOO MUCH

AMANDA
QUICK

JOVE
New York

A JOVE BOOK
Published by Berkley
An imprint of Penguin Random House LLC
375 Hudson Street, New York, New York 10014

Copyright © 2017 by Jayne Ann Krentz
Excerpt from *The Other Lady Vanishes* by Amanda Quick © 2018 by Jayne Ann Krentz
Penguin Random House supports copyright. Copyright fuels creativity, encourages
diverse voices, promotes free speech, and creates a vibrant culture. Thank you for buying
an authorized edition of this book and for complying with copyright laws by not
reproducing, scanning, or distributing any part of it in any form without permission.
You are supporting writers and allowing Penguin Random House to continue to
publish books for every reader.

A JOVE BOOK and BERKLEY are registered trademarks and the B colophon
is a trademark of Penguin Random House LLC.

ISBN: 9780515156379

Berkley hardcover edition / May 2017
Jove mass-market edition / March 2018

Printed in the United States of America
1 3 5 7 9 10 8 6 4 2

Cover photo © Peter Zelei / Getty Images
Cover design by Rita Frangie
Book design by Laura K. Corless

*This one is for my wonderful editor,
Cindy Hwang,
who said, "Go for it!"*

Thank you for believing in me and in this book.

Chapter 1

The abstract painting on the bedroom wall was new. It had been painted in fresh blood.

There was blood everywhere in the elegant, white-on-white boudoir. It soaked the dead woman's silver satin evening gown and the carpet beneath her body. There was blood on the white velvet seat of the dainty chair in front of the pretty little dressing table.

Anna Harris's first thought was that she had walked into the middle of a nightmare. The scene simply could not be real. She was asleep and dreaming.

But she had grown up on a farm. She had hunted deer with her grandfather. Caught and cleaned fish. Helped deliver calves. She knew the cycle of life and the smell of death.

Still, she could not leave the room until she made certain. Helen had collapsed on her side, facing the wall. Anna crouched next to the body and reached out to check for a pulse. There wasn't one, of course.

There was a gun, however. A small one. It lay on the carpet not far from Helen's right hand. Acting on instinct—she certainly wasn't thinking clearly now—Anna scooped up the weapon.

It was then that she saw the message. Helen had used her own blood to write it on the silver-flocked wallpaper just above the baseboard. *Run.*

And in that moment, Anna knew that the perfect new life she had been living for the past year was an illusion. The reality was a dark fairy tale.

Run.

She rushed down the hall to her lovely blue and white bedroom, pulled a suitcase out of the closet, and started flinging clothes into it. Like the shoes and the frock she was wearing, almost all of her wardrobe was new, the gift of her generous employer. *Can't have my private secretary looking like she shops at a secondhand store*, Helen had said on several occasions.

Anna was shaking so badly she could barely get the suitcase closed and locked. With effort she managed to haul it off the bed.

She went back to the closet and took the shoebox off the top shelf. Tossing the lid aside, she started to reach into the box for the money she kept inside. She had been in her late teens a few years earlier when the crash occurred, but like so many others who had lived through the experience, she had no faith in banks. She kept her precious savings close at hand in the shoebox.

She froze at the sight of what was inside the box.

There was money, all right—too much money.

With all of her living expenses paid for by her employer, she had been able to save most of her salary for the past year, but she certainly had not saved anywhere near the amount that was in the box. Helen must have added the extra cash. It was the only explanation, but it made no sense.

In addition to the money there was a small, leather-bound notebook and a letter written on Helen's expensive stationery.

Dear Anna:

If you are reading this, it means that I have made the biggest mistake a woman can make—I have fallen in love with the wrong man. I'm afraid that I am not the person you believed me to be. I apologize for the deception. Take the notebook, the money, and the car. Run for your life. Get as far away as possible and disappear. Your only hope is to become someone else. You must not trust anyone—not the police, not the FBI. Above all, never trust a lover.

I wish I could give you the glowing reference you deserve. But for your own sake you must never let anyone know that you once worked for me.

As for the notebook, I can only tell you that it is dangerous. I do not pretend to understand the contents. I would advise you to destroy it, but if the worst happens, you may be able to use it as a bargaining chip.

I have always considered us to be two of a kind—women alone in the world who are obliged to live by our wits.

*I wish you all the best in your new life. Get as far
away as possible from this house and never look back.*

Yours with affection,
Helen

Helen Spencer had been bold, adventurous, and
daring—a woman of the modern age. She had lived
life with passion and enthusiasm, and for the past year
Anna had been caught up in her glittering, fast-paced
world. If Helen said that it was necessary to run, then
it was, indeed, vital that Anna run.

She emptied the contents of the shoebox into her
secretarial handbag. After a few seconds' hesitation
she put Helen's little gun inside, as well. She closed
the handbag, gripped it in one hand, hoisted the suitcase, and hurried out into the hall.

When she went past Helen's bedroom, she tried not
to look at the body, but she could not help herself.

Helen Spencer had been ravishingly beautiful, an
angelic blonde with sparkling blue eyes. Wealthy,
charming, and gracious, she had paid her small household staff, including her secretary, very well. In return,
she had demanded loyalty and absolute discretion
concerning her seemingly small eccentricities such as
her occasional demands for privacy and her odd travel
schedule.

Like the others on the mansion's very small staff—
the middle-aged housekeeper and the butler—Anna
had been happy to accommodate Helen. It had been
an enchanted life, but tonight it was over.

Anna went down the stairs. She had always known that her good fortune could not last. Orphans developed a realistic view of life early on.

When she reached the ground floor she went past Helen's study. She glanced inside and saw that the door of the safe was open. The desk lamp was on. There was a blue velvet bag inside the safe.

She hesitated. Something told her that she had to know what was inside the velvet bag. Perhaps the contents would explain what had happened that night. She set the suitcase on the floor, crossed the study, and reached into the safe. Scooping up the velvet bag, she loosened the cord that cinched it closed and turned it upside down over the desk.

Emeralds and diamonds glittered in the lamplight. The necklace was heavy and old-fashioned in design. It looked extremely valuable. Helen had some very good jewelry but Anna was sure she had never seen the necklace. It wasn't Helen's style. Perhaps it was a family heirloom.

But the more pressing question was, why would the killer open the safe and then leave such an expensive item behind?

Because he was after something else, she thought. The notebook.

She slipped the necklace into the velvet sack and put it into the safe.

She went back into the hall, picked up the suitcase, and rushed outside. The sporty Packard coupe that Helen had insisted upon giving her was waiting in the drive. She tossed the suitcase and the handbag into the trunk and got behind the wheel—and nearly went limp with gratitude and relief when the well-tuned engine started up on the first try.

She turned on the lights, put the car in gear, and drove down the long, winding drive, through the open gates, and away from the big house.

She gripped the wheel very tightly and forced herself to concentrate. She had not learned all of Helen Spencer's secrets tonight but she had stumbled upon enough of them to make one thing blazingly clear: She had to get as far away from New York as possible.

The narrow mountain road twisted and turned on itself as it snaked down into the valley, a harrowing trip for those unaccustomed to it, especially at night. But her grandfather had taught her to drive when she was thirteen, and she had learned on bad mountain roads. She knew how to handle tight curves, and she knew this particular mountain road very well. She had driven her employer back and forth between the Manhattan apartment and the secluded mansion many times during the past year.

Helen's faithful butler, Mr. Bartlett, had doubled as her chauffeur before Anna arrived at the mansion. But Bartlett's eyesight had begun to fail. Helen had been thinking of looking for a new driver when she hired Anna. Helen had been delighted to discover that, in addition to her stenography skills, her private secretary was also a skilled driver. *Saves me from having to hire a chauffeur,* she had said.

Helen had always been very keen on keeping staff to a bare minimum. She was not a stingy employer—

just the opposite, in fact—but she had made it clear that she did not want a lot of people around her at the mansion. Tonight it occurred to Anna that the reason Helen had limited the number of people on her household staff was because she had secrets to hide.

I've been incredibly naïve, Anna thought.

She had always prided herself on taking a cold-eyed, realistic view of the world. A woman in her position could not afford the luxuries of optimism, hope, and sentiment. For the most part she considered herself to be quite intuitive when it came to forming impressions of others. But when she did make mistakes, the results tended to be nothing short of catastrophic.

She reached the small, sleepy village at the foot of the mountain and turned onto the main road. Unable to think clearly enough to come up with a destination, she pursued a random route, passing through a string of tiny towns.

Run.

She continued driving an erratic pattern straight through the next day, stopping only for gas and a sandwich. But at nightfall exhaustion forced her to pull into an autocamp. The proprietors did not ask for a name, just enough money to cover the cost of a private cabin and a hot meal.

She collapsed on a cot and slept fitfully until dawn. In her feverish dreams she fled from an unseen menace while Helen urged her to run faster.

She awoke to the smell of coffee. A newspaper delivery truck arrived while she was eating the breakfast provided by the couple who operated the camp. She bought a paper and unfolded it with a mix of dread and curiosity. The news of Helen Spencer's murder was on the front page.

WEALTHY N.Y. SOCIALITE SAVAGELY MURDERED.
PRIVATE SECRETARY MISSING.
WANTED FOR QUESTIONING.
STOLEN NECKLACE FOUND IN DEAD WOMAN'S SAFE.

Shock iced Anna's blood. She was now a suspect in the murder of Helen Spencer. Helen's warning came back to her: *You must not trust anyone—not the police, not the FBI. Above all, never trust a lover.*

The last bit, at least, was easy enough, Anna thought. She did not have a lover. She had not had one since Bradley Thorpe. That humiliating debacle was the last occasion on which her intuition had failed quite spectacularly.

She pulled herself back from the cliff-edge of panic. She was a proud graduate of the Gilbert School for Secretaries. Gilbert Girls did not panic. She had been trained to exert control over chaos. She knew how to set priorities.

First things first: It was time to choose a destination. She could not continue to drive aimlessly up and down the East Coast. The very thought of spending weeks, months, or years on the run was enough to shatter her nerves. Besides, the money would not last forever. Sooner or later she would have to go to ground. Catch her breath. Get a job. Invent a new life.

She was not the only person who had spent the night in the autocamp. The others gathered around the table for breakfast, eager to get back on the road. They chatted easily, sharing travelers' tales. All of the conversations started the same way. *Where are you headed?*

There were many answers but one in particular stood out because it sparked curiosity, wonder, and several nods of agreement around the table.

By the time she finished breakfast she had made her decision. She would do what countless others had done when they were forced to build new lives. She would head for that mythical land out west where a vast blue ocean sparkled beneath a cloudless sky, and orange trees grew in people's backyards. A land where glamorous people created magic on the silver screen and got involved in titillating scandals in their spare time. A land where everyone was too busy inventing the future to care that she had no past.

She got back behind the wheel and started driving west.

Somewhere along the line she came up with a new name for herself: Irene Glasson. It had a Hollywood ring to it, she thought.

She found the highway to her future right where the other travelers had said it would be—in downtown Chicago.

Route 66 would take her all the way to California.

Chapter 2

"You failed." Graham Enright folded his hands on top of the desk. "In addition to terminating Spencer, you were supposed to acquire the notebook."

Julian was standing in front of the art deco portrait on the wall, examining it with the intent expression of a connoisseur. He could have passed for one if necessary. Not only had he received an excellent education that included an appreciation of the fine arts, but he was a born actor.

From his artfully cut blond hair to his fashionable suit with its perfectly knotted tie and elegant pocket square, he looked as if he played polo in his spare time. The accent and manners were pure East Coast Old Money, and it wasn't an act. Julian's ancestors had not actually arrived on the *Mayflower*, but they had been on board a yacht that docked soon thereafter.

"I assumed the notebook would be in Spencer's safe," Julian said. He looked and sounded bored by the conversation. "It was the logical place to look so I cracked it. Took me several minutes, by the way. When I realized the damned notebook wasn't inside, I searched the study and Spencer's bedroom. It would have been impossible to go through the entire house. The old mansion is huge."

"Spencer probably had a second safe, maybe one hidden in the floor."

Julian inhaled deeply on his cigarette. The brand was French. Very expensive. Very exclusive.

"What did you expect me to do?" he said. He did not take his eyes off the portrait. "Pry up every floorboard in search of a hidden safe? Sorry, I'm not a carpenter. I don't do household remodeling work."

"You shouldn't have gotten rid of Spencer until you had that notebook in your hands."

"Spencer kept a gun in her bureau drawer. At some point she became suspicious. She went for the weapon. I had no choice. It's not my fault I couldn't find the damned notebook."

"The client is not going to be pleased."

"That's your problem, not mine. You're management. I'm just a field agent, remember? True, I'm your *only* field agent but, nevertheless, I'm just hired help."

Graham ignored the barb. "Enright and Enright has a contract to recover the notebook and get rid of anyone who might have had access to it. I expect you to complete the assignment."

Julian turned around. "I'll be happy to make further inquiries but I want something in return."

Graham controlled his temper with an effort. He was not in a position to bargain. The reputation of Enright & Enright was on the line.

"What do you want?" Graham asked.

"A promotion to vice president of the firm."

Graham pretended to give that some intense thought. Then he nodded curtly.

"Very well," he said. "But I will expect results and I will expect them soon."

Julian's sensual mouth curved faintly. His gem green eyes glinted with amusement. "You really are nervous about this contract, aren't you?"

"I want it completed satisfactorily, yes. The client is a new one with very deep pockets and wide-ranging interests. If we are successful, there is the potential for a great deal of future business."

"You seem particularly keen to land this particular client. Why is it so important?"

"It represents a golden opportunity for the firm to expand its business into the international sphere."

That got Julian's attention, just as Graham had known it would.

"This client has *international* interests?" Julian asked.

Graham allowed himself a small, satisfied smile. "It does, indeed."

"What sort of interests are we talking about?"

"A wide variety. You read the newspapers. The modern world is an unstable place."

Julian waved that aside. "That's hardly a new development. The world has always been an unstable place. But until now Enright and Enright has confined its activities to the United States."

Graham pushed back his chair and got to his feet. He went to stand at the window. He had a spectacular view of New York City, but in his mind's eye he saw Europe, the Middle East, Russia, and beyond—all the way to the Far East. He intended to position the firm to take advantage of the opportunities that would abound in the future. It would be his legacy, he thought, the legacy that he would leave to his son and heir, who would, in turn, provide future generations of Enrights.

Not that he planned to leave that legacy to his son anytime soon. Graham was still in his prime, healthy and fit. He came from a long-lived line. Unfortunately, the men of the Enright line were not very prolific. After two wives—both deceased—he had managed to sire only one heir.

The law firm of Enright & Enright had been founded by his father, Neville Enright, amid the chaos following the Civil War. Neville had understood that the desires for money and power and revenge were forms of lust and, therefore, immutable aspects of human nature. Firms that catered to those elemental lusts would always prosper, regardless of stock market crashes and wars.

On the surface, Enright & Enright was a respected law firm that specialized in estate planning for an exclusive, wealthy clientele. But in addition, it provided very discreet services to those willing to resort to any means to achieve their objectives so long as they could keep their own hands clean. For a hefty fee, Enright & Enright was willing to do the dirty work for its clients.

In the aftermath of the War to End All Wars it had become clear to Graham that not only would there be more wars in the future, but there would also be an unlimited demand for the services that Enright & Enright provided.

It had also become obvious that the rapid advances in modern technology—faster modes of transportation and communications as well as more efficient weaponry—would open up new markets and new opportunities.

"The times are changing," he said. "The firm must change with them. To do so we must cultivate clients such as the one that has commissioned us to retrieve the notebook."

"A client with international interests," Julian repeated softly. "Very interesting."

He no longer sounded bored. There was something new in his voice. Anticipation. Graham was pleased and more than a little relieved. Satisfied, he turned around.

"The only way to secure this client is to find the notebook and get rid of anyone who might be aware of its value," he said. "You will, of course, have the full resources of the firm at your disposal."

Julian headed toward the door. "I'll get started immediately."

"One moment, if you don't mind."

Julian paused, his hand on the doorknob. "What is it?"

"Can I assume you have some idea of where to start looking?"

"Yes, as a matter of fact, I do," Julian said. "Spencer employed only three people. One of them has gone missing."

Graham tensed. "Which one?"

"The private secretary, Anna Harris. An orphan with no family and, given her career, very little money, unless she stole some from Spencer. She is the only member of the staff who disappeared, so it seems likely that she took the notebook."

"I see."

"The thing is, Anna Harris is not a professional like Spencer. She won't know how to go about making a deal for an item as dangerous as the notebook without revealing herself to someone who is watching for it to appear on the underground market."

"Someone like you."

"Thanks to the firm's connections I can keep an eye on that market. Don't worry, Anna Harris and the notebook will show up sooner or later, and when they do, I'll deal with both issues."

"Why didn't you mention this before?"

Julian smiled his fallen-angel smile. "Because I wanted to know just how important this contract was to you."

"I see. What makes you think that this Anna Harris knows the value of the notebook?"

"I'm sure of it, because she fled without helping herself to the necklace that was in the safe. She must have seen it. Why would a poor secretary leave such a valuable item behind unless she thought she had something of even greater value to sell?"

"Good point," Graham said. "But I must say, I'm surprised that Spencer confided the truth about the notebook to her secretary."

Julian's brows rose. "Are you really? We both know that, sooner or later, private secretaries discover a great deal about their employers' confidential business."

Graham grunted. "Very true."

It was unfortunate that the very qualities that made for a skilled secretary—intelligence, organizational talents, and the ability to anticipate her employer's needs before he was even aware of them—were the same qualities that eventually caused problems.

He was always careful to hire experienced single women who lacked family and social connections. His current secretary was a fine example. Raina Kirk was in her thirties and alone in the world. There was no man in her life and no close relations. When it came time to let her go, there would be no problems.

"Don't worry," Julian said. "Anna Harris is just a secretary who made off with her employer's property. Her first objective will be to try to sell the notebook. But it will be difficult for her to find a buyer for such an exotic item. Once she starts putting out feelers, she'll give herself away very quickly."

"Let's hope you're right. One more thing."

Julian had been about to open the door. He sighed rather theatrically and turned back to face Graham.

"What is it?" he asked.

"Was it absolutely essential to make such a mess of the Spencer job? The murder is making headlines because the police believe that whoever killed the victim is a homicidal maniac."

"Which distracts them from the true reason for the kill," Julian said with exaggerated patience. "That was the point. They are now looking for a madman—or, possibly, a madwoman. They won't make the connection to the notebook."

He let himself out into the reception area. Graham saw him give Raina a warm, seductive smile just before he closed the door.

Graham sat down at his desk. Julian's explanation for the bloody death was reasonable, but he could have taken a less spectacular approach. A motor vehicle accident or a suicide might have generated headlines— Helen Spencer moved in society—but neither would have involved the police.

He realized that what concerned him was Julian's penchant for the sensational. He clearly enjoyed the thrill of the kill. Graham understood. *We're only young once*, he reminded himself. Nevertheless, it was time that Julian matured and learned to control his impulsive nature.

Graham contemplated the portrait of himself that hung on the wall. The artist, Tamara de Lempicka, had used her talent to give him an aura of mystery and glamour. He appeared both intensely masculine and darkly sensual. The light turned his blond hair to gold. His green eyes glowed like jewels. Lempicka had called him Lucifer during the sittings and tried to seduce him. Her illicit liaisons were the stuff of legend. He smiled at the memory.

Better to reign in hell, he thought, especially when one commanded such a profitable version of Hades.

He was untroubled by thoughts of heaven and hell

because he was not a religious man. He did not consider himself a vain man, either, but he had to admit
that he was quietly pleased with the portrait. He was
some thirty years older than Julian, but the similarity
between the two of them was unmistakable. Anyone
who saw Julian standing next to the Lempicka portrait
would recognize the truth immediately.

Like father, like son.

Chapter 3

When Chicago was several miles behind her, Irene pulled off Route 66 to spend yet another night at yet another anonymous autocamp.

After a dinner of stew and homemade biscuits, she retired to her cabin and took the notebook out of the handbag. She had glanced at it briefly the night she fled the mansion, but she had been too focused on getting away from New York to take a closer look.

She sat on the edge of the cot and examined it by the light of the kerosene lantern. There was a name on the first page. It had been written in a tight, precise hand. *Dr. Thomas G. Atherton.* Below the name was a phone number. The rest of the pages appeared to be covered in some sort of code, all of it in the same handwriting.

She puzzled over the strange numbers and symbols for a time before it dawned on her that she was looking at scientific notations. It struck her that she was in possession of the personal notebook of a mathematician or a chemist. But that made no sense. Helen Spencer had never displayed any interest in either subject.

At dawn Irene awoke from a restless sleep with a sense of resolve. She was running. She needed to know more about what she was running from.

After a breakfast of eggs and toast, she used the autocamp phone booth to call the number on the first page of the notebook. The operator requested several coins.

"Where is this number located?" Irene asked, chucking money into the slot.

"New Jersey," the operator said.

A moment later a polished female voice answered.

"Saltwood Laboratory. How may I direct your call?"

Irene took a deep breath. "Dr. Atherton, please."

There was a short, brittle pause on the other end of the line.

"I'm sorry but Dr. Atherton is no longer with us."

"Do you mean he is no longer employed there?"

"Unfortunately, Dr. Atherton is deceased. Would you care to speak to someone else in his department?"

"No. What happened to Dr. Atherton?"

There was another short pause on the other end of the line before the receptionist spoke.

"I'm sorry, who did you say was calling?"

"Looks like I've got the wrong Atherton," Irene said. "Sorry for the inconvenience."

She hung up the phone and got back on the road. Two people connected to the notebook were dead. That did not bode well for her future. She would have to do a very good job of disappearing.

Chapter 4

Burning Cove, California
Four months later . . .

Irene stopped at the edge of the long lap pool and looked down at the body sprawled gracefully on the bottom. It was fifteen minutes past midnight. The lights had been dimmed in the grand spa chamber, but in the low glow of a nearby wall sconce, it was possible to make out the dead woman's hair floating around her pretty face in a nightmarish imitation of a wedding veil.

Irene turned away from the pool, intending to run to the entrance of the spa to summon help. Somewhere in the shadows, shoe leather scraped on tiles. She knew then that she was not alone with the dead woman. There was a faint click and the wall sconces went dark.

The vast spa chamber was abruptly plunged into dense shadows. The only light now was the ghostly glow from the moon. It illuminated the section of the spa where Irene stood. She might as well have been pinned in a spotlight.

Her pulse pounded and she was suddenly fighting to breathe. The nearest exit was the row of French doors behind her. But they were on the opposite side of the long lap pool. The side door that she had used to enter the spa was even farther away.

She concluded that her best option was to sound as if she was in command of herself and the situation.

"There's been an accident," she said, raising her voice in what she hoped was a firm, authoritative manner. "A woman fell into the water. We've got to get her out. There might still be time to revive her."

That was highly unlikely. The woman at the bottom of the pool looked very, very dead.

There was no response. No one moved in the shadows.

Somewhere in the darkness water dripped, the faint sound echoing eerily. The humid atmosphere was rapidly becoming oppressive.

There were two possible reasons why the other person on the scene might not come forward, Irene thought. The first was fear of scandal. The Burning Cove Hotel was one of the most exclusive on the West Coast. Located almost a hundred miles north of Los Angeles, it offered a guarantee of privacy and discretion to those who could afford it. If the rumors were true, it had sheltered a list of guests that ranged from powerful figures of the criminal underworld to Hollywood stars and European royalty. Times might be hard elsewhere in the country, but you'd never know it from the luxury and opulence of the Burning Cove Hotel.

The stars and aspiring stars came to the hotel to escape the prying eyes of the always hungry reporters of the Los Angeles newspapers and the Hollywood gossip columnists. So, yes, it was possible that the watcher in the shadows feared being discovered in the vicinity of a woman who had just drowned. That kind of scandal could certainly taint a budding film career.

But there was another reason the other person might not want to assist in what would no doubt be a futile rescue effort. Perhaps he or she had been directly responsible for the death of the woman in the pool.

The thought that she might be trying to coax a killer out of hiding sent another jolt through Irene. She decided to make a run back to the side door.

But she had waited too long. Running footsteps sounded in the darkness, ringing and echoing off the tiled walls and floor. The other person was not fleeing the scene, Irene realized. Instead, he or she—it was impossible to tell which—was coming toward her.

Standing there in the glowing moonlight and silhouetted against the wall of glass doors behind her on the far side of the lap pool, she made an ideal target.

She kicked off her shoes, whirled around, and hurled her handbag across the narrow lap pool. She had spent her youth pitching hay and stacking firewood. She was tall for a woman, and the single life had kept her fit and strong. A lady on her own in the world could not afford the luxury of being delicate.

The handbag landed on the tiles on the opposite side of the pool with a solid thud.

She jumped into the water and started swimming. She would reach the opposite side within seconds. Unless the watcher followed her into the water, she would have a good chance of escape. There was no way the other person could get around either end of the pool in time to intercept her.

She was a good swimmer but her fashionable, wide-legged trousers were immediately transformed into lead weights. She swam harder, resisting the downward pull of the clothing.

It was not the first time that she had gone into water fully dressed. There had been a river near the farm where she was raised. Her grandfather had made certain that she learned how to swim almost as soon as she learned how to walk.

The knowledge that she was swimming over the body of the dead woman was unnerving, but not nearly as unnerving as the realization that she was probably being chased by a killer.

She reached the far side and dragged herself up out of the water. It took every ounce of strength she possessed, but she discovered that fear was a terrific motivator. She managed to scramble to her feet.

Breathless, she paused to look back. She saw no one in the shadows, but she heard rapid footsteps again. This time they were headed away from the pool. A short time later a door opened and closed on the far side of the spa chamber.

Irene gripped the handle of her handbag and hurried to the glass doors that fronted the spa. She fled into the moonlit gardens.

Once again she was running from the scene of a murder, running from a killer.

Just when she had begun to think that her new life in California might have a Hollywood ending.

Chapter 5

"Now that Detective Brandon and the officer have taken their leave, Miss Glasson, I think you and I should have a private conversation," Oliver Ward said.

Irene considered her options. She had an uneasy feeling that her first choice—concocting an excuse to decline the chat—was not going to work. In her short time in California she had learned to expect the unexpected, and Oliver Ward definitely qualified as a disturbing example of the unexpected.

She glanced across the living room, gauging the distance between the big leather armchair in which she sat and the front door. She just might make it. She had one very big advantage—Ward had a bad leg. His gait was stiff and halting. He was forced to rely on a cane.

The cause of the injury was no secret. It was, in fact, something of a show business legend. Oliver Ward was once a world-famous magician who had performed amazing illusions at some of the biggest theaters in the United States. He had toured Europe. But two years ago things had gone terribly wrong. Ward was nearly killed in what proved to be his final performance. The disaster made headlines across the country. *Blood on the Stage. Famous Magician Badly Injured in Front of Audience, May Not Survive.*

What, precisely, had gone wrong had been a matter of conjecture in the press for months. All anyone knew for certain was that there had been real ammunition in the gun that was used in the illusion. Ward had steadfastly refused to give any interviews on the subject. After he was released from the hospital, he had seemingly vanished from the scene.

Tonight Irene discovered that he had gone into the hotel business.

At the moment, he was on the far side of the room, standing at an elegant black-lacquer liquor cabinet where he was in the process of pouring two whiskies. He appeared to be in excellent health but, given his serious limp, she was almost certain she could get to the door before he could.

It was, however, highly unlikely that she could escape the grounds without being stopped. Ward employed an impressive array of well-dressed security guards. Their evening uniforms consisted of black-and-white formal attire, but the good clothes did not disguise their muscular builds. Not that any of them had been around earlier in the spa when she could have used a little help.

Just like cops, she thought, *never around when you needed one*.

She abandoned the idea of making a dash for the door.

"It's been a very trying night," she said instead, striving to appear pathetic. She certainly looked the part, swathed in a thick spa robe with her hair bound up in a turban made from a hotel towel. "I'm exhausted. If you don't mind, I would like to go back to the Cove Inn. I've got a room there. Perhaps we could talk in the morning?"

With a little luck she would be in her car, heading back to Los Angeles, before Ward realized she had left town.

"I'd prefer to have the conversation now," he said.

She abandoned the pathetic approach and went for icy outrage.

"Detective Brandon declined to arrest me," she said. "Most likely because I'm innocent. Are you planning to keep me here against my will? Because, if so, I would like to remind you that I am a member of the press. I'm sure you don't want this scandal to get any bigger than it is already."

All right, claiming to be a member of the press was pushing things a bit—technically she was a mere assistant at *Whispers*, a Hollywood gossip paper. But she was in Burning Cove with her editor's approval, and she was on the trail of what she was sure would be a headline-making story—murder and scandal that involved a leading man who was considered by many to be the next Clark Gable.

A short time ago, Ward had summoned his manager and the head concierge. They had been instructed to do everything in their power to stanch rumors and speculation. Their primary job was to keep the press at bay. The fact that it was a reporter, or an *aspiring* reporter, who had found the body in the spa was going to be a very big problem for Oliver Ward.

She could expect threats, she thought, but Ward had to know it was unlikely that any force on earth could squelch the story of murder in his hotel spa. Furthermore, she doubted that Ward would want to add fuel to the fire by ordering his people to forcibly detain her—not in front of witnesses, at least.

Unfortunately, at the moment there were no witnesses. She was alone with Oliver Ward in the living room of his private villa, Casa del Mar.

"We both know that there is no avoiding the headlines," Oliver said. He put the stopper back into the cut glass decanter. "The best I can do at this point is try to contain and control the story."

"At least you are honest about your intentions. How do you intend to contain and control the scandal?"

He gave her a cool, assessing smile. "I'm working on that problem. Perhaps you can help me."

"Why?"

"It would be in your own best interests."

She managed what she hoped was a smile as cold as his own. "Threats, Mr. Ward?"

"I never make threats. Just statements of fact. I do have some questions I would like to ask before you leave here tonight." Oliver picked up one of the glasses and turned to face her. "Save yourself the effort of making a run for the front door. It's true that I am no longer a working magician, but I've still got a few tricks up my sleeve. I'm not quite as slow as I appear."

She believed him.

"I don't care if you are the owner of this hotel, Mr. Ward," she said. "You have no right to keep me a prisoner here."

"I hope you will consider yourself my guest," Oliver said. He gripped his cane and made his way across the living room. "You are, after all, sitting in my home, wearing a robe and slippers provided by my hotel."

He stopped in front of her and held out the glass of whiskey. She was briefly distracted by the masculine grace of the gesture. In his hands the glass seemed to materialize out of thin air.

She looked up from the glass and found herself briefly ensnared by his compelling eyes. They were an unusual color—a feral shade of dark amber. She refused to admit that there was anything genuinely mesmeric about his gaze, but she was intensely aware of the sheer power of his will. She was dealing with a very intelligent, very coolheaded man. She was certain that once he settled on a goal or a course of action, it would be difficult—make that *impossible*—to distract him or turn him aside.

It wasn't just his eyes that caught and held her attention. He was not handsome in the way of the leading men of the silver screen, but there was a certain kind of raw power about his boldly carved features, broad shoulders, and lean build. Oliver Ward possessed that magical quality called *presence*. No wonder he had been able to enthrall audiences.

Her first inclination was to refuse the whiskey. She needed to keep her wits about her. But her nerves deserved some consideration, she thought. The events in the spa had rattled her.

She took the whiskey and swallowed a healthy dose of the spirits. The stuff burned all the way down but it had a fortifying effect.

She immediately regretted the action because Oliver looked quietly pleased. *Too late now,* she decided. She took another sip.

Oliver went back across the room and picked up the other glass. He made his way to the big, heavily padded chair across from her and lowered himself into it. He stretched out his bad leg with some care.

"Tell me again how you managed to get access to my hotel," he said.

"You heard me explain to Detective Brandon that Gloria Maitland asked me to meet her in the spa. She left my name at the front desk. I was her guest for the evening."

"The guest of a woman who is now dead."

"Are you implying I'm responsible? Detective Brandon certainly didn't seem to think so."

But she was clutching at straws now. Brandon had been summoned by the head of hotel security. He had arrived with an officer from the Burning Cove Police Department. It was obvious that the detective had been roused from his bed, but he was professional and polite.

Unfortunately, it had also been evident from the

moment he arrived that he and Oliver Ward were well acquainted. Irene had no doubt but that Brandon would defer to Ward's desire to try to contain the scandal. Burning Cove might be a small town, but it appeared to operate under L.A. rules—money and power controlled everything, including the local police.

"I checked with the front desk," Oliver said. "While it's true that Miss Maitland invited you here this evening, she failed to mention that you were a member of the press. Reporters are never allowed on the property."

"Yes, well, I'm afraid you'll have to take that up with Miss Maitland."

"Who is now deceased. We keep coming back to that unpleasant fact, don't we?"

"It's not my fault that Gloria Maitland didn't obey your rules," Irene said. "And while we're on the subject of security, it would appear that the Burning Cove Hotel has a few problems in that regard. A woman was murdered in your fancy spa tonight. That doesn't make your security people look good, does it?"

"No," Oliver conceded. "But the fact that you were the one who found the body doesn't make you look good." He paused a beat. "Some would say that makes you the primary suspect."

Don't panic, she thought. *There will be plenty of time to do that later.*

"I told Detective Brandon the truth," she said, managing to keep her voice steady. "I'm a journalist. I had an appointment with Miss Maitland. She chose the time and the location."

"You work for a Hollywood gossip sheet. I'm not

sure that position entitles you to call yourself a journalist."

"You are hardly in a position to lecture me on the
subject of sensational headlines. You're an ex-magician
who built a name for himself by making exactly those
kinds of headlines with your very daring performances.
I'm sure that when you were touring you wanted all
the newspaper coverage you could get."

"I'm in a different profession these days."

"We both know that your patrons don't just come
to the Burning Cove Hotel because they crave privacy.
The actors and actresses book rooms here because they
want to be seen checking in to such an exclusive establishment. The rich come because they want to rub
shoulders with the famous and the infamous. Admit
it, Mr. Ward, people are attracted to this hotel precisely
because they want their names mentioned in the same
breath as Hollywood royalty and wealthy tycoons and
notorious gangsters. Your guests will do just about
anything to be the subject of the kind of journalism
that appears in *Whispers*."

To her chagrin, Oliver inclined his head once in
acknowledgment of the counterattack.

"That's all true," he said. "However, I'm sure you
understand that the policy against allowing journalists
onto the grounds is part of the illusion. Obviously, if
I did let them wander around the hotel, it would no
longer appear exclusive."

"It's all about appearances, then?"

"It's all about maintaining the illusion, Miss
Glasson."

"What do you want from me, Mr. Ward?"

He turned the whiskey glass absently between his fingers.

"Tonight a woman died in my hotel under mysterious circumstances," he said. "You claim that you had an appointment with her in the spa. That appointment was at a rather late hour."

"A quarter past midnight. And it didn't strike me as a strange time at all. It made perfect sense. Your hotel was in full swing at that hour. The lounge was crowded. People were dancing, drinking heavily, and no doubt meeting other people's spouses and lovers in various rooms and pool cabanas. Gloria Maitland had every reason to think that no one would notice her slipping off to the spa for an interview with a journalist."

"You seem to have a somewhat jaded view of what goes on here at the Burning Cove."

Irene gave him her best you-can-trust-me, everything-is-off-the-record smile. "Care to set me straight?"

"I never discuss the personal lives of my guests."

"Of course not."

"I would like to know what you expected to learn from Maitland."

"We're back to that, are we?"

"I'm afraid so."

There was something implacable about Oliver Ward. Short of screaming for help, she did not see an easy way out of the situation. Given that he owned the hotel and paid the salaries of everyone who worked there, she was not certain that screaming for help would be of much use.

It occurred to her that there was another angle to consider, as well. If there was one thing she had learned in her short career at *Whispers*, it was that two could play the information game.

Trying to give the impression that she was willing to humor him, she sank deeper into her chair. The effect of languid grace was somewhat marred because she had to fumble with the oversized robe to make certain that it did not fall open. She was not wearing anything underneath. All of her clothes had been handed off to the housekeeping department for cleaning and drying.

To his credit, Oliver's fierce eyes never once dropped below her face. Either he was a real gentleman or he was not attracted to women, she thought. Her feminine intuition told her that the latter was not the case.

She decided there was a third possibility—he simply wasn't interested in her.

"You heard me answer all of Detective Brandon's questions," she said. "Gloria Maitland phoned me long-distance at my office in L.A. yesterday. I might add that she reversed the charges. My boss was not pleased with that."

"You told Detective Brandon that Maitland was vague about why she wanted to speak to you, yet you made the long drive from Los Angeles to keep the appointment."

"She assured me that the gossip she had for me was very hot. To be honest, Mr. Ward, I could use a good story. I'm relatively new at *Whispers*. I'm trying to make my mark. If I don't come up with a solid headline soon, I might be looking for other employment. All I can tell you is that I went to the spa a little after midnight, just as Gloria Maitland instructed. She was dead at the bottom of the pool when I arrived."

Oliver narrowed his eyes ever so slightly. "You said someone else was there."

"Yes. I wasn't sure at first but then I heard the footsteps. Someone was running toward me. That made me very nervous. I went into the water to avoid him. That's it. I don't know what else I can tell you."

"You went into the water to avoid him."

"Yes."

"You told Detective Brandon that you weren't sure if the other person was a man or a woman."

"Sound echoes in your spa, Mr. Ward. Also, I couldn't see anything clearly—just shadows. I can't be absolutely certain whether it was a man or a woman who ran toward me. I have to admit I wasn't paying close attention to the details."

"But your first thought was that the other person was a man."

Irene drank some more of her whiskey while she recalled the scene in the spa. She nodded once.

"Yes," she said. "I'm almost sure of it."

"What makes you *almost* sure?"

Irene eyed him warily. "Why are you pushing so hard on this particular subject?"

"Because I think that you have a specific reason to believe that the person who murdered Gloria Maitland was male." Oliver paused for emphasis. "Perhaps because of what Maitland said to you in that phone call that made you get into a car and drive all the way to Burning Cove to meet her."

Irene took a deep breath and exhaled slowly. "Good guess, Mr. Ward. Yes, I have a reason to think that Gloria Maitland might have been murdered by a man."

"While I'm on a roll, I'm going to make another guess. You didn't drive all the way to Burning Cove just to pick up a little Hollywood gossip from an aspiring actress. I'm sure you've got better sources in Los Angeles. I think you came here for a very specific reason. So I'm going to ask you again, what did Gloria Maitland tell you in that phone call that brought you to this town and my hotel?"

Irene rocked her glass back and forth a little, sending the whiskey into a slow swirl. In the past nine days she had chased too many false leads and run into too many stone walls. She had nothing left to lose.

She set the whiskey glass aside and met Oliver Ward's unusual eyes.

"I came here to meet Gloria Maitland because she said she had something very important to tell me about Nick Tremayne."

"The actor?"

Oliver sounded curious but not startled, Irene thought.

"Yes, Mr. Ward, the actor. I'm sure you know him. I believe that he is currently registered here as a guest. Tremayne and Maitland were involved in an affair that ended rather badly, at least from Maitland's point of view. But I'm sure you know that. The news was in all the Hollywood papers."

"I never give out personal information on my guests," Oliver said.

"Yes, you keep mentioning that policy. Look, I'm

not asking you to confirm or deny Tremayne's presence in this hotel. I know he's here because Gloria Maitland told me that much when she called my office."

"You think that the other person in the spa tonight was Tremayne."

It wasn't a question.

She was on treacherous ground now. Nick Tremayne was under contract with one of the most powerful movie studios in Hollywood. His first film, *Sea of Shadows*, had been an unexpected hit. His latest, *Fortune's Rogue*, had transformed Tremayne from rising talent to box office gold. He was suddenly worth a lot of money to his employers, which meant that they would go to great lengths to protect their investment.

She had been in Los Angeles long enough to know that the men at the top of the big studios ran Hollywood and, by extension, much of the city of Los Angeles. They routinely paid off cops, judges, and assorted politicians. Making an inexperienced reporter from a small-time gossip paper disappear would be no problem at all. She had to be very careful.

The studio execs weren't the only ones with a vested interest in Nick Tremayne. Oliver Ward made a very good living providing at least the illusion of privacy to his Hollywood clientele. He had every reason to protect guests like Tremayne.

She had probably said far too much already, thanks to the whiskey and the state of her nerves. Time to take a step back.

She managed a steely smile. "I have no idea what you're talking about, Mr. Ward. I wouldn't dream of implying that I thought Nick Tremayne was the other person in your spa tonight."

He accepted that statement with equanimity. He had probably seen it coming, she decided.

"I understand your reluctance to confide in me," he said. "But if you're telling the truth about what happened this evening, then you might want to reconsider."

"Why would I do that?"

"Because if you are being honest, then I give you my word that we share the same goal."

"Which is?"

"Finding out who killed Gloria Maitland."

She went very still. For some inexplicable reason she was inclined to believe him. But she had learned the hard way that her intuition was not to be trusted.

"What happens if it turns out that one of your guests is the killer?" she asked. "A wealthy guest who has powerful connections? One who has every reason to expect you to keep his or her secrets?"

Oliver gave her a politely quizzical look. "If my guests choose to assume that I will keep all of their secrets, that's up to them."

"But you allow them to think that you will protect them."

"My services do not extend to protecting a killer."

She gripped the lapels of her robe. "I want to go back to the Cove Inn now, Mr. Ward. I need to think about this."

"If you insist." He pushed himself to his feet and gripped his cane. "You said you left your car on a side road behind the hotel?"

She leaped to her feet. "Yes. I didn't want to ask one of the valets to park it for me."

"In case you decided to leave in a hurry and didn't want to have to wait while the valet fetched your vehicle? Never mind. You don't have to answer that question. I'll walk you to your car."

"That's not necessary, really."

"It's going on two o'clock in the morning, Miss Glasson, and if you are telling the truth, there is a murderer on the loose. He or she may still be on the grounds of this hotel. I insist on seeing you safely off the premises."

He had a point, she thought. The one thing she knew for certain tonight was that Oliver Ward was not the person she had encountered in the spa chamber. The killer had not limped or used a cane.

There was another reason she was sure that Ward was not the murderer. She had a feeling that if he wanted to get rid of someone, he would handle the business with efficiency and finesse. He would have created a convincing illusion of an accident.

But not even the most practiced killer could plan for every detail, she reminded herself. Sometimes things went wrong, even for one of the world's greatest magicians.

Oliver Ward, after all, was in a new line of work because two years ago things had gone very, very wrong for him.

Chapter 6

The shrill screech of the printing machine hurt Oliver's ears and made conversation in a normal tone of voice impossible.

He looked at his uncle, who was watching the stylus move slowly back and forth across the paper with the air of an alchemist observing the results of his latest attempt to transmute lead into gold.

"Can you shut that damned thing down?" Oliver said, projecting his voice the way he had once done onstage.

"Almost finished with the test run," Chester yelled back. "I'm telling you, Oliver, this machine is the future of newspapers. All you need is a radio equipped with a printing device like this one."

With his wild mane of gray hair, round gold-rimmed spectacles, and faded coveralls, Chester Ward looked

like a cross between an absentminded professor and
an eccentric mechanic. The reality was that he was a
combination of both. He was an inventor.

Chester loved to take machines apart to see how
they worked. When he was satisfied that he understood the design of a particular instrument or device,
he invariably made some modifications and reassem-
bled it in a way that made it function faster or more
efficiently or even perform an entirely different task.
He currently held a number of patents on everything
from slot machines to hydrofoil engines. Unfortunately, the hydrofoil design had failed to catch the attention of the military, so there was no income from
that source.

The slot machine patent was a very different story.
Chester had licensed his design to a man with extensive
interests in the gaming industry. Luther Pell had recently installed the Ches. J. Ward Gaming Machines in
his Reno casino and his offshore gambling ship anchored in Santa Monica Bay. It was hard to go broke in
the gaming business, Oliver reflected. Chester might
never have another moneymaking patent, but he
wouldn't need one. The steady income from the slot
machines guaranteed him the cash he needed to finance
his endless projects.

It was Chester's innovative machines and devices
that had elevated the Amazing Oliver Ward Show to
a level never before seen in the world of magic. Until
disaster had struck, Oliver had been well on his way
to joining the ranks of Houdini and Blackstone, and
Chester had been his secret weapon.

Chester could design and build anything that Oliver

had been able to imagine. Audiences had left the theater thrilled by a flawless performance of magic and convinced that they had witnessed working prototypes of exotic, highly advanced technology.

Self-driving speedsters, one-man submarines, robots, ovens that cooked entire meals at the touch of a button—the Amazing Oliver Ward Show invited people to "See the Future." It had been a great publicity hook. The advance press releases had played up the educational aspect of the performances, which inspired parents to take their children to the show. Science teachers across the country had encouraged their students to attend. Afterward, there were invariably front-page stories in the local papers rhapsodizing about the futuristic engineering marvels witnessed onstage.

Of course, after the disaster, the press had taken a different tack. The mystery of what went wrong with Oliver Ward's final performance had made headlines for weeks. Eventually the reporters moved on to other sensational stories, but the questions surrounding the bloody end of one of the world's most famous magic acts had achieved something close to legendary status. It was his own fault, Oliver thought. Speculation had run wild primarily because he flatly refused to discuss the subject. In addition, he forbade his employees to talk about the disaster.

"You know, in the length of time it will take you to print out just the front page of one of those radio newspapers, you can read the *Burning Cove Herald* and several L.A. papers as well," Oliver said. He held up the copy of *Hollywood Whispers* that he had picked up at the front desk. "This was delivered to the hotel fifteen minutes ago, for example."

"Old technology," Chester shouted. He patted the massive, waist-high radio with its screeching printer. "In the future you won't have to wait for the news to be printed and distributed. It will be delivered directly into every home and office by one of these babies."

The shill screech ended abruptly. Oliver exhaled in relief. He watched Chester remove the freshly printed page.

"Here you go." Beaming like a proud father showing off his firstborn, Chester held out the printed page. "This just in from a small radio station a few miles up the coast. They've agreed to work with me on the testing phase."

Oliver looked at the page. The headline read *Test*. The story was short. *Weather sunny and warm.*

"There's no news," Oliver said.

"Course not. Still running tests."

"The ink is still wet. No one's going to want to read a wet paper. And at the rate it was printing, it's going to take a very long time to get the front page out of the machine."

Chester grunted. His bushy brows scrunched together. "The slow speed of the printer and the fact that the ink needs time to dry are problems, but I'm working on them." He looked up and squinted at the headline of *Whispers*. "What's it say?"

Oliver read the headline aloud.

ACTRESS FOUND DEAD IN BURNING COVE HOTEL SPA.
WAS IT MURDER?

"Well, damn," Chester muttered. "That reporter lady didn't waste any time, did she?"

"No," Oliver said grimly. "She did not. Must have telephoned her editor right after she got back to the Cove Inn last night. The editor, in turn, must have moved heaven and earth to get the story on the front page in time for today's edition."

"Huh," Chester said. "Well, *Whispers* is a small paper. Doubt if very many people read it."

"They will read it today," Oliver said. "And by tomorrow morning, the story will be in every paper in the country."

"Nah. Gloria Maitland wasn't a famous actress. She was just another pretty face who went to Hollywood to become a star. She didn't make it."

"True, but Nick Tremayne is fast becoming a household name, and he is mentioned in the piece."

Chester started to look worried. "How bad is the story?"

"The article states that Tremayne happens to be vacationing at the same hotel as the dead woman. But the big problem is that there is a thinly veiled reference to a rumor that Tremayne and Maitland once enjoyed a romantic liaison."

Chester pursed his lips. "That's not good."

"No," Oliver said. "It's not."

Chester clapped him on the shoulder. "Cheer up. Not the first time we've had a little scandal here at the hotel. It will all blow over in a day or two. You'll see. Just more publicity."

Oliver tossed his copy of *Whispers* down on the nearest workbench. It landed on top of the latest issue of

Popular Science, Chester's favorite reading material. The cover of the magazine featured an artist's rendering of a futuristic war machine designed to navigate on land and sea.

"This isn't the kind of publicity the hotel needs," Oliver said.

Chester squinted thoughtfully. "Are the police looking into the death of Miss Maitland?"

"I don't know. Haven't talked to Brandon this morning. He's a good man. I know he has his suspicions but I'll be surprised if Chief Richards allows him to conduct a serious investigation."

Chester snorted. "Everyone knows that Richards owes his cushy job to the city council, and the council likes to pretend that there is no crime in Burning Cove. Bad for business."

"Right. So unless Brandon comes up with some hard evidence, Maitland's death will go down as a tragic accident."

"How did the *Burning Cove Herald* cover the drowning?"

"As an accident, unsurprisingly. When was the last time the *Herald* covered anything in depth except charity luncheons and the thrilling activities of the Burning Cove Gardening Club?" Oliver said.

"Y'know, they say that once upon a time Edwin Paisley used to be a red-hot crime reporter."

"Well, he's obviously retired from that line of journalism."

Chester picked up the copy of *Whispers* and quickly scanned the front-page story. He paused at one line, squinting a little.

"What's this about a quote from the proprietor of the Burning Cove Hotel?"

"Don't remind me," Oliver said.

"You actually gave that reporter lady a quote?"

"Her name is Irene Glasson, and I didn't exactly give her a quote. What I tried to do was warn her off the story. I told her that if she wasn't careful, the police might conclude that she had something to do with Maitland's death."

"Looks like you didn't do a very good job of scaring the daylights out of her."

"No," Oliver said. "Apparently not."

He brooded over his impressions of Irene. He didn't have to dredge up the memories. He had been thinking about her nonstop since the moment he met her. That had occurred last night when Tom O'Conner, the head of hotel security, summoned him to the spa chamber.

Irene was soaking wet, shivering in the cool night air. Someone had given her a towel, which she had wrapped around her shoulders. She clutched it closed in front of herself with one hand. In her other, she gripped a handbag that looked like something a professional woman would carry. Her whiskey brown hair hung in damp tendrils. Her wide-legged trousers and thin blouse were plastered to her slender frame.

Aware that Irene was both the only eyewitness and the principal suspect, Oliver had whisked her into his private villa before any of the guests could see her. At that point, Jean Firebrace, the head of housekeeping, had taken charge of her for a while. The two women disappeared upstairs to the guest bedroom, a room that, until that moment, had never housed a guest.

The next time Oliver saw Irene she was bundled up in a thick white robe and ensconced in one of the two big chairs in front of the fireplace.

What had surprised him the most was that he found it difficult to read her. He was usually very good when it came to figuring out what made someone tick. He could pick out a stranger in an audience and come up with an accurate character analysis in a few short minutes. All it took were some key questions and a quick study of the individual's clothes, jewelry, and voice. It was amazing how much you could tell about someone from just a pair of shoes.

One thing had been clear from the start. He was damned sure that Irene didn't trust him. But for some reason, that just made her all the more interesting. There were secrets hidden in her big eyes and a haunted quality that told him she had learned some things the hard way.

Well, that gives us something in common, lady.

She would never have survived a casting call in Hollywood because, with the exception of her fine eyes, everything else about her was too subtle for the camera. She was attractive but not spectacularly so. She had an edge, though, an intensity that aroused his curiosity. He was very sure that, like with any good illusion, there was a lot hidden under the surface of Irene Glasson.

By the time he had limped back to the villa after seeing her off in her nondescript Ford sedan, he concluded that he was more than merely curious. He was downright fascinated.

He probably ought to be worried by his reaction to her, he thought.

"So where is this famous quote from management?" Chester asked, scanning the article.

"It's somewhere near the end of the piece, and I told you, it's not a quote."

"Ah, here we go," Chester said. *"The management of the Burning Cove Hotel refused to respond to this reporter's request for clarification."*

"In other words, I wouldn't confirm that Nick Tremayne was staying in the hotel or that he was rumored to have had an affair with the dead woman."

"Which is as good as telling her straight out that he was here and that he probably did have an affair with Maitland."

"Miss Glasson already knew that much."

Chester did not look up from the article. "I wouldn't worry about it if I were you. It's just the usual Hollywood gossip."

"Except for the reporter's speculation about the possibility of murder."

"Except for that part. Where's the stuff about how the reporter had to jump into the pool to escape the killer?"

"She left out that bit of drama."

Chester frowned. "Wonder why?"

"Probably because she wants to keep the attention on the death of Gloria Maitland. She's convinced it was murder."

"Why is she so determined to prove it? Just to get the story?"

"I don't think so." He had been asking himself the same question since Irene Glasson had landed, soaking wet, in his otherwise well-organized, well-controlled world. "Got a feeling there's more to it than that. She says she needs the story in order to keep her job, but I have a hunch that she's got another reason. Something personal."

"Something personal involving murder? That strikes me as peculiar."

"Strikes me the same way."

"Well, you're usually damned good at reading people."

"I've been known to make mistakes," Oliver reminded him grimly.

"True, but I think that in this case the odds are excellent that you're right." Chester read some more of the article. "Says here that the hotel management is expected to go to great lengths to suppress any whisper of murder in order to avoid a scandal."

"Strangely enough, I don't think she believed me when I told her that I intend to find out exactly what happened to Maitland."

Chester tossed the paper aside. "Miss Glasson doesn't know you very well."

"No," Oliver said, "she doesn't."

"As if you'd let someone get away with murder right here on the grounds of your own hotel."

"Damn right. The Burning Cove doesn't set a very high bar when it comes to the behavior expected of its guests, but management does frown on murder."

"Got to have some standards," Chester said.

"Right. Besides, murder is bad for business."

"When the Amazing Oliver Ward Show was touring, we used to say that any publicity was good publicity so long as it mentioned the next appearance."

"We're not on the road anymore."

Chester took off his spectacles and began to polish the lenses with a large handkerchief. "No one's got a better eye for detail than you do. Part of what made you a good magician. What do you think happened in that spa chamber last night?"

"I took another look around this morning. It's just barely possible that Gloria Maitland slipped on the tiles at the edge of the pool and somehow managed to hit the back of her head and tumble into the water, but I doubt that's what happened. The angle of the blow makes it a lot more likely that she was struck from behind. Probably knocked out cold. I'd say that she fell into the water and drowned."

"So she was murdered."

"That's what it looks like."

Chester's bushy gray brows climbed. "Any chance it was the reporter lady who did it?"

"If I were a cop, I'd consider Miss Glasson an excellent suspect. She admitted that she had a private late-night meeting with the victim. Also, she's strong for a woman. She could have overpowered Gloria Maitland."

"What makes you say Glasson is strong?"

"She was able to swim across the pool fully dressed. Granted, she had the sense to get rid of her shoes first; still, swimming in a pair of women's trousers wouldn't have been easy. Lot of heavy fabric. Then she managed to haul herself up out of the water when she reached the opposite side. There was something else, as well."

"What?"

"She had a large handbag. Looked a bit like a small version of a doctor's medical bag."

"What about it? Women usually carry a handbag."

"She hurled it across the lap pool before she went into the water."

"Huh." Chester reflected briefly. "You think it's odd that she didn't just drop the handbag when she kicked off her shoes, don't you?"

"I think there was something very important inside that handbag."

"Money, probably, as well as the usual fripperies women carry around."

"Whatever it was, it was so important that she made a point of trying to save it before she went into the water." Oliver paused, thinking. "It looked heavy."

"The handbag?" Chester grimaced. "In my experience the average woman's bag is as heavy as one of my tool kits. Anything else strike you?"

"Lots of things. Irene Glasson is shaping up to be a regular mystery woman. I heard her give Brandon her address in L.A. and the name of her landlady."

"And?"

"I called the landlady this morning. Said I was a relative who was hoping to speak to my long-lost cousin. The landlady didn't seem to know much about Irene Glasson, just that she had appeared on the doorstep a few months ago, looking to rent an apartment. She had enough money for the first month's rent so the landlady didn't ask a lot of questions."

"Did you call the *Whispers* office?"

"Sure. Got right through to the editor, Velma Lancaster, who confirmed that Miss Glasson works for her, but that was about all she said. She sounded worried. When I told her who I was, she got even more nervous."

"That's no surprise. So, what it boils down to is that you really didn't learn much about Miss Glasson."

"Irene Glasson does not appear to have a past. All the evidence indicates that her life began four months ago when she showed up in L.A."

"She wouldn't be the first person to arrive in California looking for a fresh start. Take yourself, for example, and me, and most of the people who worked in the Amazing Oliver Ward Show."

"Yeah. For example. But we all have pasts. Irene Glasson doesn't."

Chester's expression tightened with concern. "You think she's going to be trouble, don't you?"

"She already is trouble. The question is, what do I do about her? Damned if I'll let her destroy this hotel. Every nickel I've got is tied up in this place."

"You've got a plan?"

"The plan is to figure out what happened to Gloria Maitland."

Chester eyed him with a shrewd look. "What else do you have in mind?"

"I'd really like to know what Irene Glasson has inside her handbag."

Chapter 7

"The Maitland bitch wasn't supposed to become a problem." Nick Tremayne tossed the copy of *Whispers* down on the table. "What the hell went wrong?"

"I don't know." Claudia Picton clutched her notebook to her bosom and tried to contain her anxiety. Her job depended on keeping the star calm. "Mr. Ogden assured me that everything was under control."

Nick stabbed an accusing finger at her.

"Well, that's not the case, is it?" he said. "The piece in *Whispers* says that Maitland and I were rumored to have had an affair and that I'd recently ended the romance. Everyone who reads that story will assume that Maitland followed me here to Burning Cove. That she threatened to make trouble for me. And it's all true, damn it. Talk about a motive for murder."

"I'm sure everything will be all right," Claudia said. She was practically pleading now. "The police are calling Miss Maitland's death a tragic accident. No one has labeled it murder."

"No one except a third-rate gossip rag. That's all it takes."

"I telephoned Mr. Ogden again a few minutes ago," Claudia said, striving for a soothing tone. "He said there's nothing to be concerned about. He said you are to go on with your vacation here in Burning Cove as though nothing happened. He says if you check out before you were scheduled to leave, it will only stir up more speculation."

Nick gave her a savage glare and then stalked across the villa's main room, stopping at the glass doors that opened onto a private patio.

The outdoor sitting area was enclosed with a walled garden. A sweeping view of the cove and the Pacific Ocean beyond was visible through the decorative wrought iron. The glare of the light dancing and flashing on the surface of the water was so bright it hurt Claudia's eyes.

The knowledge that Nick was seething was more than enough to tighten her already strained nerves to the breaking point. She had a job that almost any other woman in America would gladly have sold her soul to obtain—she was Nick Tremayne's personal assistant. If only those other women knew the truth. Her dream job had become a nightmare.

He had been a supporting player in his first film, *Sea of Shadows*, but he managed to steal every scene in which he appeared. He'd been cast as the lead in his second film, *Fortune's Rogue*. The movie catapulted him to instant stardom. The gossip magazines couldn't get enough of him. Female fans adored him. There were rumors that Stanley Bancroft, the star who had been expected to get top billing in the film, was drinking heavily and turning to cocaine to alleviate his depression.

"Ogden was supposed to deal with Maitland before she made real trouble," Nick said.

He gazed grimly at the view through the open doors. Claudia watched him carefully, trying to gauge his mood. Stars were notoriously temperamental and Nick Tremayne was no exception. The disconcerting thing was that he could switch from laughter to rage in the blink of an eye. It was part of his talent but it was also unnerving.

"Mr. Ogden said that he gave Miss Maitland the money she demanded," Claudia said. "He was certain that she would disappear."

"But she didn't disappear, did she?" Nick did not turn around. "Instead she followed me here to Burning Cove. And now she's dead and that damned reporter from *Whispers* has as good as implied I'm a murderer."

"Mr. Ogden said the hotel management would protect you from the press. The studio will take care of everything else."

"Easy for Ogden to say. It's not his future on the line. What am I supposed to do for the next two weeks? Hang around the hotel pool and drink martinis while I duck the press? Or maybe I should schedule a massage. That would certainly make for some interesting gossip, don't you think? I can see the headline. *Actor*

Enjoys Attentions of Lovely Masseuse in Spa Where His Lover Drowned."

"I'm sure everything will be all right. Mr. Ogden will deal with the police and the hotel management. He'll take care of the editor of *Whispers*, too. That's his job. The studio pays him to fix problems like this. He knows what he's doing. I'm sure he's handled far worse situations."

"Worse than an accusation of murder?" Nick swung around. "Ogden is powerful in L.A., but we're in Burning Cove. Things may be different here."

"I'm sure that's not true," Claudia said quickly. "Money talks and Mr. Ogden has the resources of the studio behind him. He can buy off the L.A. police and judges. He can certainly afford the Burning Cove cops."

"I refuse to sit here in this villa while that *Whispers* reporter sabotages my career. I've worked too hard to get this far. Damned if I'll stand by and let that Glasson bitch destroy me."

Claudia clenched her fingers very tightly around her notebook. "What do you want me to do?"

Nick looked at her with blazing eyes. Unlike many of Hollywood's leading men who got by on their looks and minimal talent, Nick was a genuinely gifted actor. He was endowed with an uncanny ability to project a variety of emotions ranging from smoldering passion to bone-chilling fury. It didn't hurt that he was breathtakingly handsome with a classically carved jaw, high cheekbones, and a trim, athletic physique. His dark hair was cut in the sleek, brushed-back style made fashionable by the likes of Cary Grant and Clark Gable. It gleamed with just the right amount of hair oil.

The camera loved Nick. So did directors. So did women.

Claudia was starting to think that women might prove to be Nick's downfall. The Hollywood magazines called him irresistible and he had begun to believe his own press. The result was a string of one-night flings and short-lived affairs. It had been inevitable that sooner or later a problem like Gloria Maitland would occur.

"According to the rumors flying around this hotel, the reporter who wrote that story for *Whispers* is still here in town," Nick said.

He sounded thoughtful now.

"That's right," Claudia said, relieved that he appeared to be calming down. "Mr. Ogden gave me the details. He got them from the local chief of police. Miss Glasson is registered at the Cove Inn."

"Talk to her," Nick said. "Offer her an exclusive."

Shocked, Claudia stared at him. "I don't understand. What kind of exclusive?"

"An exclusive interview with me, you stupid woman. She'll jump at the opportunity to have a private conversation with Nick Tremayne. Any reporter would, especially under these circumstances."

Claudia swallowed hard. "Do you think that's wise? Mr. Ogden instructed me to keep you away from the press."

"Ogden is in L.A. I'm the one here in Burning Cove. It's my career at stake. I'll deal with the problem. Make that appointment for today."

She wanted to argue with him. The thought of going against Ogden's orders terrified her. But Nick Tremayne could easily get her fired if he decided that he didn't want her around.

It dawned on her that the idea of an exclusive interview just might work. Nick could certainly turn on the charm when it suited him. There was no reason to think that he could not manipulate Irene Glasson.

"I'll contact her right away," she said.

She whirled around and rushed toward the front door of the villa.

When she was safely outside, she stopped and took several deep breaths of the warm, fragrant air. There had been a little fog earlier but it had been burned off by the late-September sun. Now the sky was an unreal shade of blue.

When her nerves had settled down, she made her way along a flagstone path that wound through the lush gardens of the hotel. Nick had one of the private villas, Casa de Oro, but her room was in the main building. The villas, with their secluded patios and gardens and dramatic views, were reserved for the stars and others willing to pay top dollar for luxury and privacy.

The Burning Cove Hotel crowned a gently rising hillside above the rocky cliffs. At the foot of the cliffs, splashing waves churned up white froth on a pristine beach. The main building and the villas were all constructed in a fantasy version of what they called the Spanish colonial revival style of architecture. From what she had seen, the entire town—houses, hotels, shops, even the post office and the gas stations—had been built according to the same set of design rules.

White stucco walls, red tile roofs, charming shaded courtyards, and covered walkways were everywhere.

Burning Cove was a Hollywood movie set of a town, she thought. And just like a movie, you never really knew what was going on behind the scenes.

She decided that she hated the place.

Chapter 8

"We scooped every paper in town with the Maitland story," Velma Lancaster said. The words crackled a little over the phone line. "But by now half the reporters in Los Angeles will be on the way to Burning Cove. You need to get me a follow-up headline for tomorrow's morning edition."

Irene winced and held the phone away from her ear. When Velma got excited, she tended to talk very, very fast and she got very, very loud. She was definitely excited this morning. Gloria Maitland's death with its connection to Nick Tremayne and a legendary hotel known to be the haunt of Hollywood royalty was the biggest story *Whispers* had ever printed. Velma had just spent five minutes of long-distance phone time emphasizing that it was also the most dangerous.

Forty-something and constructed along Amazonian proportions, Velma had taken control of the sleepy little paper two years earlier when her much older husband had collapsed and died at his desk. Irene had no difficulty summoning up a mental image of her new employer. An outsized woman with a personality to match, Velma colored her hair scarlet red and styled it in a short, sharply angled bob that had gone out of fashion several years earlier. She wore exotically patterned caftans, smoked cigars, and kept a bottle of whiskey in the bottom drawer of her desk.

"Don't worry," Irene said. "I'm working on a headline for you."

She lowered her voice because she was using the front desk phone in the lobby of the Cove Inn. Mildred Fordyce, the gray-haired proprietor, was puttering around behind the counter, doing her best to make it appear that she wasn't paying attention, but Irene knew she was hanging on every word.

"Call me as soon as you have something I can print," Velma rasped.

"I will but it's not going to be easy," Irene said. "The Burning Cove Hotel has tighter security than most banks."

"So what? Banks get robbed all the time. Do your job."

"Yes, Boss. But there's another problem—"

"Now what?"

"I only planned to spend one night here in Burning Cove," Irene said. Automatically she glanced down at the calf-length skirt and flutter-sleeved blouse she was wearing. "I just brought a single change of clothes with me. Housekeeping at the Burning Cove Hotel took the things I was wearing last night when I went into the pool. I haven't seen them since. I'm not sure if they survived."

"Reversing the charges for phone calls is one thing. But if you think I'm going to pay for a new wardrobe, you can think again. Go rob a bank."

Time to play her high card, Irene decided. "This is about Peggy, Boss. Her death wasn't an accident. We both know that."

There was a short, taut silence on the other end of the line.

"You don't have to remind me," Velma said finally. She sounded gruff but worried. "Promise me you'll be careful. I don't want to lose another reporter. *Whispers* is a Hollywood gossip paper. We care about which actors are sleeping with which actresses. We don't cover murder."

"Except when one of our own is a victim."

Velma heaved a sigh. "Agreed."

"We need to follow up on this story, Boss."

Ten days ago Peggy Hackett had drowned in her own bathtub. The death was called an accident. For years she had been a Hollywood legend, the gossip columnist of one of the biggest papers in L.A.

Peggy had also been a chain-smoking, martini-swilling reporter who, in her younger days, had been known to sleep with her sources—male and female—in order to get a story. As her looks began to fail, she had not been above using *leverage*, as she termed it, to convince people to talk.

In the end the drinking and hard living had exacted a toll. She was fired from the newspaper that had carried her column for so long.

Six months ago, she wound up on the doorstep of *Whispers*. Velma hired her. Peggy had gained some control over the drinking, but she was no longer young enough or pretty enough to seduce her old sources. Most of the insider secrets that she had once used as leverage had become old news involving faded stars. But she had been determined to rebuild her career.

It was Peggy who had convinced Velma to hire Irene in spite of her lack of experience. *Glasson's got the grit,* Peggy had argued. *That's what matters. Reminds me of myself when I was just starting out. Hell, I can teach her everything else she needs to know.*

Theirs had been an odd relationship, Irene thought. Jaded and afflicted with a chronic cough, Peggy had seemed to gain a new lease on life when she undertook the task of mentoring Irene. *I owe you, Glasson,* she had said more than once.

I owe you, Peggy. You were a friend when I needed one.

"All right," Velma said. "Follow the story but just be damned careful."

"Don't worry, I will," Irene promised.

But she was speaking to a dead line. Velma had hung up on her.

She set the receiver back in the cradle and gave Mildred Fordyce a bright smile.

"Don't worry," she said. "I reversed the charges."

Mildred turned around, beaming, and studied Irene

with rapt attention. "So you're the reporter who found
the body of that poor woman last night."

"I see you read *Whispers*."

"Not until today," Mildred said cheerfully. "But I
picked up a copy at the newsstand this morning after
I saw the front page of the local paper. Can't rely on
the *Herald* to give you the whole story, not when the
story involves Oliver Ward's hotel."

She pushed a copy of the *Burning Cove Herald* across
the desk, turning it around so that Irene could read
the headline.

TRAGIC ACCIDENT AT LOCAL HOTEL

"Yes, I saw the piece that ran in the *Herald*," Irene
said. "You're right. It's not the whole story, not by a
country mile. More like a small obituary notice."

Mildred tapped the front page of the *Herald*. "According to this, that woman's death was accidental. It
says the cops think she slipped and fell on some wet
tiles. Cracked her head and went into the pool. Probably unconscious so she drowned."

"That does seem to be the prevailing theory at the
moment," Irene said.

Mildred got a speculative expression. "But the article in *Whispers* claims that there was someone else
in the spa."

"There was someone else there," Irene said. "I didn't
get a good look but I heard him. Or her."

"You couldn't tell whether it was a man or a woman?"

"No. It was quite dark and sound gets distorted in
that big, tiled room."

"How do you know that person killed Gloria Maitland?"

"I don't know for sure," Irene admitted. "But I think that, under the circumstances, the situation warrants a full investigation."

"You mean because Miss Maitland had an affair with Nick Tremayne? And because rumor has it that he ended things, and because Tremayne just happened to be staying at the Burning Cove Hotel at the time of the death?"

"I see you read my story very carefully."

"Yes, indeed," Mildred said.

"There was someone else in the spa last night," Irene said. "I think that at the very least the police should find and interview that individual, don't you?"

Mildred pursed her lips. "I'm afraid it's not going to be that simple. This is Burning Cove."

"You mean the authorities here are as corrupt as they are back in L.A.?"

"You didn't hear me say that." Mildred raised one shoulder in a dismissive shrug. "According to the *Herald*, the lady who discovered the body was very upset. It says she was likely suffering from a case of shattered nerves."

"Do I look like I'm suffering from a case of bad nerves?"

"No," Mildred admitted. "What are you going to do next?"

"I'm here to cover a story," Irene said. "That's what I intend to do."

"We'll see. Good luck to you is all I can say."

Chapter 9

"W hat is it with actors?" Earnest Ogden tossed the copy of *Whispers* onto his desk, got to his feet, and walked to the window. "They're all the same. I swear, the hotter the star, the more likely he is to get into trouble. If only their brains matched their looks and their talent. Damned fools, all of them. Pardon my language, Miss Ross."

Maxine Ross glanced up from her stenography notebook. "Of course, Mr. Ogden."

As usual, she was cool and unruffled. It was, after all, not the first time she had heard the lament about temperamental, neurotic actors or a bit of rough language. She was a professional. She also happened to be one of the few females employed by the studio who had never had aspirations to become a star. She was unflappable, a steady, calming influence in a business built on overheated passions, dreams, ambitions, and too much money.

Glumly, Ogden contemplated the scene outside his second-floor office window. From where he stood he could see an array of large, enclosed soundstages, the commissary, and the wardrobe department. Beyond was the big backlot used for outdoor scenes. That week they were filming a western, a staple of the business. You could always sell westerns, Ogden thought. The façade of a frontier town had been set up—a saloon, the sheriff's office, the bank that was destined to be robbed, and a general store—and all of it fake. That was the movie business for you. It sold illusions. He did love it so.

The whole establishment, from backlot to executive offices, was, in effect, a secure compound surrounded by high walls. Access was controlled through high, ornate gates manned by tough security guards. Theoretically the walls and the guards were there to protect the privacy of the stars and prevent interference with the filmmaking process. But sometimes it felt as if he worked for a fancy prison or a secret government agency.

He was a very well-paid nanny to a bunch of spoiled actors and actresses. He routinely saved prominent talents who went on drinking binges and got involved in hit-and-run incidents. He made morals charges against actors with a fondness for underage sex partners disappear. He paid off women who claimed a star had raped them or that they were pregnant with a star's love child. He hushed up rumors of homosexuality. And so it went. He could fix just about any problem that came up.

"What's done is done," he said. "Nick Tremayne is

very important to the studio, so obviously we will have to clean up this mess."

"Yes, sir," Maxine said.

She waited, pen poised above her notebook.

Ogden considered his options. He lived by three simple rules. Rule Number One: Identify the problem. Rule Number Two: Identify the source of the problem. Rule Number Three: Identify the pressure points and apply whatever pressure was required to make a problem disappear.

Most of the time, money was all that was needed. Money persuaded cops and judges to look the other way. Money persuaded women to cease making accusations of rape. Money kept blackmailers quiet.

But sometimes more forceful measures were required.

"The problem, Miss Ross, is that a gossip columnist has published completely false rumors about Nick Tremayne in a cheap Hollywood scandal sheet."

"Yes, Mr. Ogden."

"The source of the problem would appear to be the reporter who wrote the piece, Irene Glasson."

"Yes, sir."

"Get the editor of *Whispers* on the phone for me. It's time that Velma Lancaster and I had a little chat."

"Yes, Mr. Ogden. Will that be all, sir?"

"No. Tremayne's personal assistant called again this morning. She told me that Tremayne is very nervous. Nervous stars are always a problem. They become even more temperamental and unpredictable than they usually are."

"Yes, sir."

Ogden turned around. "Get ahold of Hollywood Mack, too. Tell him to stand by. I might have a job for him."

"Yes, sir."

Maxine rose, unfazed by the instructions to contact a man who consorted with shady characters and known criminals. She left, closing the door very quietly.

Ogden went back to the window and watched a familiar limousine pull up to the big gate. The driver flashed a badge at the guard and was waved through. It wasn't that long ago that the arrival of Stanley Bancroft, the star of *Sea of Shadows*, would have created a buzz of excitement on the grounds of the studio. But today few people bothered to look at the big car. Bancroft was not yet box office poison, but everyone knew that his career was fading fast.

All glory is fleeting, my friend, Ogden thought. A few years earlier, at the dawn of talking movies, Bancroft had displaced another leading man who, as it turned out, had a high, grating voice. That hadn't been a problem during the heyday of the silents but it was a career-killer in the era of sound.

Ogden turned away from the window and sat down at his desk. He thought about the various steps he could take to control the damage that threatened one of the studio's most important investments. After a while he came up with a plan.

This is why you get the big bucks and the corner office, pal.

But he knew that long ago it had ceased to be about the money. What he truly relished these days was the power that he wielded. It was more intoxicating than any drug.

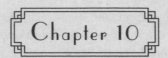

Chapter 10

I t was his job to protect the star. *That's what friends are for,* Henry Oakes reminded himself.

He sat at the counter of the small café, hunched over a cup of coffee and a copy of *Whispers*, and contemplated the task that he had set for himself.

The problem was that Nick Tremayne did not understand he was in danger. Henry wanted to warn him but he didn't dare reveal himself. The time was not right.

It should have been the studio's job to protect Nick Tremayne, but whoever was in charge of his security was obviously not paying attention. The studio had missed the threat that the first *Whispers* reporter, Hackett, had presented. They had not dealt with the Gloria Maitland problem.

Henry had talked to both women. Tried to reason

with them. But they had treated him as if he was crazy. Hackett had actually called him crazy to his face. It had reminded him of his mother's words. *You have to stop obsessing over movie stars, Henry. People will think you're not right in the head.*

One thing was certain—neither the Maitland woman nor the nosy newspaper reporter, Hackett, would call him crazy again. With them out of the picture, it had appeared that Nick Tremayne was safe, at least for a time.

But now another reporter from *Whispers* had arrived on the scene, and it was obvious that Irene Glasson posed a serious threat to the star.

Henry folded the copy of *Whispers* very carefully so that the terrible headline was concealed. Nick Tremayne was not the first star with whom he'd shared a special kind of friendship. Before he had developed the relationship with Tremayne, he was very close to another leading man. But the studio had come between them. Two goons found him outside the star's home one night. They had hurt him badly, beaten him nearly senseless. They told him that if he ever got close to the star again, they would kill him. He believed them.

For a while he tried to avoid having any more close friendships with stars. But he couldn't resist the movies, and one afternoon he'd gone to see *Fortune's Rogue.* He had been transported by the power of Nick Tremayne's acting. By the time he left the theater, he'd understood that he and Tremayne were destined to share a special relationship.

He'd also comprehended that this time he had to be careful. He could not allow the studio to discover his friendship with the star. Nick Tremayne would be forced to deny it. So, for Tremayne's sake, he had remained in the shadows.

Someday, when the time was right, he would reveal himself to Tremayne, but until that day he would do what he was meant to do—he would protect his friend, the star.

Chapter 11

I rene was in her room, trying to come up with another hook for the next story, when Mildred Fordyce bellowed from the bottom of the stairs.

"Someone is here to see you, Miss Glasson."

Oliver Ward. It had to be him. Irene couldn't think of anyone else in Burning Cove who might want to speak with her. A little rush of anticipation swept through her. She told herself it was because a visit from Ward boded well for her story. Perhaps he had decided to give her a real quote, after all.

But a small, secret voice whispered that it wasn't just the prospect of getting a useful quote that made her hurry to the door. The truth was that she was very, very curious to see Oliver Ward again. It would be interesting to find out whether her initial impressions of him held up in the light of day or if she had allowed her imagination to mislead her last night.

She opened the door and leaned out into the upstairs hall. "I'll be right down, Mrs. Fordyce."

She closed the door again and hurried back across the room to check her image in the mirror. After returning to the inn last night, she had made the phone call to Velma and then gone upstairs. She had been energized and feeling jumpy, but she took the time to pin several big curls into her damp hair before collapsing onto the bed. Now she was very glad she had done so. At least she no longer looked like she'd been dunked in a pool. She certainly wouldn't be mistaken for Ginger Rogers or Katharine Hepburn, but she looked presentable with her hair brushed back off her face and tucked behind her ears. The soft, easy waves fell to her shoulders.

She put on some lipstick, took a deep breath, and went out into the hall.

It wasn't Oliver Ward who was waiting in the lobby.

A tall, thin woman in her early twenties looked up as Irene came down the stairs. The newcomer wore a severely cut brown suit with a narrow, calf-length skirt and a tight jacket that did little to enhance her figure. Her dark hair was parted in the middle and pinned in a tightly rolled set of curls that started at one ear and looped down around the back of her neck to end at the other ear. It was a very businesslike hairstyle. She clutched a notebook as though it were a life preserver.

Irene's first thought was that the woman would have been quite pretty if she didn't look so anxious.

"Miss Irene Glasson?" the woman asked.

The voice fit with the rest of the image—thin and nervous.

"I'm Irene Glasson." Irene tried to sound cool and professional. She was a journalist now. The new role was not so very different from her previous career as a private secretary. Success in both fields, she had discovered, depended on organizational skills and the ability to think on one's feet. "What can I do for you, Miss—?"

The woman looked almost pathetically relieved.

"Picton, Claudia Picton. I'm Mr. Tremayne's personal assistant. I wonder if I might have a word with you? It's very important."

"What is this about?" Irene asked. But she was sure she knew the answer. Excitement splashed through her.

Claudia cast a quick, uneasy look at Mildred and then lowered her voice. "I'm afraid it's a private matter."

"Of course," Irene said. "My room is too small. There's only one chair. Let's go out on the patio. We can talk there."

Ignoring Mildred's disappointed expression, she went quickly toward the glass-paned doors that opened onto a small garden. Claudia followed, practically trotting.

Irene motioned toward two green wrought iron chairs shaded by an awning. Claudia hesitated and then perched on the edge of one of the chairs. Irene sat down across from her.

"How did you find me, Miss Picton?"

Claudia flinched and then reddened. She made a visible effort to square her already rigid shoulders.

"Someone at the studio gave me your name," she said.

Irene nodded. "Of course. That explains it."

"I beg your pardon?"

"You're here because you were assigned to handle Nick Tremayne's little public relations problem. Some fixer at the studio made a phone call to the local police and offered a nice gratuity in exchange for the address of the reporter who broke the story of Gloria Maitland's death. Obviously the helpful local policeman obliged."

Claudia's jaw tensed. "I did get a call from someone who represents the studio. But I'm here because Mr. Tremayne, himself, asked me to speak with you."

"Did he? That's very interesting. What is he going to offer me in exchange for dropping the story?"

"You don't understand. He wants to give you an exclusive one-on-one interview."

"That's very generous of him. Why would he do that?"

"Mr. Tremayne feels there has been a grave misunderstanding concerning his prior association with Miss Maitland. He would like to clarify the nature of his relationship with her."

"That should be interesting. Naturally I'll be delighted to conduct an interview with Mr. Tremayne, provided he understands that everything will be on the record."

"I'll make sure he knows that before he meets with you." Claudia paused. "You do realize that Mr.

Tremayne was nowhere near the spa last night at the time of Miss Maitland's death."

Irene caught her breath but managed to maintain what she thought was a serviceable air of unconcern.

"Is that so?" she said.

"He was at the Paradise Club," Claudia said. "It's a popular nightspot here in Burning Cove. He was seen by any number of people. The police will be able to confirm that if they feel it necessary to do so."

Damn, Irene thought. That was not good news.

"In that case, there is no reason for Mr. Tremayne to be concerned about an investigation into the death of Miss Maitland, is there?" she said.

"I hope you will try to understand his situation," Claudia said. "Mr. Tremayne has no reason to be concerned about an appearance of guilt. But he and Miss Maitland were . . . acquainted."

"Well acquainted, apparently. Can you confirm that they had a romantic liaison?"

"No, nothing like that. Mr. Tremayne considered Miss Maitland to be a friend, that's all. And because of that friendship, he doesn't want to see her reputation impugned."

"Miss Maitland is dead. She is no longer concerned about her reputation."

"I would hope you would consider her family's feelings in this matter."

"She has no close family," Irene said. "I checked."

Claudia leaped to her feet. She was thoroughly flustered now. "I think it would be best if Mr. Tremayne, himself, explained the nature of his association with Miss Maitland."

"I agree. I'll look forward to the interview. When and where?"

"Mr. Tremayne asked me to invite you to meet with him in his villa at the Burning Cove Hotel."

Irene almost smiled. "I don't think that would be a very good idea under the circumstances. Appearances, you know."

Claudia froze. It was clear that she had not expected the invitation to be refused.

"You don't want the interview?" she asked.

"I want the interview but I would prefer to conduct it somewhere other than Nick Tremayne's private hotel suite."

Claudia looked stricken. "I don't understand. Surely you aren't afraid of Mr. Tremayne?"

"Let's just say that I would be more comfortable if the interview were conducted out in the open. I'd prefer a location where there will be other people around. That way if Mr. Tremayne tries to threaten me or offer a bribe, I can round up a couple of witnesses."

Claudia was torn between shock and outrage. "That's ridiculous. Mr. Tremayne just wants to tell you his side of the story."

"Which I will be only too happy to hear. I suggest we meet for coffee at one of the local cafés."

"I'm afraid that would be difficult to arrange. Mr. Tremayne is famous. He can't just walk into a café and expect to go unrecognized. He would soon be surrounded by a crowd of people wanting his autograph. The reason he stays at the Burning Cove Hotel is precisely because he knows he can expect that his privacy will be respected."

Irene shrugged. "All right. I'll meet with him at the hotel but not in his villa. I want a more public location. And keep in mind that it might not be easy to arrange for me to get through the front gate of the Burning Cove. I understand management has a strict policy when it comes to members of the press. Evidently journalists are not allowed on the premises."

"I'm sure the hotel management will make an exception for Mr. Tremayne," Claudia said. "Would this afternoon be convenient for you?"

"Certainly."

"I suggest three o'clock. You and Mr. Tremayne could meet for tea in the Garden Room at the Burning Cove Hotel."

"I'll be there at three. If you don't see me, it will be because I couldn't get past the guards at the gate."

"Don't worry, I'll take care of that end of things. Thank you, Miss Glasson. You won't regret this, I promise you."

Irene gave her a cool smile. "I'm sure you didn't expect me to turn down an interview with Nick Tremayne."

Claudia looked pathetically grateful. "To be honest, I didn't know what to expect. Miss Maitland's death has been so upsetting for everyone, especially Mr. Tremayne. Three o'clock."

Claudia turned and fled back into the lobby.

Irene waited a moment before she opened her handbag and took out her notebook. She unclipped the pencil and started to jot down her impressions of Claudia Picton. *Nervous. Anxious. Scared?*

I know how you feel, Claudia Picton. I've been nervous, anxious, and scared for the past four months.

She had driven some three thousand miles, traded her prize Packard for a far more anonymous car, changed her name, changed her career, and invented a new life. But she was still looking over her shoulder, still listening for footsteps in the night, still jumping at shadows.

Finding another body last night certainly hadn't helped soothe her nerves. Three women whose lives had touched hers were dead within four months: Helen Spencer, Peggy Hackett, and Gloria Maitland.

Logic and common sense told her that the deaths of Peggy Hackett and Gloria Maitland could not possibly be connected to the grisly murder of Helen Spencer. But logic and common sense did little to allay the fear that churned deep inside her. It was fear of a link between the three dead women that had caused her to become obsessed with finding out the truth about Peggy Hackett's death.

So be it, she thought. She had run as far as she could, all the way to the opposite edge of the country. There was nowhere else to run. She had to discover the truth for the sake of her own sanity.

A large shadow fell across the open page of her notebook.

"I doubt that she'll last very long," Oliver said.

Irene was so startled she nearly levitated out of her chair. She took a sharp breath and looked up. Oliver was standing slightly behind her, his cane gripped tightly in one hand.

She should have heard him approach, she thought.

She had been so lost in her own thoughts that she hadn't heard the tapping of his cane or the hitch in his stride.

She glanced down and saw that there was a thick rubber cap on the end of the cane. That no doubt explained why she hadn't heard it thumping on the paving stones of the patio. Oliver had moved very quietly for a man with a bad leg. The word *stealthy* came to mind.

He was dressed in a pair of excellently tailored trousers, a crisply pressed shirt, and a lightweight linen jacket cut in the drape style. The fashion had become very popular because the design emphasized the width of a man's upper chest and shoulders. But Oliver didn't need the illusion created by a good tailor, she thought. His shoulders would have looked good with or without the jacket.

It occurred to her that the style had something else going for it. The slightly angled drape of the fabric above the waistline was far less restrictive than the older style, which fit the body quite snugly. The ease of movement allowed by the new fashion probably appealed to a man who needed to use a cane.

"I didn't hear you," she said.

She knew the comment sounded like a thinly veiled accusation.

"Sorry," he said. "Didn't mean to startle you. Do you mind if I join you?"

"No," she said.

She slipped the pencil into her notebook and closed the cover.

He eased into the chair that Claudia had just vacated. Irene watched the small action carefully, trying to determine if he really did need the cane or if he used it as a prop. As if an otherwise healthy specimen of manhood would deliberately go about with a fake limp, she thought. *I'm suspicious of everyone these days.*

"Was that shorthand you were using to record your notes?" Oliver asked.

She tensed. "Every reporter develops his or her own version of shorthand."

"I know, but I've seen notes made by other journalists. They aren't nearly so neat." Oliver smiled faintly. "Not so impossible to decipher, either. I'm guessing that only another trained stenographer could read your notes."

He was fishing for information about her.

"That's the thing about a private code, isn't it?" she said. "No one else can read it. What did you mean when you said that Claudia Picton wouldn't last very long?"

"I assume you've met other studio publicists and assistants?"

"Sure. Usually on the phone, though."

"Still, you must know what they're like."

"They're your best friends when they want coverage for their stars and your worst enemies if you don't print the kind of coverage they want."

Oliver's mouth curved faintly in wry amusement. "Exactly. Reporters aren't the only ones who have to deal with publicists and assistants. The hotel has to handle them all the time."

"Yes, I'm sure you've had a lot of experience with the species."

"The appeal of the Burning Cove Hotel is based in

part on the fact that it has become a fashionable retreat for famous film stars. Ambitious publicists and assistants want their actors and actresses to be seen checking in, but they don't want photographers to catch the stars in compromising positions. The result is that my security staff exists primarily to make sure reporters and photographers don't get on the grounds without my permission."

"Which brings you to me."

"Yes, it does." Oliver watched her with unreadable eyes. "I couldn't help but overhear that last part of your conversation with Miss Picton. You have an appointment to meet with Tremayne at my hotel this afternoon."

"Yes, I do. I've been invited to conduct an exclusive interview with Tremayne over tea in something called the Garden Room. Will you allow me on the grounds, Mr. Ward?"

"You're welcome to do the interview in the Garden Room. But I wouldn't be too hopeful of getting anything useful out of Tremayne, if I were you. He'll do his best to charm you. I understand he has a real talent for that sort of thing."

"I'm sure he'll try to dazzle me, but I'm not naïve, Mr. Ward. I fully anticipate that Nick Tremayne will try to convince me that his former girlfriend's death was nothing more than a tragic accident."

Oliver nodded, satisfied. "A word of warning. He really is a very talented actor."

"I know. I saw him in *Fortune's Rogue*."

"I see. Well, in that case, good luck with the interview."

"So you will allow me into your hotel."

"Yes, Miss Glasson. You are free to come and go at will. All I ask in return is that you keep me updated on whatever you learn."

She thought about that for a few seconds and then nodded. "Fair enough, so long as you let me know whatever you find out about Gloria Maitland's death."

"Agreed." Oliver looked amused. "Are you saying that you trust me, Miss Glasson?"

She smiled her reassuring reporter's smile, the one Peggy had taught her. Peggy had called it the just-the-two-of-us-chatting smile.

"No more than you trust me, Mr. Ward," she said. "However, as you pointed out last night, at the moment we do seem to share some similar interests."

"One of which is the security of my hotel. This morning I went over events with the head of my security department. We retraced your steps. As a rule, the spa chamber is locked at night, but there was no sign of forced entry. I assume the side door was unlocked when you arrived?"

"Yes."

"Who unlocked it for you?"

"I assumed Miss Maitland unlocked it. She chose the spa as the location for our meeting. She said it would be empty at that hour of the night. Would it have been difficult for her to get her hands on the key?"

"Unfortunately, no," Oliver said. He sounded grim. "There are several keys to the spa because various departments have reason to go in at various times—housekeeping stocks the robes and towels, the maintenance people have a key, and several members of the spa staff have keys."

"In other words, someone who wanted to borrow a key for a short time could probably figure out how to do it."

"Yes." Oliver hesitated briefly. "Something else has come up. My security people talked to the housekeeping staff."

"Why?"

"The maids are one of the front lines when it comes to hotel security. No one ever notices them."

"I see what you mean," Irene said.

"One of the housekeepers witnessed what was evidently a very hot quarrel between Tremayne and Miss Maitland the day before Miss Maitland died. The maid didn't catch all the details, but Tremayne appeared to be threatening Maitland."

"Very interesting," Irene said.

Oliver watched her intently for an endless moment.

"What?" she finally asked.

"There is one other possibility that should be considered."

Irene did not move. "Are you about to suggest that I stole the key?"

"It did occur to me."

"For what it's worth, I didn't take it."

"For what it's worth," Oliver said, "I'm inclined to believe you."

"Really? Why?"

"As far as I can tell, you had no motive to kill Gloria Maitland."

"All I wanted from her was information."

"As I said, I'm inclined to believe you."

"Be still my beating heart."

Oliver stretched out his bad leg and contemplated her with an unreadable expression. A shiver of knowing iced her nerves. He was waiting for her to make some small slip.

"I'm sure you've heard that Nick Tremayne has a fairly good alibi for last night," she said. "Miss Picton told me he was at a nightclub here in Burning Cove."

Oliver nodded. "The Paradise Club."

"You checked?"

"Last night, after you left."

"Miss Picton said that Tremayne spent the evening there and that several people saw him."

"People who had been drinking heavily all evening are not the most reliable witnesses. But, yes, it seems he was at the club for at least some portion of the night. Would you care to talk to someone who can provide more details?"

"Of course." She raised her brows. "I take it you have a witness in mind?"

"The owner of the club, Luther Pell."

"I would definitely like to ask him a few questions, although he has no reason to tell me the truth."

"You don't trust anyone, do you?"

She smiled a thin smile. "Everyone has secrets."

"Including you."

It was a statement, not a question. It sent another little chill through her.

"When can I talk to Luther Pell?" she said.

"He invited us to have dinner with him this evening at his club."

"Us?"

"Like you, I have a few questions for him myself. I

realize you don't believe me, Miss Glasson, but I can promise that I want the truth as badly as you do, if not more so. I am willing to go to great lengths to protect the privacy of my guests, but I won't protect a killer."

"Even if it means a full-blown scandal?"

To her surprise, Oliver smiled.

"My guests claim they want privacy," he said. "But the truth is, their careers depend on making headlines in papers like *Whispers*. Properly managed, there is nothing like an interesting scandal to boost the career of an aspiring actor or actress. Does wonders for my hotel business, too."

"We're talking about a scandal involving the murder of a woman who is said to have had an affair with a fast-rising star."

"Which makes it a very interesting scandal."

"That you intend to see is properly managed."

"I had to reinvent myself after a disastrous conclusion to my previous career, Miss Glasson. Reinvention is an expensive process. I survived it once. I don't intend to start over a third time if I can avoid it. So, yes, I'm going to try to manage the scandal."

"Do you really think I'll let you dictate the story?" she asked.

"Without my help, you won't get any story at all."

"Is that so?"

"Without my assistance, this town might as well be a fortified castle, as far as you're concerned," Oliver said. "They will lock the gates, pull up the drawbridge, and fill the moat with alligators."

"And in exchange for my accepting your help, you will try to control what I write."

"I may make a few suggestions from time to time," Oliver admitted.

"And if you don't like what I write, you'll withdraw your assistance."

"I thought I made it clear, we share the same goal. I want the killer found."

"Why?"

"Because the Burning Cove Hotel belongs to me. I protect what is mine. No one gets away with committing murder on the premises."

"No exceptions?" she asked.

His smile was as cold as his eyes. "One exception."

And suddenly she knew.

"You," she said.

"Me."

She took a short, tight breath.

"But you didn't kill Gloria Maitland," she said.

"What makes you so sure I didn't murder her?"

"You're a magician. You would have done a better job of it."

Chapter 12

Nick Tremayne's smile was dazzling, a combination of masculine heat and smooth assurance. His eyes were as seductive in real life as they were on the screen. He wore an elegantly cut navy blazer and white linen trousers. His white shirt was accented with a beautifully knotted striped tie. He looked as if he had just stepped off his private yacht.

"Thank you for agreeing to let me give you my side of the story, Miss Glasson," he said. "I appreciate your time."

Humility, gratitude, and sincerity shimmered in the atmosphere around him. Irene had been prepared for his good looks and a whole lot of charm, but she was forced to admit that she was impressed in spite of herself. There was something almost unreal about the man. She felt as though she were doing a scene with him in front of a camera.

Oliver's warning echoed in her head. *He really is a very talented actor.*

The Garden Room of the Burning Cove Hotel was a glass-walled conservatory fronted by a broad terrace overlooking the cove. Well-dressed guests drank their Darjeeling and nibbled dainty pastries amid an assortment of potted plants, hanging ferns, and colorful flowers. Sparkling fountains were scattered around the elegantly tiled room. Beyond the cove the Pacific glinted and flashed in the afternoon sun.

Irene and Nick were seated in a corner that was screened off from the rest of the tearoom by a half dozen artfully placed palms. The position allowed for private conversation but was also a public venue, just as she had requested.

"I know you have questions for me," Nick said. "But before we begin, I'd like to make it clear that my relationship with Miss Maitland lasted for only a couple of weeks. It ended about a month ago. At least, it did on my side."

"How, exactly, did it end?"

"I admit that things got complicated. Look, Gloria and I had some fun together at first. I met her at a Hollywood party. She was vivacious and very pretty. I made it clear that I was not interested in a serious, long-lasting relationship. At this point in my life I am focused exclusively on my art. I thought she understood that."

"But she didn't?"

Nick sighed. "To be honest, I don't know what Gloria

understood. It took me a while to figure out that the woman was not entirely stable."

"What do you mean?"

"I'll be blunt. I think she was unhinged. When we first met, she was a lot of fun. But it wasn't long before she revealed a real talent for high drama. She would cry at the least provocation. She started accusing me of cheating on her. When I reminded her that I had never promised her anything beyond a good time, she threatened to harm herself."

"Do you think she was serious?"

"I don't have a clue," Nick said. "But I made it clear that I was not about to let her manipulate me. I suggested quite strongly that she see a doctor. But that infuriated her. In the end I had to cut things off very forcefully. I told my studio about the situation and I was assured that it would be handled."

"What did you think the studio would do?"

"I never gave it much thought. I was told that Gloria Maitland would no longer be a problem, and that was the end of it as far as I was concerned. The next thing I knew, she turned up here at the hotel. She threatened to make a scene. I told her to get lost. And now she's dead."

"After making an appointment to speak to me."

"I can't begin to guess her intentions, Miss Glasson. But I will repeat, the woman was unstable."

"What do you think happened last night?"

"I think it was an accident, just as the police have concluded," Nick said. "I suspect that Gloria planned some sort of petty revenge but before she could carry it out, she slipped on the tiles, hit her head, and fell into the pool. I'm sure she had been drinking all evening. She liked her Manhattans."

"You think you were intended to be the target of her petty revenge?"

"Sure. In her bizarre fantasy world, she concluded that she was a woman scorned. You know what they say. Hell hath no fury."

"What do you think she planned to tell me?"

"I have no idea," Nick said. "Whatever it was, I'm sure it was guaranteed to make me look bad."

"Why do you think she dragged me here to Burning Cove? Why not speak to me in L.A.?"

Nick closed his eyes briefly. When he opened them, she could have sworn she glimpsed some deep, wrenching emotion.

He's an actor, she reminded herself.

"You want the truth, Miss Glasson? I'll give it to you. But I'm hoping you won't print it. As I said, I think she planned to tell you something that would make me look bad. But I have a feeling that she intended to take her own life after she met with you, or, more likely, stage such an attempt. She wanted the whole act to take place here at the Burning Cove Hotel because she knew that I was staying here. She knew that there would be a scandal that could easily damage my reputation. And thanks to that piece you wrote for *Whispers,* that is exactly what is happening. I've become the subject of a lot of baseless rumors and speculation."

Neatly done, Irene thought. Nick Tremayne was playing his role brilliantly. He had concocted a script that made her look guilty of using the power of the gossip press to hound an innocent man.

It might have worked if she hadn't found Peggy Hackett's body a week ago.

She jotted down a few meaningless scribbles in her notebook, aware that Nick was watching intently. When she looked up without warning, he narrowed his eyes a little. She knew he was trying to figure out if he had given a convincing performance.

"That is all very interesting, Mr. Tremayne," she said. She snapped the notebook closed. "But it leaves me with the same question I had when I agreed to this interview."

"What?" he asked.

There was an edge on the single word.

"I still have no idea what Gloria Maitland planned to tell me." She rose from the table. "Now you must excuse me. I have a few more people to interview."

Nick leaped to his feet. She could have sworn that he started to reach across the table, perhaps to grab her wrist and force her to stay. But in the next heartbeat he had himself under control.

He smiled, startling her. His eyes warmed.

"I appreciate your time, Miss Glasson," he said very earnestly. "I hope you'll at least consider my side of things before you write another piece for *Whispers*."

"Definitely."

He lowered his voice and infused it with meaningful intensity.

"I had nothing to do with Gloria Maitland's accident last night," he said. "All I'm asking is that *Whispers* prints the truth. If it does, I will be very . . . grateful."

She angled her head slightly as though she hadn't heard him clearly.

"Grateful?" she repeated.

"My career took off with *Fortune's Rogue*. As a result, I am besieged with requests for interviews. Let's just say that I am now in a position to pick and choose which reporters get the real inside information regarding my career and my personal life. Naturally I'll tell my publicist that I will only talk to the members of the press I know I can trust."

She gave him her most winning smile. "No need to make threats, Mr. Tremayne. Your assistant already did that for you."

"I wasn't threatening you."

"Yes, you were." She turned to go and then stopped.

"One more thing," she said, trying to make it sound as if a last-minute thought had just occurred to her. "Would you care to comment on why you refused to talk to my predecessor?"

"What?" He looked wary now.

"Peggy Hackett. I'm sure you remember her. She was a reporter for *Whispers*. She tried to schedule an interview with you shortly before she suffered an unfortunate accident and drowned. An interesting coincidence, don't you think? Two women associated with you have recently drowned. You're sure you don't have a comment?"

For a beat he looked as if he had been struck by lightning. An unnatural stillness came over him.

It was all over in the next instant. He gave her a pitying look, as if she were not very intelligent.

"I have no idea what you mean, Miss Glasson," he said. "I had no relationship of any kind with Peggy Hackett. Everyone knows that she was a washed-up drunk. The studio publicist mentioned that she had begged for an interview but it never happened. The publicist turned her down cold."

"Did Gloria Maitland speak to Hackett?"

"I have no idea. A word of advice, Miss Glasson. You're playing with fire. The studio can destroy you and your cheap newspaper in the blink of an eye."

"Thanks for the quote."

She turned quickly, instinctively wanting to escape— and collided with a very solid, very unmovable object blocking her path. The shock of the impact rattled her. She gasped, lurched back a step, and found herself off balance.

Oliver used his free hand to steady her.

"Sorry," he said. But his attention was on Nick Tremayne, not her. "I've been looking for you, Miss Glasson," he said. "The front desk just had a telephone call from Mildred Fordyce at the Cove Inn. Evidently someone in L.A. is trying to reach you. Mildred said it sounded important."

"Thanks," Irene mumbled. She pushed her hair back behind her ears and collected herself. "If you'll excuse me, I'll go back to the inn and return the call."

"No need to do that," Oliver said. "You can use the telephone in my office."

Startled all over again, she stared at him. "Thanks, but that's not necessary. Really."

"I insist." He took her arm. "You'll have privacy here. You can't say the same about the telephone in the lobby at the inn."

She started to argue but something in his eyes made her change her mind.

"Fine," she said. "Your office. I appreciate it. Don't worry, if I have to telephone my editor, I'll reverse the charges."

"We can discuss the charges later." Oliver kept his attention on Nick. "I trust you're enjoying your stay with us, Mr. Tremayne?"

"It's been interesting," Nick growled. He did not take his eyes off Irene. "You'll remember what I said, won't you, Miss Glasson?"

"Every word," she vowed.

A shiver whispered through her. She knew that Oliver felt it, because his hand tightened around her elbow in a reassuring way.

"I'll take you to my office," he said.

Chapter 13

She did not succeed in taking a deep breath until they were out of the Garden Room. Oliver steered her through the graceful, arched walkway that ran the length of the hotel's main building.

"Are you all right?" he asked quietly.

"Yes, of course." She glanced at him. "Was there really a telephone call for me?"

Oliver's mouth curved faintly. "Yes."

"Why did you insist that I return it from your office?"

"Just trying to be helpful. The Burning Cove Hotel prides itself on offering our guests every convenience."

"I'm not a guest."

"Details."

"You were trying to send a message to Nick Tremayne,

weren't you? You wanted him to know that you were keeping an eye on me."

"Maybe."

"I realize you meant well, but I can't do my job if you insist on hovering over me."

"I wasn't hovering."

"What would you call it?"

"I was observing," Oliver said. "From afar. I didn't hear a word of your conversation with Tremayne. As promised, you had privacy. But when you got to your feet and he started to grab your arm, I had the impression that he had reached the stage of making a few threats."

She winced. "Something about the studio destroying my career and *Whispers*."

"Had a hunch that was what was happening."

"So you stepped in to let Tremayne know that I had a little muscle on my side, is that it?"

"I thought we agreed that we were partners in this venture," Oliver said.

He had the nerve to sound offended, as if she had somehow reneged on a promise.

"That doesn't give you the right to take charge whenever you feel like it," she said.

"Did you get anything useful out of Tremayne?"

"You're changing the subject."

"It's called distraction. It's a classic technique in my former profession."

There was no point in arguing with him. She had agreed to the partnership. Besides, she had to admit that there was a great deal to be said for having him in her corner. He was both mysterious and intimidating. She knew that Tremayne had not been oblivious to the impact Oliver made.

The problem, she thought, was that she wasn't accustomed to having anyone else in her corner, least of all a man like Oliver. She wasn't sure what to do with him.

She had dated and flirted in the light, casual way of the modern woman but she had only been seriously involved with one man—Bradley Thorpe. He had been her employer. Charming and good-looking, he'd had a great job and given every appearance of being in love with her. She still cringed whenever she reflected on how remarkably naïve she had been.

Afterward she had discovered that she was merely the latest in a long line of naïve young women who had occupied her position in Thorpe's plush offices. He seduced secretaries the same way he collected sports trophies. As far as he was concerned, both were fair game.

Oliver stopped and opened a door.

"Here we are," he said.

She pushed the unpleasant memories aside with the motto her grandfather had taught her—*it's only a mistake if it kills you or if you fail to learn from it*—and walked through the doorway of a handsomely appointed reception area.

A trim, forty-something woman with striking features and warm brown eyes sat at the desk. Her jet-black hair was shot through with silver. She wore it caught back in a sleek, elegant knot at the nape of her neck. There was a gold band on her ring finger.

She stopped typing on the handsome Remington, looked up, and removed her glasses.

"Oh, there you are, Mr. Ward," she said. "I was wondering if you got my message. I assume this is Miss Glasson?"

"Yes, it is. Irene, this is Elena Torres. She runs this office. Actually, she keeps the entire hotel running. I just try to stay out of her way."

"How do you do," Irene said.

"A pleasure to meet you, Miss Glasson."

"Please, call me Irene."

"And you must call me Elena."

"I told Irene that she could use the telephone in my office," Oliver said.

Irene thought Elena's brows rose ever so slightly in reaction to that statement. She could not tell if it was surprise or curiosity or amusement that she detected. Perhaps a mix of all three. Whatever the case, she got the clear impression that Oliver was not in the habit of offering the convenience and privacy of his office telephone to his guests.

Oliver had already crossed the room and opened the door, revealing a second, handsomely paneled room.

"Do you have the number of the inn?" he asked.

"Yes," she said.

"Take your time. I'll wait out here with Elena."

"Thank you," she said.

He closed the door very quietly.

She glanced around the office. It was a large space decorated with warm gold walls and dark wood trim. The high, arched windows looked out over a private patio and the ocean beyond. The elegantly inlaid desk glowed from extensive polishing. The chairs and sofa were padded in rich, saddle brown leather. A tall vase of fresh flowers stood in the corner.

There were two paintings on the wall. Both were a contrast to the serene surroundings. They were coastal scenes, but they were not pleasantly languid pictures of sunny beaches and cloudless skies. Instead, they depicted wild, violent storms. Waves crashed and dark clouds swirled. A strange, eerie, ominous light infused each picture.

There was a signature in the lower right-hand corner of each picture. She took a closer look. *Pell.*

With the glaring exception of the two paintings, Oliver's office looked exactly like one would expect the office of the proprietor of a fine hotel to appear. Oliver's office was a Hollywood stage set of an office.

He said he had been forced to reinvent himself two years earlier but she wondered if he had created an illusion for himself, one that he thought would appear convincing to others. That was exactly what she had done. It seemed that they had both constructed new lives for themselves but neither of them felt truly at home in that new life—not yet, at any rate. Maybe never.

She knew why some part of her was always prepared to pack her bags, grab the notebook, Helen's gun, and some money, and run. The message that Helen Spencer had written in blood haunted her. She could not escape the fear that someone might be hunting her.

She wondered why Oliver was having trouble settling into his new life. It was difficult to imagine that he spent any time looking over his shoulder. He seemed in command of both himself and his world in Burning Cove. But everyone had secrets.

Perhaps we have a few things in common, Mr. Ward.

She went to the desk, took the business card out of her handbag, picked up the receiver, and dialed the number of the inn. Mrs. Fordyce answered on the first ring.

"There you are, dear. I'm so glad you got my message."

"I was told that you were looking for me. Is something wrong?"

"I had a very odd call from a Velma Lancaster. She said she was your editor and that you were to telephone her immediately. She said it was an emergency."

"Is that all? Relax. As far as Velma is concerned, everything is an emergency."

"She made it sound very urgent so I thought I'd better let you know immediately."

"Thank you. I'll call her now."

"Good. Well, that's that. By the way, the clothes that got soaked when you jumped into the spa pool were returned by someone from the Burning Cove Hotel staff a short time ago. Everything looks like it has been nicely laundered and pressed."

"That's a relief. I just hope nothing shrank in the wash. The trousers were new."

"I'm sure they're fine. Everything at the Burning Cove Hotel is first-class. And I must say the dress is lovely."

"What dress?"

"An adorable cocktail frock. Wait until you see it."

"There must be some mistake."

"No. I asked George, the man who delivered the clothes, if there was some mistake but he assured me there wasn't. Said it was a gift from the hotel management. I suppose it's a sort of apology."

"An apology? For what?"

"For nearly getting murdered on the hotel grounds, of course. I expect that the hotel management wanted to compensate you."

"Or bribe me in an attempt to persuade me to go easy on the follow-up stories."

"Oh, no, dear." Mrs. Fordyce was clearly shocked. "I can't imagine that Oliver Ward would resort to bribery."

"I'm not so sure. Is it an expensive-looking dress?"

"Oh, yes. Silk, the real thing, not rayon. And the shoes are adorable."

"There are shoes, too?"

"Yes, dear, and a divine little wrap. It can get chilly here in Burning Cove after the sun goes down. All in all, very nice compensation, I'd say. Not worth nearly getting killed for, of course. Still—"

"Thank you, Mrs. Fordyce. I'm going to hang up and call my editor now."

"Good-bye, dear."

Irene put the phone down and eyed the closed door. In the end she decided that she would deal with the dress bribe after she dealt with Velma.

She got the operator on the line, gave her the number, and reversed the charges. If Velma refused to accept the collect call, it would be a strong indication that there wasn't much of an emergency.

Velma accepted the charges immediately.

"Your landlady called an hour ago," she said.

"Why would Mrs. Drysdale do that? I'm up to date with my rent."

"She said that someone broke into your apartment earlier today. She was out at the time."

"What?"

"She was very upset. She said the place was ransacked."

Irene sat down hard in the big desk chair. Panic rolled through her in a wave that threatened to choke her. Automatically she touched her handbag, reassuring herself that the notebook was safely tucked inside. She never let it out of her sight.

But if Helen Spencer's killer had found her, he would have no way of knowing that she never left the notebook behind. He would assume that she had done what most people did with a valuable item—stashed it in a secret hiding place.

She looked down at her hand and was shocked to see that it was trembling ever so slightly.

Calm down. Don't panic. Think.

Mentally she cataloged the few possessions she had acquired in the months that she had been living in Los Angeles. There was very little of value—her clothes, the new radio, some inexpensive furniture, and the kitchen things.

"Was anything taken?" she asked.

"Mrs. Drysdale didn't think so but how would she know?" Velma said. "She told me that she called the cops. An officer filled out a report but there's not much chance that anyone will be picked up. I told Mrs. Drysdale that it was probably just a random burglary, but between you and me, I'm not so sure."

Neither am I, Irene thought. She was suddenly very glad that she had refilled the gas tank when she arrived in Burning Cove. She wouldn't have to waste time stopping at a filling station. She could pick up her things at the Cove Inn, throw them into the car, and leave. Time enough to decide on a destination after she got on the road.

Unaware of the turmoil she had created with her news, Velma continued speaking.

"I think we have to consider the possibility that the break-in at your apartment is connected to your Maitland story," she said. "I had a call from Tremayne's studio—Ernie Ogden himself."

The name rang a faint bell but it took Irene a couple of beats to make the connection.

"Peggy mentioned him a couple of times," she said.

"No surprise. He's the fixer at Tremayne's studio. Rumor has it that he and Peggy had an affair back in the day. He told me he'd heard that I'd hired her and he appreciated it. I think he was genuinely fond of her, which is probably why he cut me some slack today. Regardless, he was not happy."

Irene gripped the telephone cord. "Did he threaten you?"

"Let's just say he made it clear that it would be very unwise of me to print another story about Tremayne—not unless Tremayne actually gets himself arrested for murder. What I'm getting at is that it wouldn't surprise me if Ogden paid someone to go through your apartment."

Relief crashed through Irene. She started to breathe again.

"A private detective, maybe," she said, seizing on the possibility. "Looking for something to use as leverage against us. Well, against me, at any rate."

"Exactly," Velma said. "It's the timing of the break-in that makes me think someone from the studio is responsible. We ran the Maitland story this morning. I got a telephone call warning me off the story a couple hours later. And then, early this afternoon, someone broke into your apartment. It all adds up."

"You're right," Irene said. "Probably not a coincidence."

There was a small hesitation on the other end of the line.

"Correct me if I'm wrong, but you seem damned cheerful for someone who's just been told that a burglar broke into her apartment," Velma said.

"I'm looking on the bright side. The studio is clearly nervous. Here's the good news, Boss. I just concluded a one-on-one interview with Tremayne—at his request, no less."

"Okay, I'm impressed. I assume he went heavy on the charm."

"So thick you could have cut it with a knife."

"Learn anything?"

"When the charm didn't work, he made some threats. Peggy said that was typical behavior for stars. They figure their studios will take care of them."

"They're right," Velma said, her voice very dry. "If the star is important to the studio's bottom line. Tremayne is certainly a box office draw now, but he's no Clark Gable or Gary Cooper. Not yet, at any rate."

"We're onto something here. I can feel it."

"I agree," Velma said. "The story of a leading man who murdered a lover and the reporter who uncovered the crime could make or break my paper. But we've got to get some hard proof before we run any more stories that feature Tremayne's name."

"I'm working on it. As a matter of fact, I've got an interview scheduled with Luther Pell tonight."

"Why does that name sound familiar?"

"He owns the Paradise Club here in Burning Cove."

"Damn. *That* Luther Pell. Be careful. Pell has always managed to keep his hands clean but they say he's got mob connections from Reno to New Jersey."

Irene glanced at the storm-filled paintings on the wall. They looked as if they had been inspired by violence.

"Tremayne claims he was at the Paradise Club when Gloria Maitland was murdered," she said. "I want to find out if his alibi is solid."

"Pell agreed to talk to you about one of his customers? Got to say I'm damned surprised."

Irene glanced at the closed door. "Oliver Ward, the owner of the Burning Cove Hotel, told me that Pell was his friend. Ward made the arrangements."

"That's even more interesting. How did you convince Ward to cooperate?"

"He thinks he can control the story if he gets involved."

"He's probably right, damn it. He's got a few connections, too."

"I think Ward is serious about wanting to find out what happened to Maitland. He doesn't like the idea that someone thought he could get away with murder in the hotel. He took it as a personal affront or something."

"Huh." Velma cleared her throat. "Sorry to pry, but I've got to ask you if there's any chance the burglar might have found something in your place that the studio can use to silence you?"

Irene tightened her grip on her handbag. "No. There wasn't anything for the bastard to find."

"That's a relief. All right, stay on the story, at least for now. Let me know if you get anything solid. Until then we'll keep our heads down. Let Ogden think that his threats are working. And, Glasson?"

"Yes, Boss?"

"Be careful. Good reporters are hard to find. I don't want to have to replace you."

"You think I'm a good reporter, Boss?"

"Peggy said you had what it takes. Just be damned careful."

"I will. Don't worry, Boss."

The line went dead. Irene put down the receiver and sat quietly for a moment, contemplating the very convincing illusion that was Oliver's office.

What are you concealing behind the scenes, Magician?

She got to her feet, crossed the room, and yanked open the door.

"What's up with the dress and the shoes?" she said.

Oliver was standing in front of Elena's desk, reading a typewritten letter. He looked at Irene.

"Mrs. Firebrace in housekeeping suggested that you might not have anything to wear to the Paradise Club this evening."

"It's just an interview," Irene said. "If I wear a cocktail dress and heels, people will get the idea that I'm your date for the evening."

"That's the plan," Oliver said.

"What plan is that?"

"After we are seen together at Pell's club, people will assume that the management of the Burning Cove Hotel does not consider you a threat to the hotel or its guests."

He had a point, Irene thought. There was, of course, the very real possibility that people would think she had allowed herself to be seduced by the owner of the Burning Cove Hotel, but so what? As far as everyone in town was concerned she was just a small-time reporter chasing a Hollywood gossip story for a third-rate paper. Pretending to be Oliver's date for the evening might be a very useful cover.

"It could work," she said.

Elena turned away very quickly and concentrated on inserting a blank sheet of paper into her typewriter. But Irene was pretty sure she had caught the glint of amusement in the secretary's dark eyes.

"It's all about creating an illusion," Oliver said. "One that will distract the attention of the audience from the real purpose of your visit to the club. It's called misdirection."

"I get to be the magician's assistant for the evening, is that it?"

It was Oliver's turn to look amused.

"That's it," he said.

Chapter 14

Oliver Ward was waiting for her in the lobby of the Cove Inn. Irene paused at the top of the stairs and allowed herself a few seconds to deal with the impact he made on her senses.

He wore a white dinner jacket, a white shirt, a perfectly knotted black bow tie, and dark trousers with the ease of a man accustomed to formal attire. *No surprise there*, she thought. He had, after all, spent his first career onstage.

The aura of cool, controlled power and masculine grace should have been undercut by the ebony cane, but the effect was the opposite. The cane served notice that Oliver was a survivor.

She started down the stairs, intensely aware of a little rush of heat and a pulse-quickening flicker of excitement. She reminded herself that she was not going out on a date. She was working on an assignment. Nevertheless, she was suddenly very, very glad that she was wearing the clothes that had been given to her as compensation for her ordeal in the spa.

The dress was fashioned of midnight blue silk cut on the bias so that it glided over her curves and flared out around her ankles whenever she took a step. Combined with the stacked-heel evening sandals and the light wrap, the overall effect hit all the right notes— California casual infused with a subtle touch of Hollywood glamour.

Dresses this lovely and this expensive were called gowns, Irene thought. It was a fantasy gown designed for a fantasy evening in the fantasy world that was Burning Cove. When she got the dress home to her little apartment in L.A., it would go to the back of her closet because she would probably never have another occasion to wear it.

She reached the foot of the stairs and paused because she could have sworn she saw some heat in Oliver's eyes. He smiled and took her arm.

"I see the dress fits," he said.

Mrs. Fordyce folded her arms on the front desk and regarded Irene with an appraising expression.

"It's lovely on you, dear," she said. "But your handbag rather spoils the effect. Where is the little beaded bag that came with the dress and the shoes?"

Irene tightened her grip on her handbag. "I couldn't fit my notebook into it."

Or Atherton's notes or my gun, she added silently.

"Oh, but surely you're not going to be conducting interviews this evening," Mrs. Fordyce said.

"You never know," Irene said. "Readers of *Whispers* will be thrilled with an inside peek at the Paradise Club. I may spot a star or two."

Oliver tightened his grip on her arm and steered her toward the door. "Time to go. Cocktails at seven. Dinner at eight."

Irene allowed herself to be escorted out into the balmy night.

A sleek, dark blue speedster waited in front of the inn. Irene had seen a lot of expensive vehicles in the year that she had worked for Helen Spencer, but never one like Oliver Ward's. The bold, sweeping curves reminded her of a yacht or an airplane.

"My dress matches your car," she said.

Oliver smiled. "I like blue."

He opened the passenger side door for her. She slipped into a cockpit of a front seat. It was uphol-stered in rich, hand-tooled leather the color of butter and just as soft. The instrument panel looked like it had been designed by an artist working in the art deco style.

"I can put up the top," Oliver said.

"No, thanks." She took a scarf out of her handbag. "It's a beautiful evening. I'd like to enjoy it."

"So would I," Oliver said.

But he was looking at her, not at the evening sky.

He closed her door gently, as if he were tucking her into bed. She flushed at the image and busied herself with knotting her scarf under her chin.

Oliver rounded the front of the car and got behind the wheel. The narrow front seat suddenly seemed a thousand times smaller and much more intimate.

He put the car in gear and eased it away from the curb. The big engine purred like a tame leopard.

At the end of the street, he turned onto Cliff Road, a narrow, winding strip of pavement that followed the ragged coastline. She was not surprised to discover that he was an expert driver. He eased gently into each turn and accelerated smoothly on the other side.

The last light of a fiery sunset was fading fast. The red tile roofs and stucco walls that characterized so much of the town's architecture were bathed in the colors of twilight. Out on the horizon the ocean blended into the evening sky.

Irene suddenly wished that she and Oliver were setting out on a long night drive with no destination in mind.

"This car is gorgeous," she said. She touched the gleaming instrument panel with an appreciative finger. "But I don't recognize the make and model."

"It's built on a Cord chassis but the rest—the engine, steering wheel, brakes, instrument panel, and exterior body—are all custom. My uncle designed it."

"It looks so sleek. Where do you get this kind of custom work done?"

Oliver smiled. "My uncle knows some people. But letting him make so many modifications may have been a mistake."

"Why?"

"I don't dare let a regular mechanic touch it. Chester is the only one who can work on the car because he's the only one who knows how it operates."

"What kind of changes did your uncle make to the engine?"

"Don't ask me, ask Chester. All I know is that this car can go very fast."

She understood. "You like to drive fast."

"Sometimes." Oliver shifted into another gear with the finesse of a considerate lover. "It makes for a pleasant change once in a while."

"A change from having to rely on a cane," she said before she stopped to think.

He gave her a quick, appraising glance before returning his attention to his driving. She got the feeling that she had not exactly surprised him; rather, she had confirmed some impression that he had already formed.

"Yes," he said.

The one-word answer was devoid of all emotion, but it told her just how much he hated the cane and what it represented.

"Understandable," she said.

"Don't worry, I don't indulge my taste for speed when there is a passenger in the car."

"I don't have a problem with speed," she said, "so long as I trust the driver."

"Given that I am permanently hobbled with a cane due to a serious failure of judgment that nearly got me killed, I won't ask the obvious question."

"You won't ask me if I trust you?"

"No. Too soon for that."

"Nothing personal," she said, "but I've experienced some rather serious failures of judgment, myself. I've concluded it's probably best not to trust anyone."

"Safer that way."

"Yes."

"So much for trust. Aren't you going to ask me the question that everyone else wants to ask?"

"You mean, what really went wrong at your final performance?"

"Right," he said. His hands flexed a little on the steering wheel. "That question."

"No," she said.

"Why not? You're a reporter. Aren't you curious?"

"You have always maintained that it was an accident and that the rumors of attempted murder were baseless. There's no reason to think you would change your story tonight, not for a reporter from a scandal sheet. Besides, I'm in Burning Cove to cover another story, remember?"

"I remember. About this other story you're chasing."

"Yes?"

"This isn't just another movie-star-scandal piece, is it? I can tell this is personal for you."

"Yes," she said. "It's personal."

"Do I get an explanation?"

She had known that sooner or later he would ask for more information. That afternoon as she had used pins to set the deep waves in her hair, she pondered just how much to tell him.

"Ten days ago another *Whispers* reporter died," she said at last. "Her name was Peggy Hackett."

"Hackett? The gossip columnist who became a raging alcoholic and managed to get herself fired from her own column?"

"My boss hired her about six months ago. Peggy was working on a story involving Nick Tremayne when she died. According to the authorities, she slipped and fell in the bathtub. She drowned."

She waited for Oliver to make the connection. He did. Immediately.

"Like Gloria Maitland," he said quietly.

"Peggy died in a bathtub, not a pool, but, yes, almost exactly like Gloria Maitland."

"You're absolutely certain?"

"I'm the one who found Peggy's body. Trust me, there are a lot of similarities between the two death scenes. Blow to the back of the head. Blood on the tiles. Death by drowning. A link to Nick Tremayne."

"And you don't believe in coincidences."

She studied his hard profile. "Do you?"

"No," he said. "Any idea what Hackett's Tremayne story involved?"

"Peggy was pursuing the usual angle—*Tremayne Rumored to Be Smitten with Aspiring Actress. This Time It Looks Serious.* That kind of thing. But I think something happened in the course of Peggy's research."

"What makes you say that?"

"When she started the piece, she treated it like any other assignment. It was going to be a very nice little scoop for *Whispers.* But at the last minute, just before deadline, Peggy told our editor that she needed more time. She said she had uncovered something much bigger than another *Hot Star Seduces Young Actress* story. But a few days later she was dead."

Oliver contemplated that for a moment. "How did it happen to be you who found the body?"

Irene watched the road unwind in front of the powerful car. "There's no big mystery about that. One morning Peggy didn't show up at the office. When Velma couldn't get her on the telephone, she sent me to Peggy's apartment to make sure everything was all right. She was afraid that Peggy had started drinking heavily again. When I got there, the door was unlocked. I went in and . . . found the body in the tub."

"I can see why a second drowning death would make you start to wonder about a pattern."

"I went into the living room and telephoned for the police and an ambulance, but it seemed to take forever for them to arrive." Irene shivered. "I was going to wait outside on the front step but I kept thinking about the scene in the bathroom."

"What about it?"

"Something didn't look right."

"It was a death scene. No surprise that it didn't look right."

"I know, but—"

"You went back for another look, didn't you?"

She winced. "How did you know? You're right. I don't know why I felt like I had to do that. Maybe it was just to reassure myself that she really was dead and that there was nothing more I could do. But in hindsight I think it was the blood that bothered me."

"The blood in the water?"

"No. Well, there was blood in the water, of course, because of the gash on Peggy's head. But there was also some blood on the floor behind one of the claw-feet on the tub. I found a little more on the tiles under the sink."

Oliver said nothing. He just listened.

"But here's what really bothered me," she said.

"There was no bath mat on the floor and no towel hanging on the hook near the tub."

She waited, wondering if he would conclude she was crazy, paranoid, or simply over-imaginative.

"You think the killer used the bath mat and a towel to clean up after the murder," he said.

He said it as calmly as if she had made a casual observation on the weather.

She concentrated hard on the view of the road through the windshield, but all she could see were Peggy's blank eyes staring up at her from under the bloody water.

She took a deep breath and let it out slowly, with control. "Yes. I think she was struck from behind before she got into the tub. I think there was too much blood on the floor and maybe on the walls to be consistent with a fall in the tub."

"Anything else?"

"One more thing. I couldn't find Peggy's notes. She may have had a problem with the bottle but at her core she was a crack reporter. She kept very good notes. She's the one who taught me how to get the quotes right and how to make it look as if you'd gotten a quote when the subject never actually gave you one."

"Don't remind me."

Irene shot him a quick, searching glance. He didn't look annoyed, she concluded. More like resigned.

"Just doing my job," she said.

"Forget it. All right, so you think the killer took Hackett's notebook."

"Yes, I do. I never found her notebook but I did find

something interesting when I cleaned out her desk at the office."

"What?"

"A piece of paper with the name Betty Scott written on it in Peggy's handwriting. It looked like she had jotted down some quick notes while on the phone. In addition to the name, there was a phone number."

"You called the number?" Oliver asked.

"Sure."

"And?"

"Turned out to be a Seattle number. A woman answered. Said her name was Mrs. Kemp. She seemed surprised when I asked for Betty Scott. She said that Scott had rented a room from her at one time but that she had died about a year ago."

"Why do I have the feeling that you are going to tell me Scott's death was a tragic drowning accident?" Oliver asked.

"Probably because you're a magician. According to Mrs. Kemp, Betty Scott slipped and fell in the bathtub. Struck her head. Drowned."

Oliver whistled softly. "Any connection with Nick Tremayne?"

"None that I could find."

"That would have been too easy."

"Yes. But when I started asking questions, Mrs. Kemp said that another reporter had called about Betty Scott."

"Hackett."

"I think so, yes. Mrs. Kemp said she could only tell me what she had told the first reporter—Betty Scott had been a waitress who'd had dreams of going to Hollywood."

"So there is a vague Hollywood connection," Oliver said.

"Very vague. A lot of people, including a lot of waitresses, dream of going to Hollywood and getting discovered."

"Where does Nick Tremayne come from?" Oliver asked after a moment.

Irene gave him another quick, searching glance. "We think alike on some things. I looked into Tremayne's background. According to his bio, he's from the Midwest. Chicago, I believe."

"I don't think so."

"Well, it's no secret that film star bios are largely fiction. The publicists write them. What makes you doubt Tremayne's?"

"Something about his accent. I can't place it exactly but I don't think it's Chicago. More West Coast. So, you've got three women dead in drowning accidents; two of the deceased were definitely connected to Tremayne. No wonder you think you're onto a story. You're sure you don't know what Gloria Maitland wanted to tell you last night?"

"No, only that it had something to do with Tremayne and that it was red-hot."

Oliver slowed in preparation for turning off Cliff Road. "How did Gloria Maitland know that you might be interested in whatever she had to tell you about Tremayne?"

"That," Irene said, "is an excellent question. I'm guessing that she had talked to Peggy. When she called the *Whispers* office, she asked for whoever had taken over Peggy Hackett's job."

Oliver eased into a paved parking lot in front of yet another red-tile-and-white-stucco structure. This one looked like a mansion. It was surrounded by luxurious gardens and was protected by a high wall. An ornate wrought iron gate barred the entrance.

There was a group of young men clustered around the valet parking stand. Their expressions brightened at the sight of Oliver's car. They were visibly crushed when Oliver cruised past them and deftly maneuvered the vehicle into a space marked *Private*.

"I think you just ruined their evening," Irene said.

"I can't trust any of them with the key," Oliver said. He shut down the engine. "They wouldn't be able to resist taking the car for a spin as soon as we were out of sight."

"Who wouldn't want to drive this car?"

He gave her a speculative look. "Do you want to get behind the wheel?"

"Are you kidding? I'd love to give it a whirl."

He smiled. "Forget it. No one drives this car except me."

She sighed. "If it were mine, I'd be possessive about it, too."

He opened his door and climbed out.

Automatically she started to open her own door.

"It's supposed to look like we're on a date, remember?" Oliver said.

"Oh, right."

She sat back and untied her scarf while Oliver retrieved his cane and made his way around the front of the car to her door.

He got her door open and reached down to assist her out of the passenger seat. She wasn't sure what to do with the powerful hand that he offered. She was afraid that if she took it, she might accidentally pull him off balance.

Flummoxed, she grabbed the top of the windshield frame instead, intending to use it to lever herself up out of the low-slung seat.

"Are you usually this difficult?" Oliver asked. "Or am I getting special treatment?"

Before she could respond, he took her arm in a vise-like grip. He hauled her up out of the seat so quickly and with such force that for a second she was afraid she would be propelled into flight.

"Sorry," she mumbled. "I didn't want to—"

She broke off awkwardly, not wanting to put her concern into words. She knew he wouldn't appreciate it.

"In the future don't worry about it," he said. "I'll let you know if I'm in danger of falling on my face."

She was almost certain that he was speaking to her with his back teeth clamped together. It was not an auspicious start to the evening.

"Sorry," she said.

"Do me a favor. Don't say sorry for the rest of the evening, all right?"

"Right. Sorry. I mean—"

"Forget it."

He steered her toward the wrought iron gate where two large, muscular men dressed in formal black and white waited. Irene suspected that they were supposed to look like butlers or majordomos, but they bore a striking resemblance to prizefighters or gangsters. It occurred to her that the fashionable drape cut of their jackets could easily conceal shoulder holsters.

And maybe her imagination was getting out of control.

"Good evening, Joe, Ned," Oliver said. He inclined his head in casual recognition of the pair. "Nice night, isn't it? I believe Miss Glasson and I are expected."

"Evening, Mr. Ward," Joe said.

"Mr. Ward, sir," Ned said.

Both men nodded politely at Irene.

"Mr. Pell said you'd be along," Joe said. "The boss is waiting for you upstairs in his private quarters. Need an escort?"

"I know the way, thanks," Oliver said.

Ned pulled open one half of the big gate. Oliver steered Irene into the walled garden.

She stopped short at the sight of the fairyland that surrounded the club. Small electric lights sparkled amid the lush greenery and illuminated a graceful fountain.

Oliver was amused. "Not quite what you expected, I take it?"

"Well, no," she admitted. "I imagined an old, re-modeled speakeasy joint with an entrance in some dark alley."

"Years ago Pell's father, Jonathan Pell, made a great deal of money running gambling halls, taverns, and clubs in London. He retired young and moved the family to America. Figured it was the land of opportunity, a place where he could bury his shady past and get respectable. He invested heavily in the stock market."

"Of course. They said you couldn't lose."

"After the old man got wiped out in twenty-nine, Luther took over the finances."

"He decided that the best way to recover was to go back into the original family business?"

"Right. He operated a number of speakeasies during the dry spell. After repeal, he bought a Reno casino. He also has a gambling ship anchored in Santa Monica Bay. But the Paradise Club is his star property. It's also his home."

"He lives in a nightclub?"

"I live on the grounds of a hotel."

"True, but somehow that doesn't seem quite so . . . unusual."

"Luther and I like to keep a close eye on our investments."

"I see. You know, I can't help but notice that some of these men might be carrying guns."

"Uh-huh."

"Do your security guards carry weapons?"

"No," Oliver said. "I operate a hotel, not a nightclub. The last thing I want on the grounds of the Burning Cove is gunplay."

"I take your point."

"I'm not a fan of guns," he added. "They give people who carry them a false sense of security. Guns tend to jam when you need them most. In addition, it can be extremely difficult to hit a moving target, especially under stressful conditions."

Obviously he felt quite strongly about the matter. She decided not to mention that she was carrying Helen's little gun in her handbag.

Oliver stopped in front of another stout wrought iron gate and pressed the button on the intercom.

"Ward and Miss Glasson here to see Mr. Pell," he said.

A deep masculine voice rendered somewhat scratchy by the device responded.

"Welcome, Mr. Ward," the voice said. "I'll be right down to let you in."

"Thanks, Blake."

Oliver released the button. "Blake runs Pell's household."

"A butler?"

"Who doubles as a bodyguard."

"There seem to be a lot of those around here."

"It's a nightclub, Irene, run by a man who made his money in speakeasies and the gaming business."

"I take your point. Again."

"I've got a question for you."

She had been starting to enjoy the adventure but that stopped her cold.

"What?" she asked.

"It's about the blood."

Startled, she looked at him. "The blood?"

"The little splashes of blood that you noticed under the bathtub and the sink in Peggy Hackett's bathroom. I'm also interested in the fact that you noticed that the towel and bath mat were missing. A lot of people who stumbled onto a scene like the one you described would have been too shocked to take in such small details. Just wondered what made you pay attention to them."

For a couple of seconds she was too stunned to respond. She could not tell him the truth—that after the discovery of Helen Spencer's body, she had become unnaturally sensitive to the details that indicated an act of violence. Some people might say she had developed a phobia. Others would conclude that her nerves had been strained to the breaking point.

She turned her attention back to the ornate gate. A tall, burly man dressed in butler's attire was coming toward them. Another man with a coat cut to conceal a weapon, she thought.

It suddenly occurred to her that in some surreal way, the scene—a graceful, luxurious garden and an elegant mansion protected by men who probably carried guns—somehow represented the entire town of Burning Cove. She had entered a charming, glamorous paradise that hid dark and dangerous secrets.

This is my new life, she thought. *Everything looks great on the surface. I've made a fresh start, got a good job and my very own car, and tonight I'm going out to dinner with the most interesting man I've ever met and I'm wearing an amazing dress. But underneath it all I'm keeping some very scary secrets.*

"Oh, the blood?" she said, striving to sound as cool as possible. "I probably noticed it because I'm a journalist. In my profession, you learn to pick up on the details."

"Same in my field," Oliver said.

The butler was almost at the gate. Irene shot a quick, sidelong glance at Oliver.

She had a feeling that he wasn't buying her answer—
not for a second.

"Which field would that be?" she asked. "The business of magic or the business of running a classy
hotel?"

"Both. I told you, they have a lot in common."

Chapter 15

S he had lied about the blood. The question was, why?

Oliver tasted the martini that Blake had mixed, and watched their host try to charm Irene, who was sipping a pink lady and pretending to appear enthralled.

It wasn't entirely an act, Oliver thought. It was clear that she was curious about Luther but it was also plain that she wasn't falling under his spell. That was interesting because Luther was very good at charming others, especially women, when it suited him. Very few looked beneath the surface.

Oliver had long ago concluded that the real Luther Pell was revealed in the dark seascapes that hung on the wall. He found it interesting that Irene had cast several covert glances at the paintings as if she was searching for something in them.

Pell was tall and lean. His jet-black hair was cut in the sleek, discreetly oiled Hollywood style—parted on the side and combed straight back. He was a well-educated man with wide-ranging interests. He could converse on almost any subject—the latest books, the economy, the news, or the results of a recent polo match—with an easy, polished manner.

It was obvious that he was as curious about Irene as she was about him, but Luther wasn't making any progress getting past her invisible defenses. For some reason Oliver found that both entertaining and gratifying.

There was nothing more intriguing than a woman with secrets, he thought, and Pell was definitely intrigued. *We both are*, Oliver thought. The hot flash of possessiveness that burned through him caught him off guard. Damned if he would let Pell be successful where he, himself, had failed. *I'm going to be the man who solves the mystery*.

He suppressed his unexpectedly fierce reaction with an act of will, but the fact that he'd even experienced the electrifying heat left him bemused.

"Enough about me, Mr. Pell," Irene said. "I'm just a journalist working a story. Mr. Ward said that you had agreed to answer a few questions about Nick Tremayne."

Oliver had been about to drink some of the martini. He paused and lowered the glass.

"Oliver," he said.

Irene glanced at him, bewildered. "What?"

"My name is Oliver," he said.

"Oh, right." Irene flushed and turned back to Luther. "About my questions, Mr. Pell."

Luther smiled. Oliver swallowed a groan. The smile was just as much an illusion as the Lady Vanishes in the Mirror act that had been a signature of the Amazing Oliver Ward Show.

"I understand that you want to know if I can vouch for Tremayne's alibi," Luther said. "He's letting it be known that he was here in my club at the time Miss Maitland died."

"That's right." Irene set her pink lady on a table, opened her large handbag, and removed a notebook and pencil. "The police have established that Gloria Maitland died sometime between eleven forty-five and about twelve fifteen, which is when I found the body."

Luther eyed the notebook. "You do realize that by answering your questions, I'm doing a favor for Ward."

Irene hesitated, wary now. "A favor?"

Luther's smile got a little brighter. "He'll owe me one in return."

Irene looked at Oliver. "Is there a problem?"

"Don't worry about it," Oliver said. "Stop teasing the lady, Pell. Answer her questions so that we can finish our drinks and have dinner."

"Very well." Luther turned back to Irene. "But I want to make it clear that anything I say is off the record."

Irene's mouth tightened. "If you insist."

"I'm afraid I must. I'm a businessman, Miss Glasson. I can't afford to make any more enemies. I've got enough as it is. If my name shows up in your paper in a story that hurts my club, I'll make sure that *Whispers* goes out of business before the ink is dry."

Irene gave him an icy smile. "I understand, Mr. Pell. I'll add your name to the list of people who have threatened to destroy *Whispers*."

Luther's black brows rose. "Is it a long list?"

"And getting longer by the minute. Which tells me that I'm on the right track."

"No, Miss Glasson. It tells you that you are putting your hand into a bag that may be filled with rattlesnakes."

"Don't waste your time trying to scare her," Oliver said. "It won't work. Believe me, I've tried."

Luther exhaled slowly. "I see. Well, in that case, I'll tell you what I can, Miss Glasson, but I don't think it will do you much good. According to my security staff, Tremayne arrived around ten last night. He had evidently spent the earlier part of the evening at the Carousel."

"What's that?" Irene asked.

"It's a former speakeasy just outside of town. The owner runs an illegal casino disguised as a private club. In addition to liquor and gambling, the management also provides other forms of entertainment aimed at the gentlemen's market."

"Prostitutes?"

"As I was saying, my boys tell me Tremayne was at the Carousel before he showed up here."

"All right." Irene made a few quick notes. "Please go on."

"Tremayne had obviously been drinking when he arrived. My bartenders tell me he drank steadily throughout the evening, danced with every attractive woman in the room, and seemed to enjoy the entertainment."

Irene looked up quickly. "Are you saying that he was in sight of one of your people at all times?"

"Not exactly."

"What does that mean?" Irene demanded.

"As far as I can determine, none of my people actually saw Tremayne between approximately eleven forty-five and twelve thirty."

Irene tensed. "He disappeared?"

"That's a matter of interpretation."

"What is that supposed to mean?"

"When he returned to the bar to order another drink, there was a woman with him. Both were somewhat . . . disheveled."

Irene got a blank expression. "Disheveled? As if they had been involved in some sort of violence? I never considered the possibility that there might have been two people in the spa last night."

Oliver stifled a small sigh. Irene was so obsessed with proving that murder had been done that she had missed Luther's attempt to be diplomatic.

Luther caught his eye, one brow cocked inquiringly. Oliver shook his head and gave him a don't-expect-any-help-from-me, I'm-just-a-bystander look.

Amused, Luther turned back to Irene.

"The lady's hair was mussed and her lipstick was smeared. The back of her dress was partially unfastened. Tremayne had a smudge of lipstick on the side of his face. His hair was tousled. His tie was undone.

Allowances should be made, however. It isn't easy to tie a bow tie without a mirror."

Irene flushed. "I see. In other words, Nick Tremayne and the lady were out in the garden during the time frame when no one saw them inside the club."

"Yes," Luther said.

Irene tapped her pencil against the notebook and looked grim. "I was so sure."

"I'm sorry," Luther said.

He said it almost gently, as though he genuinely regretted not being of more assistance.

Oliver set his unfinished drink aside, tightened his grip on his cane, and moved to stand at the window. He looked down into the walled garden. Although there were lights scattered around the enclosed space, the thick foliage created deep pockets of shadow.

It would be so easy to disappear into the darkness, he thought. It was emerging back into the light that was the hard part.

"Mr. Ward?" Irene said rather sharply. "Oliver? Is something wrong?"

He refocused on the problem of how to pull off the illusion.

"It wouldn't be all that difficult to get out of this garden by going over the wall or even through the delivery gate at the rear," he said.

Irene moved quickly to stand beside him. Luther approached from the opposite side. Together the three of them looked down into the shadows.

"It's really quite dark in several places along the wall, isn't it?" Irene said. There was a thread of excitement in her voice. "Tremayne appears to be a physically fit man. I'll bet he could climb over it."

"Probably not without the aid of a rope or ladder, but it wouldn't be hard to get hold of one or the other," Oliver said. "I imagine there are any number of handy items available in the gardening shed."

"Unfortunately, that's true," Luther said. For the first time he sounded troubled. "But the delivery gate is always locked when not in use."

Oliver glanced at him. "Keys are easy enough to snag and replace, as I discovered last night at the spa."

Luther grimaced. "There is also the faint but very real possibility that Tremayne managed to persuade someone on my staff to assist him."

"So there are ways he could have escaped this club without being seen," Irene said.

Oliver looked at Luther and then turned back to Irene. "As a rule, Luther and I have a problem keeping would-be trespassers such as the press and party crashers *out* of our establishments. Our guests certainly aren't prisoners. Our security is designed to protect them, not keep them from escaping."

"Regardless of how he got out, it would only take a few minutes for Tremayne to drive to the hotel and back, right?" Irene said.

Luther looked at Oliver and then shrugged. "It would be tight but I suppose it could be done. It would take some advance planning, though."

Irene confronted them, her notebook tightly clutched in one hand. Her eyes were brilliant with a feverish excitement. A whisper of dread ignited Oliver's senses. *If she keeps this up, she's going to get herself killed.*

But he could not think of any way to stop her.

"What do you mean?" she asked.

Luther swallowed some of his martini and assumed a thoughtful air. "He'd need a car."

Irene frowned. "He has one. I checked. He drove his own vehicle here to Burning Cove."

"Tremayne left his car with the valet attendants," Luther said. "He did not ask to have his vehicle brought around until after three in the morning."

"He could have had another car waiting in a side street," Irene said quickly.

"True," Luther conceded. "But even if you are correct, you're forgetting the lady, the one who came in from the garden with him looking as if she had been enjoying a romantic interlude."

"I need to talk to her," Irene said. "You must know her name and where I can find her."

"Daisy Jennings," Luther said. "And before you ask, she's a regular. Likes to rub shoulders with the Hollywood crowd. She's a stunner, and both men and women enjoy her company. I have no objection to her as a customer. But if you're right about Tremayne's activities last night, it means that he persuaded Daisy to help him with his story. If that's the case, you can bet that she'll tell you exactly what Tremayne and his studio want her to tell you."

"You mean they'll pay her to lie to me."

"Or they'll threaten her," Oliver said evenly. "Or Tremayne will make it clear that she will no longer be allowed inside his circle of party friends if she doesn't cooperate. One way or another, I doubt that you'll get the truth from her."

Luther looked thoughtful. "I would remind both of you that Tremayne's story might be the truth. Maybe he really was out in the garden with Daisy Jennings during that forty-five-minute window of time. Regardless, Oliver's right, Miss Glasson. You'll only get the story that Tremayne and his studio want you to hear."

Irene contemplated the view of the gardens. "There might be another way to find out if Tremayne left this place last night. If he parked another car on a side street, someone might have noticed it. After all, he would have had to park it again near the hotel before he went into the spa, then get back into it and return here. And that begs the question, whose car did he borrow? Daisy Jennings's, perhaps?"

Luther looked at Oliver. "Does she ever give up?"

"Not that I've noticed," Oliver said.

"That could be a problem," Luther said. "For her future well-being."

"You're welcome to try to explain that to her," Oliver said. "I tried. Didn't get very far."

Irene snapped her notebook closed. "If the two of you continue to talk about me as if I weren't here, I'll leave and find my own way back."

"My apologies," Luther said.

Blake loomed in the doorway. "Dinner is served."

Luther smiled. "Your timing is excellent, Blake."

"We need a good distraction," Oliver said. "Dinner will work."

He took Irene's arm. On the way into the formal dining room, she took one last look at Pell's seascapes.

"These are your paintings, Luther?" she asked.

"Yes," he said.

"They are . . . interesting."

Luther chuckled. "In other words, you wouldn't want them hanging in your home."

"I can't say for sure," Irene said. "I don't have a home. Just an apartment in L.A."

Chapter 16

Oliver eased the car into a space at the curb in front of the Cove Inn. The guest rooms in the small establishment were all darkened, but a porch light glowed weakly over the front door.

"Looks like Mrs. Fordyce decided not to wait up for you," he said.

"She gave me a key to the front door," Irene said. "Told me to let myself in."

Oliver thought about the lonely bed waiting for him, and then he thought about how he had grown accustomed to sleeping alone. Most nights it didn't bother him. But tonight would be different. Tonight when he went to bed, he was going to be thinking about Irene. He had a hunch he would lie awake for a long time.

He took his time climbing out from behind the wheel. The fog had rolled in across the waters of the cove, but he could see the lights of the marina and the old fishing pier.

He wondered what Irene would say if he suggested a stroll on the pier before she went back to her room at the inn.

What the hell. The worst that could happen was she would say no.

He rounded the front of the car and opened the passenger side door. This time when he reached down to help her, Irene didn't resist. Her fingers were warm and delicate, but there was strength in the light, firm way she grasped his hand.

This time she didn't act as if her weight might pull him off balance. She trusted him not to fall on his face. Progress.

"Would you like to take a walk?" he asked, trying to make it casual, trying not to let her know that everything in him was willing her to say yes.

There was a short silence during which he was sure he actually stopped breathing.

"It's late," she said finally. She adjusted the light shawl. "And a bit damp."

But she had stopped on the sidewalk, making no attempt to move toward the front porch steps.

The wrap wasn't much protection against the cool night air off the ocean. Without a word he unfastened his dinner jacket and draped it around her shoulders. It was hugely oversized for her slender frame. It enveloped her like a cape. But she made no attempt to remove it. He savored the sight of her in the coat.

He offered her his arm. She took it. He started breathing normally again. But his blood was heating.

They walked slowly along the sidewalk, the streetlamps lighting their way for a time. He was grimly aware of the hitch in his stride. He wanted to snap the cane like a twig. But Irene paid no attention to it—probably because her thoughts were focused on someone else, namely Nick Tremayne.

"Well?" he said after a time. "What did you make of Pell?"

"I think I can understand why you consider him a trusted friend, even though he's a few years older than you."

That was not the answer he was expecting.

"What makes you think we're good friends?" he asked.

Irene smiled. "You have two of his paintings on your office wall."

"You noticed them, did you? Perhaps I like his work."

"It's more than that. I think you understand his work. I expect that you two have a few things in common."

"Because we both offer glossy illusions to the public?"

"No, because you both have a surface image that conceals something deeper and more complicated," Irene said.

"I've never considered myself complicated. But Luther Pell is definitely more complicated than most people realize."

"Why is that?"

"As you said, he is a few years older than me. He went off to fight in the Great War when he was nineteen. He was fortunate. He returned with no visible wounds. But not all wounds are visible."

"No," she said.

They reached the entrance to the pier. Twin rows of lights illuminated the wooden-planked walkway. The far end was lost in moon-infused fog.

Irene did not object when he guided her onto the pier. The silence was interrupted by the gentle lapping of the waves beneath the wooden boards.

Irene was so close that now and again he caught a trace of her scent, a mix of some flowery cologne and her own feminine essence. He was sure his pulse was beating a little harder than usual. Instinctively he tightened his grip on her arm. He wanted to keep her there, next to him, for as long as possible.

"Sorry Pell couldn't give you what you wanted tonight," he said at last.

She sighed. "I didn't think it would be easy to prove that Tremayne is a killer."

"No. It won't be easy. More likely impossible."

"You think I'm wasting my time, don't you?"

"What I think," he said slowly, "is that you are taking some very big risks."

She slanted him a sidelong look. "Risks you're willing to take, as well. What will you do if we find out for certain that Nick Tremayne murdered three women but we can't prove it?"

"I'll worry about that problem if it becomes a problem."

She stopped short. "What does that mean?"

He was forced to stop, too. He released her, hooked

the handle of the cane over the railing, and leaned against the wooden barrier.

"It means that this is Burning Cove, not L.A.," he said. "The rules are a little different here."

"Mr. Ward—"

"Oliver."

"Oliver. I appreciate that you have an interest in finding out what happened in your spa and I'm grateful for your help, but I don't want to be responsible for you doing something that could get you arrested."

He smiled a little at that. "Trust me, if I get arrested, it will be my own fault."

She folded her arms under the protective cloak of his coat and looked at him. In the weak glow of the nearby lamp, he could see the shadows in her eyes.

"I assume your next step is to try to interview Daisy Jennings?" he asked.

"Yes."

"Luther was right, you know. She won't talk. By now the studio people will have gotten to her."

Irene angled her head a little and studied his face in the dim light. He realized that she was trying to read him.

"It's worth a try," she said. "I don't have any other leads."

"You're not going to let it go, are you?"

"No," she said. "I can't. By any chance, do you know Miss Jennings?"

"I know her," he said. "She's all right but she's wasting her life chasing a dream."

"She wants to be an actress?"

"Daisy Jennings spends her nights at the Paradise

Club and sometimes in the lounge at my hotel because she hopes that if she sleeps with the right person, she'll finally get that screen test, the one that will transform her into a movie star."

"That's so sad."

"She's hardly alone. Hollywood is filled with dreamers like her. Some of them find their way to Burning Cove because the stars and directors come here."

"I know," Irene said. "In the time I've been working at *Whispers,* I've met a lot of people with stars in their eyes. Everyone has dreams."

"What's your dream?" he asked.

"Dreams change. I lost my parents when I was little. My grandfather raised me. I used to dream about traveling around the world. But Grandpa died when I was fourteen. I wound up in an orphanage for a couple of years. For a while my dream was to have a family of my own. But it soon became obvious that what I really needed was a way to make a living. My dreams are a lot more pragmatic these days. What about you?"

"Like you said, dreams change. There was a time when I wanted to become the next Houdini. Now my goal is to make sure the Burning Cove Hotel keeps turning a profit."

"Sounds like we've both been able to adapt our dreams to our circumstances."

"Probably less frustrating that way," he said.

"Probably."

"What happens if your investigation goes nowhere?" he asked.

"I'll go back to my job and find another story to cover. Speaking of my big story, I'm grateful to you for opening some doors for me. It was nice of you to introduce me to Luther Pell tonight."

"You can skip the gratitude," he said. "I don't want it."

He had evidently spoken more sharply than he had intended because she stiffened and then threw him a quick, searching glance.

"I was trying to be polite and civil," she said coldly. "Are you always this prickly?"

He groaned. "Sorry. Didn't mean to snap at you. Just wanted to make sure you knew I wasn't expecting anything more out of this partnership."

"Anything more?" she repeated much too carefully.

The wooden boards on which he was standing might as well have been transformed into eggshells. He was afraid to make another move but he felt compelled to try to explain.

"Gratitude can be misunderstood," he said.

"Really? I have no problem understanding exactly what it means."

"I'm trying to tell you that I don't expect you to fall into bed with me as a way of thanking me for opening those damned doors."

"Don't worry," she said. "I have absolutely no intention whatsoever of sleeping with you as a way of repaying you for your help. Are we clear on that?"

"Perfectly clear."

"Good. In that case, I'm going back to my room. Alone."

She stepped smartly to the side, whipped around him, and marched swiftly back along the pier.

"Damn it, Irene, you're twisting my words."

He grabbed his cane off the railing and started after her. Pain ripped through his bad leg. For a couple of seconds, he could scarcely breathe through the agony. He gritted his teeth, tightened his grip on the cane, and kept going.

Irene did not look back but her dainty heels slowed her down. He had closed most of the distance between them by the time she reached the front steps of the Cove Inn.

He saw the two men hunkered down in the shadows on the porch before Irene did because she was busy rummaging around in her big handbag for the key.

"Irene, stop," he said, using his stage voice, the one that carried all the way to the back row of the theater.

Startled, she froze.

"What?" she asked.

The two men surged out of the shadows. One of them held a boxlike object in his hands.

Oliver braced himself on his cane and grabbed Irene. He pulled her close, trying to shield her from what he knew was coming.

The flashbulb exploded. Oliver turned his head to avoid being blinded by the dazzling light.

"Comment for the press, Mr. Ward?" one of the men said. "How long have you and Miss Glasson been seeing each other?"

The second man fired his camera. The flashbulb went off, searing the night.

"What about you, Miss Glasson?" the first man said. "Care to comment on the nature of your relationship with Mr. Ward?"

"We're friends," Irene said, her voice very tight.

She managed to find her key. Oliver took it from her, got her up the steps, and opened the door.

"You heard the lady," he said over his shoulder. "Just friends."

He hauled her into the lobby and slammed the door shut.

Footsteps pounded away down the sidewalk. Somewhere out on the street a car engine roared to life.

"Damn," Irene said. She freed herself from the circle of Oliver's arm and slipped off his jacket. "I'm supposed to be the one writing the story—not the subject of the story. How bad is this going to be?"

"I have no idea," Oliver said. "Someone sent that pair to ambush us."

"Tremayne's studio?"

"Probably. The question is, what do they plan to do with the photos?"

"Neither of us is a star," Irene said. "I can't imagine any newspaper or Hollywood magazine paying for those shots."

"You know, for an orphan who stopped dreaming fanciful dreams when she was fourteen, you've got a very optimistic attitude."

Chapter 17

"What the devil is going on there in Burning Cove?" Velma Lancaster's voice roared through the telephone line. "According to *Silver Screen Secrets*, you're dating that ex-magician, the owner of the Burning Cove Hotel. And the competition gets the story? What am I paying you for?"

Irene clutched the phone and gazed, dumbfounded, at the front page of *Silver Screen Secrets*. Mrs. Fordyce had thoughtfully left the paper on the front desk counter where Irene could not miss seeing the large photo.

The picture was not a flattering one. Her mouth was open. Her eyes were wide with shock. All in all she had the horrified expression of a woman caught in flagrante delicto. It did not help that Oliver's white dinner jacket was draped around her shoulders and that he had her in a viselike grip.

It struck her as grossly unfair that Oliver somehow managed to appear both coldly dangerous and compellingly attractive. The fact that he was no longer wearing his dinner jacket added what could only be described as an extremely sensual element to the picture.

The caption that accompanied the photo had been written to put the worst possible light on the subject.

Ex-magician Mr. Oliver Ward and his new romantic interest, Miss Irene Glasson, reporter.

Irene huddled over the phone and lowered her voice to a whisper.

"It's not what it looks like," she said.

"What?" Velma shouted. "I can't hear you."

Irene raised her voice a little. "I said it's not what it looks like."

Mrs. Fordyce was pretending to be busy behind the counter but she was practically vibrating with curiosity. It was clear that she was listening to every word.

"You're in the newspaper business," Velma snapped. "You know damned well that a photo or a story is exactly what it looks like. Perception is everything. It looks like you're involved in a murder investigation and you're dating the owner of the hotel in which the murder occurred. What's more, said hotel owner just happens to be the famous ex-magician who was nearly killed onstage in his final act."

"This doesn't make any sense. Why would anyone outside Burning Cove give a darn about my personal life?"

"With the exception of me and your colleagues here at *Whispers*, no one *does* give a damn about your personal life. It's Ward's personal life that made the picture newsworthy."

"I don't understand. He said he wasn't worried about the L.A. press because he was no longer a headliner."

"Turns out he's wrong. Evidently the press is still mighty curious about a famous magician who disappeared after nearly getting himself killed onstage. Nice dress, by the way. How in the hell did you afford that frock on what I'm paying you?"

"I got it as a loan courtesy of Mr. Ward's hotel."

"Oliver Ward gave it to you?"

"Don't start with the innuendos. My association with Oliver Ward is strictly business."

"Interesting business you're in these days."

"Mr. Ward is assisting me in my investigation," Irene said coldly.

"Yeah? Read the rest of the story."

Irene scanned the piece quickly.

That legendary man of magic, Mr. Oliver Ward, who pulled off a disappearing act after a disastrous accident onstage, has materialized in the community of Burning Cove, California. He now operates an exclusive hotel that caters to the rich and famous of Hollywood.

Last night Mr. Ward was seen escorting Miss Irene Glasson to a notorious nightclub in the seaside community.

One wonders if the once-great magician knows that he is dating a member of the press who works for a small-time L.A. newspaper. Evidently Miss Glasson has been questioned in connection with the drowning death of one of Mr. Ward's hotel guests.

Perhaps even a skilled illusionist can be deceived by cheap goods.

"Cheap goods?" Irene repeated.

"Afraid so."

"My reputation aside, evidently Oliver Ward was right."

"Speaking personally, I take great exception to the description of *Whispers* as a small-time paper," Velma said. "*Secrets* didn't even print the name of my paper." There was a slight pause. "What do you mean, Ward was right?"

"Our date last night was supposed to be an act of misdirection. Evidently it worked."

"How is this an example of misdirection? In case you didn't notice, there is a strong hint that you had something to do with Maitland's death. Guilt by association, I think it's called—not misdirection."

"Never mind, Boss. Look, things are happening here. I need to talk to some more people in Burning Cove. I've got to stay on a couple more days."

"Bad idea."

Irene ignored her. "I didn't pack for an extended stay, so I'm going to drive back to L.A. today to pick up some fresh clothes. I also need to see if anything was stolen from my apartment during the burglary. I'll stop by the office and fill you in on what's going on here. Once I have a chance to lay it out for you, you'll realize this story is red-hot."

"I suppose you expect me to keep paying the tab at that inn where you're staying in Burning Cove."

"This is going to be the story that makes *Whispers* the number one newspaper in Los Angeles, Boss."

"Or puts it out of business," Velma said.

"This isn't just about Tremayne," Irene said. "It's about Peggy, remember?"

"All right, all right, I'll spring for another couple of days at the inn. But don't bother writing up another story with Tremayne's name in it unless you've got rock-solid proof that he's guilty."

"Thanks. You won't regret it."

"What about the dress?"

"What dress?"

"The one you were wearing in the photo," Velma said patiently. "The one that is probably worth more than I pay you in a year."

Irene thought about the gown hanging in the closet in her room. "I told you, it was just on loan. I'll be returning it to the management of the Burning Cove Hotel today."

"Too bad. It looked good on you."

"It was just a prop."

Chapter 18

Nick Tremayne tossed the copy of *Silver Screen Secrets* onto the patio table and pushed himself up out of the rattan chair.

"Ogden thinks that photo is going to solve my problems?" he asked.

"He's quite pleased with it." Claudia swallowed hard. "He says that today everyone in L.A. will be talking about the reclusive former illusionist who is dating a female reporter who is cheap goods, one who is now directly linked to the death of Miss Maitland. Mr. Ogden is sure that the story will nullify any damage done by the piece Miss Glasson wrote in *Whispers*."

"I'm not so sure about that," Nick said.

Breakfast had been served on his private patio. He had dined alone because he was not in the mood to make conversation with anyone. Claudia did not count.

He had let her stand there, briefing him on the contents of the *Secrets* story, while he finished his eggs Benedict. He had not bothered to offer her a cup of coffee. She could get her own coffee. She was supposed to be his assistant, after all.

He went to the edge of the patio and stood looking out over the cove. The morning fog had burned off, leaving another sparkling day—another California-perfect day in what should have been his picture-perfect life.

Everything had been on track until recently. He was on a very fast elevator, headed for the top. Sure, he still had to put up with a studio contract, but soon he would have the kind of power it took to pick and choose the roles he wanted. Hell, he'd be rich enough to buy his way out of the damned contract if that's what he wanted to do.

But a few weeks ago the first reporter from *Whispers* had started nosing around in his past. After Hackett's fatal accident, however, he'd been sure he was in the clear. Then Gloria Maitland had reappeared, threatening to go to the press, demanding money in exchange for her silence. Ogden had come through but the pay-off wasn't enough to stop Gloria. Deep down he'd known that the cash probably wouldn't be enough to keep her quiet, Nick thought. Gloria had wanted something more—she'd wanted revenge.

With Gloria out of the way, he had dared to hope that he was once again in the clear. He hadn't expected any trouble from the local starstruck tramp, Daisy Jennings. She had sworn she would be his alibi for the night of Maitland's death. *I'll do anything for you, Nick.*

She had wanted a screen test in exchange for protecting him. He knew he didn't have that kind of power at the studio—not yet. But he'd made the promise. With luck, that would be enough to keep her quiet until he could figure out how to stop Glasson.

It was always a woman who got in his way, he reflected—Betty Scott in Seattle; the washed-up gossip reporter, Hackett; Gloria Maitland; Irene Glasson.

It was always a woman.

"It's true that people will probably assume that Glasson is sleeping with Ward," he said. "They may even wonder if she was responsible for Maitland's death. But it doesn't follow that Glasson won't write another story about me. And people will read it, even if they do think she is a cheap little whore. I can't afford any more gossip linking me to murder. Ogden has got to make sure Glasson doesn't write another piece for *Whispers*."

"Mr. Ogden said to tell you again that everything was under control," Claudia said. "He promised he'd deal with Irene Glasson."

"You're useless. Get out of my sight. I need time to think."

Claudia hurried back into the front room of the villa. A few seconds later the front door closed behind her.

Nick turned back to the dazzling view of the cove. He would not allow a woman to derail his damned-near-perfect life.

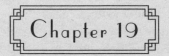

Chapter 19

Just when he had begun to think that Los Angeles would defeat him.

"Are you sure?" Julian Enright said into the phone.

"See for yourself, sir," Marcus Goodman said. "Get a copy of *Silver Screen Secrets*. If that isn't the woman in the picture you sent to our office, I'll eat my filing cabinet."

Marcus Goodman was the latest in a long line of private investigators and cops who had been paid to make inquiries about Anna Harris. For months all the leads had hit brick walls.

Back at the start it had all looked so easy, Julian reflected. When he'd returned again to Helen Spencer's mansion, the place was abandoned. The police had given up. The housekeeper and butler had packed up and left. The lawyers were still trying to locate an heir to the big house.

The result was that he'd been able to take his time going through the mansion. He thought he'd gotten lucky when he found the framed photograph of Anna Harris and her new yellow Packard.

In the picture she was standing beside the car looking as thrilled and delighted as a child who had just opened a surprise birthday present. It was clear from her expression that she was not accustomed to such gifts. He'd found the receipt for the car in Spencer's study.

He'd left the mansion with an excellent photo of his quarry and a full description of the car she was driving. It shouldn't have been hard to track her. He had played one logical hunch after another, checking hotels and inns within a day's driving distance. It finally dawned on him that she was either sleeping in her car or staying at cheap autocamps. It was the last thing he had expected. She had, after all, become accustomed to fine hotels and excellent restaurants in the course of her employment with Spencer.

He'd hit another snag because he assumed that she would stay on the East Coast while she tried to find a buyer for the notebook. In his experience, when people ran, they usually ran to places they knew, often quite well. They felt safe in familiar haunts. In addition, as Spencer's private secretary, Harris must have had some idea of whom to contact in the underground market that catered to thieves and espionage agents.

But there had been no hint of a certain scientific notebook coming up for auction on the black market.

By the time he'd figured out that she might not be on the East Coast, nearly two months had passed. His father had been furious.

He thought the tide had turned when an investigator finally located the Packard. It was parked in a farmer's yard. The farmer explained that he had found it sitting, abandoned, on the side of a dirt road one morning.

For the first time it had occurred to Julian that his quarry might have resorted to hitchhiking.

Another dead end.

Finally, after more weeks of fruitless searching, he had at last picked up the first hint that Anna Harris had taken the path that so many others in search of new lives had followed. She'd found her way to Chicago and headed west on Route 66.

By the time he'd arrived at that realization, however, another month had passed. Anna Harris was no longer an intriguing challenge; she had become an obsession.

There was another factor in play now, as well. The old man had learned that Atherton's notebook was worth far more than he had originally believed. There was more than one potential buyer with very deep pockets.

Route 66 ended in Santa Monica, California. The town was bordered on three sides by the city of Los Angeles. The fourth side faced the Pacific. Julian was sure that Anna Harris had disappeared into L.A. True, she could have continued north to San Francisco, but his intuition told him that she would feel safer in the fabulous sprawl of Los Angeles. It was, after all, a place where nothing was what it seemed. It was Hollywood, the perfect setting for a woman on the run. A new name, a new past, a new future? No problem.

There was no reason for Anna Harris to keep going. She had reached the edge of the continent.

But it soon became evident that L.A. was an even better hiding place than he had initially feared. He had been in town for nearly a month and thus far had found no trace of her. Los Angeles and the surrounding towns and communities were filled with people, including a lot of single women, trying to reinvent themselves. In California, it seemed, no one had a past.

He and the investigators he employed had hit another brick wall.

He'd settled in at the Beverly Hills Hotel for what had become a long, hard slog. There was no point in being rich if you didn't enjoy the benefits. The hotel, with its Sunset Boulevard address, acres of groomed gardens, and palm trees, was a California dream made real.

Attractive, exciting people, including movie stars, populated the bar and reclined around the pool reading celebrity-obsessed papers like *Daily Variety* and the *Hollywood Reporter*. Two days ago he'd spotted Carole Lombard and yesterday afternoon he was sure he'd seen Fred Astaire.

The place reeked of glamour—and glamour, he had concluded, was what had been missing from his life. This impossibly gorgeous world was made for him.

"I'll call you after I've had a chance to take a look at the paper," he said into the phone.

He dropped the receiver into the cradle and caught the eye of a passing bellhop.

"Get me a copy of *Silver Screen Secrets*," he said. "I'll be out by the pool."

"Yes, sir."

The bellhop found him a short time later. As soon as he saw the photo splashed across the front page, a rush of exultation hit him. He had studied the picture of Anna Harris every day for nearly four months. He'd had it enlarged so that he could get to know every angle of her face, the arch of her brows, the shape of her mouth.

Her hair was styled differently in the newspaper photo. It was no longer confined in the rolled and pinned style suited to a private secretary. Instead it fell to her shoulders in deep waves. Very modern. Very Hollywood. But there was no doubt that the woman in the photo was a dead ringer for the target he had been hunting for so long.

According to the caption, her name was Irene Glasson, a reporter. She had changed her name and her occupation. *Smart girl, but not smart enough,* he thought. *You're mine now.*

He studied the man who had his arm around Anna-Irene. The name, Oliver Ward, was vaguely familiar. He noticed the cane, and memory stirred. He read the full story.

That legendary man of magic Mr. Oliver Ward, who pulled off a disappearing act after a disastrous accident onstage, has materialized in the community of Burning Cove, California. He now operates an exclusive hotel that caters to the rich and famous of Hollywood.

Last night Mr. Ward was seen escorting Miss
Irene Glasson to a notorious nightclub in the seaside
community . . .

Julian put the paper aside, slipped on his sunglasses,
and sat quietly, contemplating the sunlight dancing
on the surface of the pool. After a moment, he smiled.

He had long ago discovered that the hunt was far
more exciting than seduction and foreplay. And the
kill surpassed any act of sexual release he had ever
experienced.

It was at that moment when he held another person's
life in his hands—when he saw the stark terror in the
eyes of a target—that he knew what it was to be fully
alive.

But first things first. He had to find the notebook
before he could take his time with Irene. The old man
wouldn't stop nagging him until the damned notebook
was recovered.

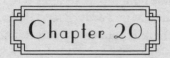

Chapter 20

I rene was in her room, getting ready for the long drive to Los Angeles, when she heard Mrs. Fordyce calling to her from the foot of the stairs.

"Phone call, Miss Glasson."

Mentally she ran through the very short list of people who knew she was staying at the inn and who might have a reason to call her. She came up with two names: Velma Lancaster and Oliver Ward. Considering the fact that Velma had phoned a short time ago, the odds were good that Oliver was the caller.

Anticipation sparked inside her. She tried to squelch it. They were partners in the investigation, she reminded herself. That was the extent of their association.

She went out into the hall and hurried down the

stairs. Mrs. Fordyce motioned toward the receiver lying on the front desk.

"If you continue tying up my telephone, there will be an extra charge," she warned.

"Just put it on the bill. My paper will cover it."

"I'll do that," Mrs. Fordyce said. "Now I've got to get back to the kitchen. Got a full house this morning."

She bustled off. Irene glanced over her shoulder into the cozy breakfast room. All of the tables were occupied by guests, and every last one of them seemed to be watching her from behind a copy of the morning newspaper.

I'm getting paranoid, she thought.

She picked up the phone and composed herself. She wanted to sound cool and professional—not like a woman who had been waiting by the phone for a man to call.

"This is Irene Glasson."

"Miss Glasson, you don't know me but I think we should talk."

Not Oliver. Anticipation evaporated. Not Velma, either. The voice on the other end of the line was female, husky, and a little breathless. It was pitched at the level of a whisper.

Another kind of excitement spiked.

"Who is this?" she asked.

"Someone with information you want. I'm willing to sell it to you."

Irene tightened her grip on the phone.

"I'm afraid you'll have to be more specific," she said, doing her best to sound disinterested. "I'm a journalist.

I get crank calls all the time from people who claim to have useful information to sell."

There was a short, startled pause on the other end of the line. Evidently the would-be informant had not expected to be brushed aside.

"Trust me, you'll want to hear what I've got to tell you. I know what really happened the night Gloria Maitland died."

"Is that so?" Irene injected a tincture of mild curiosity into her voice. "Were you at the scene?"

"What? No." Panic spiked in the whispery voice now. "I was nowhere near the Burning Cove Hotel that night."

"Then I doubt you have anything useful to tell me. I'm going to hang up now."

"Wait. I wasn't at the hotel but I was at the Paradise Club."

"You've got sixty seconds," Irene said. "Talk fast. Tell me something I can believe."

"I am the woman who was in the garden with Nick Tremayne at the Paradise Club." The words came out in a rush.

"You're Daisy Jennings?"

Another startled pause.

"How did you know my name?" Daisy demanded.

"I consulted a psychic."

"Really?" Daisy sounded uncertain, half believing. "Which one? There are several in town."

"We're wasting time, Daisy."

"I'll tell you what happened the night that woman drowned in the spa, but not on the phone, understand? The money comes first. Then I'll talk."

"Why would you tell me anything about Nick Tremayne?"

"Because I need some money and I need it in a hurry. I'm going to leave Burning Cove on the morning train. Are you interested or not?"

"How much money?"

"A hundred bucks."

"Forget it," Irene said. "Who do you think you're talking to? Rockefeller? I don't carry that kind of money on me."

She did have her emergency stash in her handbag. She could dig into it if necessary. But if Daisy had solid information to sell, Velma would be willing to cover the expense of purchasing it. She wouldn't go as high as a hundred dollars, however.

"All right, all right, make it fifty," Daisy said.

"My rate for useless information is zero," Irene said. "But if I like what I hear, we can negotiate."

"Twenty?" Daisy said quickly.

"I can manage that much if the information is good. When and where do we meet?"

"There's a phone booth on the corner of Olive and Palm streets. Be there at eleven thirty tonight. I'll call you and tell you where to meet me. Make sure you come alone or the deal's off, understand?"

The line went dead before Irene could get in another question.

She closed her notebook and stood quietly for a moment, thinking. One thing was certain—she wouldn't be making the drive to Los Angeles that day. If she got delayed for any reason—engine trouble or a road closure—she might not be able to get back to Burning Cove in time to make the rendezvous that night.

She picked up the phone and dialed Oliver's office number. Elena put her through immediately. Oliver did not bother with the usual pleasantries.

"What's wrong?" he asked.

"How did you know—? Never mind. I'd like to talk to you privately as soon as possible."

"I'll pick you up in fifteen minutes."

She hesitated. "That will probably cause more gossip."

"Misdirection, remember?"

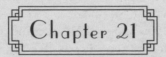

Chapter 21

"Have you lost your mind?" Oliver said. "A late-night meeting with an informant who wants cash? You can't be serious."

"Got a better idea?" Irene asked. "It's not like we have any other leads. I wanted to talk to Daisy Jennings. This is my big chance."

She was regretting her decision to tell Oliver about Daisy's call. She was also starting to get mad.

Oliver had pulled up in front of the Cove Inn less than ten minutes after he had hung up the phone. Eager to tell him her news, she had jumped into the front seat before he could extricate himself from behind the wheel.

He had listened closely, his mood darkening with every word, while driving to a small, secluded beach. She had not realized just how angry he was until he switched off the ignition and angled himself in the seat to confront her. She had expected him to be concerned but she did not anticipate the lecture. They were partners, after all.

"Don't you get it?" he said. "It's a setup. It has to be."

"You don't know that. What would be the purpose?"

"If you're right, we're dealing with a man who has murdered several women. One more probably won't matter to him."

"I agree, but we're also dealing with a man who has been very, very careful to protect himself. All of the murders have been made to look like accidents."

"Here's a bulletin for you, Miss Reporter, the corner of Olive and Palm is a shopping street. It will be deserted at eleven thirty at night. A great place for a lethal auto accident."

She took a breath. "All right, I admit I didn't know the neighborhood where the phone booth was located, but believe it or not, it did occur to me that Daisy might not have been entirely truthful with me. Why do you think I called you to discuss the situation?"

"I'd like to believe it was because you had an attack of common sense, but that could be wishful thinking on my part."

"Damn it, stop treating me like I'm an idiot. I do know there is some risk involved, but there is also the very real possibility that Daisy Jennings has solid information to sell. She told me that she needs money because she's leaving town on the train first thing in the morning."

"Did she say why?"

"No, but obviously it's because she's scared."

"There's nothing obvious about this situation. It's getting murkier by the day."

Oliver turned abruptly in the seat and opened the door. He levered himself up from behind the wheel and grabbed his cane. She watched him make his way down the short path to the beach. She knew that he was in pain. His limp was a little more pronounced. Walking on the rocky, uneven landscape likely wasn't helping matters. It occurred to her that he had probably put some strain on his bad leg during the night when he had attempted to protect her from the photographer. Today he was paying for his act of chivalry.

He came to a halt at the water's edge and stood silently, contemplating the crashing waves through his sunglasses. His profile was as hard as the cliffs. The breeze off the ocean tangled his hair and whipped at the edges of his linen jacket. She waited a moment. When he showed no signs of returning to the car, she opened her own door and got out.

She picked a path down to the beach and came to a halt beside Oliver.

"I'm sorry I dragged you into this," she said.

He turned his head to look at her, his eyes unreadable through the lenses of the sunglasses. But, then, his eyes were often unreadable, she thought.

"I thought we agreed that you would stop apologizing," he said.

"Sorry."

"I made it clear back at the start of our partnership that I'm involved in this investigation of yours because I want to know what really happened to one of my guests."

"Right."

He groaned. "I'm the one who should be apologizing. I shouldn't have snapped at you."

"I absolutely agree with you on that point."

There was a brittle silence.

"How did Daisy Jennings find out that you want to talk to her?" Oliver asked.

Irene thought back to the phone call. "She didn't actually say that she knew I wanted to interview her. She just said that she was with Nick Tremayne in the garden at the Paradise Club the night Gloria Maitland was found dead. She said she had information to sell."

"How much did she want?"

"The asking price was one hundred dollars."

He whistled softly. "That's a lot of cash to expect a reporter to come up with on short notice."

"I told her I didn't have that kind of money. She immediately dropped the price to fifty and, finally, to twenty bucks. In the end she agreed to negotiate. I got the feeling she'll take whatever I'm willing to pay. I'm sure my editor will cover the expense, provided the end result sells newspapers."

"I'll take care of paying our informant," Oliver said.

"That's not necessary."

"I said I'll take care of it," he repeated evenly.

"If you insist. I can't believe we're arguing about who will pay Daisy Jennings."

"Neither can I." Oliver was silent for a beat. "Doesn't sound like she bargained very hard."

"I think she's desperate. And very nervous. She knows something, Oliver. I have to talk to her."

"I'll come with you to the meeting tonight."

"I had a hunch you were going to suggest that."

"It's not a suggestion."

"I'll admit, I'd like to have you with me. But Daisy was adamant that I show up alone. Like I said, she is scared."

"Don't worry, she won't see me."

Irene thought about that. Then she smiled.

"Of course not," she said. "You're the Amazing Oliver Ward."

"Not so amazing, not anymore. But I can still pull off a reasonably convincing disappearing act."

She used one hand to hold her wind-tossed hair out of her eyes and turned to look at him.

"I believe you," she said.

"Do you?"

"Yes."

"Why?"

"I have no idea—except that in some ways you remind me of someone I knew a long time ago. If he made a promise, you knew he'd keep it or go down trying."

"Yeah? Who was he?"

"My grandfather."

Oliver winced. "I'm a few years older than you, Irene, but I'm not that much older."

"Oh, for pity's sake, I didn't mean to imply that I thought you were elderly—just . . . reliable. Dependable. Trustworthy."

"Like a good dog?"

"Where I come from, reliable, dependable, and trustworthy are all valuable things. They are also, I have discovered, rare."

"How the hell do you know I'm all of those things?"

"You can tell a lot about a man by the people around him. Your friend Luther Pell trusts you. I doubt that he has many friends that he does trust."

"Pell's business enterprises drastically limit the number of trustworthy people he meets."

She smiled. "Which makes it even more interesting that you and he are friends."

Oliver watched her intently. "Some would say that the fact that my closest friend in Burning Cove has underworld connections is not a particularly good character reference."

"I work for a newspaper that specializes in celebrity scandals and sordid gossip. I'm a little short on sterling references, too. Does that worry you?"

"No," he said. "No, it doesn't."

He did not say anything else but she was intensely aware of the electric tension in the atmosphere between them. She was almost certain that he was going to kiss her. She did not know if that was a very good idea or a very bad one. She only knew that she wanted to find out what it would be like to kiss Oliver Ward.

"Irene," he said.

She touched her fingertips to his mouth.

"Probably best not to talk about it," she said. "Just do it."

Heat flared in his eyes. His hand tightened around the back of her neck, and then his mouth was on hers.

It was a long, slow burn of a kiss. She went into it with no particular expectations, just a compelling curiosity. That, she concluded, was probably why she was blindsided by the sheer force of the desire that swept through her.

She had never been kissed like this. Oliver crushed her mouth under his as if he had been thirsting for the taste of her for a very long time, perhaps forever. He kissed her as if nothing else in the world was more important than that moment and the embrace, as if he wanted her more than he wanted his next breath.

If it was an illusion crafted by a skilled lover, it was a completely convincing one. She did not want to know the secret behind the trick. She wanted only to savor the magic.

A thrilling excitement made her head spin. She wound her arms around his neck and returned the kiss with a sensual abandon that stunned her. If she had been asked, she would have said she wasn't physically capable of such a response. A small voice in her head whispered that Bradley Thorpe would have concurred with that opinion. But, then, Bradley Thorpe was a lying, cheating bastard, she reminded herself, and, in hindsight, a boring lover.

The kiss made her giddy, downright euphoric. She felt as if she had accidentally opened a long-forgotten closet and discovered some bright, shiny dreams that had been locked away since she was fourteen years old.

The illusion ended with the honking of a horn. A car pulled off the road and stopped next to Oliver's car. The vehicle overflowed with a pack of young people in their teens, male and female. Someone had borrowed his father's car for the day, Irene thought.

The kids waved and laughed as they bailed out of

the front and back seats. They opened the trunk and hauled out blankets and a large picnic basket.

The driver grinned at Oliver as the teens made their way to the beach.

"Say, you're the magician who owns the big hotel in town, right?" he said enthusiastically. "You were in the paper this morning, sir." The kid switched his attention to Irene. "Are you the reporter who found the body in the spa?"

"Time to go," Oliver said.

He tucked Irene's hand in his. Together they made their way up the short beach path. The teens followed, clustering around and pelting them with questions. The girls wanted to know more about the dead woman in the spa but the boys soon switched their attention to Oliver's car.

"Is it true it's the fastest car in California?"

"How fast does it go?"

"What does it have under the hood, sir?"

"Say, would you mind if I took your car for a spin, Mr. Ward?"

"Not today," Oliver said.

One of the girls studied Oliver's cane.

"Daddy took me to see you perform once," she said. "I loved the part where you made the woman vanish in the mirror."

Oliver got the passenger side door open and bundled Irene into the seat.

"Glad you enjoyed the act," he said to the young woman.

He rounded the front of the car and got behind the wheel.

"Daddy says no one really knows what went wrong the night you nearly died onstage," the girl continued in a voice laced with ghoulish excitement. "He says there were rumors that someone tried to murder you."

"The rumors were wrong," Oliver said. "Have fun with your picnic. Keep an eye on the waves. Never turn your back on the ocean. It will take you by surprise every time. There's a strong riptide just offshore here."

There was a polite chorus of *yes, sir*s.

Oliver fired up the engine and drove onto the road. "Sorry about that," he said after a moment.

"What, exactly, are you apologizing for?" Irene asked. She held her breath waiting for the answer.

"The interruption. I should have found a more private location."

She started breathing again. "Not the kiss, then."

He gave her a quick, searching glance.

"Should I apologize for the kiss?" he asked.

"No," she said.

He nodded once. "Good. The kids will talk, and Burning Cove is a small town. There will be more gossip."

Irene laughed, feeling lighter and more carefree than she had in a very long time.

"Misdirection," she said.

Oliver laughed. It was, she realized, the first time she had seen him laugh.

"Right," he said. "Misdirection."

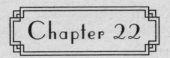

Chapter 22

The skull-faced man was sitting at the counter, reading *Silver Screen Secrets*. He looked like an extra from a horror film, Irene thought. He wasn't ugly, she decided, he was just weird.

She took a seat at the end of the counter and ordered a lettuce-and-tomato sandwich and a cup of coffee. It wasn't much of a dinner, but she was too nervous about the late-night meeting with Daisy Jennings to eat anything else.

The skull-faced man folded his paper very precisely and got to his feet. He walked toward her. She was careful not to look at him, but when he stopped a short distance away, she knew she was doomed.

"You're Irene Glasson, aren't you," he said in a voice that sounded like it emanated from a crypt. "You wrote that piece about the woman who drowned in the pool."

"Yes," Irene said. "Who are you?"

"You don't need to know that."

"Good point," she said. "Would you mind leaving me alone? I'd like to eat my dinner in peace."

"You should stop making trouble for Mr. Tremayne."

Irene went still and then, very deliberately, she swiveled around on the stool and confronted the skull-faced man. For the first time she got a good look at his eyes. She had been wrong about the resemblance to an extra in a horror movie, she decided. The stranger looked more like one of the fanatics who carried signs announcing that the world was coming to an end.

"Why are you so concerned with Mr. Tremayne?" she said, going for a softer tone.

"Mr. Tremayne is my friend. You'll leave him alone if you know what's good for you."

"Do you know anything about Gloria Maitland?" Irene asked. "Do you have some information that I should know about?"

"Stop asking questions."

The skull-faced man turned and walked out of the restaurant.

Irene looked at the waitress for some guidance.

"Don't mind him, honey." The waitress picked up the coffeepot. "He's crazy but he seems harmless. Got a thing for movie stars."

"I know the type." Irene paused. "Has he been in town long?"

"Couldn't say. He showed up here at Mel's about a week ago. Comes in twice a day, regular as clockwork. He's always got some of those Hollywood papers and magazines with him. Like I said, he's crazy about movie stars."

"Does he have a name?"

The waitress snorted. "I'm sure he does. But he never bothered to introduce himself."

Chapter 23

S hortly before eleven thirty that evening, Irene
eased her Ford to the side of the street. Oliver
had been right; the neighborhood was deserted
at that hour. The streetlamps provided some illumina-
tion but the windows were dark for the most part. She
was very conscious of night pressing in on all sides.
An eerie silence gripped the scene.

As promised, there was a wooden telephone booth
at the corner of Olive and Palm. The glass-paned doors
were open.

She switched off the engine and lowered the driver's
side window so that she would be sure to hear the
phone ring. *If it rings,* she thought.

"I don't see any other cars around," she said.

"That's a good sign," Oliver said from the dark
place on the floor behind the front seat. "It may mean

she was serious about wanting to sell you some information. Still, we're going to assume that someone is watching."

Irene folded her arms. "Sorry about the accommodations back there."

"It's a little cramped but not nearly as bad as the compartment I used for the Corridor of Infinity effect."

"Was that the trick that nearly got you killed?"

For a moment she thought he wasn't going to answer.

"No," he said finally. "That was the Cage of Death."

She wanted to ask what, exactly, had gone wrong, but her intuition told her that the question was far too intrusive, the kind of question that only a very close friend or a lover could ask. He had kissed her, but that did not make them close friends or lovers.

"I ran into one of Nick Tremayne's biggest fans today," she said. "He tried to warn me off the story. He said I shouldn't make trouble for Tremayne."

"Think he was from the studio?"

"No. He wasn't a tough guy, just a fanatical fan. The waitress at Mel's Café says he's been a regular for about a week. She thinks he's harmless."

"Tremayne checked in a week ago."

"I know."

"I'll have O'Conner, the head of hotel security, see what he can find out about the guy."

"All right. But I'm pretty sure he's just another obsessed fan."

The phone rang. She flinched. Even though she had been waiting for the summons, the sound nevertheless startled her.

"Here we go," she whispered.

She jumped out of the car and grabbed the receiver.

"This is Irene Glasson," she said.

"There's an old abandoned warehouse at the end of Miramar Road," Daisy said. Her voice was infused with the same whispery quality, but this time she spoke very slowly and with great precision. "Bootleggers used it during Prohibition but it's been empty since repeal. I'll wait for you there. Remember, come alone. Deal's off if I see anyone else." There was a short pause. "And don't forget the twenty bucks."

"Wait a minute, how am I supposed to find this place? I'm new in town, remember? I'm assuming you don't want me to ask directions at the nearest bar or gas station."

"*No.*" Panic edged the word. "Don't let anyone know where you're going. I'll give you directions."

Daisy rattled off a string of instructions and hung up the phone.

Irene got back into her car and fired up the engine. "We're heading for an abandoned warehouse at the end of Miramar Road. Know it?"

"It's located several miles outside of town on a bad road. It will take us a good forty-five minutes to get there from here. According to the locals, the warehouse used to be a bootlegger distribution point."

"Daisy mentioned that."

"Did she happen to mention that there's a dock and a boathouse attached?"

That stopped her for a few seconds. "A dock and a boathouse?"

"That old warehouse sits on the edge of a small,

hidden cove. That's why the bootleggers used it. They could bring in boatloads of illegal liquor without drawing the attention of the authorities." Oliver paused for emphasis. "They also used it to get rid of bodies."

"Bodies?"

"The business was very competitive."

"I see."

"All in all, sounds like the ideal location for another drowning accident," Oliver said.

She caught her breath. "Yes, it does. All right, you've made your point. Do you really think Daisy intends to try to murder me?"

"I think it's more likely that our killer is using Daisy to lure you to the scene. I warned you this was probably a setup."

She drummed the fingers of her left hand on the wheel. "But what if Daisy is telling the truth?"

"In that case, you're right. We may come away from the meeting with some hard information that we can use to figure out who murdered Gloria Maitland."

There was a new note in his voice, she thought, one that she had not heard before. She struggled to come up with a description and finally settled on *anticipation*. He sounded like a man who was looking forward to a little excitement.

"What if you're right, after all?" she said. "What if this meeting with Daisy is a setup?"

"We pull a rabbit out of the hat."

Chapter 24

Daisy Jennings struck another match to light another cigarette—the last one in the pack. She had been chain-smoking ever since she made the first phone call to the reporter earlier in the day. Her throat was raw and her nerves were frayed. Her pulse was beating much too fast. The match shook a little in her fingers.

It was the damned warehouse that was making her jumpy. No wonder the local kids claimed that it was haunted by the ghosts of the gangsters' victims. She had brought a kerosene lantern with her but it was burning low. She should have taken the time to refill it before driving out to the warehouse, she thought. Too late now. She could only hope that the reporter would be on time.

She got the cigarette lit and hastily blew out the match. She dropped it into the empty tin can she had found in a corner. She was being very careful with the matches and the butts. The warehouse was a firetrap.

The wide door that opened onto the loading dock at the back of the structure hung on its hinges. She could hear the water lapping and the creak of rotting wood. It sounded like some creepy monster of the deep feasting on the bodies that had been dumped into the cove. Maybe she had seen a few too many horror movies.

Occasionally she heard ominous rustlings in the shadows. Each time she hoisted the lantern to take a closer look, she caught sight of a furry body with a hairless, snakelike tail. The bootleggers had pulled up stakes and moved on to other business ventures, but the rats had set up shop amid the heaps of moldy straw, wooden crates, and leftover packing materials that littered the place.

She tossed the empty pack aside and inhaled deeply. The action triggered another coughing fit. So much for the brand's promise that its product had a soothing effect on the throat. It just went to show that you couldn't trust the claims made in the magazine ads. Couldn't trust the movie stars or the doctors who made those claims for the cigarette companies, either.

But, then, a smart woman didn't trust anyone, she thought, least of all a charming, good-looking movie star. Nick Tremayne was a dream man and he had promised to fulfill her dreams. He had said he would get her a screen test at his studio. She knew now that he had lied, just like all the others before him.

But at least Tremayne had come through with some cash—a lot of it. None of the others had been so generous. The first half was paid up front. After tonight she would collect the second half. That would give her enough money to buy the clothes she would need to start over in L.A.

No more Hollywood dreams. Her looks would start to fade soon. It was time to find a rich older man, preferably one who was going senile, a guy who could give her the financial security she would need to get through the years ahead.

The extra twenty bucks from Irene Glasson hardly mattered, Daisy thought. She had been told to make the demand for money so the scene looked authentic. A reporter expected to pay for a tip.

She stopped pacing and sat down on an empty crate to finish the cigarette.

Somewhere in the darkness the thick floorboards groaned again. She shuddered and glanced over her shoulder. There was nothing to see except darkness and shadows.

She checked her watch. She had arrived early, as instructed, after making the eleven thirty call from the last gas station phone booth on Miramar Road. The reporter would have to drive back through town, find Miramar Road, and then negotiate the dirt lane down the hillside to the warehouse. She wouldn't be here for another half hour or so, maybe longer if she got lost.

Please don't get lost, Irene Glasson. I need to get away from this place.

She finished the cigarette and started to grind out the butt in the makeshift ashtray. But her fingers were trembling so badly that she accidentally knocked the tin can onto its side. Dead matches and butts spilled out.

Thankfully, they didn't fall onto a pile of straw, but

the very idea of all the used smoking materials in such close proximity to the flammable items that cluttered the warehouse made her shudder.

Hastily she bent down to scoop the discarded matches and butts back into the tin can. The safest thing to do was dump them into the water.

She went out the freight door and walked a short distance along the dock. There was enough light from the lantern and the moon to allow her to see what she was doing.

She tipped the can upside down and dumped the contents into the black water.

Only about another half hour to wait—another half hour and she would have earned the rest of the money she needed to start a new life in L.A.

What a joke, she thought. This was her first and only real acting job, unless you counted all the sex scenes she had starred in over the years. She had given some very fine performances in the gardens of the Paradise Club and in various hotel room beds. The vacationing stars and directors and studio executives had all made promises, and they had all lied.

At least she was going to get paid for this night's work. All she had to do was stick to the script.

She heard the creak of wood behind her. A footstep. It was the only warning she got.

Panic flashed, threatening to choke her. She started to turn but it was too late.

The blow to her head stunned her. She was dimly aware of tumbling off the dock into the water.

She fell endlessly into darkness, and then there was nothing.

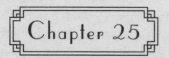

Chapter 25

"There's a clearing around the front of the warehouse," Irene announced from the driver's seat.
"One car. It must be Daisy's."

Oliver stayed where he was, crouched behind the
front seat, and tried to visualize the scene in his head.

"Any sign of Jennings?"

"My headlights are shining directly on her car.
Doesn't look like she's in it. There's some light coming
from inside the warehouse, though. A lantern."

"I'm going to take a look. Stay here. Keep the car
running, headlights on, until I get out. The glare will
blind anyone who might be watching from inside the
warehouse."

"What, exactly, are you going to do?" Irene asked.

She was worried, he thought. He rather liked the
idea that she might be concerned for his safety, but it

was far more likely that she was afraid he would ruin her chance at the big story.

"I just want to check out the area," he said.

"Are you sure that's a good idea?"

"It struck me as a better idea than walking straight into an ambush. If everything looks legit, I'll wave you in. Got that?"

"Yes."

She did not sound happy about the plan but she had agreed to it. That was good enough, he decided.

He cracked the door open, grabbed the cane, and worked his way out of the back seat and into the shadows at the side of the narrow road. The maneuver sent a couple of shock waves through his leg. His forehead was suddenly damp with sweat.

He breathed into the pain. It receded somewhat.

He was really out of shape, he reflected. There had been a time when he could maneuver his way out of a locked trunk or a steel cage. Underwater. Bound hand and foot.

But in spite of the damned leg he was strangely energized. It had been two long years since he'd experienced the old thrill. And this time it was the real deal. No magic involved.

He had Irene to thank for the druglike rush of excitement that was coursing through him. He would pay a price later. The leg was going to bother him more than usual for a couple of days but it would be worth it. He had a bottle full of aspirin and some excellent whiskey waiting for him at Casa del Mar.

Irene had lowered the window on the driver's side of the car. He spoke to her from the shadows.

"Are you all right?" she asked uneasily.

Irritation crackled through him.

"I'm fine," he said. "Give me a few minutes to go around behind the warehouse and make sure there isn't anyone except Jennings inside. Douse the lights and the car engine as soon as I give the signal. We don't want to attract any attention if we can avoid it."

"There was no traffic on Miramar Road."

"You never know. If a couple of kids out for a late-night cruise happen to see the lights, they might get curious."

"All right," she said.

"Remember, stay in the car until I wave you in. If anything looks like it's not going well, get the hell out of here, understand?"

"Yes, yes, I've got it. What about you?"

"Appearances to the contrary, I can take care of myself."

He did not wait for her to acknowledge the order. He was accustomed to people doing what he told them to do. He'd had a lot of experience in the role of boss, first onstage, where even small mistakes in a carefully staged illusion could destroy a career or get someone badly injured, even killed. Now, as the owner of a hotel that catered to a fickle and often bizarre clientele, he'd managed to keep a lot of people employed during the worst of the hard times.

The country was finally emerging from the aftermath of the crash, but his staff was loyal. No one had left to seek other opportunities.

So, yes, he'd become accustomed to people doing what they were told.

He reached inside his jacket and took the gun out of the holster.

Cane in one hand, weapon in the other, he continued toward the warehouse, hugging the deep night just beyond the headlight beams. He knew from his experience establishing lines of sight on a brightly lit stage that the audience never noticed the assistants dressed in black who worked in the shadows.

When he got close to Daisy's car, he saw that Irene was right. There was no one sitting in the vehicle. He took a chance and moved to stand next to the driver's door. Nobody was hiding in the rear seat.

He eased his way around to the rear of the warehouse. The full moon, combined with the lantern light spilling out through the open freight door, allowed him to see the old dock and the squat shape of the boathouse.

He flattened his back against the wall at one side of the freight door.

"Daisy Jennings?" he said.

There was no response.

He raised his voice a little but kept his tone cool and unthreatening. "I'm Oliver Ward. We've met. I insisted on accompanying Miss Glasson tonight. I didn't want her to take the risk of coming alone. I'm sure you can understand. Sorry for the change of plan but I brought a hundred bucks with me. I hope that will serve as an apology."

Nothing.

Gun extended, he leaned forward slightly and took a quick look around the interior of the warehouse. The lantern provided enough light to reveal that there was no sign of anyone inside. It also revealed the handbag sitting on a wooden crate.

Not good, he decided. Daisy Jennings should have been greeting him and his hundred-dollar apology with open arms.

Time to leave.

He grabbed his cane and started back around the warehouse. His only goal now was to get Irene as far away as possible.

The moonlight glinted on a small object on the dock. He had not noticed it earlier. He told himself it wasn't important but he paused anyway, hooked the handle of the cane over his arm, and took out the flashlight. He switched it on and pinned the object in the beam.

A woman's shoe lay on its side.

He went a little closer and aimed the light at the water.

The body bobbed just under the surface.

Daisy Jennings.

A setup, just as he had feared from the start, but the victim was Jennings. Evidently she really had known something that could have hurt Tremayne.

He turned off the flashlight and dropped it into the pocket of his jacket. Cane in one hand, gun in the other, he made his way as swiftly as possible around the side of the warehouse.

The growl of heavy motorcycle engines approaching at speed on Miramar Road reverberated through the night.

There was no good reason for motorcycles to be prowling the empty stretch of road at that hour.

It looked like the cleanup crew was about to arrive.

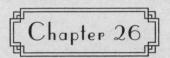

Chapter 26

Irene heard the thunder of motorcycle engines on Miramar Road and knew that Oliver had been right. It was a setup.

She did the first thing she could think of—she killed the headlights. She kept the Ford's engine running, ready for a fast getaway, and watched the shadows around the front of the warehouse, willing Oliver to appear.

He did. She could see him silhouetted against the lantern light. But he wasn't coming toward her. He was signaling her to get out of the vehicle.

Light sparked in her car mirrors. The motorcycles had reached the entrance of the dirt road that led down to the warehouse. She realized that her Ford was directly in their path.

She turned off the engine, grabbed her handbag,

jumped out of the front seat, and ran toward Oliver. She stumbled a little on the uneven road.

"Careful," he shouted.

By the time she reached him, he had the front door of the warehouse open. She rushed inside. Oliver followed.

"Turn down the lantern," he said.

She heard him slam the old, rusty bolt home, locking the door. Unfortunately, that left the two windows. Both had been shattered long ago, leaving only a few shards of glass in the frames.

She hurried to the lantern and put it out. At least they would no longer be silhouetted in its glare.

She whirled around to see what was happening. The headlights of two motorcycles were halfway down the warehouse road. They were forced to halt behind her Ford.

The engines roared, the riders enraged by the obstacle.

"Your car is blocking their path," Oliver said. He spoke from somewhere near one of the empty windows. "They'll have to get off their motorcycles if they want to come any closer. That will even the odds a little. Get down. Stay away from the windows."

She lowered herself to her hands and knees. In the glare of the motorcycle headlights shining through the windows, she saw the silhouette of Oliver's gun.

She fumbled with the catch of her handbag. Her fingers closed around the grip of the small pistol she kept inside.

"I've got one, too," she said.

"Of course you do," Oliver said. He sounded resigned. "Ever fired it?"

"No. How hard could it be?"

"You'd be surprised."

"There are bullets in it," she said, offended by his tone.

"That helps."

She ignored the sarcasm. "Do you really think they mean to kill us?"

"Damned if I know," he said. "But whatever they came here to do, they intend to do it to you. They don't know I'm here. Not yet, at any rate. That gives us an edge."

"Daisy Jennings?"

"She's dead in the water out back."

"Dear heaven. Another drowning. Just as you predicted."

There was some shouting from outside. Two men, Irene realized. One man yelled at the other.

"Do it. Hurry."

"One of them is off his motorcycle," Oliver reported. "He's coming toward the warehouse. He's got something in his hand."

"Gun?"

"Yes, in one hand," Oliver said. "That's not what's worrying me. It's what he's got in his other hand that could be a very big problem. I just saw a flash of light. The bastard lit a fuse. Stay down."

A rapid staccato of gunshots roared in the night. Irene heard some of them thud into the wall behind her.

"Cover fire," Oliver said. His tone was devoid of all emotion.

"Cover for what?" Irene asked.

A fiery object sailed through one of the empty windows and landed on the floor. It exploded on impact. Flames leaped.

"Cover for a firebomb," Oliver said.

His gun roared once, twice.

"*The bitch has a gun,*" one of the motorcyclists screamed. "No one said she was armed."

"*Oliver,*" Irene said.

He fired two more quick shots.

There was another scream from outside the warehouse, an unmistakable howl of agony.

One of the motorcycle engines roared furiously in the night.

"Dallas, I'm hit," a man yelled. "Wait for me."

The single motorcycle howled away on the dirt lane, the sound of the engine fading rapidly.

"One down," Oliver reported. "The other one is leaving. We have to get out of here. Rear door."

The hungry flames had begun to consume everything in their path. The heat was mounting but Irene knew that the real danger was the smoke.

She dropped her gun into her handbag, leaped to her feet, and ran for the wedge of moonlight that marked the freight door.

She heard the heart-stopping thud behind her and knew instantly what had happened. She stopped and whirled around.

In the blazing light she saw Oliver sprawled on the floor.

"Oliver."

"Go." The order was ice-cold and infused with savage determination. "Get the hell out of here."

"I'm not leaving without you."

She rushed back to him and grabbed his arm.

"Damn it, Irene—"

She crouched and got her shoulder under his arm. Calling on every ounce of strength she possessed, she straightened.

Somehow, between her desperation and the leverage he was able to apply with his undamaged leg, he was able to regain his feet. She grabbed his cane and handed it to him.

Together they made their way toward the freight door. Oliver's limp was worse than ever—he was staggering now, forced to lean on her to keep himself upright. She knew he must have been in agony but he did not say another word. Neither did she. There was no point. Either they both made it out of the inferno or they didn't.

They passed the crate where Jennings's handbag sat.

"Get it if you can," Oliver said, his voice harsh.

She snagged the strap of the handbag with the same hand she was using to grip her own bag.

Oliver regained some ability to keep his balance. He no longer needed so much support from her. They got through the loading dock doorway and kept going. Irene knew they had to get as far away as possible before the warehouse collapsed in flames.

They made their way around to the front of the burning building and into the clearing.

The fiery light revealed a man in a leather jacket

crumpled on the ground. At first Irene thought he was dead. But when they got closer, she heard him groan.

"Help me," he gasped. He levered himself into a sitting position and clutched his shoulder with one hand. "You can't leave me here."

"Sorry," Irene said. "You created the problem. You're stuck with it."

"Please," he gritted out. "Never meant to kill you, just scare you. Didn't know the place would go up like a torch. You gotta help me."

"Let's get him into the front seat of the car," Oliver said.

Irene stared at him, astonished. "Why? He just tried to murder both of us."

"No," the man yelped. "Didn't mean to kill anyone."

"We've got questions, and at the moment this bastard is the only one available with answers," Oliver said. "I'll keep an eye on him from the back seat."

"Bad idea," Irene said. "He has a gun."

"No gun," the man assured her. "Dropped it when you shot me. Name's Springer. I'll tell you anything you wanna know. Just get me to a hospital. Please."

"There's the gun," Oliver said. He steadied himself on his cane and pulled a handkerchief out of his pocket. "Use this to pick it up. The cops might be able to get some prints off of it."

Irene used the handkerchief to scoop up the gun. It was still warm. She wrapped it in the square of white linen.

"Got it," she said.

"Search him," Oliver said.

She found a knife strapped to Springer's leg.

"Forgot about the blade," Springer muttered.

"Sure you did," Irene said.

"I'll take that," Oliver said. He grasped the knife in his free hand and looked down at Springer. "Neither of us can get you on your feet. Can you make it to the car on your own?"

"I think so. Yeah."

Springer managed to haul himself upright. Irene opened the passenger side door. Hand clamped to his shoulder, Springer crawled into the seat. Irene closed the door.

Springer groaned and passed out.

Oliver opened the rear door and climbed into the back of the Ford. He leaned forward and clamped a hand around Springer's wound.

Irene got behind the wheel. She fired up the engine, put the car in gear, turned around in the clearing, and started up the dirt road. Rocks spit under the tires.

"What are we going to do with Springer?" she asked.

"We'll take him to the Burning Cove hospital. I'll call Detective Brandon and let him know what happened. If Springer makes it through the night, Brandon should be able to get some answers out of him."

"What about the fire?"

"We'll stop at the first place we see that might have a phone, and notify the fire department. With luck the clearing around the warehouse will keep the fire from jumping up the hillside. There's nothing but water at the back."

She reached the end of the lane and paused before turning onto Miramar Road. She glanced back at Oliver. He was pressing hard on Springer's wound. In the weak glow of the dashboard lights his face was set in hard, grim lines.

"Are you all right?" she asked.

"Never better. Drive."

She pulled out onto Miramar Road and floored the accelerator.

"You know," she said, "in the movies this sort of thing always looks a lot more thrilling."

"I've noticed that," Oliver said.

Chapter 27

"I thought you didn't like guns," Irene said.

"I don't," Oliver said. He drank some whiskey, lowered the glass, and rested his head against the back of the armchair. "But that doesn't mean they aren't occasionally useful."

Irene came to a halt in the middle of the living room and surveyed him with a critical eye. He knew the look all too well. He had been getting it every few minutes since they had walked through his front door a short time ago.

"Are you sure you're all right?" she asked. Again.

"I'm fine," he said, lying through his teeth.

He was heartily tired of the question but he told himself she meant well. He tried to sort through his mixed reactions to her concern. Sure, it was nice that she cared. But he hated knowing that she had seen him at his weakest that night.

He downed a healthy dose of whiskey to take his mind off the pain and his own miserable performance.

He was sitting in one of the big leather chairs in front of the fireplace, his damned leg propped on a hassock. Shortly after Irene had brought him home, he ordered a large quantity of ice from room service. He now had three ice bags draped over his bad leg.

Irene swallowed some of her own whiskey and resumed her pacing.

"Nick Tremayne used poor Daisy Jennings to lure us to that warehouse tonight and then he murdered her," she said.

"I agree that's how it looks," Oliver said. He drank some more whiskey. "But it will probably be impossible to prove unless Springer wakes up and starts talking."

Irene shook her head. "I never meant to drag you into this situation."

"We've already had that conversation. I'd just as soon not reopen it, if you don't mind."

She stopped pacing and met his eyes. Whatever she saw there must have convinced her he meant every word.

"All right," she said, uncharacteristically meek. She waved one hand in a vague gesture. "The problem now is, I don't know what to do next."

"Let's see what Detective Brandon does. The cops can't brush off Springer and his pal, not now that there's another dead woman."

"Another drowning victim who just happens to be one of Nick Tremayne's lovers," Irene said.

Oliver paused the whiskey glass halfway to his mouth and watched her very deliberately, willing her to understand the significance of what had happened.

"Daisy Jennings is dead, but she was not the only target tonight," he said.

"I realize that." Irene put her glass down. "You and I were also targets."

"Not me," he said. "You. No one knew I was along for the ride. Not until it was all over."

She watched him, stricken. "I'm so—"

He held up a hand. "Don't say it. What I'm getting at is that we now know for certain that someone is prepared to do whatever it takes to stop you. Springer said he and his pal were hired to scare you. That may be true. They may even believe it was the objective. But I think that whoever hired that pair to set fire to the warehouse would have been quite satisfied if you had died in the blaze."

Irene took a deep breath and went to stand at the window, looking out at the patio and the moonlit ocean.

"My death in that warehouse would have made things simpler for him," she said.

"Yes. In addition, it would have provided a neat explanation for Jennings's death."

"The cops would have assumed that I killed her and then died when I accidentally knocked over a lantern and set fire to the warehouse. But what's my motive? Why would I murder Daisy Jennings?"

"I agree that the story is weak when it comes to motive, but I doubt if anyone would worry about that too much. The police would be happy to have it all tied up in a neat package."

Irene turned around. "Tonight was different because Tremayne used fire against me. Daisy and Gloria Maitland and the others were all made to look like cases of accidental drowning."

"There could have been any number of reasons for the change in his pattern. Magicians rework the same illusions in a variety of ways to keep the act convincing. The killer probably decided that two drowning victims at the same scene tonight would have been a little hard for the cops to ignore. Besides, fire has a number of advantages."

"Advantages?"

"It's a classic and highly effective way of destroying evidence."

Irene pondered that. "I see what you mean."

"The real question is, where did the killer find Springer and Dallas?"

"Springer implied that he and his pal were hired muscle," Irene said.

"Tremayne is from out of town. He wouldn't know how to find local muscle."

"So he brought Springer and Dallas in from L.A."

"Maybe," Oliver said. "Or maybe the studio provided the pair to clean up the mess Tremayne made here in Burning Cove. There's no point speculating tonight. We need more information. We do know one thing, however."

Irene frowned. "What?"

"It's obvious now that you're a target. You should not be alone, not until we find out who tried to kill you tonight."

She gave him a sharp, unreadable look and then

turned her back to him. Her shoulders were very straight.

"I can't afford to hire a bodyguard, if that's what you're about to suggest," she said. "And I'm sure my editor won't pay for one—not for long, at least. How does one even go about hiring a bodyguard, anyway?"

"Forget the bodyguard. Finding one who knows his business and can be trusted isn't easy. You'll be better off staying here, with me, until this situation gets resolved."

She turned around. "Here? At the hotel, you mean?"

"Here, in my private quarters. In spite of what happened to Gloria Maitland, I can promise you that I really do have good security, certainly better than the security at the Cove Inn. You'll be reasonably safe if you stay on the grounds of the hotel."

She stared at him, floored. It took her a moment to recover.

"Thank you," she said. "That's a very generous offer but, really, it's not necessary."

"My bedroom is down the hall," he said. He spoke very deliberately. "On this floor. The guest suite is upstairs, if you will recall. You saw it the night you found Maitland's body in the spa."

He waited for his meaning to sink in.

She flushed. "I never meant to imply—"

"Trust me when I tell you that I avoid going up and down stairs whenever possible. You'll have plenty of privacy."

She turned red. "I don't doubt for a moment that you would be a perfect gentleman."

He wasn't sure that was a compliment but he let it go.

"Good," he said. "It's settled, then."

She got a stubborn look. "We both know I can't stay holed up here at the Burning Cove Hotel indefinitely; I've got a job that I can't afford to lose. I've also got an apartment in L.A. My editor told me that someone broke in while I've been out of town."

"What the hell? Your apartment was burglarized?"

"Evidently. I was planning to drive to the city today to get some fresh clothes and take a look around to see if the burglar stole anything. I'll have to go tomorrow, instead." She glanced at the clock. "Make that today."

"Has it occurred to you that the break-in might be connected to your Nick Tremayne story?"

"Of course. Probably a studio job."

"I can't help but notice that you don't seem overly concerned."

"Naturally I'm concerned. But it tells me I'm on the right track."

"You're going to keep working on the Tremayne story?" He grimaced. "Of course you are. What was I thinking?"

"If I give up now, Nick Tremayne will continue to murder his lovers and get away with it. Tonight was a turning point. I can feel it. He's starting to panic."

"We can't solve all of your problems tonight, but we can deal with one of them—your safety. Spend the night here. I'll send someone to the inn to pick up your things. We'll get more information from the cops in the morning. That should help us decide what to do next."

She blinked. "Us?"

He swallowed the last of the whiskey and lowered the glass.

"Us," he said.

She fell silent, as if she could not think of a response. He should probably take her lack of enthusiasm as a personal affront.

She started to resume her pacing but stopped midway across the room.

"Daisy's handbag," she said. "I forgot about it. I suppose we should give it to Detective Brandon."

They both looked at the green handbag sitting on the coffee table where Irene had dropped it earlier.

"Open it," Oliver said.

Irene went to the coffee table, picked up the bag, and opened it. She took out a lipstick, a compact, a hankie, a small coin purse, and a sheet of folded paper.

She unfolded the paper. "Looks like notes. Handwritten."

She read a few sentences out loud.

"Trust me, you'll want to hear what I've got to tell you. I know what really happened the night Gloria Maitland died.

"There's a phone booth on the corner of Olive and Palm streets. Be there at eleven thirty tonight. I'll call you and tell you where to meet me.

"There's an old abandoned warehouse at the end of Miramar Road . . . Remember, come alone. Deal's off if I see anyone else."

Irene stopped and looked up, shocked.

"It's a script," she said. "Someone gave Daisy Jennings a script to make sure she got all her lines right."

"Is that the end of the script?"

Irene looked down again. "No. There's another line. It's scribbled in on the side of the page. A last-minute addition, maybe. *Ask Tremayne about* Island Nights *and* Pirate's Captive."

"Those sound like film titles," Oliver said.

"But those aren't the two movies that Tremayne made in Hollywood."

"Tremayne wouldn't be the first fast-rising star to have a couple of pornographic movies in his past."

"That's the sort of problem that studios fix all the time," Irene said. "You don't kill someone because of a pornographic film." She hesitated. "Do you?"

"That probably depends on what's on the film."

"Are we going to give this script to Detective Brandon?" Irene asked.

"Not until we know for sure what's going on."

Chapter 28

*T*he assistant had given him the wrong key. It did not
fit the lock that secured the chains. He was trapped
in the steel cage.

That was all the warning he got.

*He wasted precious seconds extracting the backup key
from its hiding place and unlocking the chains that bound
him. He knew then that he had not been given the wrong
key by mistake. There were no mistakes in an Oliver Ward
illusion.*

He was going to die if he did not free himself.

*The first shot ripped into his thigh. Blood poured out in
a hot fountain. The second shot grazed the same leg.*

*The third shot missed, just barely. He heard the shriek of
metal as the bullet struck the chains.*

*He could hear the audience screaming now. The sound
seemed to come from another dimension. He could not see*

anything because of the black curtains draped around the Cage of Death.

The horrified shouts and screams got louder. He realized the blood was leaking out of the cage and falling onto the stage.

His leg burned with cold fire. So did the truth. What had happened was not an accident . . .

Oliver came awake in an icy sweat, the way he always did when the nightmare struck. He sat up slowly, wincing at the throbbing ache in his thigh. The combination of whiskey, aspirin, and ice had taken the edge off earlier, allowing him to fall into a restless sleep, but the effects had worn off.

He thought about the medication that his doctor had given him for the really bad nights and decided against it. He hated the stuff. It dulled his mind and his senses for hours and put him into a peculiar twilight state.

It was close to dawn. He had to be sharp in the morning. The killer was now targeting Irene. Plans had to be made. Action had to be taken.

Energized by that reality, he grabbed his cane and stood up. He shoved his feet into slippers, pulled on a bathrobe, and let himself out into the hall.

For a moment he stood in the shadows, listening intently. He was accustomed to solitude. At night Casa del Mar echoed with silence.

Tonight was different. All was quiet on the floor above, but he did not feel the deep sense of aloneness that he usually experienced in the hours between midnight and dawn. Irene was there.

He walked across the moon-streaked living room, opened the French doors, and went out onto the patio. He stopped at the edge of his private pool.

The atmosphere was infused with the first faint light of dawn. The scents of the garden and the sea mingled in an invigorating tonic.

Dawn was always the best antidote to the nightmare and the memories.

He lowered himself onto the cushion of one of the fan-back rattan chairs and absently rubbed his leg while he contemplated options.

He heard the soft sound of Irene's footsteps when she came down the stairs, walked through the living room, and emerged onto the patio. It occurred to him that he was not surprised that she had awakened. Her presence felt right. He could get used to this feeling of not being alone in Casa del Mar. *Just an illusion*, he thought.

"Couldn't sleep?" he asked.

"I got some rest," she said, "thanks to the whiskey."

"The universal if temporary cure. Doesn't last forever but while it does, it works fairly well."

"Yes."

She sat down in one of the other rattan chairs. In the early light he could see that she once again wore one of the hotel's thick white spa robes. Her hair looked as if she had raked it back behind her ears with her fingers. He could sense the anxiety that was riding her but he could also feel the gritty determination that was so much a part of her being. *What secrets are you keeping, mystery woman?*

"I'll drive to L.A. with you today to pick up your things and check out the situation at your apartment," he said.

She gave him a quick, skittering, sidelong glance. He knew he had touched on the mystery beneath the surface.

"There's no need for you to make that long drive," she said. "I'm sure it would be uncomfortable for you, given your poor leg."

Irritation sparked through him. "It's my leg. Let me worry about it."

"If you're so convinced that I need a bodyguard, perhaps one of the people on your hotel security staff could go with me."

She wasn't objecting to the idea of having someone accompany her, but she was definitely uneasy with the prospect of having him as her companion. He realized that she didn't want him with her when she examined her apartment to see if anything had been stolen. She was afraid of what he might observe.

"I'll stay out of your way," he said.

She stiffened. "I didn't mean that I didn't want you along."

He smiled. "Sure you did."

"Look, you're welcome to drive to L.A. with me," she said. Her voice sharpened. "I was just concerned about your leg, that's all."

"I told you, I'll take care of it."

"Fine. It's your leg."

"Yes, it is my leg."

She gave him a frosty look. "You're annoyed."

"Possibly."

"Are you always this irritable?"

"I don't know. You'll have to ask my staff."

She startled him with a steely smile. "No need to do that. I'm quite capable of forming my own opinion."

He watched her warily. "And just what is your opinion?"

"I think certain subjects, such as a mention of your leg, annoy you."

"It's a mention of my *poor* leg that annoys me."

"I'll try to remember that." She glanced around the patio as if searching for another topic of conversation. "I see you have your own pool."

"I use it for exercising my poor leg."

"Right." She rose, clamping the lapels of the robe with one hand. "I think I've irritated you enough for one day and the sun isn't even up yet. I had better go upstairs and see about getting dressed. We've got a long trip ahead of us."

She turned and took two steps back toward the shadowed interior of the villa.

"Irene?"

She paused and looked at him over her shoulder. "Yes?"

"It's going to be all right. We'll figure this out together. Partners, remember?"

She walked back and came to a halt in front of him.

"Not just partners," she said. "Not after last night."

"What, then?"

"I don't know," she admitted. "I told you I knew that your friend Luther Pell trusted you. I found that . . .

reassuring. But after what happened last night, I know I can trust you. That means a lot, believe me."

"You know hardly anything about me."

"Everyone has secrets," she said. "It doesn't mean I can't trust you."

"That's good to know," he said. "Because I trust you, too."

"Why?"

"Hell, I don't know. Maybe because you refused to leave me alone in a burning building?"

"You wouldn't have left me there, either."

"So we know that much about each other. Is that enough?"

"It is for me. For now."

Then, before he realized what she intended, she bent down and brushed her lips lightly across his cheek.

The heat of her body whispered to his senses. An unfamiliar certainty flashed through him. He started to reach for her but she was already stepping back.

He watched her disappear into the shadows of the living room.

It was only after she was gone that he realized that for the past few minutes he had been entirely unaware of the pain in his leg.

He smiled, bemused by his own reaction to the woman and the dawn of the new day.

Magic.

Chapter 29

They were finishing a breakfast of fresh melon, creamy scrambled eggs, and toast on the patio when the phone rang. Oliver grabbed his cane and got to his feet.

"With luck that will be Brandon with an update," he said.

He disappeared into the living room to take the call. Irene slathered butter on a slice of toast and watched the sun dance on Oliver's private pool.

She tried to ignore the nervy sensation that abruptly knotted her stomach. She reminded herself that she and Oliver had been expecting the call. The problem was that she had been savoring the intimacy of the moment—a perfect breakfast on the patio at the start of another perfect California morning.

It was all a little too perfect. Reality had been bound to intrude.

Oliver reappeared a few minutes later. His expression was severe but she could sense the energy in the atmosphere around him.

"Well?" she said.

He lowered himself into the chair across from her. He seemed to be moving more easily this morning, she thought. She took that as a sign that he had not inflicted too much damage on his poor leg during the night. Scratch the *poor*, she thought. The man had his pride. She respected that.

"Brandon says Springer and his pal—a guy who goes by the name of Dallas—are both hired muscle," Oliver said.

"We guessed that much. The question is, who hired them?"

"According to Springer, he and Dallas are both professional stuntmen. Seems work at the studios has been a little slow lately, so they've been picking up some extra cash by doing odd jobs for a shady character named McAllister, otherwise known as Hollywood Mack. Springer claims that he and his pal don't know who commissioned the arson last night. He says Hollywood Mack never tells them the name of the so-called client, but Brandon made some telephone calls to a pal in the L.A. police department. Evidently Hollywood Mack is reputed to perform certain services for some of the studios—including the one that has Tremayne under contract."

"In other words, Hollywood Mack rents out his tough guys to the fixers who are in charge of cleaning up the messes created by the studios' stars."

"Cleaners, fixers, studio execs, whatever you call

them, it's their job to make scandals disappear," Oliver said.

"So, someone at Tremayne's studio hired those two stuntmen to get rid of me?"

"Brandon says Springer is sticking to his story. He was hired to torch the warehouse. He and his pal knew you would be there. But the idea was to scare you, not kill you."

"But what about Daisy Jennings? How did Springer explain her body?"

"That's the really interesting part," Oliver said. "Springer swears up and down that he didn't know there was a dead woman at the scene. Says all he and his pal were told was that a woman would be there and that they were to scare the hell out of her by setting fire to the place. You weren't supposed to die, Springer says. He insists they didn't know that old warehouse would go up like a torch. He expected you to come running out."

"No. I'm sure that I was supposed to be dead or unconscious in that warehouse before Springer and Dallas arrived. The fire would have destroyed all the evidence at the scene. You were right. It would have looked like I accidentally died in a blaze that I started to cover up the murder of Daisy Jennings."

"Yes," Oliver said evenly. "I think that was the killer's plan."

"But everything went wrong because you accompanied me to the warehouse."

"Finish your coffee. My car should be ready by now. Chester checked it over this morning and topped off the gas tank."

A little thrill of excitement pulsed through her.

"We're taking your car?" she asked, trying to make it sound casual.

"Yeah. I don't trust that old sedan of yours. It's a long drive to L.A. and back, and most of it is open, empty country. Not a lot of gas stations on the way. We don't want to get stranded."

"Right. A long trip. No need for you to do all the driving. I'll be happy to give you a break."

"No."

"Several hours of driving will be hard on your leg."

"No."

"It's a lovely day. We can put the top down."

"Yes."

"Do you ever let *anyone* drive your car?"

"No."

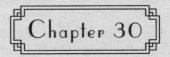

Chapter 30

The offices of *Hollywood Whispers* were on the second floor of a small nondescript building. Oliver looked around the grimy lobby, hoping to spot an elevator. There wasn't one.

Irene paused at the foot of the stairs. "Why don't you wait here? I won't be long."

He managed to squelch the flare of temper but it wasn't easy. She was just being thoughtful, he told himself. But, damn it to hell, he was really tired of having his infirmity pointed out. The last thing he wanted from Irene was sympathy.

"I'll come with you," he said.

He was careful to keep his tone neutral but she blinked and looked a little taken aback. He realized she must have seen something in his eyes warning her that she was getting too close to the invisible line he had drawn.

"Suit yourself," she said.

She took the stairs like a gazelle.

He watched her curvy rear disappear down a hallway. While the view was gratifying, he knew he probably deserved to get left behind in her dust. He was too touchy about the damned leg. He tightened his grip on his cane, grasped the handrail, and started up the stairs.

At the top, the relentless clacking of typewriter keys emanated from a large room crowded with desks and reporters. Several office doors stood open but the one labeled *Editor* was closed.

He raised his hand to knock but the door was yanked open before he could do so. Irene glared at him. Her cheeks were flushed and her eyes were hot with temper.

"We're leaving," she announced. "I've been fired."

Behind her, a large, middle-aged woman with improbably red hair sat behind a battered desk. Velma Lancaster, he decided. Although she was sitting very still, she seemed to vibrate with nervy energy.

She studied Oliver through a pair of spectacles perched on her sharp nose.

"So you're the Amazing Oliver Ward," she said.

"And you're Irene's ex-boss."

"It's a little more complicated than that," Velma said. "Why don't you both sit down and we'll discuss this like civilized people?"

She had a voice that would have projected quite well from a stage.

Irene rounded on her. "I'm not feeling very civilized today. Last night I almost got burned alive and now you tell me I'm out of a job."

Velma waved that off with an impatient gesture.

"Sit down," she snapped.

To Oliver's surprise, Irene sank reluctantly into a wooden chair. She clutched her precious handbag on her lap and fixed Velma with a wary, narrow-eyed gaze.

Velma turned her attention back to Oliver.

"What's your relationship to Irene, Mr. Ward?"

"We're partners," Irene said. "He was with me last night when we found another body and two goons tried to torch a warehouse with us inside."

Velma did not take her eyes off Oliver. "Well, Ward? What do you have to say for yourself?"

"You heard her," Oliver said. "We're partners." He walked into the room, closed the door, and sat down. "Are you going to explain why the situation here is more complicated than it appears?"

"Yep, that's exactly what I'm going to do." Velma leaned back. Her chair squeaked in protest. "Can you protect Irene?"

"My security people are good," he said. "And Luther Pell is a friend of mine. He has offered his assistance if needed."

Irene's head snapped around. Her eyes widened.

"You didn't tell me that," she said.

He waved that off. "There wasn't any reason to until now. I thought it might make you uneasy."

Velma got a knowing look. "That would be the same Luther Pell who owns the Paradise Club and some casinos?"

"Yes," Oliver said. "That Luther Pell."

"In other words, you've got access to some serious muscle."

"Yes," Oliver said again.

Irene looked at Velma and then at Oliver and back again. "Where are you going with this conversation, Velma?"

"Here's the deal," Velma said. She sat forward and lowered her voice. "This morning I got another call from Ernie Ogden at Tremayne's studio. I was given a second warning. This time things got a lot more serious. It was strongly implied that *Whispers* would be out of business within a week if I didn't get rid of the reporter who was causing trouble for Tremayne. So, naturally, I assured Mr. Ogden that I would fire Irene Glasson. And that's what I've done. I even instructed Alice in bookkeeping to cut one last check with a week's extra pay. It's waiting for you at the reception desk."

Irene groaned. "I'm sorry, Velma. I didn't mean to put *Whispers* at risk. I thought I could prove Tremayne murdered Peggy and it would be a huge scoop for the paper."

"I agreed to let you run with the story because of Peggy. I do not take kindly to having my employees murdered. But I am now in the position of having to protect the rest of the staff and this business."

"I understand," Irene said. She got to her feet. "Let's go, Oliver."

"Hang on for one damn minute," Velma said.

"Why?" Irene asked.

"This doesn't have to be the end of the line. You can work freelance. If you do get proof that Tremayne murdered Peggy or anyone else and if Tremayne is arrested, I'll buy the story from you."

"I'll think about it," Irene said. "But keep in mind that I might get a better offer from some other paper."

She headed for the door. Oliver followed her out into the hall.

"What are you going to do?" he asked.

"Get the story."

He nodded, satisfied. "I had a feeling you were going to say that."

The receptionist looked up as they approached her desk. She gave Irene a sympathetic smile and handed her an envelope.

"Sorry about what just happened," she said softly.

"Thanks," Irene said.

"Did your cousin get ahold of you?"

Irene stopped, turning sharply. "What cousin?"

"A man telephoned for you yesterday. Sounded like he was from back east. Real classy accent. Said he was your cousin or something and that he was in town on business for a few days. He wanted to see about getting together with you. I gave him your address and phone number. Warned him that you were out of town, though."

"Thanks," Irene said. She looked at Oliver. There was shock and confusion in her eyes. "The studio? Trying to find out where I live?"

"Probably," he said. "Let's go."

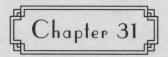

Chapter 31

The first clue that she had other problems in addition to getting fired came when she inserted her key into the lock on her apartment door.

Nothing happened.

"Wrong key?" Oliver suggested.

Irene looked at the key she was holding. "No, this is the right one."

They were standing in the hall outside her apartment. She was very conscious of the general gloom that seemed to infuse the slightly shabby, two-story building. The contrast between it and the warm, gracious architecture of the Burning Cove Hotel was impossible to ignore.

Oliver studied the lock. "Looks new."

"Of course, that explains it," Irene said. Relief flashed

through her. "The burglar must have broken the lock when he forced his way into my apartment. Mrs. Drysdale, my landlady, replaced it. I'll go downstairs and let her know I'm back and that I need the new key."

"I'll come with you," Oliver said.

She had started down the hall, but at that she stopped and turned around. "No need for you to go down those stairs twice."

"I'll come with you," he said again. "Just in case."

"In case of what?"

"We're wasting time, Irene."

"Right."

She was very conscious of Oliver making his way down the stairs behind her. His cane thudded on each step. She heard the hitch in his stride. He never said a word, but she knew that the descent must have been painful for him, considering what he had gone through in recent days.

When she reached the first floor, she went along another dingy hallway and knocked on Norma Drysdale's door.

"Hold your horses," Norma yelled in the harsh, hoarse voice of a lifelong smoker. "I'm coming."

The door swung open. Norma appeared, wearing a faded housedress and an invisible cloak of stale smoke. Her bleached hair was set in tight marcel waves, a style that had been the height of fashion until recently but that now, thanks to stars like Ginger Rogers and Katharine Hepburn, had a decidedly dated look.

Norma peered at Irene as though trying to recall her name.

"Oh, it's you," she rasped. "Wondered when you'd show up. I was getting ready to sell your things. Figured I'd give you a week to collect 'em."

"What?" It took Irene a couple of seconds to gather her wits. "But I'm current on my rent."

Norma's expression softened fractionally. "Sorry, but you're trouble, honey, and I don't need any more of that particular commodity. Got plenty as it is."

Norma paused to indulge a coughing fit.

"What are you talking about?" Irene asked. "I've been a model tenant. I pay my rent on time. I don't bring men back to my apartment. I don't make a lot of noise."

Norma got a sorrowful expression. "Things change, honey. Like I said, sorry, but that's how it is."

Oliver studied Norma. "I assume you've had a visit or a phone call from someone who advised you that it was in your best interests to evict Miss Glasson."

"Yeah, the studio sent a goon around." Norma squinted at him. "Probably the same one that broke into 2B a couple of times."

"He broke in twice?" Oliver said.

"Yeah."

"Why would he do that?" Irene asked.

"How should I know?" Norma shrugged. "First time he made a mess. It looked like the real deal—a straight-up burglary—so I called the cops and then I called you to let you know what had happened. But after the second break-in last night, I figured the bastards were trying to send a message."

"What message?" Oliver asked.

"Just trying to scare Irene, I guess. Let her know she wasn't safe anywhere—that they could get to her."

Norma broke off to cough a few more times. When she had composed herself, she eyed him more closely. "You're the Amazing Oliver Ward, aren't you? The magician who bungled his last act and nearly got himself killed? There was a picture of you and Irene in *Silver Screen Secrets* yesterday morning."

He ignored that. "What was the threat that convinced you to toss Miss Glasson out into the street?"

Norma shrugged. "I was told that if I didn't get rid of a certain troublesome tenant, there would be an accidental fire. Might lose the whole apartment house. This building is my retirement. Can't afford to risk it."

Irene pulled herself together and took a step back. "I'm sorry I got you involved, Mrs. Drysdale. Where are my things? I'll get them and leave you in peace."

"I put your stuff in some boxes," Norma mumbled. She did not make eye contact. "Broom closet at the end of the hall."

"I'll get them," Irene said.

She started to turn away.

Norma grunted. "Here's a tip, honey. The studios own this town. You don't cross 'em, not if you want to make a living. The sooner you figure that out, the better off you'll be."

Irene paused. "I'm getting the message."

Norma switched her attention back to Oliver. "Saw your act once. You were darn good, at least back before you messed up. I liked the way you made that pretty woman in the skimpy dress walk straight into the mirror and disappear. What went wrong that day you were almost killed?"

"I can't tell you," Oliver said. "Magicians' Code."

"Huh?"

Oliver looked at Irene. "Let's get your things."

Irene turned on her heel and started down the hall. She heard the door slam shut behind her. There was a very final-sounding snick as the bolt slid home.

An odd sensation ghosted through her, a mix of wistfulness and resignation. The Ocean View Apartments—for rent by week or month—didn't have an actual view of the ocean. It didn't offer much in the way of amenities. But it had been her home since she had arrived in Los Angeles.

It wasn't the first time she had lost a roof over her head, she reminded herself. Maybe permanent homes were for other people.

She glanced back at Oliver, who was following her down the hall.

"You knew what had happened when my key didn't work," she said. "You realized my landlady had locked me out of my apartment. That's why you insisted on coming back downstairs with me to see about getting a key."

"Someone once gave me the wrong key."

"I see."

"Had a feeling that whoever is trying to make you back off the story might have decided to put the squeeze on you in every way possible."

She stopped in front of the broom closet and opened the door. Three boxes tied up with string sat on the floor next to a bucket, mop, and broom. The name *Glasson* was scrawled on each box. She reached down to hoist one.

"Aren't you going to open them to make sure all

your things are inside?" Oliver said. "Norma Drysdale may have helped herself to a few items."

"It doesn't matter." Irene started back down the hall with the first box. "There was nothing valuable in my apartment. It was just a place to sleep."

Chapter 32

The Ocean View Apartments had been more than just a place to sleep, Oliver thought. It had been Irene's home or, at least, her refuge from the world. And now it was gone, stolen by a studio fixer who made a nice living paying off corrupt cops and judges and threatening the Norma Drysdales of the world.

He arranged the last of the three pitifully small boxes in the back of the car and got behind the wheel. For a moment he sat quietly, watching Irene. She was gazing straight ahead at the front door of the apartment house. Her coolly composed expression gave nothing away, but he could feel the storm brewing just under the surface.

It was the second break-in that had unnerved her the most, he realized. She'd had herself under control until Norma Drysdale told her that 2B had been broken into twice. Now Irene looked like she was in a trance.

"It's all right," he said. "You're staying with me until we figure out what is going on, remember?"

At that, she finally looked at him.

"Thank you," she said very politely. "But we both know that won't work indefinitely. I need to make some progress in my investigation before anyone else gets killed."

"I agree." He turned the key in the ignition. "But I think we'll have more luck back in Burning Cove than we will here in L.A."

"Because of the power of Tremayne's studio here in the city?"

He put the car in gear and drove away from the curb. "The studios may control Hollywood and, by extension, L.A., but their reach does have limitations. They're not the only game in town in Burning Cove. Neither Luther Pell nor I take orders from the studios."

"Still, the studios have a lot of influence. If they were to forbid their stars from patronizing your hotel or the Paradise Club—"

"You need to keep some perspective, Irene. First of all, we're only dealing with one studio—Tremayne's— and it's not even the biggest or most powerful one in Hollywood. Second, as far as the studio is concerned, this is all about business. Yes, Tremayne is a valuable property, at least for now. They're trying to protect their investment. But if the executives at the top conclude that he's more trouble than he's worth, they'll drop him without a second's hesitation."

"Just business."

"Exactly."

"So I have to find some evidence that will convince the studio that Tremayne isn't worth protecting."

"That's our goal. Ready to go home?"

She shook her head and turned back to contemplate the front door of the Ocean View Apartments.

"I can't go home," she said. "I just got kicked out of my apartment."

"Slip of the tongue. I mean, are you ready to go back to Burning Cove?"

"I guess so. It's not like I've got anywhere else to go."

"Your enthusiasm is a little underwhelming."

She took a deep, steadying breath and tightened her grip on her handbag. "I'm still feeling . . . disoriented. I can't believe that the studio sent someone to break into my place *twice*."

"Neither can I."

She cast him a quick, pleading look. "You're supposed to reassure me. Tell me the studio is just trying to frighten me."

"I could use some reassurance, too. Correct me if I'm wrong, but I have the distinct impression that you consider the studio threats to be preferable to something else that might be even worse."

She sat very still. He knew she was trying to decide whether or not to confide in him.

"You've got a right to your secrets, Irene," he said. "But we're dealing with murder. If there's something else going on, I need to know about it."

She said nothing for a moment, and then she evidently came to a decision.

"It's a nightmare," she said quietly. "I don't even know where to start."

"How about starting with whatever you're carrying around in your handbag."

She looked at him, speechless and maybe even appalled. "How did you know?"

"Maybe because you've always got a death grip on it?"

She groaned. "Is it that obvious?"

"Probably not to most people."

She gave him a wary look. "But you notice details."

"Call it a personality quirk. I know you keep your reporter's notebook and that little gun you pulled out last night in your handbag. But there's something else inside, isn't there?"

"Yes."

"Tell me about the nightmare."

Chapter 33

S he told him everything.

Once she got started she could not stop. The relief of confiding the terrible secret that she had been keeping for four months was so overwhelming that she started to cry. She had not cried in so long she was surprised to discover that she remembered how.

L.A. was a few miles behind them by the time she finished. Oliver pulled off on a scenic turnout overlooking the ocean, and shut down the powerful engine.

She opened her handbag, took out a hankie, and dabbed at her eyes.

"Sorry," she mumbled. "I've been a little tense lately."

"No surprise, given what you've just told me."

She pulled herself together and dropped the damp hankie into the handbag. "That's it, the whole story. My previous employer was murdered. She left a message in her own blood telling me to run. She wrote a letter letting me know that the notebook was dangerous, that I must not trust anyone, not even the FBI. She said that if the worst happened, I might be able to use it as a bargaining chip. I've been looking over my shoulder ever since that horrible night."

Oliver turned in the seat and rested his left arm on the steering wheel. The tinted lenses of his round sunglasses made it impossible to read his eyes. Not that you could read them anyway, she thought, not if he didn't want you to read them.

"You came to California because you're running from a killer," he said. "But you have no idea who is after you."

"No," she said. "None. I've been afraid to trust anyone."

"Which brings us back to the problem of the second break-in at your apartment."

"It must be a coincidence. What are the odds that whoever is after Atherton's notebook would show up after four months and break into my place within twenty-four hours of when the studio goon broke in?"

"The odds might be very good if Spencer's killer managed to track you as far as Los Angeles."

"But the timing—" She broke off, shattered. "Damn. The photo of you and me outside the Cove Inn."

"Yesterday morning your picture was on the front page of one of the biggest gossip rags in L.A."

"But I changed my name, my job." She stopped because it sounded weak even to her own ears. "How would he know what I looked like?"

"All he needed was a reasonably current photograph of you and a good eye for detail."

"Miss Spencer loved photography. It was her hobby. She took some pictures of me while I lived with her, including one that showed me standing next to the beautiful car she gave me. I kept it on the dresser in my bedroom. If someone found it, he would not only know what I looked like but he'd have a description of the Packard."

"What happened to the car?"

"I decided it was too memorable. I abandoned it on the side of a farm road and hitchhiked for a day. Then I used some of the money that Helen Spencer left in the shoebox to buy an inexpensive used car. When I got to L.A., I sold that one and bought the Ford I'm driving now."

"Smart," Oliver said. "Switching cars and hitchhiking for a time may have been what saved your life. Tell me more about this notebook that's supposed to be so dangerous."

"Evidently it belonged to someone named Dr. Thomas Atherton, who worked at that laboratory I told you about."

"Saltwood. You said someone there told you that Atherton is dead?"

"Yes."

"Mind if I take a look at the notebook?"

She hesitated. *Force of habit,* she thought. For four long months she had been obsessed with concealing the notebook. It felt strange to bring it out into the light of day and show it to someone else.

Oliver waited, not rushing her.

She took the stenography notebook out of her bag and flipped it open to reveal the hidden compartment she had created beneath the pad of paper.

"Very clever," Oliver said.

She pried Atherton's notebook out of the small compartment and handed it to him. He took off his sunglasses and opened the leather cover. She watched him slowly turn the pages.

"It's filled with numbers and charts and calculations, but they mean nothing to me," she said. "There weren't a lot of science or math classes at the Gilbert School for Secretaries."

Oliver turned a few more pages. "They didn't spend much time on either of those subjects at the magicians school, either."

"There's a school for magicians?"

"Sorry. Poor joke." He closed the notebook and handed it back to her. "I have no idea what any of those calculations mean, but I know someone who might be able to help us."

"We must not show it to anyone else. I told you, I have no idea who can be trusted."

"Relax, we can trust Uncle Chester."

Chapter 34

No doubt about it, Julian Enright thought, he had fallen in love with California, and the Burning Cove Hotel was the very essence of everything he adored about the state. From the palm trees that lined the long, elegant drive to the gracious Spanish colonial walkways and sparkling fountains, the place was a real-life version of a movie set.

His kind of hotel.

He chose a seat at the long, polished bar. The French doors on one side of the lounge stood wide, providing an unobstructed view of the sparkling pool and the swimsuit-clad bodies lounging around it.

The bartender was remarkably good-looking. His coppery brown hair was slicked straight back off his high forehead. He had a slender, graceful build and big blue eyes framed with long lashes.

"What can I get you, sir?" he asked.

The voice went with the rest—low and smooth with just the right touch of smoky sensuality.

"What do you recommend?" Julian asked, mostly because he wanted to hear more of the lush voice.

"House special is the sunrise. Rum and pineapple juice."

"Sounds a little too sweet for me. I'll have a scotch and soda."

"Coming right up."

Julian smiled. "You know, you ought to be in pictures."

"I've heard that."

"Mind if I ask your name?"

"Willie."

"Got a last name?"

"Yes, sir, I do have one of those."

Willie smiled faintly and glided off to prepare the drink. Julian watched him for a moment, trying to figure out just what it was about the bartender that made him so interesting. Generally speaking, he was not attracted to men. But beauty, regardless of gender, always drew his eye.

He waited until Willie put the drink on the bar in front of him and moved off to attend to another customer. Then he smiled at the morose-looking man sitting next to him. Another very handsome specimen, Julian thought, but in a more conventional way.

"You're Nick Tremayne, aren't you?" he said.

Nick swallowed some of his gin and tonic and set the glass down hard.

"So they tell me," he said.

"According to the papers, you've got a problem."

Nick shot him a wary look. "Who the hell are you?"

"Relax. I'm here to help."

"Did Ogden send you?"

Julian looked around, making it appear that he was deeply concerned about the possibility of being overheard. Then he lowered his voice.

"No names," he said. "If the press gets wind of my purpose for being in Burning Cove, the studio will deny all knowledge of me. Is that clear?"

"Yeah, sure." Nick lowered his own voice but there was a note of hope in his words. "They sent you to clean up the mess?"

"Someone has to do it. It isn't just your future that is at stake here. The studio has made a considerable investment in you."

"Don't you think I know that?"

"Let's go someplace where we can talk in private."

"My private villa," Nick said. "Casa de Oro."

"Sounds good. But finish your drink first. Make it look casual. You're not in a hurry. You're not worried. You're enjoying your vacation in Burning Cove."

"What did you say your name was?"

"I didn't. It's Julian. Julian Enright."

He didn't hesitate to use his real name. No one here on the West Coast knew him or his family, but even if someone did think to make inquiries, the cover would hold up. It always held up. The Enright name and the long history of the family law firm made an ideal cover. No one ever suspected that Enright & Enright engaged in anything except the most reputable business practices.

"Nice to meet you, Julian. You don't sound like you're from this side of the country."

"Back east," Julian said.

"How long have you been out here?"

Julian smiled. "Not long enough."

He made casual conversation with Tremayne while they finished their drinks. From time to time he studied Willie the bartender.

It took him a while to figure it out, but he was good with details. By the time his glass was empty, he was almost certain he knew what it was about Willie that had aroused his interest. Willie was a woman passing as a very attractive man.

Pleased with his deduction, he smiled at her.

Willie pretended not to notice.

Got you, babe, he thought.

Having solved the puzzle, Julian lost interest. He had not come to Burning Cove to seduce anyone, male or female. He had a job to do and he had already wasted enough time. His father had telephoned again that morning, demanding an update and urging immediate action. Evidently the competition for the auction of Atherton's notebook was heating up.

Nick put his glass down. "Let's get moving."

"Take it easy," Julian said. "Everything is going to be just fine."

"It's not your career on the line."

That was true, Julian thought. If he failed to secure the notebook, his father would be annoyed but there would be other commissions. After all, there was no shortage of people seeking the firm's unique services.

But he prided himself on his perfect record. He always got the job done and he never left loose ends.

He and Tremayne ambled through the lobby, making a point of discussing the possibility of a game of golf the next morning.

They were strolling along the covered walkway that led to Tremayne's villa when a beautiful car cruised into the long driveway. There was a man at the wheel. He wore sunglasses and an open-collared shirt. A woman, her hair partially covered by a scarf knotted under her chin, sat in the passenger seat. She, too, wore sunglasses, an oversized pair that concealed much of her face. But something about the line of her jaw snagged Julian's attention.

"Nice car," he said. "Looks custom."

Nick turned his head to look. He grimaced. "They say it's the fastest car in California."

"Belong to anyone you know?"

"That's Oliver Ward's car. Damn. I'd heard the bitch was sleeping with him. What the hell is she up to?"

"The bitch?"

"That's her, the reporter who's trying to destroy me. The one Ogden sent you to take care of."

"Irene Glasson?"

"Yeah."

Well, well, well. Hello, Anna Harris. We meet at last.

"She's sleeping with Ward?" Julian asked.

"He's a cripple. Bungled his last act. Plenty of good-looking women around the pool but a guy in his condition probably can't get any of them to fuck him. So he ends up with the bitch."

Chapter 35

"**I**t feels like she's stalking me," Nick said.

He led the way through the living room of the villa and out onto the shaded patio. They sat down on the big rattan chairs.

Julian Enright didn't look anything like Ogden's usual tough guys, he thought. Enright wasn't some beat-up ex-stuntman, and he didn't have the brutish edge of a mob guy. Hell, Enright could have been in pictures, himself. He was handsome in a classy, well-bred way—a blond Cary Grant, maybe. He moved like Grant, too, with a casual elegance that announced to the world that it could wait on him. What's more, the hair looked real, not bleached. His clothes were obviously hand-tailored, and with his tall, lean, athletic build, he looked very good in them.

Luckily Enright wasn't an aspiring actor, Nick

thought. He would have been serious competition in the leading man category.

"Tell me everything from start to finish," Julian Enright said. "Don't leave out any details. I need to know exactly what I'm dealing with."

"Didn't Ogden fill you in?"

"I prefer to do my own background research."

"Research?"

"Fact gathering. Call it whatever you want. Talk to me, Tremayne."

"I told you, it's like she's gunning for me."

"You're sure that you and Miss Glasson have never crossed paths? No one-night stands? A brief affair?"

"I'm positive. She's not my type." Too restless to sit still, Nick got to his feet, clawed his fingers through his hair, and began to pace the patio. "She's got it in for me, I tell you."

"Any idea why she might harbor a grudge against you?" Julian asked in mild tones.

"Maybe." Nick paused and then shrugged. "Something happened to one of the other reporters at that gossip rag she works for."

"What, exactly, happened to the other reporter?"

"Slipped in the bathtub. Hit her head and drowned. It was an accident. The authorities said so."

"But Miss Glasson believes otherwise?"

"I guess so," Nick muttered. "Then there was another drowning."

"I assume you mean the one that occurred here at the hotel."

"Apparently Maitland planned to meet Glasson in the spa that night. Pretty sure she was going to feed

Glasson some gossip about me. But Glasson told the cops that she found Maitland dead in the pool. Next thing I know there's a hit piece on the front page of *Whispers* linking my name with Maitland's. Reporters from papers clear across the country started calling the studio asking for interviews with me."

"Under other circumstances that would be a good thing."

Cold fingers touched the back of Nick's neck. Enright sounded as if he didn't understand the implications.

"This isn't a joking matter, Enright. Glasson is trying to tie me to the accidental deaths of two women. If this story gets out of control, my career will be ruined."

"Anything else I should know?" Julian asked.

He sounded almost bored now. Nick fought back the red tide of anger. He could not afford to lose his temper. He needed Julian Enright.

"There was another drowning last night," he said. "A local gold digger named Daisy Jennings."

"Did you know Jennings?"

"I fucked her once in the garden of the Paradise Club. That was the same night that Gloria Maitland drowned. Jennings was my alibi."

"And now she's dead?"

Nick hesitated. "It gets worse. Glasson and the magician found the body. Looks like Jennings intended to meet with that damned reporter."

"Did Jennings have something on you?"

"*No.*" Nick struggled to contain his rage. "Look, your job is to keep Glasson from making more trouble, not dig into my sex life. Why don't you go to work?"

"Thorough research is the key to success in my profession."

"Yeah? What, exactly, is your profession?"

Julian smiled. "I'm the person people like Ogden call in when they discover that they can't deal with a problem themselves. Now, then, are you sure you don't have any idea what made Irene Glasson conclude that you were the cause of her colleague's drowning accident?"

"I'm sure."

There was no way that Irene Glasson could know about Betty Scott, Nick thought. It was impossible. Betty Scott was his past—his *buried* past.

"There must have been some reason why she thinks you were responsible," Julian continued in that same languid tone.

"All I can tell you is that the other reporter—the one who died—was asking around about me. Looking for anything she could find."

"But you have no idea what she might have been searching for?"

Nick grunted. "No. None."

He needed Enright but damned if he was going to spill his secrets to him.

"Interesting," Julian mused.

"What's that supposed to mean?"

"Irene Glasson seems to have come across a lot of bodies," Julian said.

Nick stared at him. "What are you thinking?"

"You may be right. Glasson may be setting you up."

"You think she killed Gloria and the others?"

"I have no idea, but it occurs to me that she may be trying to manufacture a story that would make her career. If she can pin a murder rap on you, she would become the top Hollywood gossip columnist in the country, at least for a while."

"Yes, that's it," Nick said. Excitement snapped through him. "That's it exactly. She's out to destroy me so that she can grab a headline or two."

"Don't worry about it." Julian got to his feet. "I'm here to make your problem disappear, remember?"

"Yeah," Nick said. "I remember."

"I'll let myself out," Julian said. He paused briefly. "One more thing. Absolutely no one is to know my real reason for being here. Understand?"

"What about my personal assistant?"

Julian shook his head. "No one. As far as everyone around you knows, you and I are just a couple of guys on vacation who struck up a friendship. Got it?"

"Got it."

Julian disappeared into the shadows of the living room. Nick watched, more than a little awed. The man moved as silently as a snake.

I'm here to make your problem disappear.

A moment later the front door of the villa opened and then closed very quietly.

For the first time since the nightmare began, Nick allowed himself a measure of optimism. Maybe, just maybe, he would survive the rolling disaster that had overtaken him.

The doorbell chimed. He pulled himself out of his trance.

"Come in," he called.

The door opened. Tentative footsteps echoed on the tiles.

He stifled a sigh. "I'm out here on the patio."

Claudia appeared in the doorway, clutching her notebook.

"Who was that man I saw leaving here?" she asked.

"Just someone I met in the bar. We're going to play golf together tomorrow."

"I see," Claudia said. "I came to tell you that Mr. Ogden called again. He told me to tell you that everything is under control."

Nick's spirits soared. "I think Ogden might be right this time."

"This time?"

"Go on, get out of here. I want to work on my lines for *Lost Weekend*."

Claudia fled.

Chapter 36

"Interesting." Chester adjusted his spectacles on his nose and studied one of the pages in Atherton's notebook with acute interest. "These look like mathematical formulas, the kind used to calculate distances and angles." He turned a few more pages. "Huh."

"What is it?" Oliver asked.

Chester looked up. "I can't answer all your questions yet. I need time to study these notes. It would be helpful to know what Atherton was working on at the Saltwood lab. I can make a telephone call to the company."

"No," Irene said, her voice sharpening. "I called the lab back at the start. That's how I found out that Dr. Atherton was dead. The person who took the call immediately started to grill me. She tried to find out who I was and why I was calling. It was frightening. My former boss is dead because of that notebook."

"Yet she entrusted it to your care," Oliver said. "She didn't tell you to destroy it."

"No. But she made it clear that I couldn't trust anyone—not even the FBI or the cops. She said she made the mistake of trusting the wrong man."

Chester looked at her. "But she suggested that you might be able to use the notebook as a bargaining chip if the worst happened?"

"Yes."

Oliver studied her. "Did Spencer spell out what the worst possibility might be?"

"I think it's obvious," Irene said. "She meant that if whoever is after the notebook found me, I might be able to make a deal."

"Considering what happened to Helen Spencer, I doubt that any deal for the notebook would end well for you," Oliver said.

Irene winced. "I came to the same conclusion. But the notebook is all I've got so I keep it close. Maybe the second break-in at my apartment has nothing to do with Atherton's notes. Maybe Tremayne's studio really did send someone to break in a second time."

Chester and Oliver looked at her. Neither of them said a word.

She exhaled slowly. "I know. What are the odds?"

"Not good," Oliver said. "Unless and until proven otherwise, we have to go with the theory that the second break-in was linked to Atherton's notebook."

Irene locked her arms around herself. "Which means that whoever is after it managed to track me all the way to California."

Oliver's brows rose. "It took him four months to

find you. I'd say you did a damned good job of disappearing."

"Not good enough, apparently."

Oliver got a very intent, very thoughtful expression. "Someone lost you and the notebook for four long months. Whoever it is will be very, very relieved to know that he has finally found you. I think he will also be in a great hurry to recover the notebook before you vanish again. Or before someone else finds you."

Alarmed, Irene stared at him. "Someone else?"

"If that notebook was worth killing for, I think it's safe to assume that there may be others after it," Oliver said.

Irene groaned. "That's not a comforting thought."

"If it makes you feel any better, you can bet that whoever killed Spencer is probably concerned about the competition, too," Oliver said.

She eyed him warily. "Why should that make me feel better?"

"It means that whoever found you in L.A. will be strongly motivated to take some risks. And that leads to the very strong possibility that he'll make mistakes—especially if he's pushed to act quickly."

Chester snapped the notebook shut. "We need to know why these notes are so important. I've licensed a few of my patents to various firms around the country. I know some people. Someone out there will have some idea of what is going on at Saltwood."

"You must be very careful," Irene said.

"Take it easy," Oliver said. "Chester knows what he's doing. Meanwhile, I think we should put that notebook in a more secure place. No offense, but your handbag is not exactly Fort Knox."

Instinctively Irene tightened her grip on the strap of her handbag. "I've been afraid to let it out of my sight."

"Don't worry," Chester said. "After I've finished examining it, I'll put it in a very safe place."

"All right. I guess."

"You two go on now," Chester said. "I need peace and quiet to work on this project."

Oliver grasped Irene's shoulder and gently turned her toward the door. Reluctantly she allowed him to steer her out of the workshop.

"It feels weird," she said.

"Giving Atherton's notebook to someone else? I understand. But we need to know what makes that notebook worth the risk of a murder rap."

"If we're right about the killer—if he found my apartment in L.A.—then by now he knows that I'm here in Burning Cove."

"Yes, but he's in my territory now. We've got a good chance of picking him out of the crowd."

"How?"

He got her outside into the gardens. The sun felt very good, she thought, and the ocean looked especially dazzling.

"This is a small town," Oliver said. "It will be no trouble at all for Detective Brandon to get us a list of people who have recently checked in to the local inns and hotels."

"Including this one?" she said. "I thought you kept your guest list secret."

Oliver looked amused. "We don't give it out to the

press but I make it a policy to always know who is staying in my hotel."

"Do you really think the killer would be so bold as to check in to your hotel?"

"I think," Oliver said, "that it would be a very smart thing for him to do."

"Why?"

"Because it's the last thing you would expect."

"Misdirection."

"Either that or a breathtaking degree of arrogance." Oliver sounded very thoughtful now.

"What makes you so sure you can tell what he's thinking?" Irene demanded. "You've never met the monster who murdered Helen Spencer."

"But I already know a great deal about him, starting with the fact that he is a human monster. There was, after all, no need to murder Spencer in the grisly manner you described."

She shuddered. "No."

"It sounds like he enjoyed himself. That definitely makes him a monster. In addition, I'm very sure it also makes him arrogant. The receptionist at *Whispers* mentioned his accent."

"What about it?"

"That fits with the fact that he seems to have been acquainted with Helen Spencer. Odds are the man we're looking for is from the East Coast."

"Yes. Helen's acquaintances all moved in very exclusive social circles back east. It's possible she met someone from outside that world, though. I just can't say. It's obvious I didn't know nearly as much about her as I thought I did."

"We get our share of guests from the East Coast. They tend to stand out."

"How? Clothes? Manners?"

"And the accent. Gives them away every time. It would appear that we are dealing with two killers. I think we need some assistance."

"The police?"

"No, someone who can afford to be somewhat more flexible than the local cops. Luther Pell. Let's go to my office. I'll telephone him and ask him to meet with us as soon as possible."

"You're sure you can trust him?"

"Yes," Oliver said.

A short time later he put down the telephone and looked at Irene.

"Luther will be here in an hour," he said.

She took a deep breath. "All right."

Oliver got the look of a man who had just made a life-altering decision. He grabbed his cane and levered himself to his feet.

"Come with me," he said. "I want to show you something."

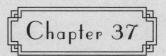

Chapter 37

I t was an act of pure impulse, but once the desire to show her the artifacts of his other life had struck, he knew it was what he wanted to do. He did not know why he wanted her to see the relics of the past; he only knew that he needed to show them to her and that now was the time.

He guided her away from the hotel and the surrounding villas. They walked through the gardens and stopped at a wrought iron gate.

He unlocked the gate and ushered her through.

"Behold the secrets of the illusion of the Burning Cove Hotel," he said. "Or, at least, some of the secrets."

Irene studied the cluster of storage sheds, workshops, and the large garage. There were a number of employees scattered about working on vehicle engines, hauling paint buckets, and wielding gardening equipment. When they noticed Oliver, they called out greetings. He responded and then indicated Irene.

"Just wanted to show Miss Glasson how you keep this place operating," he said.

The men chuckled, nodded respectfully at Irene, and went back to work.

"It's like the backlot of a movie studio," she said.

"And, like the studios, the hotel makes sure everyone who works here is well-fed. The food is free in the employee cafeteria." He urged her toward one of the larger buildings. "What I want to show you is in that big storage locker."

Intrigued, she walked alongside him and paused at the large door while he took out a key.

He got the door open, took a couple of steps into the dark, high-ceilinged structure, and found the light switch. When he flipped it, the overhead fixtures came on, revealing the array of tarp-covered objects.

The light from the fixtures was not strong enough to penetrate deeply into the gloom inside the prop storage locker. Not even brilliant stage lighting could have dispelled all the shadows, he thought, because so many of them were manifestations of the ghosts of his past.

Irene moved slowly into the space and surveyed it with intense interest. Then she turned to look at him.

"This isn't old hotel furniture you've got stored in here, is it?" she asked.

"No," he said. He walked to the nearest tarp and pulled it aside, revealing a large mirror. "After I closed the show for the last time, I was stuck with a lot of stage props and equipment. There wasn't much of a market for the leftovers of a magic act, so I put them into storage."

The mirror was a little taller than she was. She moved to stand in front of it and reached out to touch it lightly with her fingertips.

"Was this part of the illusion that the girl at the beach mentioned?" she asked.

"It's one of the four mirrors I used," he said. "Want to see how it works?"

She widened her eyes. "I thought magicians weren't supposed to reveal their secrets."

"I perfected this particular illusion, the Lady Vanishes in the Mirror, so I'm entitled to reveal the secret behind it. Besides, the assistants always know the magician's secrets."

"Ah, but I'm not an assistant. We're partners."

"All the more reason why you should know some of the magician's secrets."

She smiled. "In that case, I'd love to know how the Lady Vanishes in the Mirror works."

He was pleased that he had managed to distract her, however briefly. In the few days they had known each other, her smiles had rarely lightened the shadows in her eyes. But at that moment her curiosity had temporarily overridden her fears.

He turned away before he was utterly lost in the magic, and pulled off three more tarps, revealing three more tall mirrors.

"In the illusion the lovely assistant—in this case the magician's lovely partner—stands in front of one of the mirrors," he said. "Right about where you're standing now, in fact."

She met his eyes in the looking glass.

"Shouldn't I be wearing a skimpy costume?" she asked.

He was almost certain that she was flirting with him. It was both encouraging and unnerving. In the old days he had been very good when it came to doing a cold read on a person from the audience. But Irene was still very much a mystery in so many ways.

He gave her clothes an appraising look. Her menswear trousers defined her small waist and flowed gracefully around her legs. The pale yellow blouse with its feminine bow at the neck and long, full sleeves made her look both innocent and seductive.

"The skimpier the better," he said. "After all, the assistant's main job is to distract the audience. But what you have on will do for now."

"What happens next?"

"Good question," he said.

He did not realize he had spoken aloud until he saw that she was watching him with faintly raised eyebrows.

Each of the four mirrors was mounted on a set of wheels. He rolled three of them into position around Irene. She was now surrounded on three sides.

"Notice that all of the mirrors have reflective surfaces on both sides," he said. "When properly illuminated onstage, all the mirrored surfaces tend to dazzle the audience."

"More distraction."

"Right. It's one of a magician's most valuable tools. Now, note that three of the mirrors are mounted on narrow frames. When they are turned sideways to the audience, it's obvious that there is no room for even a very slender assistant to be concealed inside."

"Aha. But the other one has a hidden compartment?"

"Yes." He opened the mirror and showed her the long, narrow box inside. "It's just wide enough to allow a slim assistant to stand upright. Next, I position the fourth mirror in place. She is now surrounded on all four sides and concealed from the audience."

He pushed the fourth mirror into position.

"The assistant opens the mirrored box and gets inside, right?" Irene said from the interior of the mirrored chamber.

"Yes, she does."

He heard a hinged door open and close. In the old days the hinges would not have squeaked. Chester had kept them well oiled.

"Are you inside?" he asked.

"Yes. This is really a very small space, isn't it?"

"The boxes are always small, which is, of course, why magicians' assistants are usually small, slender people. If we were doing this onstage, a large curtain would descend at this point, covering the four mirrors. The entire assembly, including the mirrored box with the assistant inside, would be hoisted off the ground to show the audience that there is no secret hiding place beneath the mirrors. The whole thing is then lowered back to the stage. I pull one of the mirrors aside and the audience sees that there is no assistant inside the chamber."

He rolled one of the mirrors out of the way. Irene had vanished.

"Nicely done," he said.

He pushed the mirror back into position. "Now the process is repeated. The curtain is lowered and all four mirrors are hoisted off the floor. The assembly is lowered back down to the floor. The assistant steps out of the concealed box. One of the mirrors is rolled aside and we see that our lovely assistant is back, having just magically emerged from a mirror."

He rolled one of the framed mirrors aside. Irene smiled at him.

"It's all so simple," she said.

"Most of the really dramatic illusions are fairly simple, at least technically speaking. The trick with this one is to make sure the lighting is right so that the audience never sees the wide sides of the mirrored box that conceals the compartment."

"So the real skill is in the sleight-of-hand work."

"Always," Oliver said. "In this case, the magician's job is to shuffle the four mirrors on the stage in such a way that the audience thinks they've seen all of them from every angle. But the truth is, they've only seen three of the mirrors from all sides."

"What happens if you have an assistant who gets extremely nervous in small, enclosed spaces?"

"Assistants who suffer from claustrophobia don't last long in the magic business."

"I can understand that." Irene shuddered. "I think you would have had to fire me by the end of the first performance."

"Are you all right?" he asked.

"Yes, I'm fine. I just wouldn't want to have to climb in and out of those boxes for a living."

"As it turns out, I'm not hiring any box jumpers these days."

"What happened to the ones who used to work for you?" Irene asked. She sounded curious.

"Some went their own way after I closed the show. But most of the people who worked for me in the old days decided to go into a new field."

"What field?"

"The hospitality business."

Irene gave him a knowing look. "You took care of your crew by giving them jobs here at the hotel."

"As I told you, the hotel business and the magic business have a lot in common. The skills required to keep both operating are very similar."

Irene searched his face. "Do you miss it a lot?"

"The magic business? Sometimes. But not as much as I did at first. Things change. I've changed. But, yes, occasionally I miss that moment when you know you've pulled off the perfect illusion and the audience is thrilled by the effect."

"Of course you're bound to miss it sometimes. Magic was your passion. Your art." She started to stroll slowly through the jumble of covered props, pausing here and there to peek beneath the canvas. "What will you do with these things?"

"I have absolutely no idea." He watched her lift the cover off a stack of neatly coiled ropes. "I told you, there's not much of a market for any of this stuff. One of these days I'll have it hauled away."

"No." She turned quickly. "You shouldn't destroy it. You should save it."

"For what?"

She spread her hands. "For your children or your grandchildren. Who knows? One of them might inherit your passion. At the very least, they will be curious about your life as a magician."

"I don't have any plans to have children."

"You don't?" She looked surprised at first, and then she gazed at him with what could only have been described as compassion. "I'm so very sorry. I should never have said anything about children. Please forgive me."

"For what?"

"I didn't realize the full extent of your injury." She glanced down at his leg and then hastily raised her eyes. "I had no idea it was so severe." She broke off, floundering wildly. "It hadn't occurred to me. I never gave it any thought, actually. Not after that kiss at the beach. I just assumed . . . Please, let's change the subject. Can't you see I'm absolutely mortified?"

Understanding finally dawned. He walked toward her and came to a halt a few inches away. He set the cane aside and very deliberately framed her face between his hands.

"I'd like to make one thing clear," he said. "I'm somewhat damaged but the damage was not that extensive."

"Oh. I see." She swallowed hard and came up with a shaky smile. "I'm so glad."

"So am I. And never more so than right now."

He closed the last bit of distance between them, giving her plenty of opportunity to slip away. She did not step back. Instead she gripped his shoulders with both hands as though to keep herself upright.

"Oliver," she whispered. "This probably isn't a good idea."

"Why not?"

"I don't know," she admitted.

And then, in a rush of heat and sensual energy, she released his shoulders, wound her arms around his neck, and kissed him with dizzying urgency, kissed him as if she wanted him—craved him—more than she wanted anything or anyone else in the world.

As if she wanted him almost as much as he wanted her.

The fire roared through him, hot, fierce, soul-stirring. The ice that had formed a protective shield around him during the past two years thawed. The glacier melted and became an avalanche of desire.

The eternal gloom in the storage locker was transformed into a hidden world made to welcome lovers.

Magic, Oliver thought. The real thing.

Somehow he managed to get both of them down onto one of the tarps that he had pulled off the mirrors.

"*Oliver,*" Irene said.

His name was a breathless whisper on her lips, filled with wonder and amazement.

He did not even try to speak because he knew that if he did, whatever he managed to say would sound incoherent. Instead he kissed her again, drinking in the hot, sweet taste of her.

And then he was fumbling with her clothing. An eon passed before he got the fastening of her silky brassiere undone. Another wave of hunger crashed through him when he finally cupped the sweet, gentle curves of her breasts. He kissed one tight, firm tip. She made a soft, desperate sound, arched against him, and sank her nails into his back.

He unfastened her trousers and pushed them down over her hips. She slipped her feet out of her shoes, and then the trousers were gone and she was left wearing only a pair of panties.

She started to undo his shirt but her fingers trembled. He lost patience and levered himself to a sitting position for long enough to get rid of his shoes and his trousers.

He was wearing briefs, the new style of men's underwear. The garment did little to conceal his rigid erection. But it was the wicked scar on his thigh that Irene reached out to touch, not the portion of his anatomy that ached to be clasped in her fingers.

"You could have been killed," she said. She sounded stunned. "I mean, I knew your wound must have been bad, but I didn't realize—"

The shocked sympathy in her words was maddening.

He captured her hand and very deliberately moved it from the scar to the front of his briefs, making her aware of his need.

"I could have been killed, but as it happens, I wasn't," he said. "Now, if you don't mind, I'd rather move on to a more interesting subject."

She blinked and then, tentatively, her palm closed over him. She explored him gingerly, cautiously, as though she was unsure of herself. He groaned.

Hastily she withdrew her hand.

"Aren't I doing it right?" she said anxiously.

"Irene," he got out between clenched teeth. "You have done this before, haven't you?"

"Yes, a few times, but I don't think I was very good at it."

"I'm going to faint."

"What?" Horrified, she sat up very fast. "Lie down."

"I am lying down."

"Shall I get a cold compress?"

"I don't think that will do any good."

"Do you need a doctor?"

She started to reach for her blouse.

"I don't need a doctor." He imprisoned her hand again and pulled her gently down on top of his chest. "I need you. Tell me, what went wrong when you tried this before?"

"He was a lying, cheating bastard."

"That explains it."

"It turns out that I wasn't the first secretary in the history of modern business to make a fool of herself with her boss."

"I get the picture." He cradled her face between his palms. "I want to make this special for you."

"Trust me, this is special," she said.

She kissed him and he was lost. Desire heated his senses until all he could think about was sinking himself into her soft, supple body.

The surroundings were hardly romantic but he had one thing going for him—he was very good with his hands.

When she came for him, breathless, shuddering in

his arms, then and only then did he allow himself to thrust into her.

She gasped, wound herself around him, and held on with all of her strength.

His release pounded through him, and the world outside the storage locker disappeared, taking the past with it—at least for a time.

Magic.

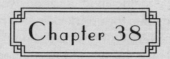

Chapter 38

uther Pell propped one forearm on the bar and considered the earthshaking news that Willie had just delivered in a very low voice and with all the drama suited to the announcement.

"He took Miss Glasson into the prop storage locker?" Luther said. "Are you absolutely certain?"

"That's straight from Hank's lips." Willie polished a wineglass with a white towel. "Hank got it from one of the gardeners, who saw the boss unlock the door himself."

Luther whistled softly. "Big news, all right."

Willie raised her brows. "What's more, they're still inside, according to Hank. He says they've been in there nearly an hour."

"Evidently Miss Glasson is very interested in a certain magician's props."

"If you ask me, the most fascinating aspect of the situation is that a certain magician seemed keen to take Miss Glasson on a tour of his props."

"You're right," Luther said. "As a matter of fact, I can't recall the magician in question ever having escorted any lady into the prop locker for a private tour."

"Neither can I." Willie slotted the wineglass into the overhead rack. "You heard what happened at the warehouse fire last night?"

"The story is all over town."

Willie smiled. "The boss ordered ice from room service. Rick in room service made the delivery. The boss explained what had happened at the warehouse. Rick told the kitchen staff, who passed the story on to housekeeping and security, and the next thing you know, it's all over town."

"Small town," Luther reminded her.

He swallowed some of the sparkling water that Willie had poured for him and thought about the meaning of it all. One thing was clear: Irene Glasson was different, and not just because she had refused to abandon Oliver in a burning building.

It wasn't that Oliver didn't like women. Oliver had escorted other ladies to the Paradise Club, and he had indulged in a couple of short, discreet affairs since arriving in Burning Cove.

But Irene Glasson was different, Luther reflected.

He and Oliver had known each other ever since Oliver purchased the hotel. In spite of the age difference between them, they had become friends from the start. Luther figured it was because each of them had recognized a kindred soul in the other—or maybe just another lost soul traveling the same path. Whatever the case, it was the kind of soul you wanted at your back in a bar fight. A soul you could trust with your secrets.

Both of them had been damaged when they arrived in Burning Cove. Each of them had made a fresh start in a town that encouraged reinvention. Each had done a good job of concealing the damage, but neither of them tried to pretend to the other that the damage didn't exist. Maybe that was the real reason for their friendship.

"Looks like the private tour is over," Willie said, glancing past Luther's shoulder. "Here comes the boss. He's alone. Wonder what happened to Miss Glasson?"

"Let's assume he didn't leave her in the prop locker."

"Probably a safe assumption."

Luther swiveled the bar stool around a quarter turn and saw Oliver coming toward them through the lightly crowded bar.

"It strikes me that Ward's bad leg doesn't seem to be bothering him as much as usual," he said.

"I do believe you're right," Willie said.

Oliver was dressed, but his shirt was open at the collar and his hair looked like it had been combed with his fingers. Aside from that, he appeared in rare good spirits.

"Afternoon, Boss," Willie said. "Can I get you anything?"

"No, thanks," Oliver said. He looked at Luther. "Front desk told me you were here. Let's go back to the villa. We can talk there."

Oliver started to turn away.

Luther stood. "Where is Miss Glasson?"

"She's at the villa," Oliver replied. "Said she wanted to freshen up."

Luther glanced at Willie. Willie suddenly became very busy polishing the already glowing top of the bar.

"Heard you took Miss Glasson on a tour of those old props you've got stored out back," Luther said.

Oliver's eyes narrowed ever so slightly. "Word travels fast around this hotel."

"I can understand why Miss Glasson would want to freshen up," Luther said.

"Is that so?" Oliver said evenly.

"Those old props have been stored in that locker for quite a while now. Probably dusty from lack of use."

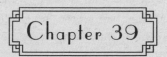

Chapter 39

Irene heard Oliver and Luther arrive just as she finished running a brush through her hair. She put on some lipstick and checked her image in the mirror. She was feeling oddly cheerful and she thought she looked unusually bright and vivacious for a woman who had just engaged in hot, sweaty sex in a storage locker.

In hindsight, maybe she shouldn't have been so cautious after the disaster with Bradley Thorpe, she thought. Life was short. Sex—at least the kind she had just enjoyed—was exhilarating. A woman had a right to grab the good things when they came around. Perhaps she should have taken advantage of the opportunities that had come her way during her year in Helen Spencer's fairy-tale world.

But even as the thought occurred, she was quite

certain that she would have wound up regretting a liaison with any of the charming, polished gentlemen she had met during the course of that year. For one thing, most of them had been jaded, bored, and utterly lacking in principles. They drank too much. They partied too hard. They were often thoughtless or downright cruel to those they considered beneath them. They lived for superficial entertainments, and they would have considered the seduction of Helen Spencer's private secretary a form of entertainment.

But everything was different with Oliver.

She gripped the edges of the pedestal sink with both hands and studied her reflection in the mirror, searching for an explanation. Perhaps the episode in the storage locker had been so intense and so freighted with meaning because she and Oliver had endured danger together. The experience had probably created some sort of bond between them.

If that was the case, she had to accept the fact that the bond was, in all likelihood, temporary. But it was real, which was a hell of a lot more than she could say about the connection she had felt with Bradley Thorpe. Then again, Bradley had been a lying, cheating bastard.

She turned away from the mirror, let herself out into the hall, and went down the stairs. Oliver and Luther were on the patio, sitting in the shade. Both men got to their feet when they saw her.

Luther smiled at her. The smile looked genuine but there was something odd about the way he was looking at her, she thought. It was almost as if he approved of what he saw. But that made no sense. He barely knew her.

"Miss Glasson," he said. "A pleasure to see you again."

She smiled and sat down. "I thought we agreed that you would call me Irene."

"We did, indeed." Luther took his seat. His dark gaze sharpened. "Tell me what's going on."

"Things have gotten complicated," Oliver said. "We need some assistance."

"How complicated?" Luther asked.

"We think that a killer may have followed Irene here to Burning Cove."

Luther's brows rose. "The one who murdered Gloria Maitland and Daisy Jennings?"

"Another one," Oliver said. "And if we're right, he is far more dangerous."

"What makes him more dangerous?"

"If I'm reading the guy right, he's a pro who enjoys his work."

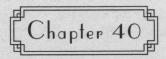

Chapter 40

That night they dined in the hotel's restaurant. The room was crowded when they walked in shortly after eight, but they were immediately seated in an intimate booth on the balcony level.

The position provided a measure of privacy while simultaneously allowing a sweeping view of the main floor. It was, Irene reflected, a lot like sitting in a box seat at the theater. From her position the dining room was a stage set lit by candlelight. The scene sparkled with crystal, polished silver, and glamorously dressed people.

Oliver's martini and Irene's pink lady materialized along with an appetizer tray that featured lobster canapés, olives, and caviar.

"I take it this is your personal booth?" Irene asked.

"I like to keep an eye on my guests, and the view is

excellent from up here," Oliver said. "Most of the people who stay in my hotel eat dinner here even if they're planning to go out to one of the local clubs later in the evening. I can get a list of those who don't have reservations here tonight and those who order room service, if necessary. But I'm betting that our visiting monster doesn't think that he has any reason to hide."

"What makes you so sure he'll be here at your hotel?"

"You're the one he's after and you're here."

"No offense, but your reasoning is quite chilling. Do you really think you can identify him?"

"If he's here, yes. I'm good at reading people in an audience, Irene. It's not that hard once you learn to pick up the cues."

"How do you do it?"

"Like most illusions it's really very simple," Oliver said. "You let the subject tell you everything."

"That actually works?"

"How do you think fortune-tellers, psychics, and mediums make their livings?"

"I've always assumed that people who claim to be psychic were all frauds."

"They are. But they wouldn't stay in business if they didn't put on very convincing acts."

"You're a magician," she said, "not a fortune-teller or a psychic or a medium. You didn't defraud people by making them believe that you could tell them their future or put them in touch with the dead."

He looked surprised by her vehemence.

"Thank you," he said. "I like to think there was a difference between my cold-read performances and the fraudulent variety, but the only real difference is that my audience understood that it was an act—just a clever trick. And for the record, I never performed the talk-to-the-dead scam."

"Of course not. People might have taken that seriously. So many do believe in spirits. You wouldn't want to be responsible for making someone think that he or she really had communicated with the dead. That would be cruel."

He seemed a little amused by the certainty in her voice.

"I was a magician, not a con artist," he said. "But as I told you, a lot of the techniques used in both careers are the same."

"So, what do you see when you look out at your audience tonight?"

He surveyed the dining room. "A lot of people with too much money and too much time on their hands. A lot of people trying desperately to have fun. A lot of people pretending to be someone else, at least for a night. But here and there, I see people who wish they were somewhere else."

"Or with someone else?"

"Oh, yeah," Oliver said. "A lot of those people. I also see some who are trying to reinvent themselves."

"Such as?"

Oliver swallowed some of his martini and angled his head very casually toward a booth down below.

"See the two women sitting together in the corner?"

Irene followed his glance and spotted an attractive blonde dressed in a yellow-gold gown with a cowl neck cut very deep. The woman with her was a brunette dressed in violet. Both were drinking martinis and watching the room like a pair of hawks sizing up the local pigeon population.

"What about them?" Irene asked.

"They both checked in today. They spent the last six weeks in Reno at a divorce ranch and now they're free."

Irene picked up her pink lady. "We in the gossip paper business call it taking the Reno cure."

The notorious quickie divorces available in Nevada were simple enough from a legal point of view, and they had certainly made things much easier for women, especially, to escape an unhappy marriage. In other states the process often took a year or longer, and the laws strongly favored the husbands.

But obtaining a Nevada divorce was not cheap, Irene reflected. For starters, you had to be able to afford to move to Nevada and establish residency for six weeks. The Reno cure carried with it a strong whiff of scandal, of course, as did any other kind of divorce. But there was no denying that the state of Nevada was doing a booming business. People who were killing time waiting for the legal process to play out spent a lot of money at hotels, restaurants, and casinos.

"What about the two women fresh in from Reno?" she asked.

"They're looking for rich husbands to replace the ones they just got rid of. My manager informed me that the blonde asked to have her room switched to one that is closer to that bald man sitting at the table with the bored-looking young woman in blue. Both he and his companion have had enough of each other. She's got her eye on another man and he's looking for someone even younger."

Irene blinked, a little shocked in spite of herself.

"And here I thought that those of us in the gossip business had a somewhat cynical view of human nature," she said.

"I'm not the one who concluded that a fast-rising movie star might be a murderer. Talk about cynical."

"Point taken. So, Mr. Magic, do you see a killer down there in the dining room?"

He contemplated the scene for a long moment. "If I'm right, we're watching for a man who checked in recently and who is traveling alone. I got the list of new guests here at the Burning Cove from the front desk. There are only a handful of names on it."

"But he might not be staying here."

"That is one of the unknowns," Oliver admitted.

"You're probably right that regardless of where he's staying he will be alone. I suppose the last thing a killer would want is a traveling companion."

"I still believe that the odds are very good that the killer is also from the East Coast," Oliver continued. "He'll have an accent and a certain style of dress. And he's rich."

"You say that because he left that necklace behind in Helen's safe?"

Oliver's smile was ice-cold. "A common thief would have been unable to resist such a tempting valuable."

"I think I'm beginning to see how you go about building up a profile of an individual you've never even met."

"Like I said, it's not that hard once you learn to pay attention to the details. Bartenders do it on a regular basis. Take Willie, for instance."

"Who is Willie?"

"The head bartender here at the hotel. She used to be one of my assistants."

"I thought most bartenders were male."

Oliver smiled. "Most are. Willie is a little different. You'll see when you meet her."

"She can do what you do when it comes to reading people?"

"She's very good at it. So is my concierge, Mr. Fontaine. Enough about our problem. It's been a very long day and I'm hungry."

"So am I," Irene said, surprised by the discovery.

"I can recommend the abalone."

"I've never had abalone," she said.

"Welcome to California."

Chapter 41

Two hours later they walked back through the front door of Casa del Mar. Oliver had a list of guests—most male but some female—who had caught his interest for one reason or another. When he needed a name to go with someone on the list, the waiter checked with the maître d' to provide it.

Irene had been so caught up in the list-making process—demanding to know why Oliver selected certain guests out of a room full of people—that she had not had an opportunity to worry about what would happen after dinner. It was, she thought, just barely possible that the pink lady and the white wine that was served with the abalone might have had something to do with her failure to think ahead.

The problem was that she and Oliver had not discussed the sleeping arrangements. It wasn't the sort of thing a lady brought up in conversation, not in a classy dining room.

A great awkwardness descended on her. The tour of the prop locker had turned her world upside down.

Unable to think of anything else to do, she paused at the foot of the stairs, one hand on the railing, and gave Oliver what she hoped was a cool, gracious smile.

"Thanks for a lovely evening," she said. "Even if we did spend most of it talking about a killer."

"Never say I don't know how to show a lady a good time."

His wry tone disturbed her. She took her hand off the railing and touched the side of his face.

"I'm not sure what I should say at this moment," she whispered.

He caught her hand in his and kissed her palm. When he looked at her, she saw a shattering honesty in his normally unreadable eyes.

"I'm not sure what I should say, either," he said. "But I know what I want to say."

She was suddenly breathless. "What is that?"

"Please don't go upstairs tonight. Please say you'll come down the hall to my bedroom instead."

"Yes," she said. She brushed her lips across his. "Yes."

Chapter 42

The following morning Luther arrived just as Irene and Oliver were finishing breakfast on the patio. Oliver waved him to a chair. Irene poured a cup of coffee for him.

"I've got news," Luther said.

"Good or bad?" Irene asked.

"Just news," Luther said. "I contacted some people I know back east. There has been no progress in the Helen Spencer murder case. Officially it remains an active investigation. But my informant told me that, unofficially, the police have given up. They've concluded that it was either a random crime committed by a deranged individual—probably a transient—or the missing private secretary."

Irene caught her breath. "So there has been no progress and I'm still a suspect."

"If it's any comfort, I think the police are leaning toward the deranged-transient theory," Luther said.

"Why?" Irene asked.

Oliver looked at her. "Probably because of the necklace."

"Yes," Luther said. "The thinking is that the secretary was not insane. According to the housekeeper and the butler, she was a skilled professional. If she had murdered her employer, the crime would most likely have been done with the goal of stealing something quite valuable."

"Such as the necklace," Oliver concluded. "Any progress on that front?"

"As reported in the newspapers, it was an extremely valuable item that went missing from a hotel safe in London shortly before Helen Spencer was murdered."

Irene gripped the arms of the rattan chair. "Miss Spencer traveled to London three weeks before she was killed."

Luther's brows rose. "Evidently your employer traveled abroad frequently and she kept an apartment in Manhattan."

"That's right," Irene said. A queasy sensation roiled her stomach. "I'm the one who booked her tickets and made her travel arrangements. I sometimes accompanied her."

"Spencer always stayed in the best hotels, didn't she?" Luther continued. "She attended parties in the homes of wealthy people."

Irene went cold. "What, exactly, are you implying?"

Oliver gave Luther a knowing look. "You think Helen Spencer was a jewel thief, don't you?"

Luther shrugged. "It would explain a lot."

Irene stared at him, stunned. "I can't believe it."

"Makes sense," Oliver said. "She probably stumbled onto Atherton's notebook when she cracked a safe in search of jewelry. She would have suspected immediately that the notebook was valuable. Why else stash it in a hotel safe?"

"I think that is the most reasonable way to explain how Spencer acquired the notebook," Luther said. "It's possible that she was a professional spy who was paid to steal the notebook, but I think it's far more likely that she was a thief who got very unlucky when she stole Atherton's notes."

"Dear heaven." Irene shook her head, dazed. "I lived in her house for nearly a year. How could I not have guessed the truth? I was so naïve. I thought she was my friend."

"It sounds like she was your friend," Oliver said quietly. "Toward the end she must have begun to realize that the notebook was not only valuable, it was dangerous. She tried her best to protect you in case something happened to her."

Irene thought about the message written in blood on the silver-flocked wallpaper. *Run.*

"Yes," she whispered.

Luther looked at her. "Did Spencer meet with anyone in the days before she was murdered?"

"I don't know," Irene said. "She had just returned from Europe. She went there alone. I spent the time at the New York apartment. She sent a telegram from London giving me the date her ship was due to arrive. I was to meet her at the pier. We were going to drive up to the country house together. But the information in the telegram was wrong. Miss Spencer was not on the ship. I discovered that she had arrived two days earlier. She must have gone straight to the country house."

"Yet she knew that you were waiting for her in New York," Oliver said.

"Yes," Irene said. "I wasn't the only one who got the wrong information. The housekeeper and butler were expecting Miss Spencer to return two days later, as well. Looking back, I think it's obvious that she deliberately deceived us. She wanted some time alone at the country house."

"Time to make a deal for the notebook, perhaps," Oliver said.

Irene looked at him. "And time to meet her lover. He murdered her for the notebook."

"That's what it looks like," Luther said. "What made you decide to drive to Spencer's country house that evening?"

"When I found out that she had arrived on a ship that docked two days earlier, I was frantic," Irene said. "I couldn't find her in New York. None of her friends had seen her. I telephoned the country house but there was no answer. I was afraid that she was there alone and had perhaps taken ill or fallen down the stairs. By then it was very late in the day. It's a long drive and I was delayed by a bridge that had been closed due to the heavy rains. I didn't arrive until nearly midnight."

"So you got into your car and drove all the way to the mansion, even though you knew you would be driving a mountain road at night," Luther concluded.

Irene looked at him. "Miss Spencer was very good to me. I would have done just about anything for her. If only I had arrived a few hours earlier."

"If you had, you, too, would probably be dead," Luther said.

Irene took a deep breath. "Yes, that thought has occurred to me every minute of every waking hour since I found Helen's body."

Oliver reached across the table and squeezed her hand. "You were alone that night. You're not alone now."

The phone rang a short time later just as Luther was preparing to leave the villa.

"Hold on," Oliver said. "That may be Brandon with some news about Springer."

He grabbed his cane and disappeared into the villa. Irene was left alone on the patio with Luther.

"I know you're involved in this mess because you're Oliver's friend," she said earnestly, "not because of me. But I want you to know how much I appreciate your help. I would apologize for bringing so much trouble to Burning Cove but that won't do any good. I can only tell you that I had no idea things would turn out to be so dangerous."

Luther drank the last of his coffee and set the cup in the saucer. "It's true you have livened things up here in our little town. But there's no need for apologies. If anything, I owe you my thanks."

Bewildered, she could only stare at him. "What on earth for?"

He gave her an unreadable smile. "Oliver and I have a tendency to sink into boredom occasionally."

"I find that difficult to believe. Each of you is responsible for a large business enterprise. I'm sure your various financial interests keep you occupied."

"It's true, our businesses do occupy much of our time. But a man can only review so many budgets before it all becomes predictable and routine."

"Murder is hardly an ideal cure for boredom."

Luther chuckled. "When you live in a small town like Burning Cove, you can't be too choosey when it comes to diversions."

"You're teasing me."

"You've got me there. But it looks to me like you're doing my friend Oliver a world of good, so I'm willing to cut you some slack when it comes to murder."

"How can you say that? I nearly got him killed at that warehouse the other night."

"Yes, well, don't get me wrong, I'm glad you didn't actually succeed. I am acquainted with a lot of people but Oliver is one of the few that I can call friend, one of the very few I trust."

"Look, Mr. Pell—"

"Luther."

"Luther, this is not a laughing matter."

"Probably not," he agreed. "But, you see, the news of exactly what happened at that warehouse is all over town."

"Then you know Oliver could have died in the fire or been shot by one of those two men on motorcycles."

"What I know," Luther said, "is that you were on

your way out of that burning warehouse when Oliver lost his balance and fell. You turned back to help him."

"Well, of course I did. It was my fault he was in harm's way in the first place. Besides, one doesn't leave one's partner behind."

"No," Luther said. "One doesn't. But not everyone understands that. You went back to help my friend. That's all that matters to me."

She studied him for a long moment. "You really have been concerned about him, haven't you?"

"Sometimes," Luther said, "he takes that souped-up Cord of his out onto an empty stretch of highway and he drives it very, very fast. I think he uses it as an antidote for the pain."

"The pain of his old injury?"

"That is the least of it," Luther said. "He lost something far more valuable than a lucrative career when he nearly died onstage. But that is for him to tell you."

"I think you understand him very well," Irene said. "I assume that is because you have also experienced real pain. You said that Oliver's antidote is to drive his car too fast. Tell me, what remedy do you use?"

The edge of Luther's mouth twitched a little in amusement. "You are very perceptive. I shall have to remember that in future."

"You paint," Irene said, very sure of her conclusion. "That is how you deal with the pain, isn't it?"

Luther narrowed his eyes. He no longer looked amused. "As I said, you are very perceptive."

Oliver emerged from the living room before Irene could say anything else.

"That was Brandon, all right," Oliver said. "Springer

was discharged from the hospital this morning. He was booked into the Burning Cove jail approximately twenty minutes later. Not long afterward a hotshot lawyer from L.A. arrived and bailed Springer out of jail."

"Who sent the lawyer?" Luther asked. "I doubt if a guy like Springer has that kind of money."

"Brandon assumes that Hollywood Mack or the studio fixer Ernie Ogden is responsible for the lawyer," Oliver said.

"So a known arsonist is running around free in Burning Cove?" Irene asked. "That's outrageous."

Oliver looked at her. "Brandon said the only good news is that Springer was last seen buying a train ticket to L.A."

Chapter 43

Graham Enright clamped his hand around the telephone. "What the hell do you mean, you were playing tennis when I called earlier? I didn't send you out to California to take a vacation. You're supposed to be working."

"Calm down," Julian said, his voice rendered distant and a bit scratchy by the long-distance connection. "I am working. I've got a plan, and Nick Tremayne is a critical element. Everything is under control."

"How much longer do you intend to spend finishing this assignment?"

"Things have gotten a little complicated."

Graham drummed his fingers on his desk. "How complicated?"

"I searched the apartment in L.A. very thoroughly. There was no sign of the notebook. Interestingly, someone got to her place before me—the studio people, I think. But I doubt that they found the notebook. Even if they had, the goons wouldn't have recognized its real value. I'm sure she brought it here to Burning Cove. I'm told she was staying at a local inn but now she's a guest at Ward's private villa."

"Who is Ward?"

"Ex-magician. Not a very good one, apparently. Almost got himself killed in his last performance."

"Are you talking about Oliver Ward?"

"Right. Ever see his act?"

"No, but I remember the headlines when he nearly got killed onstage. What does he have to do with this situation?"

"He owns the Burning Cove Hotel. Anna Harris— she's calling herself Irene Glasson now—moved in with him very soon after she arrived in Burning Cove. My guess is that she's hoping he'll be able to help her find a buyer for the notebook. Ward is friends with the owner of a local nightclub, Luther Pell. Pell's got mob connections."

"You think Ward and Harris or Glasson or whatever she's calling herself are working together now?"

"Glasson may believe that they're partners, but it's far more likely that he's running a con on her. That's the only thing that makes sense. There's no other reason why he'd be sleeping with a gossip columnist from a cheap Hollywood newspaper. Got to hang up now. I have to talk to the hotel concierge about booking a restaurant this evening."

"Damn it, what about the project? I thought I made it clear, the reputation of Enright and Enright is on the line. Our business is founded on the twin pillars of absolute discretion and successful results. We are poised to take a huge step into the global marketplace. A failure of this magnitude will do serious damage to the firm."

"I'll have this business wrapped up in just a few more days. Got to go. I'll call as soon as I have the notebook."

The line went dead.

Irritated, Graham dropped the receiver into the cradle and got to his feet. He went to stand at the window of his office and contemplated the busy Manhattan streets far below.

His son was talented and ambitious. In addition, Julian possessed the feral instincts and the intelligence required to take the helm of Enright & Enright. But there was no getting around the fact that the boy had been indulged from the cradle. The result was a spoiled, impulsive young man.

It did not matter that he was spoiled. The Enrights had always moved in wealthy, socially elite circles. Julian was a product of his upbringing. It was only natural that he was accustomed to privilege and the finer things in life.

It was the impulsiveness that was worrisome. The trait had been evident since Julian was a toddler but it was becoming increasingly pronounced. Perhaps it was a direct result of his string of successes, Graham thought. When a man got accustomed to committing murder and getting away with it time and again, it was only to be expected that he might start to think himself invincible.

Julian needed to learn control. He needed to mature. But there would be ample opportunity in the future to guide him and shape him so that he could fulfill his destiny.

First things first. It was imperative that the notebook be recovered and the woman who was calling herself Irene Glasson be terminated.

A buzzing sound interrupted his thoughts. He went back to his desk and pressed a button.

"Yes, Miss Kirk?"

"Mr. Duffield is here to see you, sir. He wishes to discuss his will."

"Thank you, Miss Kirk. Please send him in."

"Yes, sir."

The door opened and Raina Kirk ushered Duffield into the room. He was a frail man in his early eighties who was quickly going senile—just the sort of client that Graham cultivated to maintain a façade of legitimacy and respectability for the firm. It was Duffield and his ilk who unwittingly provided access to certain social circles and—most important of all—the inside information that so often proved useful to the real work of Enright & Enright.

Raina took Duffield's arm and escorted him to one of the client chairs.

"Thank you, young lady," Duffield cackled.

Raina smiled, politely ignoring the lecherous grin on the old man's face. "You're quite welcome, Mr. Duffield." She stepped back and looked at Graham.

"Will there be anything else, sir?"

"That's all for now, Miss Kirk," Graham said.

"Yes, sir."

Raina left. The door closed behind her.

Graham suppressed a small sigh. Raina Kirk was another problem that would have to be dealt with fairly soon. She had sent one too many coded telegrams, overheard one too many snippets of conversation, booked one too many hotel rooms for Julian, recorded one too many unusual financial transactions.

Lately Graham had begun to suspect that she had listened in on some of his telephone calls.

No question but that the time had come to fire Raina Kirk. She would not be the first private secretary he had been forced to let go, Graham thought. That meant he would soon be seeking a new woman for the position.

Replacing a competent secretary with an equally skilled one who had no close family was always a challenge. He had followed the policy his father set down when the business was founded. He made certain that his private secretaries were single women of a certain age who possessed no close relatives. Relatives could be a problem when it came time to terminate a secretary. And, sooner or later, each had to be fired.

The position required a woman well versed in the secretarial arts. Her typing, dictation, bookkeeping, and organizational skills had to be excellent. But such women were also quite intelligent and insightful. Eventually they learned too much about the firm's lucrative sideline.

When Julian returned from California, he would deal with Miss Kirk, just as he had dealt with her predecessor. Replacing Kirk wouldn't be easy, Graham thought. She was the most talented secretary he had ever hired. But an executive had to do what was best for the firm.

There was one benefit to firing secretaries. The exercise was an excellent way for Julian to keep his knife skills sharp.

Chapter 44

"Mr. O'Conner is here to see you, sir," Elena said over the intercom.

Oliver pressed a button. "Good. Send him in, please, Elena."

The door opened and Tom O'Conner walked into the office. He was in his forties, a big, muscular, ruddy-faced man who had handled security for the Amazing Oliver Ward Show. He wore the dark jacket, trousers, and tie that were the day uniform for the men on his staff.

Tom's clothes, like all the other staff uniforms, were supplied by the hotel. They were cleaned and pressed regularly by the housekeeping department, so Tom always started the day looking crisp and tailored. But somehow, within an hour after arriving for work, he managed to look rumpled.

Oliver lounged back and wrapped his fingers around the arms of his chair. "Have a seat, Tom. What have you got on the crazy fan?"

"Not much. His name is Henry Oakes and he's nuts about Nick Tremayne." Tom settled his bulk into a chair. "Oakes checked into the Seaside Motel a day after Tremayne showed up here. Has coffee and two fried eggs at Mel's Café every morning. Comes back for coffee and a meat loaf sandwich at dinner."

"Meat loaf?"

"It's always meat loaf at dinner, according to the waitress. Always two fried eggs in the morning. Oakes appears to be a creature of habit. The waitress said he was very precise about how he wanted his eggs and the sandwich. She also says he's creepy."

"Irene mentioned that. What does he do at night?"

"Well, that's where things get a little interesting. Parker, the guy who handles security at the Carousel Club, told me that he spotted Oakes outside the club the same night that Tremayne spent a couple of hours there."

"That was the night that Gloria Maitland drowned in the spa."

"Yeah. Parker said he noticed Oakes standing in the shadows, watching the front door of the club. Parker thought he might be a chauffeur or a bodyguard. But when Parker asked him who he was waiting for, Oakes just walked away. Hasn't shown up again, at least as far as Parker knows."

"Anything else?"

"Nothing solid. We've seen the type before, Boss.

Every month or so we catch some screwy fan trying to sneak onto the property."

"Tell everyone on the staff—I mean *everyone*: housekeepers, kitchen crew, gardeners, as well as your people—to watch for Henry Oakes. If he shows up, I want to know immediately."

"Want me to have a little talk with Oakes?" Tom raised his brows. "I could strongly advise him to leave town. I can make sure he's on the late-afternoon train to L.A."

"If we send him back to L.A., we'll lose track of him. I think we're better off knowing where he is. Like I said, if he shows up on the property, I want to know about it."

"I'll get the word out."

Chapter 45

Willie liked polishing martini glasses and sus-
pending them by their stems in the overhead
rack. She found the chore soothing, a form
of meditation. She was engaged in the practice when
Irene walked into the lounge looking like a woman
who needed a confidante.

Willie recognized the expression. When you worked
behind a bar, you saw it a lot.

It was going on ten o'clock in the morning and there
were no guests in the bar yet. That was not unusual.
Some of the early risers were playing either golf or
tennis. Several were working off the effects of the previous night's partying with a massage and a stint in
the spa's steam room. A few were sleeping late—not
necessarily with their own spouses. She had already
sent several orders of her signature eye-opener, Red

Sally—a cocktail involving tomato juice, vodka, and a lot of salt and hot sauce—to people who had ordered room service.

Irene hitched up her trousers, plunked herself down on a bar stool, and folded her arms on the polished wooden surface.

So this is the boss's new lady friend, Willie thought. She was as curious about Irene as everyone else on the staff.

"You must be Miss Glasson," she said. "Welcome to the Burning Cove Hotel. I'm Willie, by the way."

Irene had walked in with the look of a woman who was lost in her own thoughts, but at the greeting she immediately refocused her attention and smiled.

The smile was real, Willie decided. She saw all kinds. She was pretty good at separating the false ones from the genuine article. All that experience as a magician's assistant had served her well in her new career.

"You worked with Oliver in his show, didn't you?" Irene said.

"Oliver told you about me?"

"A little, not much. He mentioned that several of the people employed here at the Burning Cove, including you, had worked with him in the Amazing Oliver Ward Show."

"That's right," Willie said. "After the show closed, Mr. Ward could have let all of us go. Instead, he used every last dime he had to buy this hotel. He couldn't afford to pay us back at the start, but we had room and board so we stuck around. The place started turning a profit last year. The pay is good, so we're all still here. What can I get you?"

"Do you serve coffee in here?"

"I do."

"In that case, I'll have some, thank you."

Willie set a cup and saucer on the bar, picked up a pot, and poured the coffee.

"I see the boss let you out on your own this morning," she said. "Does that mean he thinks your problem has been resolved?"

Irene drummed her fingers on the counter. "I suppose everyone on the staff knows that Oliver thinks I need round-the-clock security."

"Sure. We also know that you helped get him out of that burning warehouse the other night."

Irene sipped some coffee. "As I keep pointing out to people, it was my fault that he was in that warehouse in the first place."

Willie picked up another glass and started polishing it. "The boss makes his own rules. If he was there with you, it was because he wanted to be there."

"That's more or less what he told me."

"It's the truth. We all know he's worried about your safety. He's always had good security here at the hotel, but during the past few days he's given orders to double down on the routine patrols, and he's cranked up the lighting at night. The grounds are lit up like a stage at three in the morning now. That said, you seem to be running free today."

Irene wrinkled her nose. "For a while. He's handling some business in his office. I didn't want to sit there, staring at him or reading a magazine while he made telephone calls and did whatever hotel executives do. He figured I'd be safe here in the bar."

"He's right. We've got good security in here, too. There's a button I can push if I don't like what's going on. One of the guards would be here in a minute or two at the most."

"That's good to know." Irene patted her handbag. "I'm not helpless. I've got a gun."

"So do I," Willie said. She held the martini glass up to the light to check her work. "I keep it under the bar."

Interest and curiosity sparked in Irene's eyes. "Really?"

"Old habit from the days when we were on the road. Some towns were rougher than others. Every so often some jerk decided to rob the ticket office or hassle one of the assistants."

"You, for instance?"

Willie gave her a humorless smile. "Me, for instance."

"Does Oliver know about the gun under the bar?"

"Yes."

"He told me he doesn't like guns."

"What do you expect? He almost got killed by one."

"He says guns give people a false sense of security. He says you never know when one will jam on you."

"Sounds like the two of you had an extensive conversation on the subject."

"Uh-huh." Irene drank some more coffee and put the cup down with great care. "Once, in another life, I had an employer who owned a gun. But in the end it didn't do her any good. She was murdered by some bastard who used a knife."

"What happened?"

"She made the mistake of trusting the wrong person."

"Trust is a dangerous thing."

"Yes, it is," Irene said. "But you get very lonely if you don't have someone you can trust."

"You can trust the boss."

Irene smiled. "He obviously trusts you."

"We go back a ways."

Irene turned thoughtful. "He says you can read people as well as he can."

"Bartenders in general are good at reading people. You could say it's a job requirement."

Irene met her eyes. "You probably know that I'm suspicious of Nick Tremayne."

"Everyone who reads the newspapers knows that."

"Care to give me your take on him?"

Willie chuckled. "Funny you should ask."

"Why?"

"Because the boss asked the same question the morning your story broke in *Whispers*. I'll tell you the same thing I told him. I think Nick Tremayne is very, very ambitious. I also think he's got a temper."

"Ever seen him lose it?"

"No. But the other day I happened to see that personal assistant of his after she came out of his villa. She looked shaken. Downright scared, I think."

"Claudia Picton? I think she's terrified of losing her job." Irene took a sip and set her cup down on the saucer with a clink. "My intuition tells me she's the weak link in this thing. I need to speak with her again. That means I have to get her alone."

"The boss might not approve."

"I've seen enough of Claudia Picton to know that she'll never open up if Oliver is with me. He'll intimidate her."

"You're probably right. It's obvious that Miss Picton's nerves are in bad shape. Wouldn't take much to send her into a complete panic."

"What else do you know about her?" Irene asked.

"Not a lot. She doesn't come into my bar."

"Maybe she doesn't drink."

"Either that or the studio won't cover her bar tab," Willie said.

"I didn't see her in the restaurant last night but I guess that's no surprise. Most women don't like to be seen dining alone."

"Maybe she went out to a local café," Willie suggested.

"Who would know?"

Willie smiled. "The concierge, Mr. Fontaine. When it comes to the habits and preferences of the guests, a good concierge is better than a private detective."

"Think Mr. Fontaine will talk to me?"

"Only if Mr. Ward tells him to talk to you."

"I need to call Oliver."

"There's a house telephone behind the bar."

"May I use it?"

"Help yourself."

Irene moved around behind the bar and reached for the receiver.

"Thanks, Willie," she said. "You've been very helpful."

Willie held another glass up to the light to check her polishing job. "Happy to be of service. Out of curiosity, how do you plan to persuade Miss Picton to meet with you in private?"

"I don't. I'm going to stage an ambush." Irene concentrated on the telephone. "Please connect me with Mr. Ward's private office. Thank you. Yes, I'll wait."

Willie smiled to herself.

"Something amusing?" Irene asked.

"I was just thinking that you're a good influence on the boss."

"A good influence? Are you joking? I found a dead body in his spa and I nearly got him killed."

"You wouldn't believe how he's perked up since you arrived at the hotel. You've done wonders. A regular tonic."

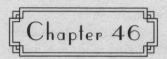

Chapter 46

E lena appeared in the office doorway.

"I just received Detective Brandon's list of guests who recently checked in at the other hotels, inns, and B and Bs in town," she said.

Oliver looked up from the list of new arrivals at the Burning Cove Hotel. "Several of the so-called singles from back east on my list are actually traveling with a personal maid or a private secretary. I've excluded them. That leaves me with eight names. How many on Brandon's list?"

"Another twenty in all, but most are from California—L.A. or San Francisco for the most part. Our hotel gets the majority of the East Coast crowd here because, like the Beverly Hills Hotel and the Biltmore in L.A., we are quite well-known."

"The benefits of advertising. Thanks, Elena."

This was, he concluded, probably one of the few times in the history of the industry that the proprietor of a hotel hoped his establishment's reputation for elegance and service had served as a lure to attract a killer.

Never a dull moment these days. Not with Irene around.

Elena put the list on his desk and went back to the doorway, where she paused and gently cleared her throat.

Oliver looked up again, suddenly wary.

"What is it?" he said.

"I just wanted to say that you are looking very well today."

"Have I been looking unwell previously?"

"No, sir. It's just that you seem to be in excellent spirits today. Especially considering the circumstances."

Nothing like hunting for a killer to put a man in an upbeat mood, Oliver reflected.

"Probably the three cups of coffee I drank at breakfast," he said.

Elena chuckled. "No doubt."

"Remember, not a word about these lists and the people on them."

"Understood."

She was about to close the door but stopped when the outer door burst open. Chester charged into the front office.

"Where's Oliver?" he demanded.

"Right here," Oliver called through the opening. "Come on in, Chester."

Chester rushed into the room, bristling with excitement. He had Atherton's notebook in one hand.

"Wait until I tell you what's in this thing," he said.

"Sit down," Oliver said. He looked at Elena. "That's all for now. Thanks."

She left, closing the door quietly behind her.

Chester put the notebook down on the desk and dropped into one of the chairs. "What do you know about radio waves?"

"I know how to turn on a radio and I know how to turn it off. Why?"

"Radio waves are a form of electromagnetic radiation and they have several very interesting properties. Most metal objects, for example, *reflect* radio waves."

"So?"

"So the British and the U.S. military have been conducting secret research designed to see if radio waves can be used to detect airplanes at a considerable distance and ships at sea."

Understanding began to dawn. "I'm listening," Oliver said.

"The work is still in the experimental stage. I'm told the Brits are ahead of us because they're so damned worried about Germany. But other nations, including Russia, Germany, and Japan, are also doing research in this area. There are serious limitations with the current equipment—the antennas are huge and the wavelengths are too long—but, theoretically, utilizing a pulsing technique and shorter wavelengths, it should be possible to build a compact device that would allow radio waves to detect ships at sea."

"To help avoid collisions?"

"Sure, but what interests the U.S. Navy is the possibility of using radio waves to find enemy vessels at a distance. Currently, the process for aiming a battleship's big guns involves the risk of getting close enough to the target to see where the shells land. After you get a visual on the first shot, you calibrate the next shot and so on. In addition, all sorts of other information must be cranked into the calculations—the pitch and roll of the ship, for example. It's complicated work that must be done at close range, which entails a lot of risk."

Oliver picked up the notebook. "Are you telling me that Atherton's calculations have something to do with engineering a device that uses radio waves to detect enemy ships?"

"Not just that," Chester said. He popped up out of his seat and began to pace the office. "If I'm right, that book contains the calculations and specifications needed to construct a very advanced rangekeeper, one that incorporates the radio wave detector I just told you about."

"A rangekeeper?"

"They're the calculating machines that the Navy uses to direct the firing of long-range guns on board a ship. If the machine described in that notebook gets built—and if it works as it's designed to work—it will give the Navy a very big advantage in the next war."

"If there is another war."

Chester stopped pacing. He heaved a sigh, took out a handkerchief, and began polishing his glasses.

"As long as human nature is what it is, I'm afraid there will always be another war," he said quietly.

"And people tell me that I'm cynical." Oliver tapped

the notebook. "What about the laboratory where Atherton worked?"

Chester put on his glasses. "It will probably come as no surprise to you that the Saltwood Laboratory is rumored to be working on a secret military project. They've got a contract with the Navy. Very hush-hush."

"And Atherton?"

Chester grunted. "No one seems to know anything about him aside from the fact that he's dead. Car accident."

"I suppose it would be too easy to just telephone the Saltwood lab and ask them to send someone out to Burning Cove to pick up this damned notebook."

Chester gave him a grim look. "You do that and the next thing you know this hotel will be crawling with government agents. You're in the middle of a major espionage case, Oliver. Anyone who knows anything about the notebook, including Miss Glasson and you, will become suspects. You might be able to talk yourselves out of trouble eventually, but once you get on a government list, you're on it for life."

"You know, my job was a lot simpler when all I had to worry about was catching a couple of killers."

Chapter 47

Irene was in the tearoom, positioned behind a massive potted palm, when Claudia arrived at precisely three fifteen just as the concierge, Mr. Fontaine, had predicted.

The waiter seated Claudia in a corner behind another potted palm. As soon as the first cup of tea had been poured, she took her notebook and a pencil out of her handbag. She opened the notebook and bent over it industriously.

Irene rose and moved as unobtrusively as possible around the room until she could approach Claudia from behind.

"Hello," she said, trying for a warm, cheery tone. She glanced at a page of Claudia's notes. "I see you know shorthand. I hadn't realized that you trained as a secretary."

Claudia jerked violently and looked up with an expression of near panic.

"Oh, it's you," she said. Her fear metamorphosed into irritation. She closed the notebook with a sharp snap. "What do you want?"

"Just a short chat. May I sit down?"

She seated herself quickly before Claudia could decide how to handle the situation.

Claudia picked up her teacup. "Mr. Ogden said you got fired from your job at *Whispers*."

"Good news travels fast."

"If you're no longer a reporter, why should I talk to you?"

"Because I plan to get my job back. To do that I need a scoop."

"If you think I'm going to help you pin Gloria Maitland's death on Nick Tremayne, you're crazy. If anything happens to Tremayne, I'm the one who will be unemployed."

"Look, you told me from the start that Tremayne's alibi for the Maitland death was solid. I didn't believe you at first but I do now."

Claudia looked wary. "Is that so?"

"I'm no longer trying to prove that Tremayne killed anyone. But I would like to know more about Daisy Jennings."

"I can't help you. I never met the woman. According to the local paper, you found the body."

"I was not alone that time. Mr. Ward was with me."

"Regardless, it strikes me as something of a coincidence that you were on the scene when another woman was found dead," Claudia said.

"Believe me, that thought did occur to me. Shortly before she died, Daisy Jennings contacted me. She claimed she had something important to tell me. Do you have any idea what it was?"

"Not unless she was trying to get revenge on Mr. Tremayne."

"Why would she do that?"

"Women are always throwing themselves at Mr. Tremayne, but the only thing he's serious about is his career."

"Where is Nick Tremayne right now?"

"At this very minute? Playing golf, not that it's any of your business."

"Alone?"

"Of course not. Men don't play golf alone. He's with a friend."

"Someone from L.A.? Another star?"

"What?" Claudia frowned. "No. Someone he met here at the hotel. Another guest. Mr. Enright. Stop asking me questions. I would have thought you'd have learned your lesson by now."

"What lesson is that?"

"According to Mr. Ogden at the studio, you lost your job and your landlady tossed you out of your apartment," Claudia said. "Isn't that bad enough? The men who run Mr. Tremayne's studio are very powerful people. If you keep asking questions about Nick Tremayne, your life will get even more unpleasant, believe me."

"Are you threatening me, Claudia?"

"Me? No. I'm just a lowly assistant. But I've worked at the studio long enough to know that men like Ogden can do a great deal of damage to people who get in their way. If I were you, Miss Glasson, I'd find another story. Leave Nick Tremayne alone."

"Sounds like you're afraid of this Mr. Ogden."

"No, Miss Glasson, I'm not afraid of Earnest Ogden. I'm absolutely terrified of him."

"Because he could get you fired?"

"In a heartbeat. Look, I'll tell you the truth. Hollywood was the biggest mistake of my life. I'm not cut out for that world or this one here in Burning Cove, either. I'm just trying to keep my job long enough to get some money together so that I can go home."

"What will you do when you go home?"

"What everyone told me I should do the day I graduated from high school." Claudia got to her feet and collected her book and her handbag. "Get a job in a department store. Meet a nice guy who can support me. Get married."

"Where is home?" Irene asked.

"A place where you don't need to wear sunglasses every day of the year."

Claudia walked swiftly toward the door of the glass-walled tearoom and disappeared out into the gardens.

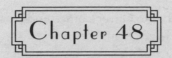

rene sat quietly, thinking about what Claudia had said. After a while she got to her feet and went along the arched walkway to Oliver's office.

Elena smiled when she opened the door. "Hello, Irene. How are you today?"

"I'm fine, thank you, Elena. And you?"

"Excellent, thanks. Are you here to see Mr. Ward?"

"Yes. Is he in his office?"

"He is. I'll let him know you're here." Elena pressed the intercom button. "Miss Glasson is here, sir."

"Send her in. I was about to go looking for her."

Elena started to get to her feet to open the door.

"Don't bother, please, I'll get it." Irene crossed the room. She paused, her hand on the knob, and looked back at Elena. "Do you ever get tired of all the sunshine here in California?"

Elena laughed. "Are you kidding? I was born and raised here. I love the light."

Irene smiled. "I'm not from around here but I agree with you. I love the light, too. Oddly enough, not everyone does."

She walked into Oliver's office and closed the door behind her. He got to his feet.

"There you are," he said. "I was about to go looking for you. Chester just briefed me on what he discovered about Atherton's notebook. Those calculations are for a highly advanced version of a military device called a rangekeeper. Saltwood evidently has a secret contract with the Navy."

"We're talking about espionage?"

"That's what it looks like. Chester agrees with the advice that Helen Spencer gave you in her letter, by the way. He says we'll be asking for a lot of trouble if we contact the FBI."

Irene shuddered. "We'll become suspects in an espionage case."

"Yes."

"Good heavens. This thing just gets deeper and deeper, doesn't it?"

"I think we're finally able to put a few pieces of the puzzle together. Did Teddy help you locate Claudia Picton?"

"Teddy?"

"Sorry," Oliver said. "He prefers his stage name. Mr. Fontaine. Occasionally I forget. To me he'll always be Teddy, the guy who somehow got the whole show, crew, props, and equipment packed up and on the right train heading for the next town. The man's brilliant when it comes to logistics."

"Claudia was right where Mr. Fontaine said she would be at three fifteen—the tearoom. I was hoping to rattle her a bit but she didn't tell me much. She did mention that Nick Tremayne was playing golf with a new acquaintance, someone he met at the hotel."

"Who?"

"A Mr. Enright."

Oliver sat down, looking thoughtful. "That is very interesting."

"Why?" she asked, taking a seat.

"There is a Julian Enright of New York on my list."

"A single man? Traveling alone?"

"Yes. A gentleman with expensive tastes and a sense of style—the sort of style that, I'm told, can only be acquired by someone who descends from several generations of moldy money. Mr. Fontaine was very impressed."

"You didn't point out this Julian Enright in the hotel restaurant last night."

"He wasn't there." Oliver held up a list with four names on it. "Enright was one of the few who chose to dine in town."

"'A gentleman with expensive tastes and a sense of style,'" Irene repeated softly. "Doesn't sound like a killer, does he?"

"Not the Hollywood movie version, perhaps. But do you think it's possible that such a man might have succeeded in deceiving Helen Spencer?"

"Maybe. Why would a killer on a mission to recover the notebook take up with a hot Hollywood talent?"

"It's quite possible that Enright is aware of your recent reporting."

"So?"

"So, since you have helpfully laid the groundwork for pointing the finger of blame at Nick Tremayne in one recent death, why not use Tremayne as cover?"

"I don't understand."

"If something were to happen to you, Irene, who do you think would come under immediate suspicion?"

She caught her breath at the sheer audacity of the idea.

"Nick Tremayne," she said. "Everyone knows he's furious with me because of that piece I wrote for *Whispers*."

"He might have a rock-solid alibi—enough to keep him from going to jail—but that wouldn't matter in the court of public opinion. I wouldn't be surprised if the murder of a certain reporter here in Burning Cove where Tremayne just happens to be vacationing might be too much for even a powerful studio to handle— especially if the murder was staged so that it was clear it was no accident."

A vision of Helen Spencer's bloody corpse flashed into Irene's mind. Her fingers trembled.

"Perception is everything," she said. "There would be a huge scandal, lots of speculation and gossip. And while all that was going on, the real killer would quietly vanish from the scene. It's a stunning idea."

"Damned brilliant piece of misdirection when you think about it."

"It certainly worked in Helen's murder. The police assumed from the outset that they were looking for an insane killer."

"A criminally insane private secretary, to be specific," Oliver said.

"No need to remind me. Such a scheme also fits with your sense of the killer's arrogance."

"Yes, but if we're right, that arrogance is the plan's fatal flaw."

"At least we know the identity of Helen's killer."

"We *may* know it," Oliver said. "We need to be certain. Did you get Claudia Picton to say anything else?"

"Well, she raised the specter of the mysterious Mr. Ogden again."

"Men like Ernie Ogden usually resort to cash payments when they want to make problems disappear. But if money doesn't do the job, he wouldn't hesitate to apply brute force to clean up a mess."

"I've been focused on Nick Tremayne from the start because of Peggy's notes. But what if she was wrong? Do you think that Ogden might go so far as to have someone murder a woman if he thought she was a threat to his star?"

"If he couldn't bribe her or frighten her, it's conceivable," Oliver said. "But I knew Daisy Jennings. Pell knew her, too. Both of us are convinced that money would have worked. There was no reason to murder her to keep her quiet."

"Unless she knew something about Nick Tremayne that was so damaging that Ogden didn't want to take any chances. What if she could implicate Tremayne in Gloria Maitland's murder?"

"Yeah, that might be enough for Ogden to send in the heavy muscle. But if that's true, it means the studio considers Tremayne absolutely crucial to the bottom line."

"I can tell you one thing: Bribery wouldn't have worked with Peggy Hackett."

"You're sure?"

"Peggy was trying to get her career back on track," Irene said. "She wasn't after money. She wanted a headline."

"Get anything else from Picton?"

"She warned me that Ogden can be ruthless. It's obvious she's scared of him. She also said she's decided she's not cut out for Hollywood or Burning Cove. She just wants to get enough money together to go home, get a job, and get married."

"Married?"

"Married. Ever tried it?"

"No," Oliver said. "Came close once upon a time. Got engaged. But it didn't work out. You?"

"Same story. I thought I was going to marry someone once. But it didn't work out."

"The lying, cheating bastard you mentioned in the prop locker?"

"He neglected to mention that he was engaged to someone. When his fiancée informed me of the facts, the lying, cheating bastard thought it was odd that I didn't want to play the part of his mistress."

Oliver nodded with a sage air. "Yeah, that lying and cheating stuff will ruin a perfectly good relationship every time."

Irene propped her elbows on the arms of her chair and put her fingertips together.

"You speak from personal experience, I assume?" she said.

"I do. She was one of my assistants. Ran off with a man I considered a trusted employee. He handled the bookings, ticket sales, and advance publicity for the act."

"I see."

"They eloped to Hawaii."

"Very romantic." Irene tapped her fingertips together once. "Costs money to travel all the way to Hawaii by steamship or airplane. And then there's the price of a hotel room. You must have paid your staff well."

"I like to think so, but evidently Dora and Hubert didn't agree. On their way out the door, they helped themselves to the cash receipts from nearly two months of performances."

"Given that the Amazing Oliver Ward usually played to packed houses, that would have been a tidy sum."

"It was," Oliver said. "They sent me a postcard from Hawaii apologizing and explaining that they could not deny their hearts. Said they hoped I would understand."

"Well, look on the bright side," Irene said. "At least the card didn't say *wish you were here*."

Oliver surprised her with a grin. "Thanks for putting things into perspective. Did you get any revenge?"

"Of the petty sort. The company was in a fierce bidding war with a competitor. The deal involved obtaining the license on a patented device used in the oil business. The lying, cheating bastard was in charge of negotiating the licensing agreement. But I was the one who had done all of the background research. I assembled all the necessary facts and figures. I was about to put everything together in a neat, tidy report for the lying, cheating bastard when the fiancée stopped by the office to inform me of the reality of my situation."

"Can I assume that something dire happened to the neat, tidy report?"

"Nothing at all happened to it because it never came into existence. That was the beauty of my revenge, you see. On my way out the door I dropped the file with all the raw data on the lying, cheating bastard's desk. I knew he wouldn't be able to make heads or tails out of my notes. They were all in shorthand—my own private version."

Oliver smiled. "They might as well have been written in a secret code."

"As for the figures, well, he was the first to admit that he never did have a head for numbers."

"I'm guessing the deal fell through?"

"The rival company obtained the license to the device."

"Was the lying, cheating bastard fired?" Oliver asked.

"Of course not. His fiancée was the daughter of the owner of the company, and she was determined to marry the lying, cheating bastard. The fiancée was daddy's little girl, so the lying, cheating bastard got promoted to vice president."

"Naturally."

"I've heard that revenge rarely works out well. Last I heard the bastard and his wife were living happily ever after somewhere in Connecticut. A real Hollywood ending."

"I doubt it."

"So do I," Irene said. "Truth be told, I even feel sorry for her. After all, she married a lying, cheating bastard."

"People don't change. They are what they are."

"That's my theory, too," Irene said.

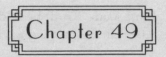

Chapter 49

The dance floor of the Paradise Club was crowded with men in expensively cut dinner jackets and women in delicate gowns. The members of the orchestra, sharply dressed in white coats and black bow ties, were playing a popular number.

The booth where Irene sat with Oliver was one of many similarly intimate seating arrangements scattered around the room. There was a martini in front of Oliver and a pink lady in front of Irene but the glasses were still full. They had not come here to enjoy themselves, Irene thought. They were here so that Oliver could get a closer look at Julian Enright.

She was very conscious of the shadows that cloaked the club. The low, floor-level lighting and the candles on the tables were designed to enhance the intimate atmosphere.

The high backs and the semicircular design of the upholstered booths ensured privacy for the couples that occupied them, but they also made it impossible to see most of the other club patrons once they were seated.

Irene leaned forward and lowered her voice. "How will we know if Enright and Tremayne show up?"

"Don't worry, Nick Tremayne is a rising movie star," Oliver said. "Stars don't walk into a nightclub, they make entrances."

"While trying to give the impression that they don't want to be noticed," Irene concluded. "But maybe he'll decide to come alone."

"Stars don't go out to fashionable nightclubs alone, either."

"I agree that's generally how it works in Hollywood but Enright might not want the attention."

"If he was concerned about being noticed, he wouldn't have become Tremayne's pal."

Irene considered that briefly. "I can't argue with that logic. But it sure seems strange that a killer would want so much attention."

"Who says professional killers can't be just as vain as movie stars? Besides, if Enright is planning to use Tremayne as cover, he has no choice but to get close to him."

Luther Pell materialized out of the shadows. He smiled at Irene, a gleam of masculine appreciation in his eyes.

"You look lovely tonight," he said.

She smiled. "Thank you."

Oliver frowned. "Any sign of Tremayne and Enright?"

"That's what I came to tell you," Luther said. "They just arrived. I've arranged for them to be seated at one of the star booths that borders the dance floor."

"Star booth?" Irene said.

"We reserve the tables around the dance floor for patrons we know want to be seen," Luther explained. "You'll have a good view of Tremayne and Enright. If either of them leaves the club for any reason, one of my security people will keep an eye on him. Let me know if you need anything else."

"Thanks," Oliver said, his tone a little gruff. "We'll do that."

Luther's mouth kicked up in an amused smile. He moved on to greet another couple in a nearby booth, playing the gracious nightclub host to the hilt.

Irene glared at Oliver. "He's not flirting with me, you know. He's just being polite. I'm sure he tells all of the women who come to his club that they look nice."

"Probably." Oliver did not sound convinced. "Here come Tremayne and Enright."

"Fine. Change the subject. See if I care."

His jaw tensed.

"I was just teasing you," she said.

"I know," he muttered.

He wasn't really jealous, she thought; he was just feeling a little possessive. Men got that way when they were sleeping with a woman. It was a perfectly natural, perfectly temporary, perfectly superficial masculine response. It didn't imply a deeper, more abiding emotion.

It occurred to her that she would be irritated if one of the glamorous women in the room happened to stop

by to tell Oliver that he looked very attractive tonight.
A perfectly natural, temporary, superficial female response. It didn't imply a deeper, more abiding emotion.

Heaven help her if it did.

Before she could reflect on that realization, she saw
Nick Tremayne and Julian Enright.

"You were right," she said. "Here they come, and it
would be hard to miss them."

The two men were escorted down an aisle by the
maître d'. A subtle beam of light appeared as if by
magic. It lingered lovingly on Nick Tremayne. Enright
was careful to remain a few steps behind the star, as
if he didn't want to steal the scene, but he managed to
catch the spotlight for a brief moment. In those few
seconds his hair glowed gold and his square-jawed
profile drew the eye. Irene heard a low buzz of excitement rise and fall in the shadows as the crowd became
aware of the new arrivals.

"So that's him," Irene whispered.

"Yes," Oliver said.

"He looks—"

"Handsome? Polished? Sophisticated?"

"Actually, I was thinking that he looks like a movie
star."

The pair was seated in one of the booths that ringed
the dance floor. The maître d' raised his hand in a
signal. A cocktail waitress arrived with a tray of
drinks. She set the glasses down on the table in front
of the men and gracefully departed.

The spotlight dimmed but there was no doubt that
everyone in the club knew that Nick Tremayne and
his friend had arrived.

"Now what?" Irene said.

"Now we wait," Oliver said.

He fell silent.

Irene looked at him. "We should probably look as if we're having a normal conversation."

"What do you want to talk about?"

"There's always the weather."

"Sure," Oliver said. He did not take his eyes off Tremayne and Enright. "Or we could talk about what you're going to do when this situation is finished."

"We could," she agreed. She felt as if she were walking across a frozen lake. One misstep and she would fall into the icy depths.

He waited a moment. When she didn't say anything else, he took his eyes off Tremayne and Enright long enough to shoot her a wary look.

"Well?" he said.

She moved a hand in a small gesture that she hoped appeared casual, as if the answer to the question was of only mild interest.

"I suppose it all depends on what happens here in Burning Cove," she said. "If we can prove that Tremayne killed Gloria Maitland and maybe implicate him in Peggy's death, and if Enright gets arrested for Helen's murder, I will have a brilliant career in journalism ahead of me. But if we can't prove anything, I'll have to change my name again, come up with a new identity, and find another job."

"My hotel can always use the services of a skilled secretary," Oliver said, his tone utterly neutral.

"You've got Elena."

"Yes, and I'm not about to replace her. She's terrific.

But there are other departments that could use a person who is skilled in organizing files and typing. Also, we frequently get calls from guests who want to employ a secretary for one reason or another while they're staying at the hotel."

"But I would be working for you," Irene said.

"Got a problem with that?"

"Yes, I do, as a matter of fact."

"Why?"

"Do I have to spell it out for you? I learned the hard way that it's not a good idea to sleep with the boss. And I'm sure you learned that it's not a good idea to have an affair with one of your employees. Or have you forgotten that postcard from Hawaii?"

Oliver winced. "Right."

She reached across the small table and patted his arm. "Thanks, anyway. I appreciate the offer. But don't worry about me. I've been taking care of myself for a long time. I'll be fine."

Something grim and edgy sparked in his eyes.

"Let's think about that statement for a moment," he said. "A few months ago you were forced to drive all the way across the country and change your name because your previous boss was a professional hotel thief who managed to steal a secret notebook that got her killed. And now the man whom we think murdered her is sitting down there on the dance floor in the same booth as the leading man you suspect of killing your colleague. You call that taking care of yourself?"

Annoyed, she was about to respond, when she saw Nick Tremayne extricate himself from the booth.

"Tremayne is leaving," she whispered.

Oliver turned to follow her gaze. "I don't think so."

They watched Nick cross to a nearby booth where two young, attractive women sat. He evidently invited one of them to dance. She slipped out from behind the table and eagerly followed him onto the dance floor. It was clear, even from a distance, that she was starstruck.

"She'll be dining out on this story for months," Irene said.

Julian Enright rose and walked purposefully up the aisle. He paused midway to speak to a waiter. A few seconds later Enright changed direction.

"He's coming our way," Oliver said. "This will be interesting."

"I can't believe this," Irene said.

"I can. The arrogant son of a bitch can't resist."

Julian came to a halt in front of the table. Irene's pulse jumped and her breath got tight. If she and Oliver were right, she was face-to-face with Helen Spencer's killer.

For his part, Oliver seemed to go preternaturally still.

"Sorry to interrupt," Julian said in an easy manner that implied he didn't give a damn. He smiled at Irene. "Allow me to introduce myself. Julian Enright. You must be Irene Glasson, the reporter for *Whispers*. My friend Nick told me all about you. Evidently you managed to annoy his studio."

"Evidently his studio was *very* annoyed," she said, "because I am now a former reporter."

"Miss Glasson is with me tonight," Oliver said.

Irene could have sworn that the temperature in the room dropped to a glacial chill.

"Is that so?" Enright did not take his eyes off Irene. "It occurs to me, Miss Glasson, that you could improve your relationship with Tremayne's studio by dancing with me. After all, he and I are friends. If we dance together, it will make people think that you are no longer hounding Tremayne."

Irene sensed that Oliver was about to intervene. She used the toe of her shoe to send a subtle under-the-table message to keep him quiet and simultaneously gave Julian a cool smile.

"Did Mr. Tremayne send you over here for that purpose, Mr. Enright?" Irene asked.

"I insist you call me Julian. And I must admit it was my own idea."

"Why?" Irene said.

"Because I'm curious about the woman who has the guts to take on a powerful movie studio."

"As it happens, I lost the fight, Mr. Enright. You can tell Nick Tremayne that he has nothing more to fear from me."

"I'll do that. I'm sure he'll be relieved to hear the news. But it doesn't mean we can't dance."

"You heard Mr. Ward. I'm here with him tonight."

"In that case, it looks like you won't be having much fun, will you? A cripple doesn't make a very good dance partner. Oh well, Irene, perhaps we'll have another opportunity to get to know each other later."

Julian glided away into the shadows. Irene remembered to breathe.

"I can't believe the gall of that man," she said.

"I can. We're right about him. He's here because of you and the notebook."

"You're sure of that?"

"I am now."

Irene watched Julian return to the booth he shared with Nick Tremayne.

"You seem very sure of your read on Julian Enright," she said. "But what about Tremayne? You haven't said too much about him."

"At the moment, Enright is the more dangerous of the two. Tremayne isn't as smart but he's far more cautious. He may be a killer, but if that's the case, he's got a clear motive—to protect his career. It's probably the only thing he cares about. He won't take chances unless he thinks he has no alternative. Right now he's hoping the studio has things under control."

"You know, when I came to Burning Cove, I never expected to spend an evening in a fancy nightclub watching a couple of killers drink and dance."

Oliver tasted his martini and lowered the glass. He watched Tremayne and Enright with an unreadable expression.

"Enright was correct about one thing," he said after a moment.

"What?"

"I'm no good on the dance floor."

She smiled.

"Lucky for you, you've got other talents," she said.

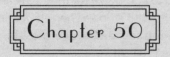

Chapter 50

She awoke to find herself alone in the bed. The sheets were still warm from Oliver's body heat. She waited a moment to see if he would return. But the clink of crystal on glass in the living room told her that he expected to be gone for a while.

She pushed aside the covers, stood, and pulled on her robe. She made her way down the darkened hall and stopped at the entrance of the moon-shadowed living room. At first she did not see him.

"Didn't mean to wake you," he said.

He spoke from the depths of the big, leather-upholstered reading chair. He was wearing a dark robe. His feet were bare. The moonlight slanted across his injured leg propped on the hassock.

She moved across the room and sat down in the other reading chair.

"How bad is it?" she asked.

"No worse than usual," Oliver said.

He swallowed some of the whiskey in his glass. It was clear that her question had irritated him.

She started to apologize for inquiring about the level of his discomfort but stopped herself in the nick of time.

"It wasn't the leg that woke me," he said after a while. "It was Enright."

"Do you think we're wrong about him?"

"No. What I'm thinking is that we need to move fast if we're going to trap him. We need to come up with a way to force his hand. Can't risk letting him take the initiative."

"What if there's nothing to our suspicions?" Irene said. "What if he really is just a rich, starstruck tourist who managed to charm a famous star?"

"If that's the case, he won't take the bait."

"What bait?"

"The notebook. He won't want to take the chance of losing it again. We'll need to set the stage. Get the props and the lighting in place. I'll talk to Chester and Luther in the morning."

"And me," Irene said. "You'll talk to me, too. This is my problem and my story."

"Don't worry, you will be a critical part of the act."

"You've got a plan?"

"I think so, yes."

"Tell me."

He did. When he was finished, she took a deep breath and released it slowly.

"That is . . . very daring," she said. "And risky."

"Like any good illusion, it is actually very simple technically."

"It relies on your read of Enright. If you're wrong—"

"No." Oliver drank some more whiskey and lowered the glass. "Tonight he confirmed everything I sensed about him. He's cold-blooded, arrogant, and impulsive."

Irene shivered. "I wonder how many people he has murdered."

"We'll probably never know," Oliver said, "but I very much doubt that Helen Spencer was the first."

He swallowed a sip of his whiskey, set the glass aside, and absently started to massage his left leg. Irene watched him for a moment and then she got up, knelt beside his chair, and put her hands on his thigh. She could feel the pain-tautened muscles and sinews beneath the fabric of his robe.

"Let me do this," she said.

"Forget it."

She ignored him and started to massage his leg, applying gentle but firm pressure.

To her surprise he stopped arguing. After a while he even seemed to relax.

"Have you ever told anyone what went wrong in your final performance?" she asked.

"Accidents sometimes happen when you mess around with dangerous things like guns."

"I don't think it was an accident."

He went very still.

"What makes you so sure?" he finally asked.

"The fact that you won't talk about it."

"No one likes to talk about a failure, certainly not a career-killing mistake."

"You've got a right to your secrets," she said.

"You had a right to your secrets, too, but now I know some of them."

"Yes, you do."

"My secrets are dead and buried," Oliver said. "But sometimes I find myself dealing with a ghost."

She didn't ask any more questions, just continued to knead his leg. After a time he started to talk.

"It was the Cage of Death illusion," he said. "Geddings created the original version but Uncle Chester and I made a few changes to enhance the audience appeal."

"Who is Geddings?"

"He was a friend and one of the most skilled magicians I have ever known. He taught me a great deal. He went by the title of the Great Geddings."

"Never heard of him."

"That was his problem. He was incredibly talented when it came to the technical aspects of an illusion but he wasn't much of a performer. Success on the stage is all about telling a story. The ability to draw the audience into the magic—make people willing participants in the illusion—is what separates the stars from the merely competent. For all his skill, Geddings couldn't read a crowd. He couldn't establish the rapport that's needed onstage. But he taught me a great deal and we made a good team."

"What happened?"

"We started out as partners. Billed the act as Geddings and Ward. But it soon became clear that, although I wasn't better than Geddings in the technical sense, I was the one who could attract and hold an audience's attention. We changed the name of the show to the Amazing Oliver Ward Show."

"Which became famous."

"We did quite well. Then the disaster occurred."

"That would have been about two years ago?"

"Right." Oliver was silent for a moment. "We were in San Francisco. We had a full house. After being suitably locked up in the usual flashy chains and manacles, I was lowered into a steel cage. The cage was hoisted several feet off the floor."

"To show the audience that you couldn't get out through a trapdoor at the bottom."

"You learn fast." Oliver drank a little more whiskey. "A curtain was lowered. The lights were focused on the draped cage. All standard effect stuff but the audience loved it. At that point a mysterious figure wearing a cape and a mask appeared. He circled the cage a few times, took out a pistol, and fired three shots into the drapery. Naturally the pistol was supposed to fire blanks."

"Obviously that wasn't the case."

"The pistol was loaded with real bullets. Two of them caught me in the thigh. Did a lot of damage to muscle and tissue but just barely missed an artery. I was lucky."

"*Lucky?* How can you say that?"

"If I had not been partway out of the cage at the time, all three bullets would have gone straight into my chest."

Stunned, Irene stopped massaging his leg. "I don't understand."

"I was wrapped in a lot of chains. They looked impressive but the whole assembly was designed to fall away when I unlocked a single lock. One of the assistants slipped the key to me just as I was lowered into the cage. I tried to use it as soon as the curtain was lowered around the cage. But it was the wrong key."

"What did you do?"

"I had never really felt comfortable relying on an assistant to slip me a key. I always carried a backup hidden in my hair. But it took me a few seconds to realize that the first key was the wrong one and then a few more seconds to get the backup key and insert it into the lock. When the masked assistant fired the first two shots, I was only partway out of the cage. I normally would have been all the way out at that point."

"So it wasn't an accident. The rumors were true. Someone tried to murder you."

"It was all carefully planned, from the false key to the real bullets."

"But who would want to kill you?" Irene paused. "That pair who eloped to Hawaii?"

"No. While I was recovering in the hospital, Chester conducted his own private investigation. It didn't take Sherlock Holmes to come up with a suspect. There was only one person who hated me enough to murder me onstage in front of a packed audience."

"Of course," Irene said. "Your friend and partner, Geddings."

"That is . . . very perceptive of you."

"You became what he had always wanted to be, a brilliant magician who could thrill audiences. A star."

"He had helped me become a skilled magician but he was jealous of his own creation."

"Geddings didn't create you, Oliver. Your talent is yours and yours alone. Geddings may have helped you perfect your skills, but he had to know that you would have become a success with or without him. That's why he was consumed with jealousy. No matter how skilled he was, he would never be the star that you became."

"Well, he made sure that my stardom came to an end."

"What happened to him?"

"Geddings? He died a few days later, shortly after the doctors concluded that I wasn't going to die or lose my leg."

"How?"

"He put some more real bullets into the gun and shot himself in the head."

"Suicide."

"He left a wife and a son behind."

"Do they know what he tried to do?"

"No," Oliver said. "There was no reason to tell them. Chester and I let the accident story stand."

"What about the other assistants? Did they figure it out?"

"I'm sure Willie did. Some of the others probably did, too. But we don't talk about it."

"A show business family secret?"

"Something like that, yes."

"What happened to Geddings's wife and son?"

"Geddings didn't leave them much. He was never good with money." Oliver set the empty glass aside. "I take care of his wife and son."

Irene smiled. "Of course you do."

Chapter 51

The following evening Julian was sharing a booth with Tremayne in the heavily shadowed hotel lounge when he heard the siren in the distance. It occurred to him that it was the first time he had been aware of a siren since his arrival in Burning Cove. One of the reasons, he reflected, was that the hotel was located nearly a mile outside of town. That lessened the odds of hearing emergency vehicles. It also increased the odds that the siren blaring in the night was headed toward the hotel.

He paused his Manhattan halfway to his mouth and glanced toward the exit he had marked the first time he walked into the lounge. It was located at the end of a darkened hallway, just past the men's room.

Regardless of whether he was working or not, whenever he entered a confined space, he always made certain to identify at least one escape route that could be utilized in the event that things went wrong. His father had insisted that he establish the habit at the start of his career, and he had to admit that it had saved his neck on more than one occasion.

"Wonder what's going on?" Nick said.

His voice was slurred by the cocktails he had been drinking steadily since dinner.

The wailing siren halted abruptly.

Julian checked the bar. Willie was reaching for the phone. She spoke quietly into the receiver and then replaced it.

"Nothing to be concerned about," Willie announced calmly. "It's not a fire. There's been an accident in one of the villas. The ambulance has just arrived. Everything is under control."

But she looked troubled, Julian decided.

"Fuck," Nick muttered. "If it's another dead woman, I've been with you all evening, right?"

"Right," Julian said.

It was the truth.

He kept his eye on Willie, who was doing her best to look cool and professional. He could tell she was concerned, though. She kept glancing out the window. There was nothing to be seen because the high hedges and the stucco walls that enclosed the hotel gardens blocked the view.

A few curiosity seekers wandered outside with their drinks to find out what was going on. Willie disappeared briefly, as well. When she returned, she was grim-faced.

The siren started to scream again.

Several of the people who had left a few minutes earlier returned. The rumors circulated swiftly through the crowd. Two men crowded up to the bar to order fresh drinks. Both were in their mid-thirties. One was going bald. The other wore a badly tailored jacket.

An attractive woman in a snug black dress and high heels slipped between the two men.

"What was all the excitement about?" the woman asked in a sultry voice.

The two men almost fell over themselves in an attempt to answer the question.

"Someone said the ambulance went to Oliver Ward's villa," Baldy announced with authority, trying to impress the woman. "Heard he fell down the stairs."

"They found him unconscious," Bad Jacket explained. "Lot of blood."

Julian listened very closely.

"Ambulance attendants told someone Ward probably broke some bones, but it's the head injury they're worried about," Baldy added. "They're taking him to the hospital. They don't know if he'll make it."

"Hell of a thing." Bad Jacket shook his head. "He survives that warehouse fire only to fall down a flight of stairs."

"Wonder what he was doing going up and down stairs with that bad leg," Baldy mused.

Bad Jacket snickered. "Five will get you ten he went up those stairs to pay his houseguest a late-night visit. Heard she was the one who called the ambulance. Someone said she went to the hospital with him."

"Women," Baldy said. "They'll get you one way or another."

Willie dabbed at her eyes with a white towel. A moment later she said something to the other bartender, a middle-aged man, and disappeared through a side door.

Julian made his way to the bar.

"What can I get for you?" the bartender asked.

"Another Manhattan," Julian said. "And one for my friend. I heard there's been an accident."

"Yeah. Just found out they took the boss to the hospital."

"Why did the other bartender leave?"

"Willie said she was going to drive to the hospital to see for herself just how bad things are. They don't know if he'll make it. If he doesn't, we'll all be looking for new jobs."

The bartender set two Manhattans on the bar. Julian carried them back to the booth. Nick grabbed his glass and took a long swallow.

A short time later Julian guided a very drunk Nick Tremayne to his villa. He did not bother to turn on the lights. He eased Tremayne down onto the bed.

Tremayne muttered something unintelligible.

Julian paused. "What?"

"Said when are you gonna take care of that damned reporter?"

"Soon."

"Good."

Julian let himself out into the night.

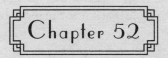

Chapter 52

The only light inside the darkened villa came from the moon. It was all Julian needed to find his way down the hall. He had brought along a small flashlight to use once he began a serious search. But first he wanted to get an overview of the place.

He had come in through the patio. The lock on the back door was good quality but it was standard issue. You'd think a magician would have installed better locks.

He did a quick walk-through, noting the exit points. There were several but they all opened onto the gardens that surrounded the villa. There were only two ways out of the gardens—the front gate and the one at the back.

Upstairs in the guest bedroom he discovered a

narrow, decorative balcony. In a pinch he could go over the railing and drop down into the gardens.

Satisfied that he had noted all the exits, he took a good look around the guest bedroom. It was obvious from the clothes in the closet and the items arranged on the dressing table that it was the room Irene Glasson was using.

He didn't expect to find the notebook conveniently stashed in a dresser drawer or under the mattress, but you never knew. People made odd decisions when it came to choosing a hiding place. Helen Spencer came to mind. She'd had a very fine safe, one he'd wasted several minutes cracking. But the only thing he found inside was the necklace.

He'd considered helping himself to the jewelry—the gems were of excellent quality—but by then he knew enough about Spencer to be certain that the damned thing was hot. He didn't have any connections in the underground gemstone market. Locating a fence he could trust would have been a high-risk venture. The old man would not have approved. Besides, he didn't need the money.

When he was satisfied that the notebook was not in the bedroom, he went downstairs to continue the search. On his initial foray, he had noted the safe in the magician's study, but he had learned his lesson at Spencer's mansion. He saved the safe for last.

Unlike the door locks, the one that secured the safe was modern and fairly sophisticated in design. He took that as a good sign. Something valuable was inside.

He slipped the knife out of its sheath and set it on

the floor within easy reach. Then he took out the stethoscope and went to work.

When he heard the last muffled click, a thrill of anticipation swept through him. He took a deep breath and opened the door. There was a thick envelope inside.

He removed the envelope, opened the unsealed flap, and switched on his flashlight.

There was a leather-bound notebook inside.

He took it out, flipped it open, and aimed the flashlight at a few of the pages. They were covered in numbers and equations. A euphoric triumph jolted through him. He had the notebook. Once it had been safely delivered to the old man, he could return to Burning Cove to take his time with Irene Glasson. She would pay for putting him to so much trouble.

He closed the safe, picked up the knife, and got to his feet.

"I've been waiting for you, Enright."

Ward's voice came from somewhere out in the shadowed hallway.

Julian froze. The realization that he had walked into a trap sent a shock of panic through him.

"Where are you, Ward? Show yourself, you bastard."

There was no response.

Now he had a choice to make. There were only two ways out of the study: the hallway and the glass doors that opened onto the patio. It seemed unlikely that Ward was working alone.

"Congratulations on your speedy recovery," Julian said. "The rumors in the bar had you at death's door."

"Don't bother running," Ward said. "All the exits from this villa are covered."

Julian listened intently. Ward's voice seemed to emanate from the living room. He had to assume Ward was armed. If he wasn't lying about the cops, they were no doubt covering all the other escape routes.

That left his one last foolproof exit strategy. The old man wouldn't be thrilled that Julian had been forced to use it. There would be another boring lecture about his inclination toward impulsive action. But the present situation was a perfect example of why he carried the license in the first place.

He went to the doorway of the study.

"I'm coming out with my hands up, Ward. This is all a huge misunderstanding."

"Let's clear up that misunderstanding," Ward said. "Who hired you to kill Helen Spencer?"

"I didn't kill her. I'm a private detective from New York. I've got a license I can show you. I work for a company called Enright Investigations. Family firm. We were hired to find the woman you know as Irene Glasson. She stole a certain notebook. Her real name is Anna Harris, by the way."

"Who hired you?"

"Let's just say our client represents a certain foreign government, one that is willing to pay very well for the notebook, no questions asked."

"What about Saltwood Laboratory?"

"I see you've been doing some investigating of your own. Unfortunately, Saltwood made the mistake of going to the FBI for help. The investigation has ground to a standstill. The G-men are wringing their hands.

Their biggest fear, of course, is that Atherton's notes will wind up in the possession of an unfriendly foreign power."

"Which is exactly what you intend, right?"

Julian tried to curb his impatience but he was getting nervous. It was time to end things.

"Business is business," he said. "The notebook will go to the highest bidder. Isn't that what you had planned? Your problem is that you don't have the connections it takes to find the deep-pocket customers for an item as exotic as Atherton's notes. You're just an innkeeper. Enright has a buyer lined up. In fact, it looks like there will be an auction. I suggest that you and I negotiate."

"What makes you think I'm trying to figure out how to market the notebook?"

"I'm not a fool. You figured out the notebook is worth a fortune. You need Enright's help to sell it."

"I'm interested."

Julian was almost giddy with relief. Now he was on firm ground. Suddenly everything made sense. He'd walked into a trap, all right, but not the kind he'd assumed at first. There were no cops waiting outside. Ward wouldn't be talking about a deal if that were the case.

Julian allowed himself a small smile. *You have no idea what you're doing, you son of a bitch. You're just a washed-up magician who bungled his last performance so badly he nearly died. You're way out of your depth. I'll show you how the Enrights do business.*

"What price did you have in mind?" he said.

"I know the notebook is worth killing for," Ward

said. "That tells me it's worth a great deal to the people who hired you."

"A hundred grand," Julian said, plucking a figure out of thin air.

"Not good enough. I need to clear a quarter mil."

"That's a lot of money," Julian said. "Planning to buy another hotel?"

He tried to sound reluctant, but it was all he could do to keep the rising tide of triumph out of his voice.

"I owe Luther Pell two fifty," Ward said.

That explained a lot, Julian thought.

"How did a smart guy like you get himself in so deep?" he said. "They say Pell's got mob connections."

"You don't need to know the details. I doubt if your client will argue about the price—not if the notebook is as important as you seem to think."

"It is. Trust me."

"All right. Make the deal. When I get the money, you'll get the notebook. Until then it stays in my safe."

Ward didn't realize that his safe had been cracked. He assumed the notebook was still inside.

Julian was dazed by his own good luck; a euphoric relief set fire to his blood.

"All right," he said. He had to fight to keep his voice reasonably cool. "I'll telephone my boss first thing in the morning. He'll have to set up the auction. It's going to take a little time to put the deal together. Maybe a couple of days."

"Fine. But meanwhile you will continue to be a guest here at my hotel where I can keep an eye on you. You don't leave the grounds."

"Understood," Julian said.

"My security people will be watching you."

"Sure."

Julian adjusted his right hand on the hilt of the knife, finding the position that allowed him the most control. Now that the bargain had been made, there was a very good possibility that the target would get careless. Talking about large sums of money had a tendency to do that to people—especially when you were having the discussion with a man who was in trouble with a shady character like Pell.

Come on, you bastard. All I need is one clear opportunity.

"Are we finished here?" he asked.

"Looks like it. See you tomorrow."

"Sure."

Just a dumb, failed magician, Julian thought.

He made his way down the shadowed hallway. When he reached the living room, he held his breath. There was always the possibility that Ward had lied to him about wanting to make a deal. But that was unlikely. He wouldn't have set up the trap if he wasn't desperate to find a buyer for the notebook.

Julian crossed the living room, hurrying through the wedge of moonlight. It was the point at which he was most visible and, therefore, most vulnerable. If Ward had deceived him, the shot would come during the second or two it took him to gain the shadows of the kitchen.

There was no flash of light. No gun roared.

He made it into the darkened front hall and paused to look back across the living room. A figure was clearly silhouetted against the glass doors that opened onto the patio. Ward's cane thudded softly on the tiles. Julian heard the rasp of shoe leather on the tiled floor.

Got you, Julian thought.

The throw was so fast and so clean that Ward never even got off a shot.

The blade went home, sinking deep into human flesh.

His target collapsed with a heavy, very final-sounding thud. The cane clattered on the floor.

Julian did not waste any time making certain of the kill. He trusted his own skill and talent. If Ward wasn't dead already, he would bleed out as soon as someone removed the knife.

He raced outside into the night. He had the notebook, but now there was a dead man, and that was a problem. Escape was his first priority. Ward's car was parked in front of the villa. The fastest car in California.

He ran across the street and opened the car door. He could start a car without a key if necessary, but he wasn't worried about having to waste time doing so. It was not uncommon for people to leave the key in the ignition. That went double in crime-free small towns like Burning Cove. Besides, who would dare to steal Oliver Ward's car? Everyone in town probably recognized it on sight. But it was unlikely that anyone in L.A. would know it. He would be in the city by dawn.

He was not disappointed. The key was in the ignition. His luck was holding.

He got behind the wheel and started the vehicle. The big engine purred to life.

He had a hundred miles to drive on a foggy, twisty road but he was a very skilled driver. The light mist would serve him well, because it would keep other drivers from venturing out.

Julian piloted the sleek vehicle quietly away from the villa, found Cliff Road, and settled down to drive.

He'd been forced to leave some good clothes and a few personal items behind in his hotel room, but they could easily be replaced. He had to get the notebook to New York as soon as possible. He would catch a plane in L.A. Once Atherton's notes were safely in the old man's hands, he would return to California to take his time with Irene Glasson.

Chapter 53

Julian had been driving for half an hour or so when the lights of another car sparked briefly in his rearview mirror.

Just another motorist braving the fog. No need to be alarmed.

He eased his foot down on the throttle and accelerated out of a tight curve.

The lights vanished from his mirror.

Five minutes went by. Ten. The lights from the other vehicle flashed again, briefly, in the mirror. Again he accelerated. Again the lights disappeared.

He sped up but almost immediately had to brake for a sharp curve in the road. The tires squealed in protest. There was no barrier at the edge of the pavement. If he miscalculated, he risked going off the high cliffs. He would plunge straight down onto the rocks at the water's edge.

He came out of the next curve a little too fast and immediately had to stomp on the brakes again. He glanced at the mirror. The lights were gone.

There was no wailing siren. The other car didn't seem to be trying to overtake him. Not the cops, he told himself. Just another late-night driver trying to make it to L.A. by dawn.

But the fog was growing thicker now. He could not risk driving any faster.

The thrill of his escape from Burning Cove faded.

He started to sweat but he reminded himself that he was driving the fastest car in California. So much power under the hood. He could outrun any other vehicle on the road.

Chapter 54

"Faster," Luther said. "We can't risk losing him in this fog."

"If he makes it to New York," Irene said, "the police and the FBI won't be able to touch him."

"We won't lose him," Oliver said.

The Oldsmobile belonged to Chester, who had done some work on it, but it wasn't nearly as fast as the modified Cord. Speed wasn't necessary, Oliver thought. The only thing that mattered was that they didn't lose the Cord. But that was unlikely. On a twisting ribbon of pavement like Cliff Road, what mattered most was the driver's skill and his knowledge of the curves.

Oliver was behind the wheel because they had all agreed that he was the best driver. Luther was in the front passenger seat. In the dim glow of the instrument panel, he looked intense. Irene was in the back, draped over the front seat, peering through the windshield.

"If he turns off on a side road—" Luther began.

"He won't," Oliver said. "I know that bastard. He thinks he won."

The first part of the act had gone off without a hitch, which was somewhat amazing given the very short span of time they'd had to put it together, Oliver thought. There had been no practical way to rehearse. He and Luther had done several walk-throughs at the villa, trying to anticipate Enright's every move. Chester had pulled a couple of the old props out of the storage locker and reworked them. He had padded a figure with material that he claimed would sound a lot like human flesh when a knife or bullet struck it.

Based on the description of Helen Spencer's murder, Oliver had been almost certain that the killer preferred to use a knife, not only because it made less noise but because he liked his work. But it hadn't really mattered which weapon Enright chose to use.

Willie had been briefed on her role, and she had performed it brilliantly. Just like old times, Oliver thought. He had a sneaking hunch that Willie had enjoyed herself.

Some of the guests had witnessed Irene following the stretcher into the back of the ambulance. She appeared to be sobbing hysterically. Persuading the ambulance crew to make a practice run to the villa that night was simple enough. Oliver had told the hospital authorities that he wanted to test the hotel's emergency response system. He had also offered a hefty donation to the hospital and paid the driver and attendants for their time.

It had all been an elaborate show for an audience of one, but until the curtain rose there had been no way to be certain that the killer would attend the performance.

Oliver had tried to persuade Irene not to accompany Luther and him on the Cliff Road chase, but there was no talking her out of it.

"He's picking up speed again," Luther said. "I think he's spotted us."

"He can't know it's us," Irene said. "He thinks Oliver is dead or very badly hurt."

"He's smart," Luther said. "Maybe he's starting to realize he's been tricked."

"If that's the case, he'll start taking even more chances," Oliver said. "That would be good."

Luther glanced at him. "You did say he was the impulsive type."

Oliver accelerated gently.

Up ahead the lights of the stolen car appeared briefly in the fog before vanishing around another curve.

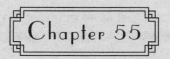

Chapter 55

Julian got only the smallest of warnings—a slight mushiness in the previously very crisp steering.

He was driving Oliver Ward's car. A real engineering marvel. There couldn't be a problem with the steering. It wasn't possible.

Ward had tricked him once tonight but there was no way the magician could have known that he would take the custom-built car.

No one would dare steal Oliver Ward's car.

No one except me.

He went into the next curve too fast. He stomped on the brakes and had to overcorrect with the steering. The tires shrieked.

The brakes and the steering suddenly went to mush. He was going into a turn much too fast. He had no control.

In the next horrifying instant, the fastest car in California was airborne, sailing over the high cliffs.

He had just enough time to realize that this time he had underestimated the target, that there was no exit strategy.

He screamed, just as so many of his targets had screamed. He wanted to beg for his life but there was no one to hear him.

His last conscious thought was that he could not be hurtling toward his own death. It was not possible. No target could fool him. He was Julian Enright.

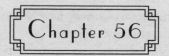

Chapter 56

Oliver accelerated out of a turn and realized that he could not see the lights of the Cord.

Luther said, "He may have found a side road."

"There aren't any near here," Oliver said.

"It's possible he's way ahead of us," Irene said.

Black skid marks came up in the Oldsmobile's headlights.

"I don't think so," Oliver said.

He braked and brought the car to a halt on a narrow turnout. Opening the door, he grabbed his cane and a flashlight and climbed out. He stood for a few seconds, listening. The only thing he could hear was the endless crash of the surf on the rocks below the cliff.

He took his gun from the holster. Luther and Irene emerged from the car and followed him. Luther took out his gun and a flashlight. Irene held her small pistol in one hand.

"Stay back," Oliver said to her. "Please. If he's still alive, he'll be armed."

It didn't take long to find the Cord. It was a crumpled mass of metal on the rocky beach below. The smell of gasoline was strong in the air.

Julian Enright had been flung out of the vehicle. He had landed on the rocks a short distance from the wreckage. His neck was twisted at an odd angle.

Luther looked at Oliver and said, "You were right about him. Definitely the impulsive type."

"He was an easy read," Oliver said. "He was so damned sure he was smarter than everyone else. He was the master puppeteer who manipulated others. People like that never believe they can be manipulated, too."

"What about the fake notebook?" Irene asked.

"He had it when he ran out of the villa," Oliver said. "It must be down there in the wreckage."

"I'll go down and take a look," Luther said.

Irene glanced at him. "Is that absolutely necessary?"

"We need to be sure," Oliver said. "I can't go down there, not with this damned leg."

"That leaves me," Luther said. "I'll get a rope."

He went to the car, opened the trunk, and took out a length of rope. He removed his jacket and pulled on a pair of driving gloves.

Irene held the flashlight steady so that Oliver was free to handle the rope.

Luther scrambled down to the wreckage. He checked the body first. He put his fingers on Enright's throat.

He looked up and shook his head. Next he went through Enright's clothes and removed a wallet. He flipped through it briefly and then stuck it back in the pocket of Enright's jacket.

A short time later he located the envelope that contained the fake notebook.

He made his way back up the cliffs, took the notebook out of the envelope, and handed it to Oliver.

"I'm amazed it survived," Oliver said.

Luther looked at him. "We should get rid of it. We don't want people asking unnecessary questions."

Oliver looked down at the wreckage. The smell of gasoline was getting stronger.

"Got a match?" he said.

"Thought you'd never ask."

Luther handed him a glossy black matchbook with the words *Paradise Club* printed in gold on the front.

Oliver struck a match and touched it to one of the pages in the notebook. When he was sure the fire had taken hold, he tossed the burning notebook down onto the wreckage.

The modified Cord exploded into flames.

"Nothing better than fire to clean up a scene," Luther said.

Chapter 57

The four of them were gathered in the living room of Casa del Mar. Oliver was in his big chair. Luther was pouring himself a whiskey. Chester was mourning the loss of his magnificent creation.

Irene paced the room, restless and unnerved, still shaky with relief. After four long months it was difficult to believe that the personal nightmare that had chased her to California was finished.

"I called the police station," Oliver said. He stretched out his bad leg. "I explained that someone broke into my place, cracked the safe, and stole my car while I was busy with the emergency drill. When they find the wreckage and recover the body, I'll identify Enright as a guest here at the hotel. I'll suggest that he must have gotten drunk and decided to pull a stunt."

"It will be interesting to see who shows up to claim the body," Irene said.

"Yes," Oliver said. "Most wealthy families would commission a funeral director to take possession of the body and accompany it back east."

"A distraught, grieving parent might feel compelled to make the trip out west himself," Irene said. "Especially if he's hoping to find a certain notebook."

"If someone from the Enright family does show up, we'll make sure that he or she is given the charred remains of the notebook. The pages will have been destroyed but some remnants of the cover will probably survive. Leather doesn't burn easily."

Irene looked at him. "Do you think it might be recognized as a fake?"

It was Chester who responded. "Nah. I did a damned good job with those calculations, if I do say so myself. It would take an expert to figure out that they're gibberish, and he'd need most of the notebook to verify that—not just the burnt leather cover and some charred pages."

Oliver sank deeper into the reading chair and rotated a glass of whiskey slowly between his palms. "The illusion is good. It will fool the audience if necessary."

Chester peered at him. "You've still got the real notebook. What are you going to do about it?"

"I'm working on that," Oliver said. "One more thing. Willie and the others know that they helped capture a suspected hotel thief. They're aware that the thief took off in my car. In the morning when the police find the accident site, everyone will know the burglar drove the Cord off a cliff. Everyone will assume he lost control."

Chester shrugged. "That was exactly what happened."

Luther lounged against the wall, whiskey glass in hand. "Obviously. Everyone knows that car was unique. That's why you never let anyone else drive it. Too dangerous."

"Just another drunk-driving accident," Chester said.

"One that took care of a professional killer," Oliver said.

"We had to be sure," Luther added. "We couldn't let him escape. He would have come back."

Irene looked at the others. They had taken a terrible risk and now they were forever bound by a dark secret. The fact that Oliver and Chester had made some last-minute modifications to the brakes and steering on the fastest car in California would never go beyond the four of them.

"More whiskey, anyone?" Luther asked.

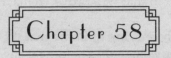

Chapter 58

He felt her leave the bed.

He opened his eyes and watched her pull on a robe and pad quietly out the door. She vanished into the shadowed hallway.

He shoved aside the covers, got up, shrugged into a robe, and followed her.

She was in the living room, gazing out over the garden and the pool to the ocean beyond. The first light of dawn was brightening the sky.

He moved to stand behind her and rested his hands lightly on her shoulders. Her tension was palpable. Gently he began to massage the taut muscles.

"Didn't mean to wake you," she said.

"You're thinking about Peggy Hackett, aren't you?" he asked.

"Now that Enright is dead, I can't stop thinking

about Peggy Hackett, Gloria Maitland, Daisy Jennings, and that other woman, Betty Scott, who died in Seattle nearly a year ago. I know I'm missing some crucial detail but I have no idea what it could be."

"Some detail that will prove Tremayne murdered all of them?"

"Yes. It's horrifying to know that I'll have to wait until another woman dies before I'll have a chance to find a fresh angle or a new source."

"I understand."

She reached up to grip one of his hands. "I know you do."

They stood quietly for a time.

"Sooner or later another woman *will* die," she said after a while.

"You're sure of that?"

"There's a pattern."

"One of the things I learned as a magician is that the mind can play tricks when it comes to seeing patterns. If we want to see them, we can usually find a way to do it. It's human nature. There are a lot of illusions and effects that rely exclusively on that fact."

She turned to face him. "Four women are dead. They're all connected to Nick Tremayne in one way or another. That's not an illusion, that's a pattern."

"You've been a little distracted lately."

"That's for sure."

"Maybe it's time to go back to the beginning and try to view everything in your notes with clear eyes," he said. "Stop looking for the pattern you think you see."

"What should I look for?"

"A new pattern."

She thought about that. "Maybe you're right. It's not like I've got a better idea. I keep circling back to the question I've had from the beginning. Maybe starting over will give me a fresh perspective."

"What's the question?"

"Nick Tremayne's name has been linked to several women in the two years he's been in Hollywood. But only four of them have died under mysterious circumstances. My question is, what did they know that got them killed?"

"Good question."

She put her arms around him. He wrapped her close and held her very tight.

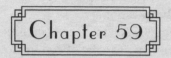

Chapter 59

They ate breakfast on the patio—fresh melon, scrambled eggs, toast, and a large pot of coffee—all delivered as if by magic.

"I could get used to room service," Irene said.

"It has its advantages," Oliver said.

"So now we wait until the police confirm Enright's identity and notify his family," Irene said. "What if it turns out he was a fraud?"

"It's possible that the man who went over the cliff in my car stole Julian Enright's identity, but I doubt it," Oliver said. "It would have been too risky, for one thing. There was always the chance that he would have run into someone from the Enrights' social circle on vacation out here in California. But that aside, I'm sure the bastard was who he claimed to be."

"Because of his arrogance?"

"He was a man born to wealth and privilege who thought he could get away with murder."

"And espionage. He was willing to sell vital national secrets to some foreign interests. That makes him a traitor, as well as a killer."

"Yes, it does."

Oliver finished his coffee, kissed her lightly on the mouth, and levered himself to his feet.

Just like a comfortably married couple, Irene thought. Except that they weren't married.

Details.

"I've got to take care of some business in the office," Oliver said. "Security is keeping a close eye on Tremayne around the clock. In addition, I'll make sure one of the guards is stationed outside of this villa. Promise me you won't leave this place alone."

"I promise," she said.

She waited until he left, and then she went back inside the villa to collect her notes. She took them outside onto the patio, determined to start at the very beginning.

She would begin the way Peggy Hackett had taught her—by setting down every hard fact she had in her possession, regardless of how ephemeral it seemed. She would follow every loose end. She would ask the question that she had been asking from the very beginning—why the four women had died.

They had each known something, she thought, or discovered something that threatened Nick Tremayne. It was the only explanation that made any sense.

An hour later she sat back and looked at her notes, searching for some pattern that she had not noticed previously. Nothing. The only thing that stood out was the fact that all of the victims except the first one had lived in Los Angeles.

She returned to the short, cryptic note that she had found when she cleaned out Peggy's desk. It included the name Betty Scott, the woman found dead in a bathtub in Seattle.

And there was a phone number.

Peggy's advice whispered through her. *When you're stuck, go back over every detail. Find one more detail—because there is always one more detail.*

She rose, went into the living room, and picked up the phone.

"Operator, I'd like to call a Seattle newspaper . . . No, I don't care which one . . . Yes, the *Post-Intelligencer* sounds fine."

The phone was answered by a receptionist who sounded rushed. "How may I direct your call?"

"I'm a reporter in Burning Cove, California. I'd like to speak with one of your crime reporters."

"Hold one moment. I'll connect you."

A short time later Irene found herself talking to a bored-sounding individual who identified himself as George.

"You want me to dig out a year-old obituary notice? Why should I do you any favors?"

"Because I'm working on an investigation that involves Nick Tremayne."

"The actor?" The boredom was replaced by a flicker of interest. "What have you got?"

"I'm chasing leads at this point. But if you give me a hand, I promise to call you as soon as I've got a story you can run with."

"Nick Tremayne, huh. All right. Give me time to go down to the morgue and pull some clips." He paused. "I'll have to reverse the charges."

"That's fine."

George called back fifteen minutes later.

"I found the Scott obit but there's not much info here," he said. "I don't see how this is going to help. Scott slipped and fell in her bathtub. Worked at a café. Survived by an aunt who lives here in Seattle."

There is always one more detail.

"I need the name of the aunt."

"Dorothy Hodges. Look, what have you got on Tremayne?"

"I have to move quickly here. I give you my word I'll contact you as soon as I've got all the facts."

Irene hung up and made the next call.

"Operator, please connect me with Dorothy Hodges in Seattle, Washington. No, I don't have the number or the address. Yes, I'll hold."

It turned out that there were three D. Hodgeses in the Seattle telephone directory. The operator connected Irene to the right one on the second attempt. A middle-aged woman answered.

"This is Dorothy Hodges. Whom did you say is calling?"

"You don't know me, Miss Hodges. I'm a journalist

doing some background research on a movie actor named Nick Tremayne."

"Heavens, dear, you must have the wrong number. I don't know Nick Tremayne. I don't know any movie stars. This is Seattle, not Hollywood."

"I have reason to believe that Tremayne may have known your niece, Betty."

"Betty? She passed almost a year ago."

"Yes, I know, Miss Hodges. Did you ever meet any of Betty's boyfriends?"

"No. I know that, for a time, she dated a young man who wanted to become an actor. Betty fancied herself in love with him. But she never brought him around to introduce him. I don't remember his name."

"I understand Betty lived in a boardinghouse."

"She was a bit wild, I'm afraid. Ran with a fast crowd. I had to insist that she move out. I just couldn't tolerate the smoking and the drinking and the partying. She visited me once in a while when she needed rent money. All she ever talked about was her dream of going to Hollywood with her boyfriend. She was sure they would both become stars. Poor, foolish girl."

"Did she ever do any real acting?"

"Oh, yes. She made a couple of films here in Seattle. She was very excited about them. But they never got released."

"What happened?"

"The studio burned down a few months before Betty died. She told me that all of the films including the ones she made were destroyed. Between you and me, I did wonder exactly what sort of movies they were, if you take my meaning."

The kind of movies that could ruin a rising star's career, maybe, Irene thought.

"I understand, Miss Hodges. You said you never met any of Betty's boyfriends. What about her girlfriends? Did you know any of them? I'd really like to talk to someone who knew Betty well."

"Why are you so curious about my poor niece?"

"It's a long story, Miss Hodges. But I think it's possible that Betty's death wasn't an accident. I think she was murdered."

"Murdered." Shock reverberated through the telephone line. "But that can't be true. They said that Betty slipped and fell in the bathtub."

"I know, Miss Hodges. But as it happens, she's not the only woman to die that way. I'm hoping that if I track down someone who knew about those films that Betty made, I might be able to get to the truth."

"I see. Well, I'm afraid the only girlfriend that Betty ever mentioned was another aspiring actress. She lived at the same boardinghouse. As I recall, she was in those films that Betty made here in Seattle."

One more detail, Irene thought.

"Do you remember the name of the other actress?" she asked, hardly daring to hope.

"No. But I'm sure the woman who ran the boardinghouse can tell you. As I said, Betty and her friend both had rooms there. Those two had a falling-out at some point. I do remember that much."

"You mean their friendship ended?"

"Oh, yes. Betty didn't talk about it much, at least not to me, but she was real cut up about it."

"What broke up the friendship?"

"What do you think? A man, of course. Betty said that her actor boyfriend ran off to Hollywood with the other girl."

"Do you remember what sort of work Betty's girlfriend did? Aspiring actresses usually have to support themselves while they wait to be discovered."

"Yes, I know. Betty was a waitress."

"What about her girlfriend?"

"I seem to recall that she worked in an office but I can't remember any details. Like I said, she ran off with that actor fellow quite a while before Betty died."

"Thank you. You've been very helpful, Miss Hodges."

"You're welcome, dear. You will let me know if you find out for certain that my niece was murdered, won't you?"

"Yes, I will."

"Poor Betty. Stars in her eyes, that girl."

Irene was about to hang up but she glanced at her notes and realized she hadn't asked all of her questions.

"One more thing, Miss Hodges."

"Yes?"

"Do you remember the name of the restaurant where Betty worked?"

"Oh, yes, the First Avenue Café. The owner is a very nice man. He was the only one who bothered to send me a note after Betty died. I drop in for coffee once in a while."

"Thank you, Miss Hodges."

Irene made a note and hung up. *Don't rush*, she told herself. *Take it step by step the way Peggy taught you.*

She picked up the phone again. "Operator, please connect me with Mrs. Phyllis Kemp in Seattle, Washington," she said. "Yes, I have the number."

Kemp answered on the third ring. She sounded annoyed.

"Kemp Apartments," she said. "If you're calling about the room that was advertised in the paper, you're too late. It's already been rented."

"This isn't about the room, Mrs. Kemp. This is Irene Glasson. We spoke over a week ago. I asked you about one of your boarders, Betty Scott."

"Yes, I remember." Kemp's tone switched from annoyed to suspicious. "Why are you calling again? I told you, it was an accident. She slipped and fell in the bathtub."

"I'm following up on a lead, Mrs. Kemp. I've just spoken with Betty Scott's aunt, who told me that Betty had a friend there at your boardinghouse, another aspiring actress who worked at an office. I'm trying to find her."

"Sorry, I can't help you. She moved out before Betty died."

"What was her name?"

"I don't recall offhand. I'd have to look it up in my files. I don't have time to do that."

"Miss Hodges seems to think that that other woman ran off with Betty's boyfriend."

"I wouldn't know about that. I make it a policy to never get involved in my boarders' private lives. I'm going to hang up now. I've got better things to do than talk to a reporter."

The line went dead.

Irene sat quietly, thinking about what she had learned. Oliver had said that Nick Tremayne's accent sounded more West Coast than Midwest. It wasn't too much of a stretch to imagine that he hailed from Seattle instead of Chicago, and that possibly he had made a couple of pornographic films before leaving town to start a career in Hollywood. Studio fixers like Ernie Ogden cleaned up that sort of problem on a regular basis.

But what if Nick Tremayne had decided to return to Seattle to erase his own past?

She picked up the phone again and asked the operator to connect her with the First Avenue Café in Seattle. The proprietor answered on the fourth ring. He sounded busy and impatient. But when she told him why she was calling, his mood changed.

"I sure do remember Betty Scott and her actor friends," he said. He chuckled. "They used to come in here and talk me into giving them free coffee. I felt sorry for 'em, y'know? They all had dreams of going to Hollywood. One of them actually made it."

"Which one?"

"Archie Guthrie. Good-looking young man. He had that certain quality. Always figured that if any of them made it, he would be the one. And sure enough he did. Changed his name, of course. They all do, I understand. First time I saw him on the screen I recognized him right away. I got kind of excited, y'know? Just think—I used to serve free coffee to Nick Tremayne."

Irene caught her breath. "You're sure Nick Tremayne's real name is Archie Guthrie?"

"Oh, yeah. Saw him in *Sea of Shadows* and then in *Fortune's Rogue*. No mistaking him."

"I understand he left town with one of the other young actresses who got coffee at your café."

"Yep. There were four of them, two young men and two young women. One of the men died in a fire at a local studio. The filmmaker died in that fire, too. As for Betty, the actress who worked for me, she was killed in a tragic accident. Slipped and fell in the bathtub. Real sad. The other two went to Hollywood."

"What happened to the woman who ran off to California with Nick Tremayne?"

"I don't know. Doubt if she'll ever make it to the silver screen, though."

"Why not?"

"She didn't have that special something."

"Can you describe her?"

"Tall. Dark hair. Pretty girl but I don't think she had much talent. She had a job in an office, as I recall. A secretary, I think. Probably should have stuck with it. I'm sure she's no longer with Archie—I mean, Nick Tremayne."

"Why not?"

"I read all the Hollywood magazines. According to them, Tremayne has a new girl on his arm every other week."

"Thank you," Irene said.

Very gently she put down the receiver.

For a long moment she simply stared, appalled, at the notes she had made during the two conversations. Shocked understanding lanced through her. It was followed by a rush of guilt.

I've been wrong from the start.

Chapter 60

Henry Oakes paused in the shady gardens just outside Oliver Ward's private villa. He had been doing a lot of thinking and had decided that he could not wait any longer. He was Nick Tremayne's special friend, after all. He had to do whatever was necessary to protect his pal. Someday Nick would understand and thank him.

It had been easy enough gaining access to the hotel grounds. He had crawled into the back of a delivery truck bringing crates of fresh vegetables to the hotel kitchen. There had been a guard at the gate but he recognized the driver and waved him through.

Henry had jumped out of the truck at the first opportunity. The driver never knew that he had a passenger.

Once on the hotel grounds Henry had made his

way into the extensive gardens. He was dressed like a maintenance man in overalls and boots. He had a cap pulled down low over his eyes. He kept his head down and walked purposefully toward his goal. He had learned long ago that no one ever paid any attention to a workingman who looked like he knew where he was going.

He stood in the shade and watched the front door of the villa. No one else had appeared after Ward left. The woman who was causing trouble for Nick Tremayne was inside.

She was still hanging around the hotel, still trying to find a way to hurt Nick Tremayne.

One of the hotel security guards was watching the front door of the villa.

Henry took the small bottle of chloroform out of his pocket.

He had warned Irene Glasson.

Chapter 61

She went painstakingly back through her notes. She had to be sure this time. She could not risk another mistake. She updated the timeline, rearranged a few details, and walked through the logic again.

In the end it all went back to Seattle, Irene thought. The answers were there at the beginning—the destruction of the films made by the small Seattle movie studio, the death of the filmmaker and one of the actors, the drowning of Betty Scott.

There had been four of them at the start. Two were now deceased. Nick had become a star. The only one missing from the timeline was the other young actress who had run off to Hollywood with Nick. For all intents and purposes, she had vanished.

Except that she hadn't.

Irene picked up the phone again and dialed the number of Oliver's office. Elena answered.

"Elena, this is Irene. Is Oliver there?"

"I'm afraid not," Elena said. "He's with Chester in the workshop. They're testing a new alarm system, I believe."

"I know where the workshop is. I'll find him."

"Mr. Ward said you weren't to leave Casa del Mar without one of the security guards," Elena said quickly.

"Don't worry. There's a guard out front. He can accompany me."

"All right."

Irene replaced the receiver, grabbed her handbag, and rushed to the door.

Henry Oakes was on the front step. He was dressed in workman's clothes, complete with a tool belt. There was a knife in the belt.

He fixed her with his disturbing gaze.

"I'm sorry, Miss Glasson," he said.

Irene tried to slam the door shut but Henry had one foot over the threshold.

"Wait," he said. "You have to let me in."

"Get away from me," Irene said. "You're crazy."

"No," Henry blurted. "You gotta let me explain. I got confused."

Claudia Picton appeared, moving away from the side of the house where she had been concealed. She had a gun in one hand and a length of iron that looked a lot like a crowbar in the other.

"Yes, I'm afraid he's very confused," she said. "Nuts, actually. Inside, both of you."

Irene retreated a few steps. Henry stumbled awkwardly into the foyer. He looked bewildered.

Claudia followed him into the villa and closed the door.

Henry gave Irene a pleading look. "I tried to warn you. I told you not to bother Mr. Tremayne."

"Where's the guard?" Irene said. "What did you do to him?"

"Nothing." Claudia smiled. "Henry took care of him for me, didn't you, Henry?"

"I put him in the gardening shed," Henry said. He looked and sounded utterly bewildered. "I had to get him out of the way. I needed to talk to you. But I didn't understand—"

"You're right, Henry," Claudia said. "You don't understand at all."

In a lightning move Claudia raised her hand and slammed the butt of the gun against the back of Henry's skull.

He dropped to his knees, grunting. Blood leaked from his head. Claudia struck him again. This time he collapsed, facedown.

Irene looked at Claudia. "You've had a lot of practice doing that, haven't you?"

"Yes." Rage glinted in Claudia's eyes. "Yes, I have had some practice. And I'm going to get some more today. I knew you were going to be a problem for my star," she said.

Chapter 62

"If you pull that trigger, someone will hear the shot," Irene said.

"I doubt it," Claudia said. She stepped over Henry's unmoving body. "This villa is quite secluded. Everyone knows that Oliver Ward likes his privacy. Even if someone did hear a shot, it would probably be dismissed as a backfire. No one expects to hear gunshots in a classy place like the Burning Cove Hotel. But I didn't come here to kill you, Irene."

"For some reason I don't believe you. I'm afraid you're a rather poor actress, Claudia."

"You think you know everything, don't you? I just want to talk to you. Turn around. Let's go into the living room. We're going to have a chat like two normal people."

Irene did not move. "As far as I can tell, there's not

much normal about you, Claudia. Lucky for you, Henry Oakes came along, right? What would you have done with the guard at the front door?"

"He wouldn't have been a problem. I would have handled him the same way I did Henry Oakes."

Out of nowhere, Irene remembered the advice that Oliver had given to the carful of young people who came across them at the secluded beach. *Never turn your back on the ocean. It will take you by surprise every time.*

Claudia was like the wild surf at the foot of the cliffs, she thought, filled with treacherous currents. Her victims had all been struck from behind. Perhaps she had a problem with looking them in the eye. Or maybe she simply couldn't come up with another way to commit murder. According to Oliver, most tricks were simple enough. The hard part was figuring out a new way to create the same illusion.

Cautiously, Irene retreated backward into the living room, never turning her back to Claudia.

"I said, turn around," Claudia said.

"We both know I can't do that," Irene said, gentling her tone. "Not until you tell me what you came here to say. You want me to know your side of the story, don't you?"

She halted next to Oliver's big, thickly cushioned reading chair, vaguely surprised to realize that she was still clutching her handbag.

Claudia stopped at the edge of the living room, several feet away.

"You've got it all wrong," she said. "I came here to explain things before anyone else gets hurt."

"I see. How many people, exactly, have been hurt so far?"

Seething anger flashed in Claudia's eyes, burning away all traces of nervy anxiety. She drew visible strength from the maelstrom.

"I didn't have any choice," she said.

Oliver had also mentioned the virtues of misdirection, Irene thought. She had to find a way to keep Claudia talking.

"I assume that not all the films you and your friends made in Seattle were destroyed in the fire at that little movie studio," she said.

"Betty told us that they were all gone but she lied. She saved the two that Nick made, *Island Nights* and *Pirate's Captive*."

"Who burned down the studio?"

"That was Betty. She was in love with Nick, you see. He was plain Archie Guthrie in those days. But after he told her that he was going to Hollywood with me, she was furious. She knew that if Archie made it big, those films would make excellent blackmail material."

"She murdered the man who made those films and the other actor."

"I honestly don't know if she intended for that creepy director and Ralph to die in the fire. But they were both there that night, probably passed out. They were heroin addicts."

"When did you learn that Betty had stolen the two pornographic films?" Irene asked.

"She made her demands right after the release of Nick's first film, *Sea of Shadows*. She telephoned him anonymously and told him how much she wanted.

Nick panicked. He planned to go straight to Ernie Ogden. But I knew that would be a disaster. Nick was
clearly an up-and-coming actor but he wasn't a real
star, not yet. I was sure the studio would drop him
rather than pay blackmail. So I told Nick that I would
take care of everything."

"He believed you?"

"Of course." Claudia smiled. "He needs me and he
knows it. I'm the one who slept with three different
directors in order to get him his first screen test. I'm the
one who came up with the name Nick Tremayne. I'm
the one who read his lines with him. I'm the one who
worked the lunch counter at Woolworth's and picked
up traveling businessmen in bars in order to pay the
rent. I did it so that Nick could focus on his acting."

"How did you land the job as his personal assistant?"

"It was obvious after the release of *Sea of Shadows*
that women loved Nick Tremayne. The studio publicist
wanted Nick to get single in a hurry. Better for his
image, they said. They told him that he had to get
divorced."

The penny dropped.

"You and Nick Tremayne were married?" Irene
asked.

"Is that so hard to believe?"

"No," Irene said. "No, it's all starting to make a lot
more sense."

"The studio said they would pay for me to spend
six weeks in Reno at a divorce ranch. For a pitiful
amount of money, I was supposed to disappear."

"They paid you to get the divorce?"

"Not nearly enough to make up for what I would lose in the long run. Not enough to compensate me for the sacrifices I had made. I knew that, unless Nick made some huge mistake, in a few years he would be worth millions. As his wife, I would have gotten a share of the money."

"But as his ex, you'd wind up with nothing."

"It wasn't fair," Claudia said. "Nick pleaded with me to get the divorce. They were threatening to cancel his contract if I didn't. I finally told him that I would get the divorce but in exchange he had to find a way to let me stay close to him. I reminded him that I was his best friend. I told him that now that he was becoming famous, the only person he could ever really trust was someone who had been his friend and his lover from the old days."

"He loved you?"

Claudia snorted. "Archie has never loved anyone but himself. But he knew that he owed me so he convinced the studio to hire me as his personal assistant. They agreed. All they cared about was that Nick Tremayne was single."

"So you went to Reno, got the divorce, changed your name, and became Nick Tremayne's personal assistant."

"Just another Hollywood story," Claudia said. "But then the blackmail started."

"How did you figure out that Betty Scott was the extortionist?"

"That wasn't hard. By then the director and Ralph were both dead. There was no one else who would have had access to those two films. It was obvious that

Betty was the one who had possession of *Island Nights* and *Pirate's Captive*."

"So you decided to get rid of Betty Scott."

"I told her that I would bring the money to her. I took the train to Seattle. We arranged to meet at the boardinghouse on a night when everyone else was out partying. I went upstairs to her room. She came out into the hall. When she realized I hadn't brought the cash with me, she was furious. I tried to reason with her. I told her that we could both make a lot of money if we just waited until Nick was a bigger star. She laughed in my face. She said that she'd rather have a bird in the hand."

"That's when you killed her?"

"The bitch called me a failed actress." Claudia's voice rose in fury. "When she turned around to go into her room, I grabbed the big flower vase off a table and I hit her."

"Betty Scott was found in the bathtub."

"It wasn't easy getting her into the tub, believe me."

"What about the films?"

"Afterward I searched her room and found the two cans of film." Claudia got herself back under control. "I now possess the negatives of each of Nick Tremayne's pornographic films. They're dynamite because they both feature Nick Tremayne having sex with Ralph."

"That would be guaranteed to kill Tremayne's career."

"Definitely," Claudia said. "But timing is everything. A year from now when Nick is the next Clark Gable those old films will be worth a fortune. The studio will pay whatever it takes to get ahold of the negatives."

Irene managed to get her handbag open behind the chair. She reached inside. Her fingers closed around the small gun.

"Blackmailing a major film studio will be a very dangerous proposition," she said.

"Don't you think I know that?" Claudia said. "I plan to disappear before I go into business."

"Does Archie—Nick Tremayne—believe that Betty's death was an accident?"

"He did at the time. He wanted to believe it, you see. But now I think he's starting to wonder. Sometimes he looks at me as if he's no longer sure he can trust me. That other reporter from *Whispers* is the one who put the doubts in his mind."

"You murdered Peggy Hackett because she was closing in on the story about the pornographic films, didn't you?"

"I had to get rid of her. I broke into her house and waited for her upstairs in a hall closet. I couldn't believe my luck when she had a couple of martinis and then decided to take a bath."

"The fireplace poker was missing. That's what you used to kill her."

"She heard me at the very last instant but by then it was too late."

"Why did you murder Gloria Maitland?"

"She got too close to Nick," Claudia said. "They had an affair. He got drunk and made the mistake of telling her about those early films. After he dumped her, she started hounding him. Ogden paid her to go away but she didn't."

"Why did she follow Nick to Burning Cove?"

"She told Nick she would give him one last chance to resume their affair. They quarreled."

"That was the fight that the hotel housekeeper witnessed."

"Nick has a temper. He lost it and told Gloria he never wanted to see her again. I kept an eye on her. No one ever notices the star's personal assistant. The next night she spent the evening drinking alone in the lounge. That wasn't like her. Gloria liked to have people around. When she left, I followed her. When she went into the spa, I knew something was up. I confronted her. She laughed at me. Told me that you would be there any minute. She said that if I came up with more money than *Whispers*, she'd keep quiet."

"What did you use to hit her?"

"A rock from the garden," Claudia said.

"You shoved her into the water to drown, and then you tried to murder me."

"I didn't know how much you knew at that point or what you'd seen. I couldn't think of anything else to do. When you escaped, I got scared. The next morning the story of Gloria Maitland's drowning was on the front page of *Whispers* and you had implicated Archie. Ogden called, demanding to know what was going on."

"You knew you had lost control of the situation. Ernie Ogden took over. He sent someone to search my apartment. He got me evicted. He even got me fired."

"That should have been enough to silence you but

you didn't go away," Claudia said. "Ogden said there was no need to worry but I knew he was wrong."

"So you cooked up the scheme to make me disappear in a fire. Was Ogden in on that plan?"

"No. He had no way of knowing how high the stakes were, you see. He thought that with you off the Gloria Maitland story, everything was under control. But I knew you weren't going to stop."

"You were afraid that eventually I'd make the connections between the murders and those two early pornographic films. You used poor Daisy Jennings to lure me to that warehouse. You killed her. If Ernie Ogden wasn't involved, how did you arrange to send Springer and Dallas to set the fire?"

"It's no secret at the studio that Ogden uses Hollywood Mack when he wants some muscle work done. I made the call to Mack. Told him that Mr. Ogden wanted Springer and Dallas to throw a real scare into a nosy reporter. I told him I knew exactly where you would be that night and that Mr. Ogden wanted the warehouse set on fire."

"But you weren't going to take any chances, were you?" Irene said. "You were going to make sure I was dead first."

"I waited for you in the old boathouse. But everything went wrong."

"Because Oliver Ward showed up first and you knew that he was probably armed."

"I realized that if he had accompanied you, he suspected a trap. So I stayed out of sight and waited for Springer and Dallas to arrive. I hoped that I'd get lucky and that you and Ward would both die in the fire."

"But that didn't happen."

"Things kept going wrong." Claudia's voice climbed in an unstable wail of frustration and rage.

"Let me see if I've got this straight," Irene said. "You murdered Betty Scott at the start and then you killed three more people to cover up your crime. I think that's all I need to write my story. You're going to make headlines in the morning, Claudia Picton. Congratulations."

"Shut up." Claudia made a jerky motion with the gun. "Outside. Move."

Irene glanced at the crowbar in Claudia's hand. "Are you planning to bash me over the head and dump me in the lap pool? You have got to be kidding me. How will you explain poor Henry Oakes's death?"

Claudia smiled. "You've got it all wrong. Again. Everyone will think this is Henry Oakes's gun. They'll assume that he's the one who shot you. And then he will put the gun to his own head. It will turn out that all the murders were committed by a crazed fan."

"You're finally going to rewrite the murder scene."

"This is the last scene. It needs to be different."

Irene looked past Claudia toward the front door. "Heard enough, Detective?"

Claudia did not bother to glance over her shoulder.

"Do you think I'm dumb enough to fall for that trick?" she asked.

"It was worth a try."

"Move."

"So you can shoot me in the back? You really have an issue with doing this sort of thing face-to-face, don't you?"

"I said, turn around. Outside. Now."

"I get it; you're planning to shoot me but you still want to finish me off in the pool. Tell me, why do you like to use water? Was it because that was how you staged the first murder? Or does it have some other significance?"

"Turn around, damn you."

Claudia was shaking with rage now. The gun wobbled.

Irene obediently started to turn as though she was about to walk out onto the patio.

She yanked Helen's gun out of her handbag and dropped to the floor behind the chair.

"Get up," Claudia screeched.

Irene leaned around the side of the chair, revealing the gun in her hand.

"Get out of this house," she said. "Run while you can."

The sight of the weapon seemed to transfix Claudia. She stared at it, horrified.

"Drop it or I swear I'll shoot," Irene said, keeping the heavy chair between herself and Claudia. "You'll probably get a shot off, but it will most likely hit the chair. I can't miss. Not at this range."

"No," Claudia whispered. "No, damn you."

She reeled backward, simultaneously squeezing the trigger.

Her gun roared. The sound was deafening but Irene realized in a rather vague way that she wasn't dead. The bullet had plowed into the heavily padded back of the chair. Evidently Claudia hadn't had much experience with guns, either.

Irene leaned around the chair again and pulled the

trigger of Helen's gun, not bothering to aim, just trying to scare the daylights out of Claudia.

There was an audible click. Nothing happened.

Jammed, she thought, *or something*. She didn't know enough about guns to even begin to guess what had gone wrong. A fine time for Oliver to be proved right about the unreliability of firearms.

She had nothing left to lose now. Damned if she would stay where she was, cowering behind the reading chair while she waited for Claudia to put a bullet in her head. She would rather go down fighting.

She leaped to her feet and hurled the useless gun at Claudia, who instinctively ducked and retreated again. This time she stumbled against Henry Oakes's inert body. She nearly lost her balance.

Irene grabbed the fireplace poker out of the iron stand, jumped to her feet, and charged.

It was the last thing Claudia was expecting.

Confused and disoriented, she stumbled again and looked down, trying to find a way to get past Henry Oakes's body. She seemed transfixed by the sight of the madwoman closing in on her with the heavy poker. Maybe she was recalling the occasions when she had used a similarly lethal object to knock her victims unconscious before drowning them. Maybe she simply panicked.

Whatever the case, she scrambled backward—and came up hard against the liquor cabinet. She squeezed the trigger convulsively but she was too panic-stricken to even try to aim. Her gun roared again but the bullet plowed into the ceiling.

Irene held the poker like a sword and drove straight for Claudia's midsection.

Claudia reeled to the side in a desperate effort to avoid the poker. She stumbled and went down. The gun fell from her hand. Irene turned aside long enough to kick the weapon across the tiled floor, out of Claudia's reach.

Gripping the poker in both hands, she stood over Claudia.

"Move and I'll smash your head just like you crushed Peggy's head," Irene said.

Crouched on the floor, Claudia stared up at her. "You're crazy."

"Right now? Definitely."

The front door slammed open.

"Nobody moves," Oliver thundered in a voice that had once electrified audiences.

Irene and Claudia went utterly still for a beat. Then they both looked at Oliver. He had a gun in his hand.

"You can put that poker down now, Irene," he said.

She took a couple of steps away from Claudia. She was breathing hard.

"She murdered Peggy," she said. "She killed all of them."

"I understand," Oliver said. "But she won't kill again. You can put the poker down."

Irene focused on the poker. She realized she still had a death grip on it. She took another deep breath.

"All right," she said. She set the poker down with great care. "The guard. I think Henry Oakes did something to him. Oakes said something about the gardening shed."

Another guard showed up at the door. He was red-faced from running. He looked at Oliver for direction.

"Find Randy Seaton," Oliver said. "He may be hurt. Search the gardening shed first."

"Yes, sir."

The guard raced off.

Irene went to Henry Oakes. She put two fingers to his throat. And nearly collapsed with relief when she found a pulse.

"He's alive," she whispered.

"Get the gun, Chester," Oliver said quietly when his uncle appeared behind him. "Use a handkerchief. There will be fingerprints."

"Don't you think I know that?" Chester muttered.

He whipped a handkerchief out of his overalls and moved to scoop up the weapon.

Another voice spoke from the front doorway.

"What's going on here?" Nick Tremayne said. He took two steps into the room and stopped short. "Claudia? What have you done?"

Oliver looked at him. "The more interesting question at the moment is, what are you doing here?"

Nick switched his attention to Irene. He looked stunned. *Probably sees his career going up in flames,* she thought.

"I couldn't find her," he explained in a dull, defeated voice. "No one seemed to know where she was. That's not like her. She usually sticks to her routine. I went to the front desk and asked if they had seen her. They said no. But the hotel operator said that Claudia had recently taken a telephone call from Seattle. That didn't make sense. I got a bad feeling."

"So you came here?" Oliver said.

Nick groaned. "Yeah. I was afraid she might have decided to confront Miss Glasson. Maybe do something terrible."

The red-faced guard reappeared in the doorway. He was panting now.

"Found Randy," he gasped. "He's tied up in the shed but he's not hurt. Kind of sick, though. Says a workman showed up saying he had been sent to fix a plumbing problem. Randy was suspicious. He started to turn around to knock on the door to see if anyone had called a plumber, and that's the last thing he remembers."

"Go take care of him," Oliver said.

"No," Claudia shrieked. She scrambled to her feet. "It doesn't end this way. Not after all I've done."

"You're wrong," Irene said. "It does end this way. And it ends now."

Claudia burst into tears. She turned to Nick, pleading now. "You need me, Archie. We're a team. The studio knows that. The studio will protect me."

"No," Oliver said. "The studio won't protect you. You're not the star. You're just Nick Tremayne's personal assistant. You can be replaced."

Claudia succumbed to another round of tears. No one offered comfort.

Oliver looked at Irene. His usually unreadable eyes were intense with some fierce emotion.

"Are you sure you're all right?" he asked.

"No," she said. "But I will be just as soon as I get to a typewriter."

rene walked into the offices of the *Burning Cove Herald* and stopped at the front desk. The sign read *Trish Harrison, Society News.*

"I'd like to speak with the editor," Irene said.

The forty-something woman behind the desk stopped typing long enough to take the cigarette out of the corner of her mouth.

"Who are—?" she began in a smoky voice. She stopped and no longer looked bored. "Hell, you're Oliver Ward's new girlfriend, aren't you? I recognize you. Your picture was in *Silver Screen Secrets.*"

"Will you direct me to your editor's office or shall I just start opening doors?"

Trish gave her a hard look. "I'm the society reporter. If you've got any news from the Burning Cove Hotel, I'm the one you should talk to."

"Sorry," Irene said. "I'm out of the gossip business."

"In that case, Paisley's office is down there," Trish said. She waved a hand toward an office at the back of the room, stuck the cigarette back in her mouth, and returned to her typing.

Irene made her way past a few more desks. The typewriters went silent. Everyone in the room was watching her now.

She ignored the stares and rapped smartly on the door marked *Edwin Paisley, Editor in Chief.*

"Door's open."

Irene opened the door, marched into the room, and closed the door very firmly. The room reeked of cigar smoke. She went straight to the window and opened it.

Edwin Paisley was balding, middle-aged, and portly. He looked like the washed-up journalist he no doubt was. Maybe, at one time, he had dreamed of becoming a crack reporter, Irene thought. But somewhere along the line he had given up on his ambitions. He had probably spent too many years putting out a small local paper that focused on garden parties, diet fads, society luncheons, and discreet hints about various stars who had been seen arriving or departing from the Burning Cove Hotel.

"Who the hell—?" he began. He stopped and squinted at her over the top of the glasses perched on his nose. "Wait, I recognize you. You're Ward's new girlfriend."

"I'm Irene Glasson, a reporter. I'm here to apply for a position on your staff."

"No job openings," Edwin said. He scowled. "Tell

Ward if he wants me to hire you, he'll have to come up with the money for your salary. He'll also need to supply a desk and an office. And a typewriter."

"You'd hire me if Oliver Ward insisted on it?"

"He owns the Burning Cove Hotel, and Luther Pell is his best friend. Between them, those two control a big chunk of this town. I'm just the editor of the local paper. Not like I'm William Randolph Hearst. So, yeah, if Ward applies pressure to hire you, I'll do it."

"But you won't like it."

"Would you?"

Irene smiled. "Relax, you've got nothing to worry about. Mr. Ward is not going to push you to hire me. In fact, I think he's rather hoping that you won't."

"That's supposed to reassure me? Look, I don't need another reporter on the local society beat, which is about the only beat this paper covers unless you count births and obituaries."

"I'm well aware of the narrow focus of the reportage one finds in the *Burning Cove Herald*."

Edwin snorted. "Reportage?"

"Never mind." She planted her handbag on his desk. "What you need is a good crime beat reporter. That's the job I want."

Edwin stared at her as if she'd turned a peculiar shade of purple. "We don't get much crime in Burning Cove. At least, we didn't until you arrived in town. I'll admit things have gotten a little more exciting lately."

"Good news, Mr. Paisley. I've decided to stick around."

"I am, of course, overjoyed that you have chosen to settle down here in our little corner of paradise. But

I'm not giving you a job unless Ward threatens to break my arm. Or make me disappear. Sometimes I forget he was a magician."

"Don't worry, I'll make sure Oliver doesn't apply any pressure. And I'm not asking you to give me a job, by the way. I'm going to earn it. Starting with my first story."

Irene opened her handbag and took out the pages she had typed that morning on Elena's typewriter.

Edwin eyed the pages. "What's this?"

"The story that will be all over the front pages of the L.A. press tomorrow. It will be in one of the Seattle papers, too. I made some promises. But it's yours to break tonight." She handed him the first page.

"Who's Claudia Picton?"

"A crazed killer who murdered four women, including Daisy Jennings, a local resident. What's more, Picton would have kept right on killing if not for the heroic actions of Nick Tremayne."

"Tremayne? The actor?"

"Right. Turns out he plays heroes not only on the silver screen, but in real life, too. Miss Picton is now in custody at the Burning Cove Police Station. The cops expect an insanity plea."

"You've got a story featuring Nick Tremayne and a deranged female killer? Why aren't you taking this to your paper, *Whispers*?"

"Because I was fired."

"Oh, yeah. Heard about that."

"Don't worry, *Whispers* will have the story along with every other paper in L.A. for their morning editions. Nick Tremayne's studio will make sure of it. But

I'm offering you an exclusive today. You can run with it in your evening edition tonight."

"We don't have an evening edition."

"Make it a special edition. All I ask is that I get a byline."

"And a job?"

"Read the story, Mr. Paisley." She put the typewritten pages on the desk. "I've got quotes from Nick Tremayne, himself, not to mention Oliver Ward and Luther Pell."

"Ward and Pell never grant interviews."

"They made an exception for me. Go ahead, read the story, and then tell me you'll print it."

Chapter 64

"Why aren't I dead?" Irene asked. "Claudia had a gun. She got off two shots. I should be dead."

The four of them were on the patio of Oliver's villa—Oliver, Chester, Luther, and herself. Oliver kept casting worried glances in her direction, so she did her best to look like the coolheaded journalist who had just concluded a successful investigation.

It was Luther who answered her question. His eyes were bleak with a dark knowledge, and there was an oddly remote quality in his voice.

"It's true that Picton had a gun, but it's surprisingly difficult to hit someone who is charging straight at you," he said. "Especially when your attacker is armed with a lethal weapon like a poker. In addition to the problem of aiming at a moving target, there is the added psychological factor. Your first instinct is to dodge the sharp object that is aimed at you."

Irene looked at him. They all did. No one commented, but she knew they were all thinking the same thing. Luther was not speaking theoretically. He was remembering scenes from nightmares. He wasn't thinking about pokers; he was thinking about fixed bayonets.

It was Oliver who broke the short silence that followed the observation.

"Luther's right," he said. "By charging Picton with that poker, you took an enormous risk but you also presented the ultimate distraction. She panicked."

"What made you realize that Claudia had come after me?" Irene said.

Her nerves were still on edge and she knew she would not sleep well that night. She might not sleep well for a long time to come. She would never be able to forget the feral expression in Claudia's eyes.

"I didn't," Oliver said. "Not until I opened the door and saw you standing over Claudia with that poker in your hand. The reason I went back to the villa was because someone in housekeeping spotted an unknown workman matching Oakes's description on the grounds."

Irene smiled. "You did say housekeeping was the front line of security here at the hotel. No one pays any attention to the maids."

Luther leaned back in his chair. He contemplated Irene. "Any idea what it was that made Claudia Picton choose today to attack you? She must have been desperate to take such a risk right here on the grounds of the hotel."

"She felt she had to act," Irene said. "She had just gotten a warning, you see. I made some telephone calls to Seattle this morning. One of them was to Phyllis Kemp, the landlady in Seattle. Peggy Hackett made the same phone call. I'm sure it was that call that led to her murder. Calling Kemp almost got me killed today. It was the second time I'd called, you see."

Chester's brows scrunched together. "Kemp called Claudia Picton and told her that you had just telephoned asking about Betty Scott?"

"Yes. The news clearly terrified Claudia," Irene said. "She panicked because she knew I was closing in on the story. She probably assumed the odds were very good that Oliver wouldn't be home during the day. He's an executive, after all. He was likely to be in his office. She took a chance and came to the villa, hoping to find me alone. She ran into Henry Oakes, who was watching me because he believed I was a threat to Nick Tremayne."

"So much for my ability to read a member of the audience," Oliver said. "I knew Claudia Picton was a nervous, overanxious woman. I assumed that she wanted to protect her job, but I've got to admit it never occurred to me she would risk her life or a murder rap to do so."

Chester shook his head. "It was the money. Reckon all Picton could see were the millions of dollars that she would someday collect."

"No, it wasn't just the money," Irene said. "She wanted revenge. I think she believed that she had sacrificed her own dreams for the sake of Nick Tremayne's career. You read her correctly, Oliver, but you didn't have all the facts. None of us did. We didn't know that Claudia had once been married to Nick Tremayne and that she had been paid to get a quickie divorce."

"That fact changes everything," Oliver said quietly. "It makes it all personal."

"Yes," Luther said. He looked thoughtful. "It does."

Oliver's eyes tightened a little. "There's only one reason why the landlady, Phyllis Kemp, would have made that phone call to Picton today. She must have been involved in Picton's blackmail scheme."

"She was." Detective Brandon spoke from the living room doorway. He walked out onto the patio. He looked at Oliver. "The housekeeper guarding your front door let me in. Hope that's all right."

"Mrs. Taylor is there to make sure no members of the press sneak into the front garden," Oliver said.

Irene raised her brows. "Except me, of course."

Brandon chuckled and lowered himself into a chair. He looked tired but satisfied.

"Phyllis Kemp is now talking to the Seattle police," he said. "Turns out she's Claudia Picton's aunt—Picton's only close relation. Kemp is maintaining her innocence but Picton says she was in on the scheme from the beginning. It was Kemp who made certain that Betty Scott was alone in the boardinghouse the night Picton confronted her about the blackmail threat. In fact, according to Picton, Phyllis Kemp helped her stage the bathtub scene."

"When I called Mrs. Kemp again and asked more questions, she realized that yet another Hollywood reporter was closing in on the truth. She hung up and immediately called Claudia."

"Who panicked," Oliver said. "She grabbed a gun and a crowbar from the trunk of her car and went looking for Irene."

"So Tremayne's ex-wife was his personal assistant?" Chester said. He snorted. "That had to be a strange setup."

"Stranger things happen in Hollywood," Luther said.

"So they tell me," Brandon said. "Speaking of Hollywood, the studio cut Claudia Picton loose immediately, as you said they would, Oliver."

"I wonder how much Daisy Jennings knew about what was going on," Luther mused.

"Very little," Brandon said. "From what I can tell she had a onetime fling with Nick Tremayne in the garden of the Paradise Club. Later, Claudia Picton offered her cash to lure Miss Glasson to the warehouse."

"Picton also gave Jennings a script to read that contained two film titles. Jennings must have known something dangerous was happening," Oliver said.

"Maybe," Brandon said. "Regardless, it looks like she took the money and didn't ask too many questions."

Chester scowled. "What about that studio executive, Ernie Ogden? How much did he know?"

"According to Claudia Picton, Ogden didn't know that his star was being blackmailed, so he couldn't have known why women with a connection to Nick Tremayne had a bad habit of turning up dead," Irene said. "But he must have been getting concerned. What's more, I think Claudia Picton knew that. It's probably why she was so desperate today. If the studio dumped

Tremayne, her blackmail scheme would go down the drain. She'd have committed several murders and have nothing to show for it. I'm sure that situation was an additional source of stress for her."

"No wonder she always looked so nervous," Chester said.

"She's looking a lot more anxious now," Brandon said. "She's doing a good job of acting like she's nuts. Got a hunch she's going to go with an insanity plea."

"What will happen to Henry Oakes?" Irene asked. "I think he's a little crazy but he wasn't a killer."

Brandon grunted. "He's going to recover from his head wound. That's the good news. The bad news is that he's still crazy. Thinks he's Nick Tremayne's special friend and that he has to protect the star. I'll have a little chat with him before he leaves the hospital, but if that doesn't work, I guess the studio will have to deal with him."

"That's what men like Ernie Ogden get paid to do," Luther said.

"I know," Brandon said. He shook his head. "I've seen that kind of crazy before and there's no cure."

Irene glanced at her watch and got to her feet. "It's almost three o'clock. If you gentlemen will excuse me, I have an appointment with Nick Tremayne."

The men rose.

Chester looked surprised. "Tremayne agreed to another interview?"

"Not exactly," Irene said. "I owe him an apology. He has graciously agreed to accept it. We're having tea together."

"Be forewarned," Oliver said. "There will be a studio photographer and a publicist present. Ogden sent them here in a chauffeured limo."

"In that case I'll go upstairs and put on some fresh lipstick," Irene said.

Brandon chuckled. "I thought the Burning Cove Hotel had a firm policy when it came to photographers and publicists. They aren't allowed on the grounds."

"It's my hotel," Oliver said. "I made the policy. I can make exceptions."

Luther gave him a knowing look. "You kept the lid on a major scandal involving a fast-rising star and you arranged things so that Tremayne came out of a messy situation looking like a real hero. His studio is going to be very grateful."

"I'm counting on it," Oliver said.

Luther smiled. "In other words, casting Tremayne as the hero is good for business. Ernie Ogden owes you a very big favor. Having him in your debt is bound to be useful. On top of that, the gossip columnists will fall all over themselves retelling the story of Tremayne's heroics, and the Burning Cove Hotel will be featured in every single piece that appears in papers across the nation."

"Nothing like good publicity," Oliver said.

Brandon got to his feet. "Sounds complicated. I think I'll stick with the detective business. If you'll excuse me, I'm going back to work."

He nodded politely at Irene and disappeared into the living room. A moment later the door closed quietly behind him.

Luther looked at Oliver. "Correct me if I'm wrong, but I believe there is one more reason for making

Nick Tremayne the star of your little story. It will dominate the news. No one will pay any attention to a much smaller piece about a certain automobile accident that took the life of another guest of the Burning Cove Hotel."

"In the magic business we call it misdirection," Oliver said.

Chapter 65

Nick Tremayne eyed the elegantly wrapped gift box with a wary expression. "What's inside?"

"Two cans of film," Irene said. "The negatives of those two movies that you made in Seattle. They were found in Claudia's hotel room. I can't guarantee that there are no copies floating around somewhere, but I very much doubt it. Claudia seemed quite sure that she was the only one who possessed *Island Nights* and *Pirate's Captive*. I had a hunch she would keep them close at hand. Her whole future was tied to them."

Nick looked up, his expression watchful. "You found them?"

"Yes."

There was no need to explain that Oliver was the one who had realized that Claudia's suitcase had a false bottom.

She and Nick were sitting in a corner of the tearoom, alone at last. The studio photographer had taken several pictures of Nick looking both heroic and modest. The publicist had jotted down several quotes from Irene and the management of the Burning Cove Hotel that verified Nick's timely arrival at the scene of the attempted murder. Both the photographer and the publicist were on their way back to L.A.

Nick studied the box as though it contained a cobra. When he turned back to Irene, there was anger and resignation in his eyes.

"How much do you want for them?" he asked, his voice flat.

"Nothing. They're yours. It's the least I can do after dragging your name into a murder case."

Nick stared at her in disbelief. In his world there was a price tag attached to everything.

Irene picked up the teapot and filled the two cups. By the time she set the pot down, Nick's expression had transformed into cautious hope. He glanced at the box again and turned back to her.

"You know what's on those films?"

"Claudia told me."

"Either film could kill my career."

"If I were you, I'd take them down to the beach and burn them."

Nick nodded slowly. He put one hand on the box.

"I'll do that," he said. "I thought she loved me, you know."

"Maybe she did back at the start."

"Something happened after I made *Sea of Shadows* and *Fortune's Rogue*."

Irene smiled. "Something happened, all right. You became a star."

"I shouldn't have pleaded with her to get the divorce. Shouldn't have let the studio pressure her into going to Reno."

"For what it's worth, I doubt that would have made much difference. Being married to you would not have been enough. She wanted what you have. She longed to be a star."

"It probably won't last, you know," Nick said.

"The stardom? Nothing lasts forever. My advice is to enjoy it while you can. Meanwhile, be careful how you invest the money."

Nick laughed. The California sun streaming through the windows caught the handsome angles of his face and gleamed on his dark hair. The atmosphere around the little table was infused with a magnetic energy. Heads turned.

A little thrill whispered through Irene. She was having tea with a movie star.

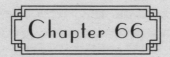

Chapter 66

The special evening edition of the *Burning Cove Herald* hit the newsstands shortly after five o'clock that afternoon.

Irene was waiting at the front desk of the Burning Cove Hotel when the newsboy arrived. She threw some money at the kid, pounced on a copy, and savored the headline.

CRAZED FEMALE KILLER
ARRESTED AT BURNING COVE HOTEL.
ACTOR NICK TREMAYNE A HERO,
SAY THOSE AT THE SCENE.

The byline read *Irene Glasson*.

One of the front desk clerks leaned toward her. "The

hotel operator says there's a telephone call for you, Miss Glasson. You can take it on the house phone."

"Thanks." Irene hurried to the ornate telephone that sat on a nearby console. She picked up the receiver. "This is Irene Glasson."

"First edition is sold out," Edwin Paisley announced. His voice vibrated with excitement. "We're going back to press. I want a follow-up piece for the morning edition. Get me some more quotes from Tremayne. I want stuff that won't be in the L.A. papers. I want exclusive material."

"Does this mean I've got a job?"

"Yeah, yeah, you got the job. You're my new reporter on the crime beat. Now go write me another hot story."

"I'll get right on it, Boss."

Edwin hung up. Irene admired her headline again, and then she hurried down the hall to Oliver's office. Elena was in the process of putting the cover on the typewriter.

"Hi, Irene. I was just about to leave for the day. Congratulations on the front-page story."

"You've seen it?"

Elena chuckled. "Are you kidding? Mr. Ward gave orders for a copy to be delivered by special courier as soon as it came off the press. To tell you the truth, I think he was a little nervous. He has this thing about reporters and photographers, you see."

"I've heard that," Irene said.

"Well, that's it for me," Elena said. "I must say it's been a busy day." She headed toward the door. "See you tomorrow."

"Bye, Elena."

Irene waited until the outer door closed behind Elena, and then she crossed the room to the door of Oliver's office and opened it.

"Good news," she said. "I've got a job."

Oliver was lounging back in his chair, his good leg propped on the corner of his desk. He had a copy of the special edition of the *Herald* in his hands.

"Figured you would after this story of a crazed female killer prowling the grounds of the Burning Cove Hotel." He took his foot off the desk and rose. "You made my security look bad but you did a great job of transforming Nick Tremayne into a real hero."

"It's the crazed female killer and the movie-star hero that people will love. That's all they'll remember. They won't care about your security." She went behind the desk and wound her arms around Oliver's neck. "Thanks for the quotes, by the way. I may need another one."

"Figures. Tell me about the job."

"Meet the new crime reporter for the *Herald*."

"According to the local authorities, we don't have much crime in Burning Cove."

"With luck, that will change now that there is an actual reporter on the beat."

"For some reason I do not find that a comforting thought," Oliver said.

"Nonsense. There's absolutely nothing to worry about. I'm a professional."

"Don't remind me." The amusement vanished from Oliver's eyes. "So, this means you'll be staying in town?"

And just like that, the frothy, sparkling sense of delight and excitement that had made her almost giddy went flat. She went very still.

"Yes," she said. "I like it here. It's not as though there is any place else that feels like home."

"Does Burning Cove feel like home?"

"I think," she said, choosing her words with care, "that under the right circumstances, Burning Cove could definitely feel like home."

"Let me be more specific. Do you think that Casa del Mar could feel like home?"

The weight of caution descended on her. Her future was hanging in the balance. She had to be certain that she understood exactly what Oliver was offering.

"Are you inviting me to move in as a permanent houseguest?"

"If that's what you want."

"No," she said. "It's not what I want."

His eyes turned bleak. "I see."

"Was it what you wanted?" she asked.

"No." His voice hardened with pain. "What I want is for you to move in as my wife. But I figured it was too soon to ask you to marry me."

"It's not," she said.

He looked startled. "It's not too soon to ask you to marry me?"

"Not if you love me."

"Why in hell would I ask you to marry me if I didn't love you?"

"I have no idea. But I need to be sure. Because I love you."

"Irene—"

She gave him a tremulous smile. "Actually, it's Anna. Anna Harris."

"Irene—Anna—call yourself whatever you want. I love you and I will keep on loving you, whether you move in with me or not."

Joy blossomed deep inside her. A moment ago she had been feeling giddy with success and the promise of a job that gave her an excuse to stay in Burning Cove. But now she was beyond delighted. She was thrilled. Intoxicated with happiness. Lighter than air.

She tightened her arms around his neck. "I would like very much to marry you and move in with you on a permanent basis."

He tightened his hold on her. "It will be permanent. Forever."

"That sounds very good. Perfect, in fact."

"Just one question."

"Yes?"

"Do I call you Anna or Irene?"

She smiled. "I found a new life here in California as Irene. I'll stick with her."

"Sounds good to me."

"Besides, it's the name on my byline."

Oliver laughed. He sounded like the happiest man on earth. He kissed her there in the golden light of a California day, and for the first time since she was fourteen years old, she knew she could plan a future filled with love and a family of her own.

Chapter 67

Raina Kirk put the updated files relating to the contract for the murder of Helen Spencer into a large envelope. She wrote the address with a neat hand. She would drop it off at the post office later.

She removed the remaining files from a locked cabinet and put them into her briefcase.

The files weren't the only items in the case. There was also several thousand dollars in cash.

She closed the briefcase and locked it. She left it sitting on her desk while she crossed the room to put on her coat and the adorable little felt hat that she had bought the day before. With its upturned brim and high crown trimmed with a jaunty feather, it was currently the height of fashion. The instant she had spotted it in the department store window she knew it was exactly the hat for her.

She glanced at the telegram on her desk. It had been delivered early the previous morning before Graham Enright had arrived at the office. Fortunately she had been there to receive it.

REGRET TO INFORM YOU THAT JULIAN ENRIGHT DIED
IN A CAR CRASH IN BURNING COVE, CALIF. THE
REMAINS ARE BEING HELD IN A LOCAL MORGUE. FOR
DETAILS CONTACT DET. BRANDON, BURNING COVE
POLICE DEPARTMENT. CONDOLENCES.

She picked up the telegram and took one last look around the office. All was in order. The plant in the corner had been watered. The desktop was clear. The typewriter was covered. It was an office that any secretary could be proud to call her own.

It was time to leave.

She crossed the room and opened the door of her employer's inner sanctum. Graham Enright was in the same position he had been in when she last peeked into the office—slumped over his desk. The delicate china cup from which he had taken his last swallow of coffee lay in pieces on the polished oak floor.

Graham Enright had been dead since yesterday morning. The body was quite cold.

She put the telegram on the desk.

Satisfied, she left the inner office, closing the door very quietly, as she always did. A well-trained secretary never slammed doors. She pulled on her gloves, picked up the briefcase, her handbag, and the envelope, and let herself out into the hall.

With luck it would be quite some time before

Graham Enright's body was discovered—days, perhaps. The janitors were called in only to clean when authorized to do so by Graham Enright himself, who always supervised the process.

When someone eventually did find the corpse, the assumption would be that a grief-stricken Enright had taken his own life after learning of the death of his only son and heir.

Anyone who thought to check the secretary's calendar would learn that, shortly before his death, Graham, a generous employer, had sent her off for a monthlong visit to relatives in Pennsylvania.

There were no relatives in Pennsylvania or anywhere else for that matter, but no one would think to question that tiny, insignificant fact, Raina thought.

When you discovered that you were working for a family of contract killers, you learned that details were important. They often made the difference between life and death. She had been planning her departure from the firm for some time, merely waiting for the right moment. The news of Julian Enright's death the day before had prompted her to hand in her notice that same day. She had done so with a cup of coffee laced with cyanide.

Graham Enright had died without ever seeing the telegram. He did, however, have a moment to realize that his secretary had poisoned him. She had seen the fury and outraged disbelief in his eyes just before he collapsed. That was an Enright for you, she thought. Both of them, father and son, had always assumed that they were smarter and more ruthless than those around them.

She took the elevator down to the lobby and went outside. The new car she had purchased with some of the cash from the firm's discretionary fund was parked on a side street. She put the briefcase into the trunk alongside her suitcase and got behind the wheel.

She stopped at the post office and hurried inside to mail the envelope containing the Helen Spencer file. It was addressed to the local office of the Federal Bureau of Investigation. There was enough material in the envelope to point the FBI to the agent of a foreign government who had commissioned Enright & Enright to retrieve a certain notebook, no questions asked. What the FBI chose to do with the information was up to them.

Raina walked out of the post office, got back into her sharp new car, and drove away from New York.

She had given a great deal of thought to her destination. In the end she concluded that any town that knew how to deal with the likes of Julian Enright was her kind of town. Burning Cove sounded like the perfect place to start her new life.

According to the map, the road to the future started in Chicago. Route 66 would take her all the way to California.

Chapter 68

There were two armed guards at the front gate of the compound, but it was three o'clock in the morning, so they were working hard to stay awake with coffee and low-voiced discussions of sports and women.

The intruder had studied the layout of the Saltwood Laboratory earlier in the day from the cover of a stand of trees. He had determined that the weakest point of entry was the loading dock gate. There was a serious-looking lock but it presented no problems. He was good with locks. He had brought along a set of wire cutters to deal with the alarm system, but in the end he didn't have to use them. He simply opened the device and unplugged it.

He found a side door, picked another lock, disarmed another alarm, and then he was inside the darkened building. He had brought a flashlight with him. The metal shielding around the bulb ensured that the device cast only a very narrow beam.

He made his way past several doors marked *Authorized Personnel Only*. Curious, he opened a couple at random and saw shadow-filled lab rooms crowded with workbenches. An assortment of instruments and mechanical equipment was arrayed on each bench. White lab coats and goggles designed to protect the eyes dangled from wall hooks.

He continued down the hall and turned the corner into another wing lined with office doors. When he located the one marked *Dr. Raymond Perry, Executive Director*, he picked the lock and entered the reception area.

He went past the secretary's desk and paused to unlock the door of the inner office. Dr. Raymond Perry's office was neat and uncluttered. A row of locked file cabinets lined one wall.

He did what he had come to do and made his way back out of the building, relocking the doors and resetting the alarms. At the far end of the compound the guards were still drinking coffee and chatting.

He made his way through the stand of trees. The new speedster was waiting in the dense shadows at the side of the road.

He got in on the passenger side. Irene turned the key in the ignition and pulled out onto the empty road.

"I take it everything went according to plan," she said.

"No problems," Oliver said. "I left the notebook on

top of the executive director's desk. He'll see it first thing when he goes into his office in the morning."

"He'll wonder how it got there."

"Sure. But it's in his own and his company's best interests to keep quiet. Besides, there's no way he'll be able to figure out how the notebook reappeared."

Irene smiled. "Magic."

"Magic."

"You weren't gone very long. I thought you would have to spend more time getting through the locks and alarms."

"Saltwood has a government contract, so they've got standard government security. They obviously gave the contract to the lowest bidder."

"Of course. So, now we're free to go on our honeymoon."

"Got any particular destination in mind?"

"I hear Burning Cove is a romantic choice for a honeymoon destination."

"I've heard that, too," Oliver said. "It's a long drive back to California but there's no rush. We can stop at some of the roadside attractions along the way."

"That would be nice." Irene patted the steering wheel affectionately. "The last time I drove across the country I was in a hurry. I didn't get a chance to do any sightseeing."

"This time will be different."

"Yes, it will," Irene said. "This time we're going home."

Read on for a special look
at Amanda Quick's new novel

THE OTHER LADY VANISHES

Available May 2018 from Berkley

The screams of the patients in ward five told Adelaide Blake that time had run out.

She stopped searching for the key to the file cabinet and went to stand at the door of the small office. She had not dared to turn on any lights in the laboratory. There was enough moonlight spilling through the high, arched windows to illuminate the long workbenches and create ominous silhouettes of the equipment and instruments.

The wails and shrieks and howls from the floor below were escalating rapidly. Something or, more likely, someone was agitating the patients. The ward on the fifth floor was reserved for the most hopelessly mad and insane. The locked rooms housed those who were forever lost in their own private hells. Some of the patients were afflicted with violent, paranoid visions and hallucinations. Others battled fearsome monsters that only they could see.

Soon after she had been locked in one of the cell-like rooms in ward five, she had learned that the patients provided an excellent alarm system, especially at night. Nights were always the worst.

The nerve-shattering chorus of the damned echoed up the stone staircase There was no one around to calm the inmates. The orderlies in the locked ward had been given the night off.

She could not delay any longer. If she did not escape now, she might not make it at all. She would have to leave the file behind.

She left the doorway of the office and started to make her way cautiously through the maze of workbenches. She had plotted her exit strategy down to the smallest detail but the last-minute decision to look for the file had put the plan in jeopardy. She had to get out of the laboratory immediately or she might not escape.

Originally, the Rushbrook Sanitarium had been the private mansion of a wealthy, eccentric industrialist who had intended to entertain on a grand scale. The result was a gothic nightmare of a house with five floors, endless hallways, and the tower room that now served as a laboratory. The single redeeming architectural virtue as far as Adelaide was concerned was that there were a number of discreetly concealed staircases intended for the use of a large staff.

Most of the servants' stairs had been permanently closed and sealed long ago. Others had disappeared under various waves of renovations and remodeling projects. But a few were still accessible. She had the key to one of the little-used staircases.

She was halfway across the lab when she heard the panicky footsteps on the tower stairs. Someone was coming up to the laboratory. Whoever it was would see her as soon as he turned on the lights.

There was nowhere to hide except behind Ormsby's desk. Discovery spelled doom. Dr. Gill would order increased security for her. She might never have another chance to escape.

A cold sense of certainty sliced through the fear. If necessary she would try to fight her way out of the sanitarium. She could not—would not—go back to the cell on the fifth floor. She would rather die.

She turned quickly, searching the shadows for something that could function as a weapon. She knew the lab all too well because it was where they brought her when Gill and Ormsby decided to give her another dose of the drug. In her desperate attempt to hold on to her sanity by focusing on an escape plan, she had memorized every inch of the tower room.

She went to the nearest cabinet, yanked open the door, and pulled a couple of bottles off the shelf. She had no idea what she grabbed—it was too dark to read the labels—but she had seen Ormsby take a variety of chemicals out of the cabinet. Many were flammable. Some were highly acidic.

With the two bottles in hand she hurried back into the office. Dr. Ormsby's desk was neat and tidy. He was a fussy little man who was obsessed with his research, but orderliness was high on his list of priorities.

Aside from the usual office accessories—telephone,

blotter, and inkwells—there was one other object on the desk. The black velvet box looked as if it had been made to hold a woman's collection of jewelry. But Adelaide knew there were no necklaces, rings, or bracelets inside. The velvet box contained a dozen elegantly cut crystal perfume bottles.

She made it behind the desk with the bottles of chemicals just as Dr. Harold Ormsby staggered into the darkened laboratory. It sounded as if he was gasping for air. He did not turn on any lights.

"Get away from me," he shrieked. "Don't touch me."

Adelaide heard other footsteps on the stone staircase, the slow, steady, determined tread of a predator stalking prey.

Ormsby wasn't trying to catch his breath, Adelaide realized. The doctor was in the grip of raw panic.

Ormsby's pursuer did not respond, at least not verbally. Crouched behind the desk, Adelaide removed the tops of the bottles. She hoped the screams of the patients covered the small sounds she made.

She tried to keep her breathing as light and shallow as possible but it wasn't easy. Like Ormsby, she found it difficult to breathe. Ice-cold perspiration dampened her skin. She shivered and her pulse skittered wildly.

Ormsby screamed again, louder this time. The high, unnatural screech affected Adelaide like a bolt of lightning. For a few seconds she wondered if it had stopped her heart.

And then she wondered if lightning actually had struck the laboratory. A narrow beam of fire blazed in the darkness. Peering around the corner of Ormsby's desk, she watched the glow move past the office doorway.

Ormsby's piercing screams rose above the cacophony from the fifth-floor patients, the cries of a man being sent into hell.

Running footsteps reverberated in the tower room. Heavy glass shattered. Night air flowed into the laboratory.

Ormsby's hopeless cries echoed in the night for another second or two. The suddenness with which they were cut off told its own story.

Adelaide froze as she realized what had just happened. Dr. Harold Ormsby had leaped straight through one of the high, arched windows. No one could survive such a fall.

In the shadows of the lab the fiery light winked out. It dawned on Adelaide that someone had lit a Bunsen burner and used the flame to drive Ormsby out the window. That didn't make sense. He had obviously been terrified but she knew something of the man. It was easy to imagine him pleading for his life or cowering in a corner, but jumping to his death seemed oddly out of character. Then, again, she was not the best judge of character. She had learned that lesson the hard way.

The screaming from the fifth-floor ward got louder. The patients sensed that something terrible had happened.

Adelaide heard rapid, purposeful footsteps crossing the stone floor, coming toward the office. She gripped the containers of chemicals and waited, aware that the only thing protecting her now was the noise from the inmates down below. The shrieks and cries would make it difficult if not impossible for the killer to hear the sound of her breathing.

The intruder stopped directly in front of the desk. A flashlight came on briefly. Adelaide prepared to fight for her life.

But the intruder turned and hurried quickly out of the office. A few seconds later footsteps sounded on the stairs.

The keening of the agitated patients rose and fell but there were more shouts now. They came from the courtyard below the broken window. Someone had found Ormsby's body and was sounding the alarm.

Adelaide waited a couple of heartbeats and then got to her feet. She was shaking so badly she had a hard time recovering her balance. She thought briefly of trying once again to find the key to the file cabinet but common sense prevailed. Escape from the sanitarium was the first priority.

She reached up to adjust the nurse's cap pinned to her tightly knotted hair. When she glanced down at the desk, she saw that the black velvet box containing the perfume bottles was gone. The intruder had taken it.

She selected one of the two open jars of chemicals to use as a weapon and left the other one behind on the desk. She picked her way through the moonlit lab. When she got to the staircase, she descended cautiously.

At the foot of the stairs she paused and looked around the edge of the door.

The inmates continued to howl and scream through the grills set into the locked doors but the hallway was empty. There was no sign of the intruder.

Her room was located at the far end of an intersecting hallway. There were no other patients in that corridor. Earlier she had arranged the pillows and blankets on her bed in an attempt to approximate the outline of a sleeping figure but it looked as if the ruse had been unnecessary. The agitation of the other inmates and the commotion in the courtyard were providing sufficient cover to conceal her movements. The white cap and the long blue cloak, familiar elements of a nurse's uniform, would do the rest. With luck anyone who chanced to see her from a distance would assume she was a member of the hospital staff.

The entrance to the old servants' stairs was in a storage closet on the opposite side of the hall. She was edging out of the stairwell doorway, preparing to make a dash for the storage closet, when the patients' screams rose in another hellish crescendo. It was all the warning she got. It was just barely enough to save her.

She retreated to the shadows of the stairwell and waited. When the screams faded a little, she risked a peek around the doorway.

A figure dressed in a doctor's coat, a white cap, and a surgical mask emerged from the hallway that led to her room. The black velvet box was in his left hand. In his right he gripped a syringe.

The only thing that saved her from being seen was that the masked doctor was intent on rushing down the hall in the opposite direction. He disappeared through the locked doors just beyond the nurses' station.

She did not think it was possible to be any more terrified than she was already was, but the sight of the masked doctor leaving the corridor that led to her room sent another jolt of horror across her nerves. Maybe he had intended to kill her, too.

With an effort of will, she pulled herself together. She certainly could not continue to dither in the stairwell indefinitely. She had to act or all was lost.

She took a deep breath, clutched the bottle in one hand, and rushed across the hallway. She opened the door of the storage closet.

A bearded face appeared at the steel grill set into a nearby door. The insane man stared at her with wild, otherworldly eyes.

"You're a ghost now, aren't you?" he said in a voice that was hoarse from endless keening and wailing. "It was just a matter of time before they killed you, just like they did the other one."

"Good-bye, Mr. Hawkins," she said gently.

"You're lucky to be dead, you know. You're better off now because you can leave this place."

"Yes, I know."

She slipped into the storage closet, closed the door, and turned on the overhead fixture. The old door to the service stairs was at the back. It was locked. To her overwhelming relief, the key she had been given worked.

By the time she made it downstairs to the darkened kitchen on the ground floor, she could hear sirens in the distance. Someone had telephoned the local authorities. The sanitarium was located a couple of miles outside the small town of Rushbrook. It would take the police and the ambulance several minutes to arrive on the scene.

There was no one around to see her when she slipped out of the kitchen. She inserted another stolen key into the lock on the massive wrought iron gate that the delivery vehicles used.

And then she was free, hurrying down a rutted lane with only the light of the moon to guide her.

She was not at all sorry that Ormsby was dead but his death could complicate her already desperate situation. It would be so easy for the authorities to conclude that the patient who had escaped the secure grounds of the Rushbrook Sanitarium on the night of the doctor's mysterious demise was, in fact, a crazed killer.

She had to get as far away as possible from the asylum before the orderlies realized she was gone.

It occurred to her that one person already knew she had disappeared—the doctor in the surgical mask who had gone to her room with the syringe.

She wanted to run but she did not dare. If, in the darkness, she stumbled over a rock or a fallen tree limb she could twist an ankle or worse.

The emergency vehicles passed her a short time later. They never noticed her hiding behind the heavy shrubbery at the side of the lane.

Dawn found her standing on the side of a highway hoping that a passing motorist would take pity on a nurse whose car had run out of gas in the middle of nowhere.

She raised her hand to wave down a truck. The gold wedding ring on her finger gleamed malevolently in the morning light.

Ready to find
your next great read?

Let us help.

Visit prh.com/nextread